Carlisle's Duty

The Eleventh Carlisle & Holbrooke Naval Adventure

Chris Durbin

Chris Durbin

To James

Our son-in-law

Carlisle's Duty

Copyright © 2022 by Chris Durbin. All Rights Reserved.

Chris Durbin has asserted his rights under the Copyright, Design and Patents Act, 1988, to be identified as the author of this work.

No part of this book may be reproduced in any form or by any electronic or mechanical means including information storage and retrieval systems, without permission in writing from the author. The only exception is by a reviewer, who may quote short excerpts in a review.

Editor: Lucia Durbin

Cover Artwork: Bob Payne

Cover Design: Book Beaver

This book is a work of historical fiction. Characters, places, and incidents either are products of the author's imagination or are used fictitiously. For further information on actual historical events, see the bibliography at the end of the book.

First Edition: January 2022

CONTENTS

	Nautical Terms	vii
	Principal Characters	viii
	Charts	x
	Introduction	1
Prologue	An Unprofitable Cruise	3
Chapter 1	Squadron Command	11
Chapter 2	A Neat Operation	21
Chapter 3	Change of Tack	31
Chapter 4	A King's Cutter	39
Chapter 5	Gresham's Day	50
Chapter 6	The Baited Bear	60
Chapter 7	Interrogation	73
Chapter 8	Restitution	85
Chapter 9	A Mystery Ship	97
Chapter 10	A Chase	106
Chapter 11	An Informer	115
Chapter 12	Salutary Neglect	125
Chapter 13	Pandora's Box	135
Chapter 14	The Tempter	144
Chapter 15	Colonial Interests	155
Chapter 16	Trade's Increase	166

Chapter 17	A Falling Glass	176
Chapter 18	The House on the Green	186
Chapter 19	A Single Shot	196
Chapter 20	The Family Property	204
Chapter 21	Borrowed Time	213
Chapter 22	Horse Latitudes	223
Chapter 23	The Sea Gods	233
Chapter 24	Something's Afoot	240
Chapter 25	A Tactical Decision	246
Chapter 26	Breaking the Line	256
Chapter 27	Cry 'Havoc'	263
Chapter 28	One More Victory	271
Chapter 29	A Blind Eye	280
Chapter 30	A Happy Hurricane Season	292
	Historical Epilogue	299
	Fact Meets Fiction	301
	The Series	304
	Bibliography	314
	The Author	317
	Feedback	319

Chris Durbin

LIST OF CHARTS

The Western Atlantic	x
The Antilles	xi
English Harbour, Antigua	xii
The Careenage, St. Lucia	xiii
Narragansett Bay and Approaches	xiv

NAUTICAL TERMS

Throughout the centuries, sailors have created their own language to describe the highly technical equipment and processes that they use to live and work at sea. This still holds true in the twenty-first century.

While counting the number of nautical terms that I've used in this series of novels, it became evident that a printed book wasn't the best place for them. I've therefore created a glossary of nautical terms on my website:

https://chris-durbin.com/glossary/

My nautical glossary is limited to those terms that I've mentioned in this series of novels as they were used in the middle of the eighteenth century. It's intended as a work of reference to accompany the Carlisle & Holbrooke series of naval adventure novels.

Some of the usages of these terms have changed over the years, so this glossary should be used with caution when referring to periods before 1740 or after 1780.

The glossary isn't exhaustive; Falconer's Universal Dictionary of the Marine, first published in 1769, contains a more comprehensive list. I haven't counted the number of terms that Falconer has defined, but he fills 328 pages with English language terms, followed by an additional eighty-three pages of French translations. It's a monumental work.

There is an online version of the 1780 edition of The Universal Dictionary (which unfortunately does not include all the excellent diagrams that are in the print version) at this website:

https://archive.org/details/universaldiction00falc/

PRINCIPAL CHARACTERS

Fictional

Captain Edward Carlisle: Commanding Officer, *Dartmouth*

Matthew Gresham: First Lieutenant, *Dartmouth*

David Wishart: Second Lieutenant, *Dartmouth*

Enrico Angelini: Third Lieutenant, *Dartmouth*

Arthur Beazley: Sailing Master, *Dartmouth*

Alfred Pontneuf: Marine First Lieutenant, *Dartmouth*

Frederick Simmonds: Captain's Clerk, *Dartmouth*

Jack Souter: Captain's Coxswain, *Dartmouth*

Nathaniel Whittle: Able Seaman, *Dartmouth*

Lady Chiara Angelini: Captain Carlisle's wife

Joseph Kendrick: Master, *Hope*

Joshua Cranston: Man of Business, Obadiah Brown & Company

Historical

William Pitt: Leader of the House of Commons

Lord George Anson: First Lord of the Admiralty

Commodore Sir James Douglas: Commander-In-Chief Leeward Islands

Commodore Lord Colville: Commander-In-Chief North America

Francis Fauquier: Lieutenant Governor of Virginia

George Wythe: Lawyer and member of the House of Burgesses, Virginia

John Brown: Partner, Obadiah Brown & Company, Rhode Island

Abraham Whipple: Master, Rhode Island Privateer *Gamecock*

Chris Durbin

The Western Atlantic

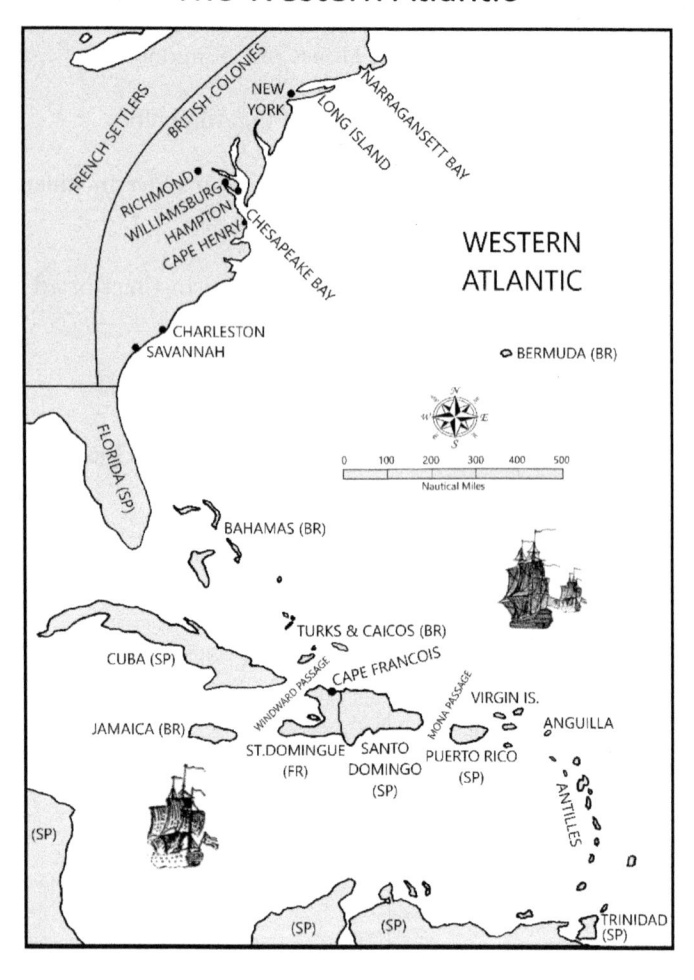

Carlisle's Duty

The Antilles

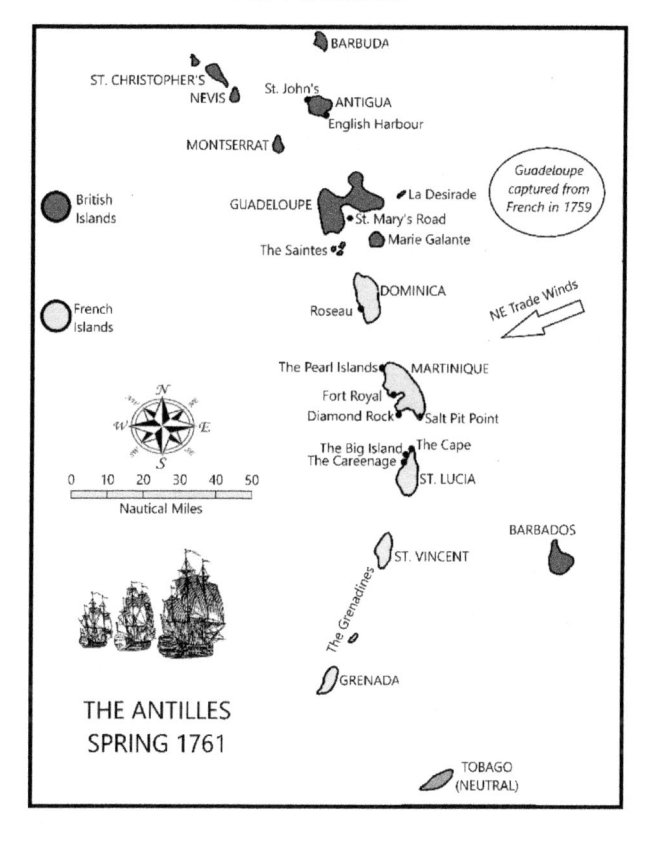

THE ANTILLES
SPRING 1761

Chris Durbin

English Harbour, Antigua

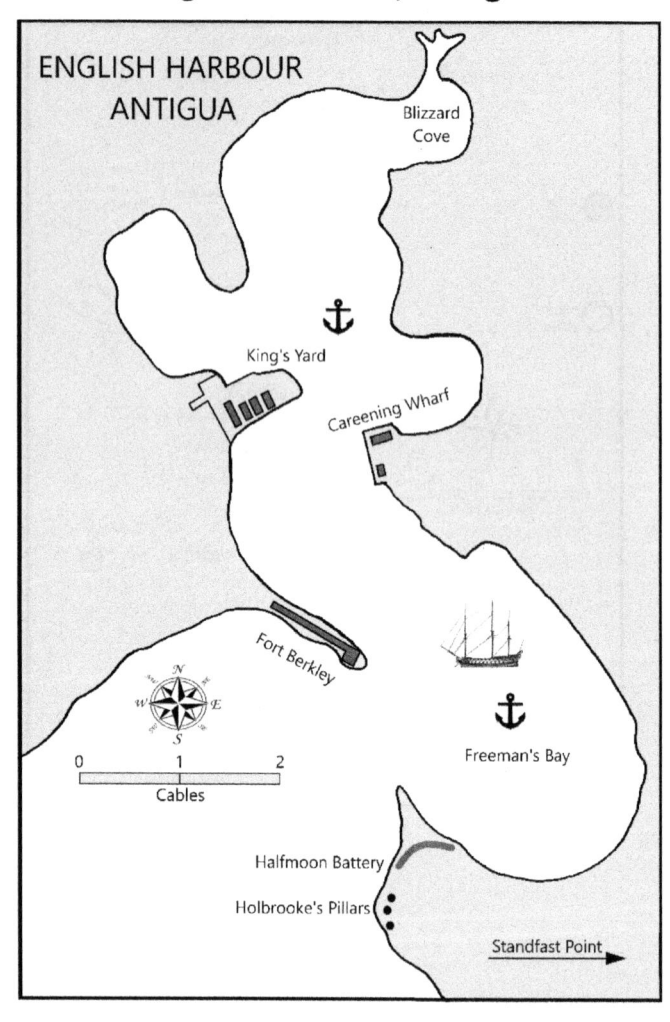

The Careenage, St. Lucia

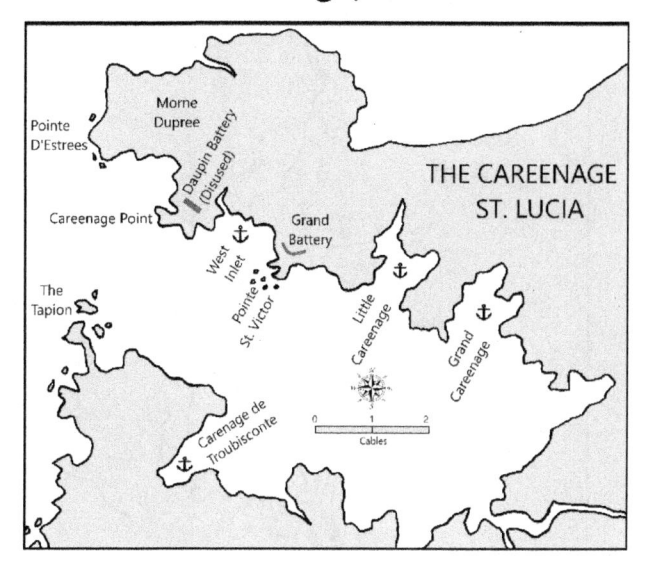

Chris Durbin

Narragansett Bay and Approaches

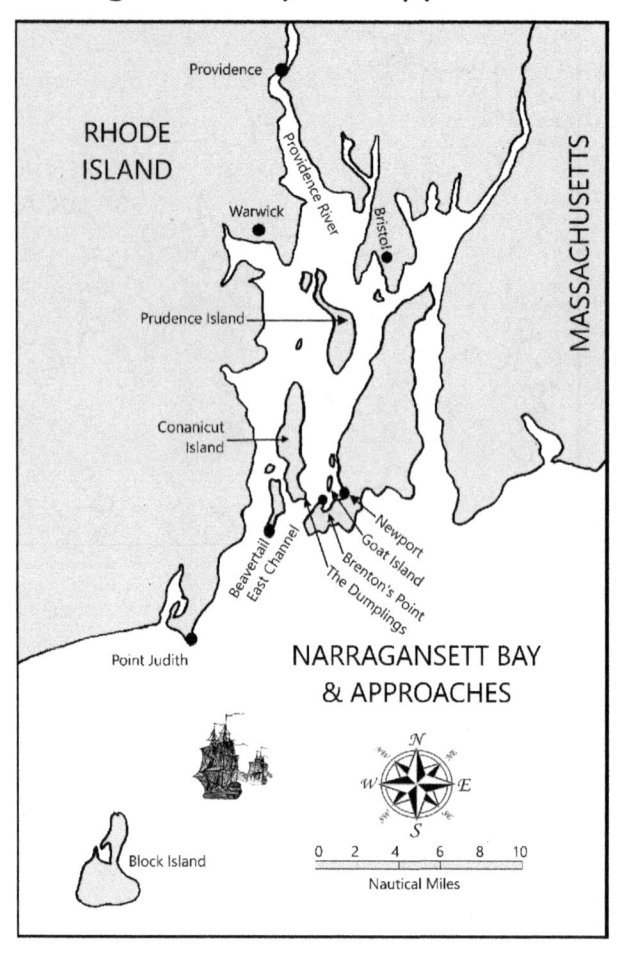

Carlisle's Duty

Every subject's duty is the king's; but every subject's soul is his own

Henry V, in disguise as Harry le Roy, speaking to his soldiers on the eve of the Battle of Agincourt,

according to William Shakespeare

Chris Durbin

INTRODUCTION

The Seven Years War at the end of 1760

The year 1760 saw something of a consolidation in the war, as Britain started to scent a victory and France sought a way out of the conflict. Without Spain, France could not see how to end the war with its colonies – and its honour – intact, yet Spain couldn't afford to enter the war. The squadron that Admiral Saunders took into the Mediterranean in 1760 was calculated not only to pin down the French in Toulon, but to make it clear to the King of Spain what awaited him should he join the war on France's side.

In North America, after a fearful winter in Quebec, the British army was defeated at the battle of Sainte-Foy in April 1760, just a short walk from where Wolfe had beaten Montcalm in the previous year. However the French commander at Sainte-Foy, the Chevalier de Lévis, was unable to follow up his success and when in May a British navy squadron sailed up the Saint Lawrence as the ice melted, it was all over for New France. The promised French naval squadron failed to materialise after the terrible defeats that the French suffered at Lagos Bay and Quiberon Bay, and the sinking of the supply ships at the Battle of Restigouche. Lacking men, provisions and even a clear means of communicating with France, and with British armies closing in on three sides, Montreal surrendered in September. By the end of 1760, the long dream of New France was over, and the American colonists turned their attention to the great tracts of land to the west that the French had given up.

For France it was a year to rebuild, and to attempt to repair its navy after the devastating defeats of 1759. And, despite its financial difficulties, money was found for building ships. In all the great ports of France and in many of those of its friends and allies, the sound of adze and saw could be heard as a new navy started to take shape. Yet it takes more than a year to build a ship-of-the-line and France went into 1761 with its navy in a parlous state.

Carlisle and Holbrooke

1760 was a good year for George Holbrooke. His promotion to post-captain had allowed him to marry his sweetheart and he had been given a new frigate – *Argonaut* – with orders to join the Downs Squadron under Commodore Boys. His ship was detached with two others to chase a French expedition that intended to make a diversionary landing in the north of Britain, and when the French squadron was cornered and defeated, Holbrooke shared in the vast amount of prize money, making him a more-than-moderately wealthy man. In *Nor'west by North*, we found Holbrooke considering the purchase of a house in his hometown of Wickham while being courted for a position in the legislature of his county.

Edward Carlisle spent most of the year of 1760 in the Mediterranean in his fourth rate ship-of-the-line *Dartmouth* where he was sent on a diplomatic mission to the capital of the Kingdom of Sardinia. He became entangled in the affairs of his wife's family and was a witness to the inexorable decline of the house of Angelini. *Dartmouth* intercepted and disrupted the delivery of new ships for the French navy being built by the Republic of Genoa and in so doing engaged a French seventy-four gun ship and was narrowly saved from defeat by the appearance of a British third rate. In July of 1760 he was sent to Antigua to reinforce the Leeward Islands Squadron where a convoy for the Chesapeake gave him the opportunity to visit his own home at Williamsburg in the Virginia colony. The end of 1760 found him in the West Indies, where this story starts.

Carlisle's Duty

PROLOGUE

An Unprofitable Cruise

Thursday, Twentieth of November 1760.
Privateer Hope, Off the Pearl Islands, Martinique.

The darkened ship pitched gently as it lay hove-to under the lee of Cape Saint-Martin, butting its bluff bow into the little waves while its backed fore-tops'l and stays'l kept its head to the wind. The sun had not yet shown itself over the looming high land of this north-western tip of Martinique. There was no moon, and the clouds that streamed off the land like endless ghostly legions in battle array were more to be imagined than seen. It was that last hour before dawn and the two men who stood at the taffrail knew how quickly the night would give way to the full brilliant light of the tropical day. The next thirty minutes were critical.

Dick Parsons shuffled restlessly as he stared to leeward, trying to penetrate the darkness. He knew that this was the last roll of the dice on this hitherto futile trip. One way or another they'd have to steer for home today and he didn't relish the thought of warping alongside at Providence with nary a prize to show for a four-month cruise. He hadn't learned to disguise his misgivings in front of the crew, and it was lucky that the night hid his face. Parsons' nervousness was in sharp contrast to Joseph Kendrick, the master of this New England privateer, who looked unconcerned. He was the only man on deck who wasn't straining his eyes into the blackness.

'Nothing yet.'

Dick's edginess showed in his need to speak. Joseph didn't respond, nor did he move; he could have been made of stone. And yet a keen observer would have seen the way his right index finger beat a tattoo on the cap of the taffrail. As the ship's master he had the most to gain from a privateering cruise, and he had the most to lose if it was unsuccessful. Like all the crew he was paid a small retainer and a share of the prize money, as well as his victuals for the duration. If there were no prizes, he would go back to his family empty-handed. For Joseph, it wasn't the serious matter that it was for some of his crew, who budgeted from cruise to cruise. His wife and son wouldn't go hungry, not yet, but if he wasn't given another cruise – and that was a distinct possibility – then things could start to get difficult.

The master and mate had concocted this plan together – this last roll of the dice – and they both felt the weight of responsibility for its success or failure, even if they showed it in different ways. They had scoured the Leeward Islands for French merchantmen and even sailed far north and west to Saint Domingue, but since the capture of Guadeloupe, it appeared that nothing was moving. The French still held the whole chain of islands between Dominica and Grenada but with the British navy pushing blockading patrols out from English Harbour and Barbados it was too dangerous for the French trade to put to sea without a strong escort. They hadn't seen a single potential prize in the past four months, and yet, the French must communicate between the islands. The sugar crop still had to be sent to Fort Royal to await convoy across the Atlantic and therefore they had to be sailing by night.

The distance between Roseau on Dominica and Fort Royal on Martinique was nearly twenty leagues on a beam reach, if the nor'east trade winds blew true. It was too far for a single overnight passage, and the French merchantmen would have to find a safe anchorage after the first night. A careful study of the charts showed that the Pearl Islands on the north-west tip of Martinique was the most likely place. The word among the privateering community was that the French had established a battery to cover the anchorage inside the islands and further batteries guarded the northerly and southerly approaches. The anchorage battery mounted six or nine pounders, just sufficient to cover the precious ships that would lie as close to the shore as they could. The approach batteries were probably nines but could be twelves.

Joseph nodded as he rehearsed the plan in his mind. He was satisfied that it was the best chance, aye, and probably the last chance. This was the third night they had waited under the lee of Mount Pelée. There would be no point in remaining after sunrise; news of their vigil would have been passed back to Roseau and no vessel would make the attempt until they heard that the passage was clear of privateers. If nothing appeared at dawn today, he would have to abandon the plan.

And that was why *Hope* was lying so close to the land, barely a mile off the rocky shore. He was relying upon his prey's natural reluctance to approach the anchorage at night. They would – he hoped – time their arrival for the half hour before sunrise when there was enough light to see the dangerous islands and ensure that they could anchor in safety. It was no use *Hope* lying further offshore, not with the trade wind blowing regularly through the night and the sea breeze unlikely to dominate until some two or three hours after sunrise. He had to be so close in that he would be to windward of anything approaching the anchorage, but not so close that dawn would find him within range of the batteries. A risky plan, for sure, but something must be attempted, and privateering wasn't a trade for the faint-hearted.

***

Slowly, almost imperceptibly, a tint of orange started to highlight the slopes of Mount Pelée. The faintest outline, no more. It did nothing to penetrate the darkness, but it did bring the promise of dawn.

Joseph turned to look astern – to the nor'west and to leeward – in a futile attempt to peer through the blackness. It was like looking into a pitch-bucket. Then something stirred, the clouds parted, just for a moment, and a spectral silvery light illuminated the sea.

'There! On the larboard quarter. A sail!'

Joseph swung around but the streaming clouds had again covered the sky and he saw nothing.

'Are you sure, Dick?'

'Certain. A brig, or a tops'l schooner perhaps, beating in towards the anchorage, right on time.'

Joseph hesitated for two heartbeats. If Dick was wrong, then he was taking his ship away from the best position to intercept any approaching vessels. But the mate looked deadly confident of what he had seen.

'Make sail! Hands to sheets and braces. Helm a-weather!'

The ship's bows paid off and she gathered way to leeward. Joseph could still see nothing.

'Take her down to where you saw the chase, Dick.'

Joseph looked around the deck. There had been no need to order the guns prepared, not with a crew whose livelihoods depended upon a capture. The stubby six-pounders were primed and ready. As the ship settled on her new course, the gun crews clustered around their own particular weapons.

Still nothing. Joseph was starting to doubt his mate, he really should have seen something by now. Then the clouds parted again, and the chase appeared, a lonely vessel on a still-dark sea. It was a brig, no more than three miles to leeward, hard on the larboard tack and clearly making for the anchorage inside the islands.

'I'll take her now. Bring her two points to windward.'

The steersman pushed the wheel over a few spokes and the ship bucked as its bows rose to the waves.

It was immediately evident that the brig couldn't make the anchorage, not with *Hope* blocking the way, but so far the chase showed no sign of having seen the danger.

A minute went by, as the two vessels approached each other rapidly.

'She's going about!'

Dick was shouting in his excitement, but Joseph could see it for himself. The sky was lightening, and the brig had become visible, revealed in the shocking light of the infant day.

'Another point to larboard.'

Damn! Joseph thumped his fist onto the binnacle. Five more minutes and it would have been too late for the brig. He could see what his enemy was doing. The brig's master had seen the unknown ship steering a course to cut him off from the anchorage, he'd guessed at its identity, and instantly decided to beat in towards Serpent Cove, where the northerly of the three batteries covered the approach to the Pearl Islands. If the brig could get under the battery, he'd be safe. *Hope* wasn't a man-o'-war, and his crew were not prepared to take undue risks in what was essentially a commercial enterprise. Certainly privateers were killed and injured in the course of taking their prizes, it was a hazard of the profession, but the risk had to be proportionate.

Dick watched the French vessel settle on her new tack.

'It'll be close.'

Joseph didn't reply, his mind was too busy assessing the situation. If this was the start of a cruise, he'd give up now, in the expectation of easier prey later. But in this case there would be no more chances. This was indeed their last realistic opportunity of taking a prize. He'd never before returned home without at least one enemy merchantman to be condemned at the Newport vice-admiralty court, and he didn't intend that this should be the first. He looked up at the sails; they were all drawing perfectly, his hungry crew had seen to it.

Joseph leaned over the taffrail and made a cup of his hands.

'Put a shot across his bow, Master Gunner.'

Like most privateers, *Hope* carried the first gun of each battery far forward on the turn of the bows so that it could fire almost right ahead. Nine times out of ten that one warning shot was enough to bring any merchantman to its senses, but this one was only a mile or so from safety.

Bang! The six-pounder leaped back on its tackles and its crew was immediately at work with the sponge, going through the drill of reloading for another shot. Dick leaned out to see the fall of shot.

'Short, but good for line. We'll soon be in range of the battery, I expect.'

Neither man knew exactly where the northerly battery was located. The opinion among the privateers at Antigua was that it was mounted on a bluff above the estuary of the Red River, just north of Serpent Cove, but the whole shoreline was still in shadow, and they could see no details.

'I expect we'll know soon enough.'

Joseph cupped his hands again.

'Give her another as soon as you're loaded.'

Bang! That was better, close enough to wet the hands on the brig's deck, but still she stood on in a desperate bid for safety.

'Sixty tons of sugar, I'll bet, and the value of the ship. It'll just about clear the cruise.'

Joseph looked at the mate in irritation. That was just tempting fate. It was no good counting your chickens until they were hatched, and he was by no means sure that he could come up to the chase before it reached safety under the guns. It all depended on what weight of metal the French had mounted on those batteries. If they were only six-pounders, then there was a chance.

'Watch your helm,' he growled.

The steersman didn't respond except to shift the quid of tobacco from one cheek to the other and spit into the can at his feet. He was already steering as close as was humanly possible; he knew the stakes as well as anyone. It was the finest of calculations and required the most exact steering. Too far to starboard and they'd end up within range of the French battery; too far to larboard and the chase would slip across *Hope's* bow and into safety.

Joseph took a careful bearing from the compass on the binnacle. Nor'-by-east.

Carlisle's Duty

Bang!

The bow chaser fired again. The ball must have passed across the brig's deck, but it had no effect as the Frenchman held his luff, making a last rush for safety.

Boom!

The battery had opened fire. Only one gun. A waterspout appeared a couple of cables to windward. The flash and smoke could just be seen high up on rising ground, although the battery itself was still hidden by the darkness and the dense vegetation.

'Looks like a twelve-pounder.'

Joseph's mouth hardened into a thin line. Dick was probably right, and if the battery mounted twelve-pounders, then that doubled their peril. The French balls would carry half as far again as nine-pounders and twice as far as *Hope's* six-pounders. Not that he intended to trade shots with a shore battery!

'Dick, get the boarders ready. I'm going to put us alongside and you can jump for it. There's no time for boats.'

The mate stared at him. True, the weather was almost perfect in the lee of the mountains but boarding a brig from a ship underway was at best a risky operation. Joseph saw his hesitation.

'It's that or nothing, Dick. He won't heave-to now, not this close to safety. Get on board, don't take any nonsense from them, and put the helm up and run out to sea. We'll sort it out when we're out of range of the battery.'

Boom, boom!

The French had brought two guns into action and the waterspouts appeared in line with *Hope's* bow. Joseph could see that he'd have to run the gauntlet – to put his ship into danger – if he wanted this prize. He bent to take another bearing. Nor'-by-east: steady. If nothing changed, they'd intercept the chase in five minutes, but the interception point would be uncomfortably within the range of those big guns.

He could see the boarding party mustering in the waist. He could sense their reluctance, but Dick was doing a good job of injecting enthusiasm, hustling them into some sort of order for what was to come.

Then it all changed. *Boom – crash!* A heavy ball smashed into *Hope's* gunwale and ploughed a furrow through the boarding party. Sailors were thrown down left and right and the fore sheets parted leaving the big foresail flapping ineffectually.

Joseph took in the situation at a single glance.

'Up helm, bring her before the wind.'

This was defeat. The chase would anchor safely under the guns of the Serpent Cove Battery and there was nothing that he could do about it. Lives had been lost, or soon would be when the wounded succumbed to their injuries, and all he could do was hurry out of range and lick his wounds.

***

CHAPTER ONE

Squadron Command

Sunday, Thirtieth of November 1760.
Dartmouth, at Sea. Off the Careenage, St. Lucia.

By a landsman's reckoning of the hours it was still early, too early for a gentleman to be about, but at sea it was exactly the time that a captain of one of His Majesty's ships-of-the-line could be found on the poop deck. Two bells in the morning watch – five o'clock to those who woke up in a bed that didn't sway – and the outline of St. Lucia to windward was just starting to show. This was the time when Carlisle liked to do his thinking; to make some sense of the day to come and decide how he would shape it to meet his own plan. Backwards and forwards he strode, forty of his long paces from the poop deck rail to the taffrail and never a great gun to break his stride, for these fifties carried only swivels on the poop deck. Even the chicken coops and the other livestock hadn't made their appearance yet, not until the captain's morning walk was over.

He was considering the disposition of his force. In fact, his decision process mirrored that of his commander-in-chief, even though Commodore Sir James Douglas had a strong force of ships-of-the-line and frigates while he had only his own ship and a handful of sloops and cutters. The constraints of geography and weather were the same for the greater and the smaller squadrons. He had to cover the three principal islands that were left to the French: Dominica, Martinique and St. Lucia. Guadeloupe to the north was already in British hands and St. Vincent, the Grenadines and Grenada to the south were being covered from Barbados. To anyone unacquainted with the Leeward Islands, the problem of blockading the two hundred and thirty or so miles of the combined coastline of the three islands would have appeared insuperable with such a small force, but

Carlisle knew this area well. The trade winds that blew eleven months out of twelve dictated that all the maritime activity happened on the west – the leeward – side of the islands. On the eastern side the near-perpetual east-nor'easterly winds brought heavy seas that burst upon the rocks in white-spumed ferocity, making it all-but impossible for any substantial commerce to take root. No naval ships could possibly make regular use of the few tiny, precarious havens that did exist on that naked, exposed shore.

Thus he only had to concern himself with less than a hundred miles of coastline, roughly thirty nautical miles for each island; more for Martinique and less for St. Lucia. The other factor in Carlisle's favour was that the French navy – what was left of it – was concentrated in Fort Royal, the town and fortress strategically placed at the entrance to the Grand Bay that was gouged deeply into the west coast of Martinique, close to the geographical centre of his area of responsibility.

The three islands didn't lie in a north-south line but trended from nor'-nor'west to sou'-sou'east. Any ship would have a hard beat to reach Fort Royal from St. Lucia if the trade wind backed a point to the north, as it did from time to time. A square rigged ship could only achieve it by making a bold tack westward into the Caribbean, but a cutter was more weatherly and could easily beat up from St. Lucia in most conditions. Those were the key considerations and they led inexorably to the outline of a plan. The sloops would deal with privateers and menace the French commerce while the cutters would be his eyes and ears and messengers so that the squadron could be concentrated in case of need. It was a classic strategy: the cutters would find the enemy and the sloops would fix them in position while the fourth rate was brought down to finish them off.

That left little doubt as to how his force should be disposed. A sloop and a cutter stationed on the leeward side of each of the northerly two islands, and a lone cutter to cover St. Lucia in the south, while *Dartmouth* cruised wherever its weight of broadside was needed. And he had another advantage: he could always leave his capable first lieutenant in command of *Dartmouth* freeing himself to embark in any of the sloops or cutters as the situation demanded.

Rabbit and *Gnat*, his fourteen-gun ship-rigged sloop and one of his six-gun cutters in the centre off Fort Royal. *Falcon* and *Mosquito*, his weakest brig-sloop with only ten guns and his strongest cutter with eight guns off Roseau on Dominica and *Kite* off the Careenage in St. Lucia. *Kite* had only six guns but there were no naval facilities at St. Lucia, and it was easy to reinforce this most leeward end of his area. He felt that he'd devised a scientific distribution of reconnaissance effort and firepower while he kept his most potent man-o'-war free to reinforce wherever she was needed. Nevertheless, it was fragile, and its effectiveness relied upon the initiative and energy of the captains of his small ships, and that was a largely unknown quality.

Today, *Dartmouth* was cruising off St. Lucia. The sun was now peeping over the peaks of the island and Carlisle realised that he'd been walking without a rest for at least an hour. He suddenly felt the protest in his legs, and he could see the heads bobbing up over the deck edge as the men who were waiting to bring up the animals impatiently checked on his progress. It was comical really, as soon as he turned to face the poop deck rail the heads disappeared below the coaming, like the game of grandmother's footsteps that he had played as a child. He suppressed a grin and turned purposefully towards the ladder, deliberately slowing his steps to allow the owners of the bobbing heads to disperse.

'Pass the word for Mister Gresham, Mister Angelini, Mister Beazley and Mister Pontneuf, if you please, Mister Wishart, I'll be in my cabin.'

He looked reflectively around the horizon, at the bold mass of the island to windward and the diminutive cutter

Kite under his lee. It was a tranquil scene without another sail in sight and over all the high, white clouds of the trade winds marched off to leeward in a stately procession.

'And Mister Wishart, I see no reason why Midshipman Young can't look after the deck for half an hour, so I would be pleased if you would also join me.'

***

Oh, the joy of commanding a fifty-gun fourth rate. They had been built with an eye to embarking a flag on foreign stations, particularly in time of peace, and the great cabin was proportioned accordingly. It was a vast, luxurious space that stretched clear across the aft end of the quarterdeck with seven nine-paned windows looking over the stern gallery to the blue sea beyond. There was a dining cabin and a sleeping cabin forward of the great cabin, and his own water closet in a quarter gallery. It was luxury indeed and as long as he didn't have to embark a senior officer, it was all his. He knew that he should be more ambitious, but he found it difficult to be envious of his fellows in their third rates, or even those in the sixty-gun fourth rates, despite their greater pay and status; they were largely confined to the line of battle with little opportunity for independent command.

His senior officers arrived together: Matthew Gresham, the first lieutenant, David Wishart, the second, Enrico Angelini, the third, Alfred Pontneuf the marine first lieutenant and Arthur Beazley, the sailing master. He looked them over with satisfaction. Wishart had been with him for five years, one of his few true followers who had clung to his patronage ever since his uncle died on the deck of the French frigate that they had taken in the Mediterranean back in the long-ago days of 'fifty-six. Enrico was his wife's cousin and he'd served with Carlisle since 'fifty-seven, first as a midshipman then a master's mate. It had seemed at one time that he would have to leave to take up his commission in the Sardinian cavalry, but at the last moment he was offered a lieutenancy in the rejuvenated Sardinian navy. He was seconded to *Dartmouth* to gain the experience that would be needed as that neutral state transitioned from a navy of rowing galleys to a modern affair of ship-rigged frigates. Enrico was a valued officer and Carlisle wasn't looking forward to the day when his country recalled him, as surely it must. Gresham and Beazley were already serving in *Dartmouth* when Carlisle was given command a little over a year ago. They were both experienced officers and after some initial misgivings about his first lieutenant, they had settled into the ways of their new captain. The marine officer – Carlisle still had to resist the temptation to call him *Monsieur* Pontneuf – had only been with him a few months. His predecessor had been killed in the Mediterranean the previous year, the first man to leap from a ship's boat onto the deck of a French schooner, and he had paid the price for his courage and zeal. Pontneuf's family had come to England fifty years before, during the worst days of the Huguenot persecutions; he was more English than Carlisle – himself a rarity as a post-captain from the American colonies – and no less so than any other of his officers.

With a clink of cups and saucers, Walker brought in the coffee. His servant had recovered from the knock on the head that he'd taken in the battle with the French seventy-four last year and Carlisle was glad of it. Like Wishart and Enrico, Walker had been with him for a number of years and knew Carlisle's ways. He was a familiar face and more than that he was visible proof that Carlisle, even with no property or friends in Britain to draw on, was still capable of collecting a modest group of loyal followers. His clerk, Simmonds, rounded out the party. He was a more-or-less permanent presence in the cabin, dealing with Carlisle's paperwork, recording meetings and advising on the enormous mass of reports and returns that had to be prepared for the commander-in-chief and the navy board. Simmonds too had come to *Dartmouth* from Carlisle's previous ship, the frigate *Medina*.

'How did Young take the news that he was to be left in

sole charge of a ship-of-the-line, Mister Wishart? All I saw was a look of utter terror.'

Wishart grinned; his captain was clearly in a good humour. He could remember being in Young's position himself and it wasn't so many years ago.

'Oh, old Eli picked him up from the deck and dusted him down, sir. He'll do well enough. He looked as solemn as a judge when I left him, pacing the quarterdeck as though his commission had grown brittle with age.'

Eli, another follower, Carlisle remembered. The old quartermaster had been with him as long as Wishart but to this day Carlisle didn't know his real surname and doubted whether Eli knew himself. The ship's muster books recorded him under whatever innocuous-sounding name the exasperated clerk or the purser chose. He'd been Smith and Davies and Jones to Carlisle's certain knowledge and still he answered to nothing other than Eli. Young couldn't go far wrong with old Eli watching over him.

There were smiles all around at the thought of Midshipman Young acting as officer of the Watch. He was a popular junior officer and would make a good lieutenant in the fullness of time, if only he would grow a few more inches, so that the examining board could square their collective conscience to certify that he appeared to be twenty years of age.

'Gentlemen, now that we know the ship is in safe hands, let's consider our first move in annoying the French in these waters. Mister Beazley, Mister Simmonds, just hold down the corners of that chart, would you?'

The chart was reluctant to be unrolled, and its two ends threatened to spring together if left to their own devices. Simmonds tactfully produced two of the ledgers that he'd been working on to relieve the master and the second lieutenant from their duties as paperweights.

He gazed reflectively at the chart, his fingers moving along the chain of islands.

'It appears that the islands are at peace, for the moment.

Carlisle's Duty

We should get warning from the commodore's frigates if any French force comes from the east.' He swept his hand across the empty spaces of the Atlantic where the wind arrows pointed resolutely westward, 'and the commodore is watching the islands to the north as far as the Mona Passage. We can't discount a French intrusion into our area from Cape François, that would be taking too much for granted, but it's unlikely.'

'A long, long beat from Saint Domingue.'

The sailing master pulled a long face as he studied the vast expanse of island-studded sea between the French naval base at Cape François and the Leeward Islands.

'Indeed, but too many battles have been lost by underestimating the enemy, Mister Beazley. However, I agree that we should concentrate our efforts on the islands and to windward, and not be constantly looking over our shoulders.'

Carlisle looked at the faces of his officers. There was a range of emotions, from the master's stoicism to the frank disappointment on the faces of the lieutenants. They all longed for action, whether it was the thunder and smoke of a fleet action or the more commercial-minded destruction of the enemy's merchant shipping, and they could see little prospect of either in these islands.

'However,' Carlisle continued, having left his audience in suspense for long enough, 'I don't intend to sit here on my backside waiting for King Louis to stir his navy into action. We'll look into every port that can take a seagoing vessel, using the sloops and cutters with *Dartmouth* to cover them…'

Wishart and Enrico glanced wistfully at each other. It sounded like the commanders and lieutenants in the smaller vessels would get all the glory while the flagship's officers were stuck with the humdrum routine of life in a ship-of-the-line.

'… and we'll use our own boats also, depending on the size of the place.'

That was more like it, and the lieutenants visibly brightened at the thought of sailing *Dartmouth's* longboat into an enemy harbour. After all, it wasn't very much smaller than the three cutters under Carlisle's command, and if the wind failed, they could always pull her out of danger.

Carlisle followed this little theatre that played out on his officers' faces. It was one aspect of commanding any ship larger than a frigate that was always difficult to resolve. Unless the lieutenants were all older and settled in their ways, resigned to remaining at their present ranks until decrepitude and a world at peace should wash them ashore, they were doomed to disappointment. It was almost impossible to give them the independent responsibilities that they craved.

'We'll start here at Fort Royal,' Carlisle's finger indicated the deep inlet in the western side of Martinique, 'that should tell us about the French strength in these waters and allow us to plan our future actions. Mister Beazley, when we have finished here, kindly put the ship on the starboard tack. The wind's veered a point or two overnight so we'll take advantage of it to beat up to Diamond Head and meet *Rabbit*.'

***

Dartmouth wasn't the fastest ship on the station, not by a long way. She didn't at all like sailing hard on the wind, but even a fourth rate two-decker could show something of the spirit of an ocean greyhound when a steady trade wind was blowing. With all plain sail set to the t'gallants, the old lady was a thing of beauty as she plunged into the long Atlantic swell, thrusting the deep green sea aside at her cutwater as she pitched and rolled to a regular, predictable beat. Twelve leagues or so to Fort Royal, but they should sight either *Rabbit* or *Gnat* off Diamond Rock some three leagues closer.

Carlisle took a deep breath as he watched the hills of St. Lucia pass in review to starboard. It was days like this that made the life of a sailor bearable. They compensated – to some degree – for the separation from family and cultural pursuits, from the fruits of the land and the association of friends. He nodded to Beazley and walked past the wheel and into the great cabin. He was tired and the cushioned bench under the stern windows was calling to him. He had an hour, perhaps, before his clerk pestered him with his books and his reports and returns, and his officers knew very well that at this time in the forenoon watch he wasn't to be disturbed for anything short of the sighting of an enemy. He stretched his length upon the cushion with his head to starboard – the high side – and his long legs braced against the larboard planking. He had no intention of sleeping; this was his time for idle thought after the mental exertion of the past few hours.

He had no cause to complain. He had a career, a beautiful wife and child and a fine home close to the governor's palace in his hometown of Williamsburg. He'd even managed to see them only six weeks ago, when he'd picked up a convoy in Hampton Roads, and that in itself was a rarity for sea officers in commission. The war would be over soon, unless Spain was tempted by French promises to join the fray, and then whether he liked it or not, his ship would be reduced to ordinary – in effect an inactive reserve – and he'd be unemployed. Even that wasn't a problem as he'd amassed a small fortune in prize money, having been lucky enough to be in command of two frigates in the early part of the war and even in *Dartmouth* he'd found a way to capture enemy ships. Yet he *was* dissatisfied. Perhaps the fault was his. Maybe he was too sensitive, but he felt that he had never really been accepted by other sea officers. He was no longer the only post-captain from the colonies, but none of the others were in any recognisable way following a normal career. Joshua Loring from Massachusetts colony, for example, was commanding a squadron of brigs and schooners on Lake Ontario, and the facts of geography insulated him from the opinion of his peers.

Carlisle had found it difficult to recruit and keep a band of followers, and he well knew how essential that was to the efficiency of a ship. Oh, he had a few, but nowhere near as many as other captains. Partly it was bad luck, but mostly it was because he had no roots in Britain, he held no land and could call on no tenants and neighbours to join him at sea.

Certainly, France must be defeated, but in his home, the American colonies, France *had* been defeated; they'd been soundly beaten at Quebec and Montreal so that they were no longer a factor in the expansion of the colonies. And he so longed to be home, with his wife and son.

***

CHAPTER TWO

A Neat Operation

Tuesday, Second of December 1760.
Sloop-Of-War Rabbit, at Sea. Off Fort Royal, Martinique.

Carlisle rested his telescope against the mizzen shrouds and stared intently over the starboard bow. An island had just come into view on the southern side of the bay, conspicuous by its angular shape against the green of the shoreline beyond. Ramier's Island. He'd seen it before in 'fifty-seven and back then it had no guns mounted, but that was four years ago, and since then the war with France had escalated. There had been plenty of time for the batteries to be armed and manned. He studied the island for a few moments. It was conical in shape – perhaps an old volcano – and as his eye moved upwards from the base, its densely wooded slopes gave it a green, lush appearance. It looked like any of a thousand small islands in the Caribbean: beautiful, uninhabited and unprofitable. No sugar could be planted on those steep slopes. His gaze lingered on the pleasant verdure before it reached the summit, then Ramier's sinister crown was revealed. The entire peak of the island had been fortified. Grey stone battlements reached above the treeline and ominous black squares revealed the embrasures from where heavy fortress guns could command the southern approaches to this, the chief French naval base in Leeward Islands.

'You have a lookout at the masthead, Captain Harrowby?'

'Mister Starbuck is up there, sir. He has good eyesight…' Harrowby looked for acknowledgement from Carlisle. Finding none he improvised, '…and he has a good head on his shoulders.'

Carlisle nodded in reply. It was a pity that Harrowby hadn't learned to say what was necessary and then close his mouth. He was a young man, even younger than his friend and protégé George Holbrooke who was commanding a frigate back in England, in the Downs Squadron. Harrowby's youth and energy set the tone for the whole ship. There was an air of recklessness, of boyish confidence that was absent in his own fourth rate *Dartmouth*. Probably Harrowby had never been under fire from thirty-two or forty-two pounders mounted behind solid masonry and sited to advantage far above the sea. The chances were high that he'd never had to walk the deck while red-hot shot plunged down, seeking the magazines that would blow them all into the next world. Perhaps that explained his lack of concern, but Carlisle was aware of another explanation for Harrowby's *sang froid*. At this point in the war, with Britain victorious on all the seas of the world and the enemy's colonies falling like wheat-sheafs in a gale, it was understandable that a young man in his first command should laugh at dangers, in whatever form they came.

'I've ordered Starbuck to watch the careenage and the anchorage, and he has a midshipman to count ships,' Harrowby added, remembering the advice that Carlisle had given him. 'We can see the forts well enough from the deck.'

That was very true. The Citadel and Ramier's Island were each only a league distant from the sloop, and a bare league of water separated them from each other. Therefore, at this instant, *Rabbit* formed one corner of an equilateral triangle, a geometric figure that was steadily flattening into an isosceles as the sloop carried the sea breeze deeper into the wide bay. Carlisle had calculated the risks before he had ordered Harrowby to carry out the reconnaissance. At their optimum elevation of ten degrees, the French forty-two pounders could send a ball just short of three thousand yards, or half a league, more-or-less. The batteries on Ramier's Island were a hundred-and-forty feet above sea level and those of the Citadel perhaps sixty feet. It was just possible to claim that between them, the two forts could close off the bay to enemy intrusion. However, at that range they would be inaccurate and a little sloop underway made a poor target; but still, it wasn't worth the risk to put *Rabbit* within range. A single shot from any of those guns could disable such a small ship and leave it an easy prey for whatever French corvettes were sheltering in the bay, or even for one of the swarm of privateers that operated out of Fort Royal.

'Very well, Captain. For want of better information, we'll assume, that the island has guns as heavy as the Citadel, so stay exactly between them, if you please. When Ramier's bears sou'east you may put the ship onto the larboard tack and beat out of the bay.'

'Aye-aye sir.'

Harrowby squinted into the low morning sun and felt the wind; it was becoming fitful, heralding a warm morning.

'Sea breeze will fail soon, sir, then the trade wind will help us.'

'Just so.'

Carlisle tried to kill the conversation. He was sure he'd never been so garrulous in the company of a senior officer.

It was the balance between the morning sea breeze and the trade wind that allowed this plan to work. There was a slight danger that they would be becalmed until the reliable nor'easterly asserted itself, but it was unlikely. In any case, if the wind should entirely fail them, these small ship-sloops still carried sweeps that could be used to make their escape.

Carlisle looked over to larboard where the grim walls of the citadel at Fort Royal stood out from a background of lush tropical green, framed by the high peaks in the distance. *Pitons* they were called locally, as they were throughout the French islands, and it was said that they were the residual cones of long-cold volcanoes. He'd read recently the latest theory on volcanoes, that they were formed when sulphur fermented with other elements – iron and suchlike – below the surface and vomited upwards, creating a mountain out of the earth and rocks brought up from far below. Perhaps that was so; he just hoped not to be in the vicinity when it happened.

He ignored the hills and looked down at the shoreline. It was difficult to discern the shape from this angle, but a sprawling, substantial seaport could be seen around the fort and a number of ships lay at anchor under its protection.

He lowered his telescope and looked covertly at the faces on the deck. Even the sailing master and the bosun were young men. They all had that same eager look about them, as though nothing was impossible. Was he ever like that? Reason told him that he must have been, but he couldn't for the life of him conjure up that feeling again. Perhaps he was growing old. In fact, to these officers, he must appear to come from a different age. At thirty-five and with only five years seniority as a post-captain, he was still at the lower end of the list. He had a long way to go before he would hoist his flag, if he ever did, but to these men he must appear of immeasurable age and gravity.

And yet, this was a significant step up the ladder. The commander-in-chief had given him a small squadron: two sloops and three cutters as well as his own fifty-gun fourth rate *Dartmouth*. There was no promotion involved and he flew no distinguishing pennant, yet he held the sole responsibility for deploying this squadron to cause distress to the King's enemies.

With a French battle squadron reputed to be heading for the Caribbean, Commodore Douglas had made the sensible decision to keep his line-of-battle intact, rather than spread his third rates and sixty-gun fourth rates out across the chain of the Leeward Islands. That was also why Carlisle had sloops but no frigates: the fifth and sixth rates – colloquially called frigates – were all out in the Atlantic to windward, the eyes and ears of the Leeward Islands Squadron, keeping a lookout for the French. It was the frigates that would alert Douglas when the French were sighted and allow him time to concentrate his force for a decisive fleet engagement, the not-so-secret dream of all commanders-in-chief.

Sir James had been almost apologetic when he outlined

Carlisle's mission and listed the ships under his command. Two sloops of ten and fourteen guns and three Caribbean-built cutters with six or eight guns apiece. He also knew why he, among all the post-captains on the Leeward Islands station, had been given this task; it was one of the blessings of commanding a fifty-gun fourth rate, the smallest of the ships-of-the-line. The harsh truth was that *Dartmouth* was too small to stand in the line of battle. She had too little firepower and her timbers would never stand up to the fire of a French seventy-four. It was an easy decision for the commodore to give Carlisle command of this little squadron. And in truth, when all the factors were considered, it was sufficient for the task. Martinique, Dominica and St. Lucia were the only three of the Leeward Islands left to the French, and Pitt's grand strategy had them marked down for invasion in the summer of 'sixty-one or 'sixty-two. Meanwhile the communication between the islands had to be cut off, and their trade strangled. With no substantial French naval force in the area, Carlisle's little band could do the job, if he wasn't reckless.

'The anchorage is rather bare, sir.'

'So it would appear,' Carlisle replied flatly, still attempting to curb the young man's prattling.

Harrowby, however, was not deterred.

'There's a frigate without her topmasts and I can see more bare masts in the careenage. Nothing to worry us.'

Carlisle had heard that before. It was in these very waters in the old *Medina* that he'd been ambushed and came close to losing his ship and his freedom. A larger French frigate had cut off their escape to the south while two ships-of-the-line slipped their cables and sailed from Fort Royal to block his way to the north. It had only been by chance, he told himself, that he'd escaped. Even after all these years he found it difficult to credit himself with the genius that had allowed him to avoid the trap. But today was different. This time the French had no warning of his arrival, so a prepared ambush was less likely. Nevertheless, he glanced covertly over the sloop's starboard quarter, but the bold headland above Black Cove cut off his view to Diamond Head to the south. Out to the west he could see the reassuring white squares of *Dartmouth's* tops'ls as she patrolled on a north-south line, covering this reconnaissance in case the sloop should encounter any trouble.

***

It was eerily quiet on deck as *Rabbit* ran gently into the bay. The lush slopes of Ramier's Island looked innocent in the early morning sunshine that crept over the tall Pitons to the east, shedding its light over the Cul de Sac Royal. And yet not so innocent. The grey, angular outline of Ramier's Fort announced to any vessel entering the bay that this was French sovereign territory, and trespassers would be met with fire and iron.

'There's a flag breaking out on the fort, sir.'

Harrowby pointed to the island now broad on the starboard bow.

Carlisle stared hard at Ramier's peak: nothing. God, his eyesight must be worse than he thought. He brought up the telescope and with its aid he could just see the flash of Bourbon white atop the fort. As he looked, he saw a puff of smoke, then another. Two seconds later a pair of waterspouts leapt skywards four or five cables off *Rabbit's* beam and the flat *boom-boom* of heavy artillery reached them.

'That'll be the warning shots, sir.'

Carlisle nodded but kept his council. They were just beyond the range of any gun that could be mounted on that lofty fortress, and the commander of the fort must know that. Why was he wasting his ammunition? Could it be that he had only thirty or thirty-two pounders and he was trying to persuade the sloop to move further north and into range of the Citadel? It was a distinct possibility, and it would explain why the fort had fired at such an extreme range. The Citadel would naturally have the heavier artillery, perhaps a battery of enormous forty-two pounders on iron fortress carriages. He could see the sailing master looking at him pointedly, willing him to give the order that would bring the sloop further to larboard, away from those ominous spouts of white water.

Harrowby was also looking questioningly at Carlisle. That was disappointing; he had his orders and Carlisle was not inclined to reiterate them, nor to discuss his reasoning.

In a moment, Harrowby realised that Carlisle wasn't about to give him any fresh directions. He took a quick bearing of Ramier's Island, picked up the speaking trumpet and pointed it towards the main masthead.

'Mister Starbuck. You have five minutes before I wear ship.'

Carlisle glanced at Negro Point at the northern entrance to the bay, just abaft the sloop's larboard beam. The sailing master caught his meaning.

'Nor'-nor'west, sir. We'll weather the point without any trouble if the wind holds steady.'

'Thank you, Master.'

Carlisle had momentarily forgotten the man's name, but Master was always an acceptable substitute for the warrant officer charged with the navigation of a ship. Nevertheless, it would have been better to use his name, if he could have remembered it. He hoped that nobody had noticed.

Another pair of spouts appeared on the starboard beam and this time, by some fluke of the air, the sound of the guns echoed from the far side of the bay.

Here was Harrowby again, removing his hat for a formal report.

'Ramier's island bears sou'east, sir.'

'Very well, you may wear ship.'

Boom-boom! The guns on the island fortress spoke again. They were still short and widely separated, but that was to be expected at such long range. Three-and-a-half minutes reload time, that was fast for such heavy guns. But of course, they were manned by professional soldiers of the French Royal Artillery.

'Up helm!'

Carlisle heard the orders that brought the sloop's stern through the failing breeze. *Rabbit's* bowsprit swung to larboard until the Citadel was obscured by the jib and stays'l.

'Boom's a-swinging!' shouted the quartermaster as the wind backed the driver, and the whole apparatus of gaff, boom and sail swung violently across the quarterdeck.

He'd never served in a ship that had a gaff-rigged mizzen sail, it was only recently that sloops-of-war had started to be so equipped and it was still a novelty to him. Of course the boom was too high to catch the head of anyone on the quarterdeck, but if someone was standing on the taffrail, for example, or the skylight, it could spoil their entire day.

Harrowby removed his hat, making this a formal report.

'The Citadel has opened fire, sir.'

Carlisle looked at him sharply. He'd been so engrossed in the working of the ship – none of his business as he would freely acknowledge – that he had missed the Citadel's desperate attempt to strike a lucky blow.

'They dropped short sir, but they're heavier guns than the island's. Forty-two pounders, I imagine.'

'Very well, Mister Harrowby.'

Carlisle assumed the look of a man who had heard only what he expected to hear and couldn't care less that he'd just been under fire from the heaviest guns that the French nation possessed.

'I'd like to hear the report from the masthead as soon as Mister Starbuck comes down.'

He paced the quarterdeck waiting for the report. It had been as neat an operation as he could wish. He'd penetrated the French bay as far as prudence allowed and he'd provoked the defenders into revealing the weight of their defences. By leaning out over the starboard railing he could see that the sloop would weather Negro Point and even now he could feel the uncertainty in the westerly wind as the nor'easterly started to gain dominance.

'I beg your pardon, sir. Would you prefer to receive Starbuck's report on the quarterdeck or below in the cabin?'

Carlisle's Duty

A young man – even younger than Harrowby – was waiting in silence, nervously fingering a slate that presumably he'd used to record his observations.

'On the quarterdeck, Mister Harrowby, if you please.'

Carlisle couldn't imagine going below when they were so close to the enemy. He needed to be on deck, even though a dozen pairs of eyes, each evidently better suited to watching the enemy than his, were eagerly scanning the shore and the horizon.

***

Starbuck was indeed a young man, no more that seventeen or eighteen, Carlisle guessed. He was as long and lean as most men at that age and his only distinguishing feature – common though it was with smallpox regularly ravaging England – was a face so scarred and pitted that it was difficult to see how he could possibly shave without drawing blood. But probably he had no need for a razor.

Starbuck drew a deep breath and stared at his slate as he delivered his report.

'Two frigates in the naval anchorage off the careening wharf, sir, both with their topmasts on deck and one with her main yard sent down. There's a brig-sloop closer inshore with her yards crossed and looking ready to sail.'

He looked up to see how the great man was receiving the report. Carlisle allowed him a brief nod of encouragement. Not enough to breed familiarity but sufficient to give him courage to continue the report; he looked as though he needed it.

'There are two merchant ships and four brigs in the anchorage, sir. The ships look like regular French West Indiamen, and the brigs could be privateers. One of the ships has lighters alongside and she's in ballast, so just starting to load or finished unloading I'd say.'

Carlisle nodded again.

'And I counted thirty-two local craft as well, sir, although there could be more; it was difficult to tally them among all the masts, but none of them fit for the Atlantic crossing.'

'Very well, Mister Starbuck. Now, Captain Harrowby, be so good as to close *Dartmouth* as quickly as possible and I'll expect Mister Starbuck's observations in writing before I leave you.'

***

Carlisle had the use of Harrowby's cabin and was making notes from Starbuck's report. It was as he had expected: commercial traffic had almost ceased and the few merchantmen at anchor or against the wharves were waiting for an escort, or for a report that there were no British ships – either men-o'-war or privateers – in the offing. Well, they'd wait in vain if he had anything to do with it. And there were no substantial French naval ships ready for sea; they too had seen how things stood and were evidently waiting for some change in their country's fortunes.

That's the modus operandi, then. This little operation had validated his plan. Now all he had to do was to set up a schedule of incursions. He'd shift into the sloops and cutters himself until he was sure that each of the captains understood what level of risk they were to take and what information was required. That should keep the squadron busy, and himself. Perhaps then he could shake of this feeling of – what was it? – not quite depression, more a sense of futility.

***

CHAPTER THREE

Change of Tack

Friday, Twelfth of December 1760.
Privateer Hope, at Providence, Rhode Island.

Joseph Kendrick paused with one foot on the gunwale and the other still on the good pine planks of the deck. He cast a lingering glance aloft then forward and aft. The crew on deck – men he'd known since boyhood, mostly – avoided his eyes or stared back reproachfully. *Hope* wasn't a happy ship and the cruise that had started four months ago with so much confidence had ended in bitter failure. They'd lost two good men, and in the close-knit seafaring community of Providence they had been counted as friends as well as occasional shipmates. Another three were so wounded with imperfectly set fractures and poorly treated wounds that their seagoing days were over, unless they could find a berth as a cook. He'd had a fast passage home, just three weeks, barely sufficient time to digest the implications of his failure. Now he had to face the owners.

'You can start swaying up the biscuit barrels, Dick, and the beef and pork, but make sure you keep a good watch on the wharf until the company storekeeper shakes the lead out of his feet.'

Dick nodded. He really didn't need to be told his job, but he knew that his friend had a lot on his mind. It was odds-on that he'd return from the meeting only to clear his gear out of the cabin, just one more failed privateer master to haunt the wharves and taverns hoping for a job.

Kendrick jumped ashore with the leather satchel containing his logs and accounts and headed for John Brown's new house on Towne Street. As he walked, he pondered why Brown had summoned him to his home rather than meeting him on the ship. If it were any other of the ship-owners of Providence, he would have suspected that he was reluctant to meet the discontented crew; their four-and-a-half months cruise was a dead loss with no prizes and no fat purses to take home. But that couldn't be true of John Brown. That hard-drinking, loud-mouthed braggart was afraid of nobody and a friend to all who didn't oppose him. It was curious also that he was meeting only the junior partner of Obadiah Brown & Company. Were the others, his uncle and brothers, out of town? Or was this more evidence of the young man stretching his wings? Either way, he was prepared for a difficult meeting. He only hoped that John Brown's recent marriage and his new house had put him in a good humour.

***

'Mister Kendrick, you are welcome.'

Brown met the privateer master at the door to his study with a grim countenance and not even the ghost of a smile. He was a short, powerfully built man who met the world with an uncompromising stare. Nobody would gladly cross swords with John Brown, young though he was.

'Wine. The Madeira, I think,' he said over his shoulder to his servant.

Welcome! Kendrick didn't believe that for one moment. The privateering cruise had cost the company a small fortune and it had turned into a complete loss of their capital outlay. And who was that serious looking man stood in the hallway? He had a lawyer's look about him.

Brown saw Kendrick's glance but chose not to introduce the stranger. He led Kendrick into a panelled study with one large desk and a few hard, straight-backed chairs. There was nothing at all homely about the room, it was for business not for pleasure. At a nod from Brown, the stranger followed them and took a seat to one side, in much the same way that Kendrick imagined that a witness to a business transaction or an inquiry into misconduct, might position himself. The stranger didn't take out a pen and ink, as Kenrick had expected, but sat expressionless, looking at nobody in particular.

'I won't ask if you had a prosperous trip.'

Brown stared hard at Kendrick, waiting for an answer to the question that he hadn't asked.

Kendrick cleared his throat. He was sure that his days in command of *Hope* were over and that he'd have to look for employment with one of the other shipping companies, but it was essential to keep on Brown's good side. He was an important man in the colony, and he knew all the other ship owners. He was even a member of the vice-admiralty court at Newport and Kendrick knew that a wrong word could end his hopes of ever commanding a Rhode Island ship again. He laid his logbook and account books on the table. Brown gave them a dismissive glance and continued to wait in silence as Kendrick collected his thoughts. The Madeira arrived just in time to prevent the silence becoming a barrier between them. He found it hard to ignore the quiet stranger and he drained half the glass in one gulp before speaking.

'We took our departure from Point Judith and shaped a course sou'east to make our offing and get into the path of any Frenchmen following the Atlantic Stream for the Saint Lawrence. We saw nothing. Then I turned west and made a landfall at Cape Hatteras…'

'Why Cape Hatteras, Captain?' Brown made no apology for interrupting. 'Why didn't you stay offshore and make for the French islands? You could have kept well out of the drift and been among the islands a week or two earlier.'

Why indeed? Kendrick knew that it was the well-trodden route for New England privateers. A fast passage to the Leeward and Windward Islands, or to Saint Domingue, keeping well beyond the influence of the Atlantic Drift; that had been the established pattern through all the French wars. He cleared his throat.

'I had a feeling they'd try to reinforce New France,' he replied simply, 'and this time of year they wouldn't take the northerly route. If I could have found a supply convoy there'd have been easy pickings at night.'

'Well, Montreal fell in September,' Brown replied

brutally. 'New France is no more, and we've seen the last of the French supply convoys running up the Saint Lawrence. Is that news to you?'

'I heard it when I anchored off Newport yesterday,' Kendrick replied ruefully.

If he'd known of the collapse of New France when he sailed from Providence he'd have acted differently. He had known of course that Quebec had fallen but the French had cherished their dream of New France for so long and so tenaciously that most people thought Montreal would hold on longer, or even that Quebec would be re-taken. It was bad luck, really, but privateer captains weren't allowed that luxury. He'd also heard yesterday that the King had died and that his grandson had taken the throne. It was George III now and perhaps that would bring some changes, but whether it would be to the benefit of the privateering trade or to the colonies, nobody could tell him.

Brown nodded and continued his hard stare.

'I coasted down the Carolinas, Georgia and Florida. There was never a Frenchman to be seen, even though that whole area used to be crawling with them. Then I made for the Caicos Passage and looked into Cape François; it was empty except for a couple of French two-deckers. I called into St. John's in Antigua and into English Harbour, just to see what the locals and the navy had to say. All I could get out of them was that the French had suffered badly in the past year and were licking their wounds. With no escorts – it appears that half the French navy was lost trying to hold their territories in Canada – almost all the French Atlantic trade had stopped, and the West Indiamen were either at home or swinging around their anchors at Fort Royal waiting for cargoes and King Louis' navy. We found nothing until two weeks ago when we chased a laden brig, but he got under the guns at the Pearl Islands, in the nor'west of Martinique, and we lost him. A shot from the battery killed John Carew, he was signed on as the cooper, and Peter Blake, able seaman. Three others are badly wounded, but they'll survive.'

A heavy silence filled the room. The company was obliged by the articles to pay pensions to widows and to disabled men. Probably the insurance would cover it, but the premiums would rise yet again. There were many accusations that Brown could hurl at Kendrick, and both men knew it. He could have sailed directly to the islands rather than dawdling down the American coast, he needn't have hazarded his ship under the French batteries, he could have been just plain luckier. Neither Brown nor Kendrick were nervous men, and each stood his ground without pacing or fidgeting.

'Well, Captain Kendrick,' Brown spoke slowly and deliberately, 'I don't expect anyone could have done better. Nigh on every privateer has come home empty-handed this year and I don't expect it will be much improved in 'sixty-one. The days when Abraham Whipple took twenty-three prizes in one cruise are over, probably never to return.'

Kendrick nodded. Whipple's cruise in his Providence privateer *Gamecock* was legendary, and in Kendrick's opinion grossly exaggerated, but the fact remained that he had brought in a good number of French merchantmen and the prize money had enriched the numerous men who had invested in the cruise. It was said that even the *Gamecock's* cook was given command of a prize, so depleted was the crew after sending ship after ship in to be condemned.

Brown still stared at Kendrick, his feet planted squarely on the rug, the only luxury in the room, a tasteful Asian pattern that his wife had chosen, but now the ghost of a smile played over his lips.

'Now, what to do with *Hope*? I don't want to lay her up, if I can help it, but she won't earn her keep privateering, not this side of the ocean.'

Kendrick kept his silence. He knew where this was leading. *Hope* wasn't a fat, slow trading ship with a cavernous hold, she was built for speed and outside of the King's service that meant one of two things: privateering or slaving.

He'd sailed in a slaver as a young man, barely out of boyhood, and he hadn't taken to it. He was thinking rapidly about how he would reply to the inevitable offer.

Brown moved at last. He walked to the other side of his desk and picked up a sheet of paper. Kendrick caught a glimpse of columns of tightly packed figures before it was turned away from him. He saw an exchange of glances between Brown and the man sat apart, but still the stranger said nothing.

'We can forget the French on this continent. The war will continue until either King George – the *new* King George, that is – or King Louis is satisfied, but as far as I am concerned, I have no more quarrel with them, so long as they stay away from New England. That's not just my opinion,' he added, 'you should see all the new houses being raised in Newport. People have confidence again, confidence to invest in this colony and grow like we did before the war, without interference from the King's ministers in London. That opens up a new opportunity – a whole world of opportunities – don't you think?'

Kendrick looked puzzled. Was Brown suggesting that he carry slaves from Guinea to the French islands? It was certainly a thought, a bold and daring notion worthy of a man of Brown's ruthless reputation, but it was an additional peril in an already dangerous trade. He frowned and started framing the words with which he would turn down the proposal. He opened his mouth to reply…

'Molasses,' Brown continued before he could speak, 'like in the old days. Nothing has changed, the brandy interests won't hear of molasses being brought into France and that depresses the price in the French islands. With the cost of Jamaican molasses so high, we can undercut the other rum distilleries, if we act quickly before they all catch on. It will need a fast ship to make a quick passage and to get past the navy and the revenue.'

Kendrick couldn't hide his surprise. It was smuggling of course, and arguably it was trading with the enemy, but before the war the British government had looked the other way for so long that it had become an established practice. He knew the quiet harbours in the islands, and he knew how to evade British cruisers. It lacked the potential for enrichment that came with the command of a privateer, but at least the pay was certain, and he could make a profit by shipping a few barrels on his own account. And it wasn't slaving.

'I can have *Hope* refitted for a cargo in four weeks and you can be away after Christmastide. What do you say? Can you find a crew for a January sailing?'

Kendrick's face broke into a slow smile. He'd been on the verge of burning his boats, but this… this was something he could get his teeth into.

'I don't doubt that my men will all be keen to sign on again, Mister Brown. The married ones won't find much welcome if their wives are having to scrimp and save and the boys won't have any money for the taverns. I won't be able to sign them all, not on a trading trip, so I'll have the pick of them, you can count on that.'

'Very well, but not a word to anyone. The crew must believe they are on a normal trading voyage, as unlikely as that sounds, until you've made your offing. I'm hoping that you'll be the first ship back to the bay with molasses at a sensible cost. That'll make them all stare, and you'll see the most unholy scramble to get their ships to sea that there has ever been.'

Brown smiled broadly. Kendrick had noticed before how mercurial a temperament his employer had.

'Now, that having been agreed, let me introduce Joshua Cranston, my man of business. Mister Cranston will sail with you, this being the start of what I trust will be a new enterprise. He'll negotiate the trades and deal with any formalities. You speak French like a native don't you, Mister Cranston?'

Kendrick knew the name Cranston, who didn't? He must be a descendent or some other sort of relative of the old governor of the colony. Brown must be serious about this new enterprise to be engaging such a man.

'I do, sir. It's a pleasure to meet you, Mister Kendrick, and I trust we will have a successful voyage.'

'Now, let's shake on it and open another of the Madeira,' Brown was smiling broadly now, 'there's never a good business deal been struck on a single bottle.'

***

CHAPTER FOUR

A King's Cutter

Tuesday, Tenth of February 1761.
Armed Cutter Kite, at Sea. Salt Pit Point, Martinique, NE 2 Leagues.

The pipes wailed as Carlisle boarded the cutter in a single step, leaving the longboat to row back to *Dartmouth*, lying hove-to just half a cable to windward. He followed the latest fashion and removed his hat until the pipes had ended. A quick look around the deck confirmed that there was little to see on this the smallest vessel in his squadron. *Kite* had been hired from a St. John's merchant a year before and the dockyard at English Harbour had made the minimum modifications to turn her into a man-o'-war. They had pierced the gunwales for three gunports on each side for her six-pounders, installed a dozen mountings for her half-pound swivel guns and laid a deck in her hold for the accommodation of her thirty men and a tiny magazine for the powder cartridges. Other than that, and the commissioning pennant that flew proudly from her main topmast head, she was indistinguishable from the hundreds of small merchant cutters that serviced the British Leeward Islands. *Kite* was a man-o'-war in name only; her frames and timbers couldn't withstand any kind of rough usage.

Roscoe, the lieutenant in command of the cutter, stepped forward. He was an elderly man, perhaps forty-five, yet he looked sprightly enough and Carlisle remembered from their previous meetings that he was energetic and inclined to make light of his burdens. And it was certainly true that these lieutenants in command of cutters carried disproportionate responsibilities. Their standing officers owned only mate's warrants and they had no purser or clerk to keep their accounts in order. They had one midshipman to keep watches opposite the master's mate and never a marine to add weight to a boarding or landing party.

Roscoe held his hat in front of his stomach, and his thinning hair fluttered in the breeze.

'May I present my officers, sir?'

They were a rough-and ready lot, compared with the rather more polished officers in his own ship. Wade, the master's mate, looked to be in his mid-twenties while Harley, the midshipman, looked much younger, barely old enough for the rank. They both had an unkept look about them but that was hardly surprising considering the standard of messing that they had to endure. The bosun, the gunner, the carpenter and the surgeon were all youngish men just serving out their time and awaiting the opportunity to move into a rated ship and the unspeakable glory of a warrant, with its better pay, its status and the comforting thought of a generous pension when their days at sea were over. The remainder of the ship's company were gathered in the waist, and even though they only numbered thirty, they filled the space between the guns on either side, the windlass forward and the tiller aft.

With the ceremony over, Carlisle looked aloft at the pennant and away to the south where the bulk of St. Lucia broke the horizon.

'East-sou'east, sir,' said Wade. 'We can make the Careenage in one board if the wind holds. It shouldn't shift now, not until we get under the Cape.'

Carlisle nodded. It was a curious feature of the French islands that so many places had been named with common nouns: *le Cap*, *le Carenage*, *le Cul de Sac*, and so forth. It had the potential to cause confusion even before they started on the *Forts Louis* and *Royal*. But in this case the mate's meaning was clear; he was referring to the headland at the northwest point of St. Lucia and the bay from whence much of the commerce and the vast majority of the privateers set sail. It was presumably well known that he was planning to look into the Careenage, and in such a small vessel it was only natural that the word should have spread rapidly.

Nevertheless, it was irritating to have his plans so freely anticipated.

'Mister Roscoe, be so kind as to set a course to round the Big Island, keep two miles off if you please.'

This time Carlisle was referring to L*e Gros Islet*, for that was its French name, that lay under the shadow of the Cape. He could see the exchanges of satisfied glances on the deck. Good God, the whole crew knew his plans!

'Would you care to use the cabin, sir,' Roscoe asked after he'd given the order to Wade and seen the cutter steady onto her new course, full and by on the larboard tack with the Cape fine on the bow.

'I'll stay on deck, thank you, Mister Roscoe.'

This was his first incursion in *Kite*. He'd been with each of the other captains, and they were now handling such affairs on their own. It had become a matter of routine to sail boldly into a French port, count the shipping, flaunt the flag and depart. The simplest of operations, carried forward without any trouble. But he'd sent *Kite* on a variety of errands to English Harbour and as far as Barbados, and this was the first time that Roscoe had ventured into an enemy harbour.

He looked again at St. Lucia and then towards *Dartmouth*, estimating the distances. A watcher on the top of the Cape could perhaps see her tops'ls, but would the French go to the bother of placing a man up there, with all the difficulties of travel and communication? Unlikely, he thought. Probably *Dartmouth's* presence had gone undetected. In any case, he felt confident that there was nothing the French could do to interfere with this mission, except perhaps to chase *Kite* away after the fact.

Carlisle had never served in a cutter. They were a relatively new innovation, and their experimental status was underlined by the fact that the navy owned not a single one; they were all hired from merchant companies. There wasn't even any consensus on how one should refer to the lieutenants in command. *Captain* seemed rather too grand whereas calling Roscoe *Lieutenant* risked undermining his authority. *Mister* was a neutral title that could be used in any situation. He'd never served in one, but he had peered below decks on other cutters, into the hutch that passed for the cabin, and he shuddered at the thought of spending the next couple of hours cooped up in such a small, fetid space. Far better to enjoy the fresh breeze on the open deck.

'I'll have some coffee brought up, sir.'

'That would be very kind of you, Mister Roscoe. Now who will be keeping the tally of the enemy? I have some particular instructions for him.'

***

The cutter heeled to the brisk trade wind, and the starboard gunwale scooped great mouthfuls of green water only to return them to the sea through the streaming scuppers. It was a wonderful day to be at sea in such a small handy vessel and Carlisle was only sorry that they had to sail so close to the wind because he would have liked to see how the square tops'l was set. Perhaps he would order a downwind course when their business with the French was complete.

Carlisle was aware of some discussion over to leeward of the tiller. Evidently Roscoe hadn't detailed anyone specifically to keep the tally, hadn't thought it was necessary with both Carlisle and he on deck and able to make their own assessment. Nevertheless, he was firm in his requirement to have a specific officer count the ships; he knew only too well how many different opinions there'd be once they had sailed away to re-join *Dartmouth*. He wanted a definitive report, and he knew that his insistence on this point would impress upon Roscoe the importance of accuracy.

'Mister Roscoe, I don't have all day.'

With a shove to his back, the midshipman broke away from the group, picked up the spare slate from the binnacle and hastened to the windward side of the quarterdeck.

'Ah, Mister Harley, it's good of you to join me,' Carlisle

said trying to keep the sarcasm from his voice. 'Mister Roscoe! You too, if you please.'

Harley's confusion showed in his face. He didn't know whether Captain Carlisle was admonishing him or merely being polite. He decided that it was better to appear contrite and mumbled his apologies for keeping the great man waiting. He had learned the hard way that in the service, contrition was rarely inappropriate in a midshipman.

Carlisle outlined his requirements: Harley was to be relieved of any ship's duties until the operation was complete, and he was to have access to pen and ink and paper and submit a written report before they should again meet *Dartmouth*.

That done there was nothing else for Carlisle to do except watch St. Lucia draw closer and drink in the utter beauty of the scene. The air was crystal clear, and the hills on the northern part of the island stood out in startling detail. The whole of the mainland was covered in tree-clad hills. Up here in the north they were gently rounded for the greater part, but down in the south they formed sharp peaks – the Pitons – similar to those on Martinique, and though smaller, their sheer drama more than compensated for their lesser size.

'The Big Island's coming into view, sir.'

Roscoe offered Carlisle his telescope.

'No thank you, Mister Roscoe, I can see it perfectly well.'

'I've a man aloft looking out for any sign of French cruisers or privateers, sir.'

'Very well.'

Carlisle resumed his study of the rapidly approaching land. He wondered why Roscoe was making such a point of the danger, which he considered minimal. With *Dartmouth* cruising in the offing – although on this occasion she was out of sight, and they had no means of communicating with her – he felt perfectly safe from anything the enemy could do to him. It was slightly annoying, in fact everything about the cutter irritated him. He didn't like the way the crew hung about on deck with nothing to do but gawp at the world, and he didn't like the attitude of the officers. And now this lieutenant was offering to make observations about the enemy's likely actions. He stamped his foot in frustration and his face twisted into an angry mask. Then he realised that his every gesture was being watched and he composed himself into what he imagined was the attitude of a great man only vaguely interested in the doings of these lowly beings.

***

The Big Island loomed hugely four points on the cutter's larboard bow with the green slopes of St. Lucia in the background.

'I'll call the hands to quarters now, sir.'

'Very well, Mister Roscoe,' Carlisle replied brightly, trying not to look quite so dissatisfied with the world in general. 'I expect this is about the right time.'

On a ship that measured only fifty-six feet from the bow to the stern, there was no need for drummers, nor even for the bosun's call, and the crew moved in a leisurely fashion to their appointed stations and started casting off the lashings to their guns. It really was quite different to his own ship, Carlisle noted in distaste. Apart from the obvious difference in size, there was no sense of urgency in this cutter, no apprehension that they may have to go into action at any moment. Oh, the job was done well enough, but Carlisle couldn't imagine these men in the sort of fight that *Dartmouth* had experienced in the Mediterranean the previous year. But then, that wasn't a cutter's role. *Kite's* job, along with *Mosquito* and *Gnat*, was to be the eyes and ears of his squadron, and on occasion to disrupt the activities of the smaller type of French vessel that traded between the islands and take as prizes those that it could overwhelm. There was no question of *Kite* engaging in a protracted fight, and they evidently deemed that clearing for action was just a formality.

He watched as the number two six pounder had trouble

passing the gun tackles. It was the last of the guns to be ready, and he saw the anxious looks of the officers on the quarterdeck. They knew that Carlisle must be contrasting their performance with the bustle and energy – and the shouting and blows – that he was used to on the deck of his own ship, and Roscoe at least must be feeling some trepidation. In fact, every eye on the ship was turned towards Carlisle with varying levels of apprehension. He was on the point of losing his temper and the tension on the little man-o'-war's deck was palpable.

'Sail ho!'

The sharp cry from the masthead broke the dangerous spell.

'Sail on the larboard bow, just coming around that island on the beam, sir!'

Carlisle spun around and squinted into the low early morning sun. Two masts. No, three, and as he looked, he could see sails being set at each one, the canvas blossoming like the petals on some exotic white flower. They were being set in a way that no short-handed merchantman could possibly achieve, and the ship – for ship she was, no mere brig – was only a mile to windward. Carlisle's gloomy reverie was cast to the same winds that sped that predator towards them.

'Bring her off the wind, Mister Roscoe. Set all the sail that you have. That's a privateer and a damned fast one! Get those men moving!'

The steersman didn't wait for Roscoe's order but pushed the tiller to larboard and the cutter turned her stern towards the wind. Roscoe cast a resentful glance at Carlisle and continued with the orders to bring the cutter before the wind and away from the fast-approaching enemy ship.

The men rushed to the tacks and sheets and a half dozen hurried up the ratlines towards the yards. As the cutter heeled over, Carlisle saw with horror that in their haste to handle the sails, the crew of number two gun hadn't completed lashing the gun to the port, and it was already running down the sharply sloping deck. It ran to the limit of its breech line and for a moment it looked as though it would be held. Then, with a dreadful rending sound, the ring bolts pulled out of the frail timber and the gun rushed to leeward, with the men on deck scattering before it, to crash into the number one gun on the starboard side. Carlisle gripped the wood of the binnacle as Roscoe and his officers attempted to bring some order out of the chaos. He'd already stepped over the line between being a visiting senior officer and assuming executive authority for manoeuvering the ship, and he bore a fair measure of responsibility for the gun running wild across the deck.

The gunner was the only man who appeared to know what to do, and he ran to the now hopelessly tangled guns and hurriedly passed the tails of the number one gun's tackles around the barrel and cascabel of the number two gun, stifling its freedom of movement, at least temporarily. Others joined the gunner, and Carlisle recognised the offending gun's captain frantically trying to make amends for his errors. Fully half of the small crew were clustered around the two guns.

'Avast there!' Roscoe shouted, waving his arms urgently from the group of men at the guns to the mast. 'Set the tops'l, damn you.'

With a sinking feeling, Carlisle looked aloft, where not a man was to be seen. In a flash the problem became clear. In a lightly manned cutter, the gun crews were also the sail handlers, and by sheer bad fortune, the captain of the top was also the captain of number two gun. When he'd seen his gun running wild across the deck, he'd abandoned the tops'l and rushed down to put things right, thinking of nothing but his own error. Without any clear direction the other topmen had followed him. What had started as an awkward situation with a ship-rigged privateer just a mile to windward had turned into a desperate race to avoid capture, with the enemy now just four cables astern and closing fast.

Carlisle's Duty

There were no orders to give, he'd done enough damage already, and Carlisle could only watch the unfolding disaster.

***

Two cables now and the privateer fired the first warning shots to bring the cutter to. Carlisle glanced at Roscoe who was deliberately not looking in his direction. The man had courage, both physical and moral, that was for sure. He was ignoring his superior officer and concentrating on saving his ship.

The gap between the two vessels narrowed steadily. No cutter could match a ship-rigged privateer sailing large. The cutter rig was designed to be fast on the wind, not running free where the privateer's big square sails – and Carlisle could see that they were all drawing well – gave her a deadly advantage. It was just possible that a bold manoeuvre may save *Kite*. Roscoe could order the helm put down and bring her hard onto the wind, but a quick glance showed that the privateer was too close. The cutter couldn't survive a single broadside from those guns and that was the least that they could expect. The privateer was well-handled, and the French captain would surely be watching for such a manoeuvre and would follow the cutter onto the wind. Three broadsides, Carlisle guessed, that would be what they could likely expect before they got to windward of the enemy, and *Kite* couldn't survive one!

Bang, bang!

The privateer's guns sounded loud and clear, and two waterspouts leaped into existence close alongside, six-pounders for sure. Those would be the warning shots. In two minutes the cutter's flimsy timbers – the ease with which the gun's ring bolts pulled through was evidence of their fragility – would be subjected to the privateer's bow chasers at what was now only a hundred yards or so; they could hardly miss. Carlisle looked at the faces on the deck. They all knew the danger and he could see that they were all drawing the same conclusion.

Now Roscoe turned towards him, his face an expressionless mask.

'Sir, I must request your permission to haul down the flag, to avoid the unnecessary waste of lives.'

Carlisle looked again at the men on deck. Everyone appeared frozen in place, their ropes idle in their hands. On this small cutter nothing that happened on the quarterdeck was private, and every man knew what was passing between their captain and this visitor. He took one more glance at the awful bulk of the privateer with the rising sun glinting through its tops'ls.

'Very well, Captain Roscoe, you may strike your colours and bring the cutter to.'

***

Carlisle drank to the full the bitter cup of defeat. The *Mont Saint-Michel* – for that was the name of the privateer – was no King's ship and although her captain was all gentlemanly courtesy and accepted his sword with dignity, the crew quickly stripped Carlisle of his valuables: his watch, his purse and the pistols that hadn't even left their case.

There had been a moment of consternation when the impressive rank of their prisoner became clear; the august person of a British post-captain had never before graced this privateer's deck, or the deck of any other French private man-o'-war, not in recent years at least. There was a brief discussion out of Carlisle's earshot and after a thoughtful glance to the east, the captain made a quick decision. Such a valuable person must be taken to Fort Royal where the French navy would pay the proper rate of head money and could be responsible for his custody. In any case, the wind was dead foul for the Careenage. Fort Royal, though further in sea-miles, could be fetched on a single board, and even after the time wasted in securing the prisoners and transferring the prize crew, with this wind he could be sure of making the anchorage before sunset. And who knew what other British cruisers were in the area? The captain must have come from a larger ship and the Frenchman had no intention of tangling with a frigate or a ship-of-the-line. The weatherly cutter and its crew could be sent into the Careenage – it also would be safe at anchor before sunset – and it could be condemned in the usual way, without the commandant at Fort Royal delaying the process while he decided whether the French navy wanted to buy it.

***

Carlisle paced up and down on the short space of deck that ran athwartships beside the privateer's taffrail. It was the only space allotted to him and even there a French seaman watched him, his hand straying to the hilt of his cutlass every time their eyes met. They were taking no chances. Apart from the remote possibility that he would try to interfere with the running of the ship, there was the greater chance that he would fling himself over the side in his shame at being caught by a mere privateer. To prevent that – and with profuse but insincere apologies for the inconvenience – Carlisle was tethered to the taffrail by a short length of rope that had been knotted around his right wrist. He could perhaps work the knot free, if he had a spike and a knife, but not with the cutlass-wielding Frenchman watching his every move. It was humiliating but Carlisle's objections had been summarily brushed aside; his was a precious skin indeed.

***

CHAPTER FIVE

Gresham's Day

Tuesday, Tenth of February 1761.
Dartmouth, at Sea. Cruising between Martinique and St. Lucia.

Gresham watched *Kite* depart to the south. The cutter was beautiful, with her lee gunwale dipping into the swell as she sailed hard on the wind to make her destination in one tack. But even that exquisite sight didn't hold his attention for long; he had a whole day in command! He didn't expect the cutter to return until the dog watches, and for the next ten or so hours he was the undisputed monarch of this fifty-gun ship and the three hundred and fifty souls on board. He had his orders, certainly, to cruise between the two great islands, keeping closer to Martinique to avoid being observed from St. Lucia. Beyond that, Captain Carlisle had left it to his own discretion.

'Pass the word for Mister Wishart,' Gresham said to the quarterdeck at large, as soon as he saw the longboat hook onto the main chains.

Gresham was conscious of this mark of his captain's trust and knew very well that nothing was expected of him but to meet the cutter at the appointed time in the place where they had parted company, preferably with *Dartmouth* undamaged and without any serious revolt among the crew. He knew that, but he could still dream, and his imagination went so far as making that once-in-a-lifetime capture of a laden French West Indiaman, homeward bound with a full cargo of sugar and coffee and indigo. Remote though the possibility was, Gresham was not a man to waste it.

'Ah, Mister Wishart.'

Gresham ignored the fact that they had been on less formal terms only half an hour ago. The departure of the captain had changed their relationship in a most fundamental way, at least for the rest of the day.

Carlisle's Duty

'I can't take *Dartmouth* much further south, not while the captain is engaged in his reconnaissance, but I can extend the area that we can watch. Take the longboat, if you please, with the boat gun and cutlasses and pistols, and I daresay Mister Pontneuf will give you a file of marines, just in case. Cruise towards St. Lucia but stay within signalling range. If I don't respond to a flag, give me a gun.'

Wishart grinned and he positively hopped from foot to foot in his enthusiasm.

'Aye-aye sir. Oh how I hope the French sugar-boats make an attempt, or even a privateer! May I take a dozen muskets too, sir, as well as the marines' arms?'

Gresham couldn't help smiling in reply. There was something essentially boyish about the second lieutenant, a pleasure in escapades and scrapes that most officers leave behind before the ink is dry on their commissions. And yet there was no doubting Wishart's capability. He had proved himself in the Mediterranean and if all that Gresham had heard was true, in the frozen Saint Lawrence river as well. The longboat would be in safe hands.

'A dozen muskets it is, Mister Wishart, and see that you bring them all back in working order.'

***

They may have been sailing on a banyan, rather than a serious wartime expedition, with the seamen eagerly looking forward to the break from routine. Even the marines' faces were wreathed in smiles as they lowered their gear into the longboat. With a wave to *Dartmouth*, Wishart brought the bows to the wind until the luff of the jib just started to lift, then he paid off a touch and the longboat gathered pace on the larboard tack, steering for the nor'western corner of St. Lucia. It was a beautifully mannered boat, built to a new design in the yard at English Harbour, and if the sheets were hauled in just so, she showed hardly any sign of weather helm.

Jack Souter eased his bones into a comfortable position against the transom and settled the tiller comfortably into the crook of his arm.

'She sails well enough, sir, I suppose, but I don't know about all that extra gear.'

He nodded towards the gaff and the enormous boom that strained to the wind above their heads.

'Aye, well it's progress.' Wishart replied shortly.

'What was wrong with the old lugs'l, that's what I want to know. There used to be room to move when we were rowing, but now all that lot,' he gestured again at the hated spars, 'clutter up the thwarts like it was a timber yard. What we'll do if we have to row double-banked, I can't say.'

Wishart looked again at the new rig. Secretly, he very much approved of the navy board's decision, but he knew that it was pointless to argue against the innate conservatism of the ship's senior seamen. Souter had been Carlisle's coxswain for nearly three years, and like most of his breed he detested change as he detested the Devil's own work. The old single lugsail had been replaced by a gaff-rigged main set loose-footed to a boom, a staysail hanked to the forestay and a jib set flying on the bowsprit. Certainly it meant more spars, but the re-rigged longboat was faster and more weatherly, and that increased performance more than compensated for any inconvenience to the oarsmen. In a moderate breeze he could eat the wind out of anything except a schooner and the entire inter-island trade became his natural prey. Yet he merely nodded in reply to Souter.

It was a big boat, thirty feet long without the bowsprit, and today it was filled with twenty-four men, himself and Pontneuf – who had requested to join the party – included, and a boat gun. In fact, *Dartmouth's* longboat was over half the length of *Kite*; it was a man-o'-war in miniature, and perfectly capable of boarding and taking any French merchantman short of a full-blown, well-manned West Indiaman.

Satisfied with the way the boat was sailing, Wishart left it to Souter and took up his telescope to scan the horizon. Nothing. In peacetime or when the navy wasn't so actively patrolling, this stretch of sea would be filled with traffic between the islands, carrying the produce of the plantations, manufactured goods from across the Atlantic and a host of fishermen, but now it was empty. The cutter had long since disappeared in the gathering haze and only the tall hills of the two islands and *Dartmouth's* lofty masts broke the purity of the horizon.

The men were chattering, but that didn't worry Wishart; nothing could spoil his feeling of impending adventure. There was something in the air that spoke of excitement; perhaps it was just the refreshing trade wind, or the release from the stifling discipline and routine of a ship-of-the-line, but then perhaps not. He settled himself in the angle of the transom from where he could sweep the whole horizon between the heads of the crew and the boom of the mainsail and didn't even care when some foolery caused a seaman to leap from his seat and obstruct his view.

***

The day passed in tacking backwards and forwards along an imaginary line perpendicular to the direct route between Fort Royal and the Careenage. The time for dinner came and although it was served cold, nobody minded because in a spirit of pure benevolence, the purser's steward had sent them away with more than enough rum for the daily ration. Soon its heady fumes pervaded every part of the boat, even though the wind whipped across the deck, and the occasional capful of spray flew far enough aft to wet Wishart and Pontneuf and Souter.

'I doubt we'll see anything now, sir,' Souter commented, as the sun started to dip from its zenith, bound for the western horizon. 'The local boats will all want to be tucked up while it's still light, so they should be well on their way, if they're coming at all.'

Wishart rested his eye from his telescope. One of the seamen in a fit of enthusiasm had shinned up the mast as far as the jaws of the gaff, using the lacing of the luff for hand and footholds. It was a precarious perch, and any sensible man would come down when the longboat tacked, but not this seaman. To the cheers of his mates, he'd hugged the mast facing aft and clung to the lacing of the gaff as it swung around in obedience to the longboat's new course, and he'd endured a battering from the leach of the stays'l as it was hauled across his body. He'd certainly be the first to see a sail, notwithstanding Wishart's excellent telescope.

'We'll join up with *Kite* and run down to *Dartmouth* at the end of the afternoon watch,' Wishart replied, 'if we haven't seen anything.'

Even Wishart was starting to lose hope, yet he still couldn't get rid of that feeling, that optimism. He could see both islands clearly, but a light haze had fallen to the south and the horizon was no longer a clear division between the elements. In any case the distance was too great to discern any vessels that may be taking their departure. *Dartmouth* was within signalling range and on this bright day with the trade wind clouds marching in disciplined array across a blue sky, his signals would easily be seen by Gresham. He fell into a reverie, and then his chin started to drop to his chest. He collected himself with a start and took up the telescope again, but soon it seemed too heavy, so he lay it down, just for a moment, and then his chin started to fall again.

'Sail ho!' shouted the lookout from his lofty eminence. 'Sail three points on the larboard bow, just under the land.'

Wishart awoke with a jump and trained his telescope over the windward bow. It took a moment, but he soon found the tiny speck of white against the greens and browns of the Cape.

'What do you make of it?' he shouted. 'Here, take the telescope.'

The seaman was an experienced lookout and had often been handed the officer of the watch's telescope, so it only took him a moment to bring the sails into focus.

'Two sails, sir, either tops'ls or t'gallants, I can't quite say for certain.'

Then it wasn't the cutter, and that in itself was ominous.

Carlisle's Duty

The sail was coming from the direction that *Kite* was expected and at about the right time. If those were tops'ls then it was probably a brig. If they were t'gallants then it could be a ship, many ship-rigged vessels only flew t'gallants from the fore and main, leaving the mizzen t'gallant mast bare. And a ship big enough to sport t'gallants was likely to be a man-o'-war or a privateer. In any case, whatever they had sighted would be more than a match for *Kite*, and Captain Carlisle would be keeping out of the way until it had passed.

'Make the signal for enemy in sight to windward, the red flag,' Wishart snapped.

All his lethargy had fled in an instant, replaced by an eagerness to know what this sail was. The signal flag was enormous, a great square of red that changed the silhouette of the longboat so that even at six miles away it would be easily seen.

'*Dartmouth's* acknowledged, sir,' Souter reported.

Wishart nodded in reply. That was quick. Now what to do. Gresham had said that he should act as he saw fit in case of an enemy sighting. He looked again at the strange sail. It appeared very much like two t'gallants. Then, as the longboat lifted on one of the great Atlantic rollers, he caught a glimpse of three squares of white below the two, strangely distorted by the haze. A ship, then. It could of course be a French West Indiaman, but that was unlikely. Most probably it was a privateer, and a big one at that. A swift glance all around the horizon; nothing had changed except this strange sail.

'Bring her off the wind, Souter, we'll run to the west-nor'west.'

'Aye-aye sir.'

Souter hauled the tiller to windward and checked away on the mainsheet. A glance at the compass and he steadied on his new course. The jib and staysail sheets were eased, and the longboat settled onto its run, with its stern rising to the regular swell, and its bows dipping as the great mass of water passed forward. He could guess what Wishart was thinking. He was trying to draw the chase – for chase it had become – out to the west to give *Dartmouth* a chance of getting to windward to cut it off from the islands.

'It looks like she's bearing away, sir,' the lookout shouted excitedly, 'she's following us!'

Wishart took another look at *Dartmouth*. Gresham had also brought his ship before the wind and furled his t'gallants. He must be hoping to delay the moment when the chase saw that it was running into a trap. If this Frenchman could only be deceived for another two hours, then his intended passage to Martinique would be cut off and he'd have the greatest difficulty in beating back to St. Lucia without being caught. Wishart blessed the navy board's wisdom; with this new gaff rig he could head-reach on any square-rigged ship in a race to windward and he had at least a fighting chance of placing himself between the chase and his southerly refuge. All he had to do now was watch for the moment when the chase started to suspect that he'd been duped, and then put the longboat onto the wind and beat up towards St. Lucia. But he was forgetting, there was one more thing that he could do.

***

Gresham paced nervously. He felt starved of information; what was going on over the horizon to the south? The single signal flag – enemy in sight to windward – was all he could realistically expect. In this age before a systematic code of signals existed, it was all he could expect if there had been a frigate out there rather than a little longboat. Yet he worried that Wishart may have hoisted the wrong flag. Certainly that was a red square, but the signals had only been agreed verbally before the longboat pushed off from *Dartmouth's* side. It was entirely possible that the second lieutenant had confused the flags and that he was trying to say that *Kite* was in sight. In that case, he was unnecessarily delaying the rendezvous. How he wished he'd taken the time to put the simple code into writing. The minutes passed as he pondered whether he should bring *Dartmouth* back onto the wind. His thoughts were interrupted by Enrico who'd been watching the longboat.

'Ha! Mister Wishart's let his mainsheet fly, just for a moment. There it is again.'

Gresham took up his telescope in time to see the longboat's mainsail flap loosely again.

'Enemy in sight,' Enrico said with deep satisfaction. 'He's making sure we don't misunderstand him.'

'So it is, Mister Angelini, so it is.'

There could be little doubt. Wishart knew how flag signals were open to misunderstanding but letting fly the mainsheets – three times – was not. It was the most ancient of ways to report an enemy sighting. Normally he'd have expected the mainsail to be let fly for perhaps a whole minute, but Wishart must be trying to hide the signal from the chase. But if that was an enemy below the horizon, where was *Kite*, and where was Captain Carlisle?

'How much light do we have left?'

'Seven hours, near enough, sir,' the master replied. 'Sunset at 6 o'clock and it'll be dark by seven.'

Gresham stared to windward where he could just see the longboat from the deck. He had to trust Wishart. He just had to believe that he was luring some unknown enemy out to leeward so that *Dartmouth* could work to windward. In that case he must stay out of sight for a few more hours and then he could spring the trap with enough hours of daylight left to close on his prey.

'Let's get the tops'ls in, Mister Beazley, and wear ship, if you please. Put the wind fine on the starboard quarter.'

That would put *Dartmouth* on a course that would diverge by a few points from Wishart's course. It was a nice calculation, but it was based on insufficient knowledge. He knew his own position in relation to the islands, the wind direction and the longboat, but he could only infer the enemy's position. Well, it would have to do.

'Let me know if there's any danger of losing sight of the

longboat, Mister Beazley.'

He looked again at the sun that was now well past its zenith and felt the steady trade wind on his cheek. Everything looked peaceful and ordered, but he knew how quickly that would change if the longboat suddenly altered course, if the chase hove over the horizon, or if *Kite* was sighted.

'Mister Angelini!'

'Sir,' Enrico replied from a mere few feet away.

'As soon as we're settled on the new course and the sails are furled, you may clear for action. There's no need for quarters just yet.'

***

This typified the sea-service, Gresham thought as he studied the chart in the master's cabin. After the bustle of getting in the tops'ls and wearing ship, and the sweat and labour of clearing for action, there was nothing more to do. If nothing changed by the end of the afternoon watch, if the enemy hadn't been sighted or if *Kite* hadn't appeared, or if the longboat hadn't altered course, then he'd have to wear ship again and run down to meet Wishart. And yet it wasn't the enemy that so concerned him, not directly, it was the absence of the cutter with his captain embarked. He should have appeared by now. Perhaps the cutter had seen this mysterious enemy and hidden somewhere along the coast between the Cape and the Careenage. In which case it would likely stay there until dark before running back to the rendezvous. That was the best case, the worst was that Wishart had sighted a French man-o'-war or a privateer that had already captured the cutter and the captain. In either case, he was probably taking the correct action. He hoped so, but he would be severely embarrassed if he'd misread the situation and *Kite* was at this moment clearing to the north of St. Lucia and expecting to see *Dartmouth's* tops'ls on the horizon.

Gresham shrugged. If he hadn't by now learned to be philosophical about the things that he couldn't change, then he'd made poor use of his service in the King's navy.

***

CHAPTER SIX

The Baited Bear

Tuesday, Tenth of February 1761.
French Privateer Mont Saint-Michel, at Sea. Off the Careenage, St. Lucia.

Carlisle tried his best to look like a man cast in the true stoic mode, but it was difficult when he knew that every mile brought him closer to a humiliating captivity. As far as he could tell his captor was planning to hand him over to the French navy at Fort Royal. That was some small consolation; he'd be exchanged without too much delay. God knew that his own navy was holding enough French post-captains, and even if Commodore Douglas didn't have one to hand at English Harbour, there were dozens of them in England. At the worst he could expect to be shipped to France with the next convoy and perhaps be back in England in two or three months. However, that was only the start of his problems. Their Lordships would certainly take a dim view of his capture. It could even lead to a court martial for the loss of *Kite*, although that would be unusual for a hired cutter that didn't even warrant a line in the navy's list of commands. Even without a court martial he may find himself without a ship. He cast a savage glare at his guard before remembering his dignity. At least with his reasonable command of the French language he could understand what was being said around him. The privateer captain seemed to have forgotten that point, or perhaps he didn't care, and he gave his orders without the least regard to Carlisle's presence.

'*Ohé le pont, ohé le pont!*' the lookout cried from far aloft, '*Voile par tribord devant.*'

Carlisle glanced upwards just in time to see the lookout pointing emphatically to leeward.

A sail! This thin haze had brought the horizon in to

Carlisle's Duty

about two leagues, and anything the lookout had seen must be quite close. Carlisle strained to see over the starboard bow, but his tether didn't allow him to get close enough to the ship's side to see past the mainsail. He tugged at the rope, but his surly guard just hauled him back with a jerk. It was clear that he wasn't going to be allowed too close to the ship's side. But a sail! It could be *Dartmouth*, although he couldn't imagine why Gresham should have strayed so far from the rendezvous. Of course *Kite* would have been expected a few hours ago, so perhaps Gresham was just moving down to investigate. His heart skipped a beat as he contemplated the possibility of his salvation.

The whole atmosphere on the deck had changed in an instant, from one of peaceful passage sailing to an almost animal excitement at the prospect of a chase and the profit it could bring. There was a conference going on just out of earshot and his guard pointedly moved to stand between Carlisle and the group of men gathered around the captain. Carlisle strove again to assume an Olympian detachment from these everyday doings of mere mortals, but he still cast sly glances to starboard where the sail was just out of his line of vision, and forward to where some sort of decision was being made.

Ah, it was over. A flurry of orders that he couldn't follow brought the privateer off the wind. They must be heading nor'west, he thought, running into the Caribbean Sea. That was strange.

'Monsieur Capitaine, a moment of your time, if you please.'

Carlisle resisted the urge to answer with a theatrical shrug. He was a prisoner, every moment of his time already belonged to the privateer.

'There is a small sail on our starboard bow. It altered course when it saw us. Can you explain that?'

Carlisle thought quickly. Most probably it was a local French trader that saw the privateer and feared the worst. But in that case, it must have seen *Dartmouth*, so why hadn't it turned back at the first sight of a ship-of-the-line? Why was it risking a sea passage in the face of the enemy? He was as mystified as the privateer and his face showed honest perplexity.

'I regret that I cannot be of any assistance, sir.'

The privateer must already have guessed – by the presence of a captain – that there was a British man-o'-war in the area, but there was no advantage in confirming it. In any case, he'd said it was a small vessel, so it couldn't be *Dartmouth*. Then, with a start, Carlisle realised it was just possible that the French lookout had spotted his longboat. He'd given Gresham permission to send it away if he thought it would be useful.

The Frenchman shrugged his shoulders, it was clearly his habitual gesture when mildly perplexed.

'A matter of no importance. It is probably French but if I find that it is English, we'll certainly be able to catch it. In that case, you will be reunited with some of your countrymen faster than you had hoped. However, we may unfortunately have to stay at sea until the morning. If you know anything that may persuade me to call off the chase, you can save yourself from an uncomfortable night.'

He motioned to the rope and the guard making it quite clear that if Carlisle co-operated, he would be allowed below overnight.

'Even so, I regret that I can be of no assistance, Monsieur.'

The Frenchman bowed with a faint mocking smile and turned away to see to the handling of the ship.

Carlisle wondered at that discussion. It seemed incredible that no man of *Kite's* crew had been persuaded to reveal the presence of *Dartmouth*, but perhaps in the privateer's haste he had omitted to question the British seamen. He must be desperate for prizes to take this risk which, after all, would probably result in chasing a local French trader far to leeward. *Mont Saint-Michel* – for that was the name of the privateer, it was carved in cursive letters on the taffrail – would have a hard beat back to Fort Royal and the chances of making it before sunset were reducing with every yard they made in this leeward chase.

***

An hour passed and the privateer closed slowly on its chase. Carlisle still had not had a glimpse of it and every time he edged towards the gunwale his guard hauled him back. His wrists were starting to protest at this treatment, and he was thirsty from standing in the hot sun. The privateer captain walked aft again.

'It has a gaff rig, and it looks British to me, Captain, but it's very small for a cruiser, more like a large ship's boat.'

He was speaking conversationally, too casually, and he was clearly fishing for information. This time Carlisle did shrug. He was becoming more hopeful that the chase was indeed his own longboat, but where was *Dartmouth*? He had reservations about Gresham's ability to respond to a new situation. Oh, he was a good first lieutenant, an excellent one even, but could he command in a difficult situation? Perhaps he was being unfair, but he found it hard to imagine Gresham managing affairs so that the longboat was leading the privateer to leeward with *Dartmouth* ready to cut off its retreat to Martinique and St. Lucia. How on earth could that have been arranged?

'I cannot imagine what it could be, *Monsieur*,' Carlisle replied with at least an element of truth. 'I cannot even see the vessel that you are chasing.'

The privateer eyed him sharply and abruptly turned on his heel without offering Carlisle the opportunity to look past the straining mainsail. If his prisoner had been a mere lieutenant or warrant officer, he'd have extracted the information that he needed by one means or another, but to offer violence to a captured post-captain would lead to more trouble than it was worth.

Carlisle could see that the French captain was troubled. There was something about the chase that he didn't like. He must be desperate for prizes to take this sort of risk, to run to leeward in chase of something so small and unprofitable. But it was that time of year when prizes were few and far between, with most substantial British merchantmen waiting safely in port for a convoy across the Atlantic.

The sentry had shifted to the larboard side of the ship and shortened the tether, so there was no chance of Carlisle seeing the chase. He settled down onto the flag locker and composed himself in patience.

***

Another hour fled by, and the sun drooped lower in the sky. Carlisle cursed the loss of his timepiece but guessed that the afternoon must be over. There was no change of the watch on *Mont Saint-Michel* as every man was on deck, speculating about the chase. He saw the captain climb aloft with his telescope and make a careful study of the northern horizon. Satisfied that they were alone, he climbed down again with a less sombre countenance. A few rapid orders and the guns were cleared away. Evidently his misgivings had been dispelled and he was now committed. Carlisle watched the last of the six-pounders being run out and saw what he assumed was the gunner lumbering aft to report to the captain.

'*Ohé le pont, ohé le pont!*'

The lookout was pointing far out on the starboard beam, well abaft where Carlisle assumed the chase must be.

'*Un mât, un mât.*' the lookout yelled.

A mast! Just a mast, no sail. That was exactly what he would be doing in *Dartmouth* now, shadowing the privateer from over the horizon with his t'gallants and tops'ls furled to hide his presence. Perhaps he'd misjudged his first lieutenant.

The captain ran aloft again. He stared through his telescope then gave a volley of urgent orders. The steersman spun the wheel to larboard and the sails flapped wildly until the sheets and tacks were adjusted, then the privateer started her long and desperate beat back towards the Careenage, now almost dead to windward.

Carlisle's Duty

Carlisle could see the chase, or what had been the chase, now that the sails didn't obstruct his view. It was most certainly *Dartmouth's* longboat, the only one on the station with the new gaff rig, and it had already followed the privateer's motions and hauled its wind. He strained his eyes to see the second ship, which he was now convinced could only be *Dartmouth*, but nothing was visible from the deck. Then by some fluke the privateer heaved upwards on the swell at exactly the same moment as the unseen ship set its t'gallants, and Carlisle saw a brief flash of white, perhaps a point to the east of north.

Now it was all clear. The longboat – he wondered who was commanding it, probably Wishart or Enrico – would use its superb ability to eat the wind in order to head-reach on the chase – for the hunter had now become the hunted – and get between the Frenchman and the safety of St. Lucia to pin him down until *Dartmouth* arrived. It was a dangerous game for the longboat with nothing but a four-pounder gun – if they had shipped a gun at all – to stand up against *Mont Saint-Michel's* twelve six-pounders. If *Dartmouth* was far behind it shouldn't even be attempted. He looked again at the two chasing ships, then at the bulk of St. Lucia on the larboard bow. It could be done, but it would be tight. It was a desperate race and Carlisle was nothing more than a spectator.

***

The privateer's bows sliced through the long swell, sending showers of spray so far aft that soon Carlisle was soaked to the skin, yet he wouldn't give his captors the satisfaction of asking for an oilskin or to be allowed into shelter. In any case, he didn't want to miss a moment of this epic race. He could see that the longboat, small though she was and disproportionately affected by the swell, was drawing ahead of the privateer. She was also steering a good point closer to the wind than the ship, and the combined affect was that the longboat would soon be between *Mont Saint-Michel* and the Careenage. A quick look at *Dartmouth* showed that his own ship too was closing in. Gresham was steering two or three points free, and Carlisle's practiced eye told him that if nothing changed the three vessels' tracks would converge at a point some eight or ten miles to leeward of the privateer's safe haven. The problem was that while the privateer and the longboat would reach that point more-or-less simultaneously, *Dartmouth* would be some way behind, perhaps a mile and a half, and that meant the longboat would have to hold the privateer for fifteen minutes or so. He tried to imagine how Wishart or Enrico would handle the situation, but he valued both of his officers and his mind rebelled at the likely outcome. The longboat could neither trade broadsides with the privateer, nor board her. She was hopelessly outgunned and outnumbered in either case.

Someone brought him a plate of food and a cup of wine; rough island bread and sliced meat and cheese and a thin, acidic wine that had clearly spent too long being tossed about at sea. He ate and drank ravenously; he hadn't realised how hungry and thirsty he was.

Now he could make out some of the details on the longboat. He could see the four-pounder in the bows, and he was almost certain that he could recognise the officer in the stern sheets. Enrico had the Mediterranean black hair and this man had not. It was Wishart without a doubt, and it was his own coxswain at the tiller. He could also see a few flashes of red which must be at least a file of marines. Somehow that was a most reassuring sight and he cast to the back of his mind the relief that it was Wishart and not Enrico in command. Wishart, he knew, was the more aggressive of the two but beyond that practical factor, Enrico was his cousin by marriage, and he dreaded the thought of telling his wife that her cousin was wounded or dead.

Another glance to the north showed that *Dartmouth* was almost hull-up, and with all plain sail set she was also heeling steeply. The difference was that the fourth rate was built for conditions such as these and she shouldered the long swell aside with ease, barely taking a drop of spray over her bows. Carlisle could imagine the scene on the deck. Beazley, impassive as ever, seeing to the steering and sail trimming with no more than a word or two, while Gresham would be staring keenly ahead, trying to calculate the best course to intercept the chase, and rehearsing in his mind how he would bring the privateer to strike its colours. It brought a lump to Carlisle's throat; he hadn't realised how much he missed his own quarterdeck.

***

Wishart was also soaked to the skin and where the sea water had been dried by the hot tropical sun it had left a rime of salt in the wrinkles around his eyes and his mouth. He had stowed his hat under the stern sheets and now his natural hair was blowing in the stiff breeze.

'Wind's got up, sir, and it's veered a point, maybe sou'-sou'-east. That'll make him think.'

Souter jerking his head towards the privateer.

'Aye, he's being pushed further south and if he's making for the Careenage he'll have to tack soon.'

Neither of them uttered their supplementary thought. When the privateer tacked the longboat would be directly between them and safety, and with a great ship-of-the-line bearing down upon them they'd want to sweep the longboat aside with minimum delay. One broadside would do it. Indeed one well aimed shot from a single six-pounder would finish the longboat. Wishart had briefly pondered whether it was worth the risk, after all it was only a privateer, not a man-o'-war, and whatever he did short of a craven retreat would endanger the boat and all the men in it. He couldn't trade shots with the enemy and nor did he have enough men to board a privateer that must necessarily be stuffed full of seamen. No, he had to find a way of slowing the privateer down without either boarding her or loitering in range of her guns. He had the advantage of speed and manoeuvrability while his weakness was firepower and manpower. And yet, he had a four-pounder gun in the bows and sixteen muskets with the four that the marines carried. The germ of an idea started to form.

***

Souter looked over his shoulder at the privateer, it was close now and its big foresail blocked the horizon, huge and menacing.

'We're about there, sir. Three points on his bow at two cables. There he goes again; much good may it do him.'

The shot flew wide, it was too much to ask for a six-pound bow chaser to hit a small longboat when fired from a ship beating hard into a stiff breeze and pitching and rolling on an Atlantic swell. The privateer had been firing for ten minutes and although it was just a little unsettling waiting for each shot, Wishart knew that it would take a dose of remarkably bad luck for them to be hit.

'You're ready, Mister Pontneuf?'

The marine lieutenant nodded from his position in the bows. He appeared cool and competent, clearly looking forward to his part in the plan.

'Gun's loaded and ready, sir,' reported the gunner's mate who was cherishing the slow match under the folds of a tarpaulin.

Wishart took one more look at the privateer. Would he be able to introduce some chaos into what had so far been an orderly affair? That was what Carlisle preached: don't let the enemy fight in a way that he was prepared for. At all costs, you must shake him up, do something utterly unexpected, and that was what Wishart was plotting.

'Helm a-weather!'

The longboat heeled alarmingly as its bows spun towards the privateer. Souter was watching the wind and the enemy. He didn't want to gybe, just to put the boat before the wind on the larboard tack.

The privateer suddenly looked very large and very close as the longboat sped towards it. Wishart could see the scramble on deck as the gunners attempted to train their weapons onto the fast-moving craft, but the rate at which the longboat passed down the ship's side was too great. He clung to the backstay, watching for the right moment.

'Helm a-lee.'

He tapped Souter on the shoulder for emphasis.

Now the longboat reversed its turn and pointed its bowsprit ahead of privateer's beam. A gun went off but flew harmlessly overhead. It was all happening too fast for him to control, but he'd given his orders.

Souter brought the longboat crashing against the privateer's side, using the impact to reduce his speed. The privateer's guns loomed over their heads for a moment. He could hear shouts and screams in French and a gun fired above him, making his ears ring, then Souter pushed the tiller hard over. The bowsprit just shaved the privateer's stern as the longboat turned into the wake, and three grapnels flew from stout arms. One of them dropped short but one caught in the timber of the taffrail, and another smashed through a stern window and dug into the frame. Wishart caught a glimpse of faces looking down on him from the enemy's quarterdeck, men in round hats and tricorns and one, bewigged and hatless. He looked again; it was Captain Carlisle. He had no time to think of the implication of that.

The longboat swung tight under the privateer's stern, tethered by the two grapnel lines and the sails came down with a rush.

'Present... Fire!'

Pontneuf's orders were precise and unhurried and before Wishart could stop them, the three marines fired a volley at the faces that peered over the taffrail. They handed their muskets back to the seamen waiting to reload them and three fresh muskets were pressed forward into their hands.

Bang! The longboat shuddered like a dog on a leash as the boat gun fired into the privateer's stern. The gunner's mate was sponging and reloading at lightning speed. He'd been ordered to aim for the rudder, the first shot had narrowly missed but it had destroyed a whole stern window. That would deter anyone from trying to dislodge the grapnel.

The marines' second volley splintered the taffrail, but the grapnel still held.

'Did you see the captain?' Souter shouted as he wrestled with the tiller. The boat was behaving like a mad thing as it was towed bodily through the water.

'Yes, but he's dropped out of sight now.'

Wishart tried to sound devil-may-care, but he'd been deeply disturbed by the sight of his captain staring down on him, just before he'd fired three muskets and a four-pound ball in that direction. He hoped – he prayed – that Carlisle had sensibly ducked out of the way. In any case, that explained the mystery of the missing cutter. In a flash if insight Wishart guessed the whole story, the capture, the decision to take the important prisoner to Fort Royal and the overwhelming temptation to chase the longboat. A line of scripture intruded on his thoughts: *Be on your guard against all kinds of greed; a man's life does not consist in the abundance of his possessions.*

The privateer's helm came over; he was trying to bring a gun to bear on his tormentor, but the longboat acted as an enormous sea-anchor, irresistibly pulling the ship's stern back into line. A few pistol shots were fired, but they were ill-aimed. It appeared that none of the Frenchman relished the thought of exposing themselves for more than a second to the longboat's fire. Pontneuf's marines were no longer firing volleys but single shots, so that there was always a musket pointed at the ship's taffrail.

Bang! The second shot from the four-pounder did the trick and the privateer's rudder shattered at the stock and fell away, to be held only by a lower gudgeon. Slowly at first, but then faster and faster her bows swung to larboard, into the wind. In just a few seconds the Frenchman was in irons, stopped dead, like a baited bear with a hound's jaws fastened

Carlisle's Duty

tightly to its hind quarters. Wishart saw the Bourbon white climb swiftly to the head of the mizzen gaff, then come just as quickly down. The privateer had struck its colours!

***

Carlisle didn't even wait to reach his quarterdeck before he was issuing volleys of orders.

'Mister Gresham, my congratulations, you appear to have saved my from some considerable embarrassment, you and Mister Wishart of course. We'll talk more of that later, but for now I want all those prisoners brought on board *Dartmouth*. Put a prize crew into the privateer and send the carpenter over to see what he can do about the rudder, Mister Angelini can command. And I want Mister Wishart and Mister Pontneuf back on board here as soon as possible. The longboat doesn't look very much knocked about; you can tow her astern. As soon as that's done shape our course for the lee of St. Vincent. The prisoners are to be strictly segregated; the captain is to be fitted with manacles and placed in isolation in the hold, the officers to be in one space and the crew in another space, the three groups are to have no communication whatsoever. Is that clear?'

Gresham couldn't help smiling. It was just like Captain Carlisle to rush straight on to the next mission before the last one had been truly digested. And there were smiles all over the quarterdeck. Not only had they rescued their captain, and surely that would warrant some kind of indulgence once the dust had settled, but they'd taken a valuable prize without any loss or serious injury. The ship already had a holiday feel to it, despite the labour that they knew was to come. There was a general jostling in the waist as the seamen strove to catch the bosun's eye to be selected for the prize crew.

'We'll start the interrogation of the French officers and crew without delay. Mister Gresham and Mister Simmonds can see to them. I want it all done today but we'll leave the captain to stew until tomorrow. Now, send for the master-at-arms. I want a strict search made for my sword, my watch and my pistols, and my damned hat!'

Carlisle turned towards his cabin and there was old Eli, the quartermaster of the watch, at his station beside the wheel. He winked, as much as to say, *I know what's in your mind, Captain Carlisle, you can't pull the wool over my eyes*. That drew a wry smile from Carlisle, and he stopped in front of the cabin door.

'We'll winkle *Kite* out of that hidey-hole, don't you worry, Eli. The French won't enjoy their prize for long, not at our expense.'

***

CHAPTER SEVEN

Interrogation

Wednesday, Eleventh of February 1761.
Dartmouth, at Sea. Off St. Vincent.

Dartmouth lay hove-to in the lee of St. Vincent, with her bows to the nor'east. The island sheltered her from the long, regular trade wind swell, and she barely pitched at all in this calm sea. The early morning sun slanted through the windows of the great cabin, creating stark shadows on the deck. Carlisle was reminded of the chapel in the college of William and Mary in his hometown, and that always led to an appraisal of how he had come from being an unruly colonial planter's son to the lofty rank of post-captain with the command of three-hundred-and-fifty men and this vastly expensive machine of war. He'd been lucky, he knew, and this present war had come at just the right time to advance his career; he should have been supremely content. Nevertheless, it was at times like this that a twinge of regret came to haunt him, a longing for his home in Virginia and the company of his wife and son. A knock on the cabin door pushed the disruptive thoughts from his mind, he had a serious business before him.

'Lieutenant Gresham, Mister Simmonds and Sergeant Wilson, sir.'

Walker held the door open, and the men entered. Gresham was a big, powerful man and his sheer size tended to dominate any space. Yet since his acknowledged success in rescuing his captain the day before, he looked disgracefully cheerful and was liable to break into a grin at any moment. Simmonds was solemn as always and brought his pen and ink and paper, ready to take notes. Wilson came last, grim of countenance and apparently unable to shape that leathery face into any kind of smile.

'Take your seats, gentlemen, if you please.'

They were gathered around the polished mahogany table in the great cabin. It was altogether too grand for four people, but today it was to provide the theatre for a particular kind or drama.

'I won't offer coffee, if you don't mind, you'll see why when I explain this morning's work.'

Gresham and Simmonds exchanged glances. They'd been messmates for a long time now, and although they were used to their captain's strange ways, they still couldn't tell what was in his mind.

'Mister Simmonds, perhaps you can summarise what we have already learned from the privateer's officers and crew.'

Simmonds opened his notebook. He looked tired; he'd been questioning the prisoners well into the first watch and the compilation of his notes – many of them contradictory and some of them outright attempts to deceive – had taken most of the middle watch. He'd been abed for less than two hours and felt decidedly groggy.

'The general opinion, sir, is that *Kite* will have been taken to either the inlet to the west of Pointe St. Victor or to what they call the Little Careenage to the east of the point, close to the customs house and the commercial wharves. The officers all said it would be the inlet, to keep out of the way of authority, but the opinion among the crew was that the commandant would want the cutter under his eye in the Little Careenage. Mister Beazley gave me a sketch plan of the whole bay.'

Simmonds placed a small octavo sheet of paper on the table. Carlisle had seen it before but now his interest was more focussed. Both of the likely anchorages were on the north side of the bay that formed the Careenage, the principal port of St. Lucia. Both were close to the bay's outlet to the sea, and each was covered by the Grand Battery that sat atop Pointe St. Victor.

'I'll be interested to hear what the captain has to say about *Kite's* anchorage,' Carlisle said as he mused over the sketch. 'What did you learn about *Kite's* officers and men?'

'They told the same tale, sir, for the most part. *Kite's* crew would be held on board until the prize agent could tally them in the presence of witnesses, and they thought that would take a few days. None of them trusted the commandant to take possession of their property until it was all properly put down on paper. The same with the stores and fittings of the cutter, nothing was to be touched until the prize agent had made a full inventory. That's the reason that the officers gave for *Kite* being kept in the western inlet.'

Carlisle nodded in agreement. It was a similar situation in Antigua where the British privateers wouldn't bring their prizes anywhere near the colonial authorities until the agents had done their initial inspection. That was the reason that prizes were rarely seen in English Harbour, even when it was a more convenient anchorage for enemy shipping taken in the Leeward Islands and despite the obvious fact that it saved the need to sail halfway around Antigua to the commercial harbour at St. John's.

'The Grand Battery appears to be the only one armed. They all said that the Dauphin Battery, being so far out of town, was never manned, and its guns had been sent to the Grand Battery. Twelve pounders, that was the general opinion, though the number varied between two and eight. They mostly agreed that it was well manned day and night, with enough artillerymen to serve the guns at a moment's notice.'

Carlisle stretched his fingers across the mouth of the bay and offered them against the scale of nautical miles.

'A cable and a half. Did the prisoners agree with that?'

'Yes, sir, they did.'

Carlisle measured the distance between Pointe D'Estrées at the north side of the entrance and the Little Careenage. If *Kite* was in the commercial port, then his boats would have to row over a mile, possibly under fire from the batteries. This wasn't new information; he'd guessed it before he'd made his mind up to cut out *Kite*. Nevertheless, he had a moment of doubt before casting it aside. He'd already stated his intention and wouldn't back down now.

'Guard boats, chains, anything of that nature?'

'No, nobody mentioned such things and I'm sure at least one of them would have told us, as they were all questioned separately.'

'It's a commercial port, sir, and a small one at that,' said Gresham. 'All the officers stressed that as though they were making excuses for its rusticity. Its defence rests on the Grand Battery alone, it appears.'

Carlisle tapped the paper of the chart. It was possible, certainly, but he'd dearly like to have some assurance about *Kite's* anchorage and the guns in those batteries.

'Now, would you bring in the privateer's captain, Sergeant Wilson? He's to have no food – he's had none since he was taken – and he's to stay in manacles. He didn't treat me with much civility, so he'll be apprehensive, no doubt. I want to keep him worried, Mister Wilson, but I'm sure you can manage that.'

'Yes, sir. He'll not get any sympathy from me.'

'Then, Mister Gresham, if you will sit on my right and Mister Simmonds on my left, you can bring him in.'

***

The privateer captain certainly looked worried enough. He had a marine on each side and Sergeant Wilson behind, holding his halberd across his chest as though he would like nothing better than to use it upon the unfortunate prisoner. He was dishevelled, unshaven and his hands and ankles were held in iron manacles. The chain that joined the two pairs of manacles was just short enough to prevent him standing upright. Nobody could look at their best under those conditions and the wretched man had little dignity left. Carlisle nodded grimly in approval, remembering the hours that he had spent tethered to the surly French seaman at *Mont Saint-Michel's* taffrail. He didn't offer the privateer a seat, nor any refreshment. The two marines left but the prisoner was in no doubt of the awful presence of the sergeant behind him with that frightful halberd.

Carlisle spoke in French, the better to be understood. He consulted a paper on the desk before him.

'Now captain, my secretary has examined your letter of marque and reprisal,' he said slowly, giving the document its full title for emphasis, and dwelling on the word *reprisal*. 'It appears to have been issued by the governor of French Martinique,' he added, turning the paper over as though it offended him.

He looked directly at the prisoner for a span of half a dozen seconds, with no humanity showing on his face.

'Yes, sir, it is a regularly issued document, recognised by your own government,' the privateer said to break the dangerous silence. 'I have been sailing under its authority for three years…'

Carlisle continued to stare at the prisoner until his monologue degenerated into incoherent mumbling.

'Perhaps so. Possibly it is a genuine document,' Carlisle didn't take his eyes from the prisoner, 'and yet, Mister Simmonds has studied many such documents and he is under the impression that the seal and the signature are forgeries.'

The prisoner jerked upright but was constrained by his chain.

'But sir, but sir, I assure you…'

Carlisle silenced him with a wave of his hand.

'If the seal and the signature are forgeries then I wonder whether your capture of my cutter was a legal act. Indeed, I wonder whether your captures over the past three years, which you have admitted to, were legal acts…'

He paused, letting this horrible proposition sink in.

'… and it occurs to me that perhaps I should treat you as a suspected pirate.'

This time the Frenchman said nothing, but his appalled face bore eloquent testimony to his distress.

'You see,' Carlisle continued, 'I can deal with you and your crew in a number of ways. I could perhaps consider you to be pirates, bring you before a court martial and hang you before the sun sets on this day.'

Now the Frenchman found his voice again, but he spoke so fast that Carlisle couldn't understand more than one word in ten. He held up his hand for silence and Sergeant Wilson reinforced it with a jab of the butt end of his weapon.

'That may be a little extreme, but I don't discount it. The next option is to take you back to Antigua and send you to Britain for trial. You have perhaps heard about the prison hulks in Portsmouth harbour? I doubt whether you are old enough to have had personal experience, but certainly you must know people who have suffered in them.'

Now the Frenchman lapsed into a sulky silence, staring at the deck between his feet.

'It would give you adequate time to repent of the way that you treated me when you had me in your power.'

The Frenchman looked up and appeared to be about to say something, but Carlisle cut him off.

'And then there is a third option. With regard to the authenticity of this document,' he tapped the letter, 'I could give you the benefit of the doubt. I could assume that it is a genuine letter of marque and reprisal, and I could take you to Antigua with a recommendation that you be exchanged at the first opportunity without the inconvenience of a passage to England, with all its uncertainty.'

A look of hope spread briefly over the Frenchman's face, to be replaced by one of caution when he realised that this offer couldn't possibly come without some conditions. He knew enough about the authority of a British post-captain to be in no doubt about Carlisle's ability to carry out his threats. *He* knew that his letter was genuine, but he feared that he wouldn't have the chance to prove it, unless he co-operated.

Carlisle could guess at the privateer's emotions; they were clearly written on his face. The poor man had spent a fearful and deeply uncomfortable night in the hold,

Carlisle's Duty

surrounded by putrid bilge water and nameless creatures scurrying in the dark, and his self-possession of the previous day was no longer in evidence.

'Now, sir, I have a few questions to ask you. Don't be concerned, your answers will remain within this cabin.'

He kept his eyes on the prisoner.

'Mr. Simmonds, you can put aside your pen for the moment.'

It was a gesture of confidentiality that weighed more in the prisoner's mental balance than all of Carlisle's assurances.

'Regarding the location of the cutter's anchorage…'

***

Carlisle saw the boy scurry forward along the gangway and a moment later he heard two strokes on the bell, muted by a wad of waste canvas in consideration of the men getting some sleep before they were called at midnight. An hour into the first watch, nine-o'clock at night for that part of humanity that didn't conduct its business in great waters. He was aware of the master busily taking bearings to starboard. He could see the Pitons and the peak of the Soufrière volcano outlined by the low crescent moon. It was gross tautology he knew, because the very word *Soufrière* – sulphuric – implied a volcano in French, and there were a number of *Soufrières* in the French islands. He could also see the solid bulk of the quartermaster each time he turned at the rail of the poop deck, but that was only the subconscious part of his mind, the active part was elsewhere. Carlisle walked steadily up and down on the windward side of the poop deck, turning by long habit and some personal superstition so that at each end of his walk, he touched the flag locker under the taffrail with his right hand and the poop deck rail with his left.

He wasn't much given to second thoughts, but he was starting to have misgivings about the expedition that in three hours would be launched upon its way. The capture of the cutter weighed heavily upon his mind, and it pulled him in two opposite directions. On the one hand, he was burning with shame at the way he'd ordered *Kite* into a position where it was an easy capture for the privateer. That shame led him to want – to need, it could almost be said – to recover the cutter, and as quickly as possible. That was why *Dartmouth* was ghosting north towards the Careenage and it gave reason to the elaborate preparations that Gresham had been making throughout the day. That was the instinctive part of Carlisle's character, the trait that made him impatient of inaction, urging him forward even when reason suggested that he should pause and consider. On the other hand he knew that this was a dangerous endeavour, and he was discarding some of his long-held principles of caution and prudence.

The privateer's captain had confirmed that he had ordered his prize crew to anchor the cutter in the westerly inlet off the Careenage, but Carlisle could sense that there was a long-standing tension between the privateering community of St. Lucia and the governor and commandant. It was entirely possible that they had sent *Kite* to the easterly inlet where the majority of the island's commerce was conducted, and in that case the expedition would be much more dangerous. The approaches to both inlets were covered by the Grand Battery, but there were more guns facing south and east than west, and any boat would have to run the gauntlet for much longer to reach the commercial anchorage. Neither anchorage could be directly covered by the battery, so his boats would be relatively safe once they had turned off the main channel, but they still had to reach the anchorage unscathed. There was no guard-boat, no chain across the entrance and no other batteries that could cover the anchorages, although the Dauphin Battery on the point at the north side of the entrance was still an unknown factor. However, that was only the testimony of his enemies, and who knew how much of it was true.

Would they be expecting a cutting-out expedition? No, he could honestly say that it was unlikely. As far as the

French were concerned their capture of *Kite* was unseen by any other British ships and it would be days before the little cutter was missed and a search party sent from Antigua. They wouldn't have seen the privateer's capture either, being too far offshore. If they thought about it at all, they'd conclude that there was no danger for a few days at least. And yet, he was sending two boats, his first lieutenant and a substantial part of his crew into an essentially unknown situation, and he wasn't at all sure that the risk was justified. With Enrico away in the prize, it would leave him with only one lieutenant – Wishart – in the event of a disaster. Wishart had come close to begging to be allowed to command the yawl, but Carlisle wouldn't hear of it, this was Gresham's chance for glory.

His train of thought was interrupted by a midshipman and a boy casting the log. The boy was a big lad who could soon be rated ordinary, and he struck a heroic pose in the moonlight as he held the reel aloft while the log-line ran out and the midshipman held the half-minute glass up to the silvery lunar glow.

'Mark!' the midshipman said, quietly but sharply.

The boy pinched the line, and it went suddenly slack. They both studied the marker knots before reeling in and walking swiftly back to the quarterdeck, with a tip of the hat from the midshipman and a knuckling of the brow from the boy as they passed by their captain.

Well, Carlisle thought, there was no point in agonising over it. He'd made the decision as he crouched below the privateer's taffrail sheltering from Pontneuf's musketry, before the privateer's colours had reached the deck. The expedition had been prepared and his ship was moving into position, and he could hardly back out now. He could read the excitement on the midshipman's face, and on the boy's, and it was certain that their enthusiasm was shared by the whole ship. And of course he had to consider how Commodore Douglas would take the news if he heard that the cutter and its entire crew had been lost. The taking of

Mont Saint-Michel would be a powerful counter, but the loss of a commissioned vessel, even a hired cutter, always looked ill in the reports that he had to send to the Admiralty. If it was a slack news day, it could even appear in the London broadsheets, along with his name as the man bearing the greatest responsibility.

Beazley's head appeared at the top of the ladder.

'Four leagues to run, sir, and we're making four knots under the courses, the mizzen, the jib and stays'l. The moon sets at ten minutes to midnight, and we'll be two miles off the mouth of the Careenage an hour after that. It'll be pitch dark by then.'

He could see that even Beazley was excited at the prospect of the night's work.

'Very well, Master.'

With that, he set his jaw and picked up the pace, hoping that the intense exercise would banish his doubts. When three bells struck, he'd go below and stretch out on the bench below his stern windows and get some rest.

***

Able Seaman Nathanial Whittle sat high up at the top of the main t'gallant mast. His legs were wrapped around the slender pole with his thighs resting comfortably on the hounds. Those shaped blocks of timber were bolted to the mast to support the shrouds and stays, but they were perfectly proportioned for the human body. And from here, with the t'gallants furled, he had an uninterrupted view of the island and the darkened sea that lay like a black blanket before him.

He wasn't on watch; he'd been excused from duties because he'd be pulling stroke in the yawl in a few hours' time when they went in for the cutter. He should be sound asleep in his hammock, but he preferred to be up here on a night like this and nobody questioned his right to do so.

He remembered when he first came to sea, how high the t'gallant head appeared and how an old seaman had taken a length of one-inch rope and wrapped it twice around his body and the mast, *'cos we don't want to have to clean up a bloody mess on the gangway, now do we, mate?*

Aye, he'd been green in those days, but that was long ago. He'd been at sea since before this war and he was counted as one of the experienced seamen now. He'd come to sea – run away, you could almost say – when Edward Carlisle had mentioned that his new frigate *Fury* needed a few more hands. Nathanial's father was an indentured servant on the Carlisle plantation in Jamestown and his papers still had a few years to run, and a future as a field hand didn't look appealing for a young man. He'd had hardly paused for thought and followed Captain Carlisle across the Atlantic in a navy sloop to join his new ship. He'd been with the captain ever since, the first of his followers and the only one to have been with him since he was first posted. He was proud of that.

He took a look around the horizon. The moon was sinking fast in the west, but he could still see the island's outline to starboard. Saint Lucia: he'd heard the captain and the master discussing it. He'd known a Lucy once, when he'd been in London waiting for *Medina* to be launched at Cuckold's Point, but she'd been no saint. But then, neither had he, come to that. Other than the island there was nothing in sight; if there had been he'd have seen it.

Whittle had always been a clever, cocky lad. His father used to beat him for it, but he just laughed it off. He knew that he was smarter than the other seamen, that he should be captain of the foretop by now, or rated bosun's mate. He knew that any time he chose to change his attitude the captain would promote him without any trouble, for old times' sake if for no other reason. But Whittle was clever enough to know his limitations, for deep inside him he was aware of his deficiency. He was lazy, bone-idle, indolent, call it what you will, but he knew that he couldn't change his nature. And yet, while the other incorrigibles of the ship suffered an endless round of punishments – stoppage of grog, cleaning the heads, a turn at the grating – he sailed through it all with a grin and a wink; it would be a bold petty officer who complained about the captain's townmate.

If he moved up the ship's hierarchy then he'd have to give up his comfortable position and possibly – horror of horrors – be required to exert himself. That was why he had wheedled his way into this self-imposed position of ship's lookout, because it was easy and required no effort. True, it was often cold and wet and uncomfortable, but none of those things bothered him unduly. At the masthead he could be his own lord and he could dismiss the seamen that were sent up to relieve him until he felt like coming down. Nobody ever challenged him for the simple reason that he was the best lookout anyone had ever known, and of course his relationship with the captain did him no harm.

He looked again around the horizon. It was clear, not a sail or a mast in sight, and now the moon had inched closer to the horizon. Soon there'd be nothing to see at all and the dark of the night would hide *Dartmouth's* doings.

'Deck there. Nothing in sight from the masthead.'

There was no harm in reminding them that he was up here.

***

CHAPTER EIGHT

Restitution

Wednesday, Eleventh of February 1761.
Dartmouth, at Sea. Off St. Lucia.

The sea was almost flat calm under the lee of St. Lucia. Gresham could feel the land breeze, still hot from the island even though the sun had set over three hours before. It wouldn't be long before the land had cooled enough for the trade wind to reassert itself, but it hardly mattered because it would come from much the same direction. It would be a long, hard pull into the Careenage, but they'd be able to sail out and more importantly, so would the cutter. He was smiling in the dark, and he had good reason. Until a year ago he would have said that he was fated to never rise above the rank of lieutenant, to be one of those commonplace officers that went from ship to ship, perpetually filling the same role as he grew in age and seniority. *A warrior for the working day*, as Shakespeare put it. Those were the kind of officers that were never, ever offered a ship when peace broke out, and he had become used to eking out a living on half pay in the intervals between the blessed wars. At some point his seniority would become an embarrassment, threatening to block the rise of a captain's chosen followers, and then he would struggle to find a berth even in time of war. Under *Dartmouth's* previous captain, the process was well on its way to its logical conclusion, but that had all changed when Carlisle took command. The ship had seen success, and Carlisle had been generous in acknowledging Gresham's contribution, even to the extent of mentioning his name in dispatches. He must be known at the Admiralty by now, perhaps even with the secretary's miracle-working pencil mark beside his entry in the books. He knew very well that Carlisle would give him the credit for his rescue and the privateer's capture, along with young Wishart, of course. A successful cutting-out tonight could just propel him into a master and commander's billet. He had to shake himself every time the thought occurred to him – which was increasingly frequent – because until recently he had given up all hope.

'The yawl's crew are all present and sober, sir,' said Torrance.

Gresham nodded. He was glad to have the young man in command of the yawl. He'd been a midshipman long enough and when a vacancy became available, Carlisle had made him a master's mate, and he'd thrived in his new position. He knew that Torrance would obey his orders and he got along well with Lieutenant Kemp who would command the yawl's marines.

'Have them muster with the longboat's crew, if you please, Mister Torrance. Seamen to starboard, marines to larboard.'

There was a stamping of booted feet on one side and a disorderly shuffling on the other. Gresham waited until they settled down and then he walked slowly down the lines of the seamen allotted to the longboat. They were a reassuring set of men, browned by years of service at sea with big, calloused hands from hauling on ropes and oars. He saw that each man had a pistol and a cutlass or a boarding pike; there was no need for muskets with such a strong detachment of marines. A quarter-gunner cradled a box of grenades; the boat gun wouldn't be shipped for this expedition, and the grenades would take its place. Souter was last in the line, and he grinned at Gresham, with the familiarity that only the captain's coxswain would dare.

The yawl's seamen were much the same although of course there were less of them. Torrance appeared to have them well in hand and he would be acting as his own coxswain in this smaller boat. Then he came to the marines.

'Lieutenant Pontneuf, your men are all prepared?'

It was an absurd question, but the formality of the occasion demanded that it was asked. He'd be taking most of *Dartmouth's* marines, twenty-two crammed into the longboat and seventeen in the yawl, leaving precious few to guard the privateer's crew who were packed below decks. It was important that there should be no doubt who commanded the expedition and demanding an answer from the marine lieutenant served to emphasise his position.

'Yes, sir. All present and correct.'

The marines were drawn up in a single body of men with Lieutenant Kemp – the second lieutenant – on the right and Sergeant Wilson on the left. Each man's head was facing front, as though fixed to his shoulders without any facility for movement. Gresham walked along the rows. He didn't even pretend to examine their weapons and equipment, the day of judgement would come before Sergeant Wilson allowed any hint of imperfection, and Pontneuf and Kemp had already carried out their own equally unnecessary inspections.

'Let the men relax before we go.'

Gresham could see that Beazley was preparing to heave-to, and already the men detailed from the watch on deck were fingering the painters that held the boats in under the stern.

***

The oars splashed noisily as the boats butted their way against the rising breeze. It was cooler now, a welcome relief from the heat of the land breeze, and now that the moon had set the night was black as pitch, with just the faintest glimmering of the stars, like the dust of a million diamonds scattered over the sea. Beazley had given him a compass course to steer for the mouth of the Careenage, and to start with Gresham had needed it but now as he drew closer, he could make out the bulk of the land ahead and the slight difference in the quality of the blackness that told him where entrance lay. He looked over his shoulder to see the yawl following obediently in his wake.

'You see it, Souter?'

'Aye, sir, it's plain enough.'

A lifetime at sea had given the coxswain the ability to make sense of shapes vaguely seen on a black night. He shifted the tiller and the longboat's bow edged to larboard until it pointed directly at the entrance. Another glance over his shoulder told him that the yawl had seen the slight alteration and had made the same course change.

'It's a fine night,' said Pontneuf. 'You rarely see the stars so clearly; even at sea there's always a sail or a stay or suchlike in the way. It makes a man want to take up poetry.'

Gresham mumbled something unintelligible in reply. He had never felt the slightest urge to take up poetry. In fact, he had barely ever read a verse and didn't feel in any way deprived by this gap in his polite skills. Shakespeare, now there was a man, as long as you stayed clear of his sonnets. Gresham revelled in the bard's descriptions of the life of fighting men: he found them realistic, and honest. Poetry was for men with too little to do, and in his opinion that pretty well summarised the life of a marine officer at sea. While the first lieutenant was managing the ship on behalf of his captain and keeping watches as well, Pontneuf had Kemp and Sergeant Wilson to manage the marine detachment. In many ways Pontneuf's position was more akin to Carlisle's than it was to Gresham's, with the notable exception that a ship's marine lieutenant had little to say about the employment of his men beyond their routine duties and drills. Marine officers always ranked lower than commissioned sea officers when they were embarked and, in all probability, they had time for poetry, if that was their inclination. Gresham didn't, and it was no loss to him.

Still, it was the marines who would bear the most danger when they found the cutter. The seamen would back them up, of course, but the marines would make the first assault. It was they who would have to hack their way through boarding nets, if any were rigged, and it was they who would face the first fury of the defenders.

Carlisle's Duty

Captain Carlisle had given him the discretion to withdraw if he found that the cutter wasn't anchored in the western inlet. Some chance! He wasn't going to tamely retreat, not while he had a boat still afloat.

The land was close now, and the hills that guarded the entrance to the Careenage loomed massively above them: Morne Dupré to larboard, rising above Pointe D'Estrées, and the unnamed hill above the tangle of wave-washed rocks called Le Tapion to starboard. There was a lookout on Morne Dupré, or so the privateer asserted. It was unlikely that even the sharpest sighted Frenchman would see the two low, black shapes rowing fast towards him, but if he did, his warning to the Grand Battery could hardly travel faster than the speeding boats.

'Keep close to larboard and look out for rocks,' Gresham said softly.

Any noise could be heard from the shore now, and the muffled oars were being pulled with more care to avoid tell-tale splashes.

Gresham studied the passing land. That must be Pointe D'Estrées on the larboard bow. He could sense rather than see the looming hill and he could hear the gentle sounds of the sea moving against the rocks at its feet. Ah, that would be the broken water around the point, glowing faintly in the starlight. It gave him an indication of what a watcher ashore would see of the two boats, nothing more than a hint of dark shapes with the faintest silvery bow wave.

'Four points to starboard, Souter.'

That should take them clear of Careenage Point. There was an old battery site above the point, but the privateer captain had sworn that it was neither armed nor manned. This would be the first test of his veracity.

Pointe D'Estrées was abaft the beam now and he should soon see the Tapion to starboard to match Careenage Point to larboard. It was only a cable and a half wide here, three hundred yards, but that information also had come from the privateer, and couldn't be entirely trusted.

'Rocks broad on the starboard bow.'

Souter was trying to whisper but it came out as a hissing sound.

Gresham strained his eyes to see, then he tried the old night lookout's trick and turned his head so that he was looking out of the corner of his eye. Ah, there it was, another wave-lapped headland with a steep hill behind it, just as he'd been told. And now he could see Careenage Point to larboard. They were too far to the south of the entrance.

'A point to larboard, Souter.'

Gresham pointed his arm into the blackness ahead, then he looked astern to confirm that the yawl was following them. Being much lighter, the yawl was faster under oars, and he could see that Torrance had no difficulty in keeping station. He was little more than a boat's length astern, so close that he could hear the heavy breathing of the men at the oars.

A light on the larboard bow! It was elevated well above the shore, so it would probably be the Grand Battery. It was only four hundred yards away, he guessed, but he could make out no shapes in that blackness, just the single light.

'I think we're right in the narrows.'

Souter's hissing whisper had turned into a hoarse croaking.

Gresham nudged him to show that he'd heard. The coxswain must be feeling the strain as much as he was.

'More lights, sir, lower down and to the left.'

He could see that the marines had also seen them, and he heard a hard thud as Wilson enforced the silence.

'Bring her slowly to larboard, Souter.'

What would it be now? Maybe two hundred yards. God, they'd be alongside in less than two minutes. There were no orders to give, everything so far was exactly as planned, yet still he couldn't make out the cutter, if it was here at all. This was the most dangerous minute as they hurtled towards the battery, closing the range all the time. There'd be no need for round shot if they were seen, a volley of grape would do for them much more efficiently. But of course, the boats would be nigh on invisible from the battery.

Three vessels at anchor, no four, he just had to pick out the right one. The nearest was just a little lugger, and so was the next, and there was something with three masts over to the west side of the bay. A ship perhaps with her upper yards on deck, or a big schooner. For just a moment Gresham dreamed of cutting it out, but his business was with the cutter not some stray French West Indiaman. Tonight was about duty and honour, not prize money.

Pontneuf pointed past the luggers to where a tall single mast towered above the two smaller craft. That must be it; thank God it was here and not in the commercial anchorage. He nudged Souter again and indicated the target, but Souter had already seen it.

A shout in the night, some lookout on one of the luggers had seen him. A musket shot rang out.

'Pull!' shouted Souter, 'Pull! don't let the damned French have our cutter!'

At that moment the dark of the night was shattered by an orange flame to starboard, followed by a blast that sounded horribly close. Gresham couldn't see where the shot landed but he was sure they were firing blind, into the narrows. Probably that was their default aiming point.

'She's stern on to us, sir,' Souter shouted, 'which side?'

'Starboard, on her starboard side, just put us alongside, blast you.'

Gresham silently blessed his foresight in telling Torrance to follow him in and board on the opposite side to the longboat, with no attempt to pre-suppose how the cutter would be lying. It appeared that the high land had created an eddy in the wind and *Kite* was lying with her head to the nor'west. In the seconds that it took for Gresham to think it through, the longboat had eaten up the last few yards and with a crash Souter threw the boat beam-on against the cutter's side. The bowman hurled his grapnel into the cutter's bowsprit and Souter grabbed hold of the main chains.

Pontneuf was already hacking at the boarding nets while his marines fired their muskets at the defending Frenchman. One of the longboat's crew, wielding a massive axe that had been brought for the single purpose of cutting *Kite's* cable, shouldered the lieutenant aside and with a couple of mighty strokes ripped a man-size hole in the net. Now the rest of the seamen were adding to the din by firing their pistols into the defenders. Pontneuf was through, then Wilson, and marine after marine wriggled through after them.

Gresham's fighting fury was up, and he cast around for a way onto the cutter's deck.

'Here, sir,' Souter shouted over the din.

Where the boarding net had been stretched around the main chains, there was necessarily a two-fathom gap where it had been impossible to fix it to the deck. Ordinarily it would have been covered by fire from the defenders, but they were all facing the bows, transfixed with horror as the number of red coats on the deck grew and grew. The marines were still outnumbered and with determined leadership it should still have been possible to push them back, but the Frenchmen were disorganised, roused from their hammocks by shouts from the deck, and many of them had not even managed to find arms. Nobody was watching the main chains.

Gresham pushed his massive body through the gap. For a moment he was stuck, lying helpless halfway on the deck and with nothing to grip with his hands nor to push with his feet. A Frenchman saw him and levelled a boarding pike at his exposed back. The man seemed to pause for a moment, unsure even in this emergency whether he should actually thrust the evil weapon into a living body, and that pause was his undoing. Gresham felt a huge push from behind and he shot through the net like a cork out of a bottle. He was on his feet in a moment and slashed at his would-be assailant. The pike dropped to the deck and Frenchman turned on his heel and fled to the stern, leaving a trail of blood where Gresham's sword had caught his shoulder.

Gresham hauled Souter through the gap just as a mighty cheer heralded the arrival of the yawl on the larboard side. With the enemy all occupied with the longboat's crew, Torrance's men easily crawled and squirmed their way onto the deck. Boarding nets – like all obstacles at sea or on land – were only effective if defended by determined men, otherwise they were just a minor inconvenience that slowed a boarding by less than half a minute.

Gresham paused, trying to bring his mind to order. It was difficult to make any sense of what was happening. He heard splashes from the stern and saw men – Frenchmen – leaping over the taffrail into the sea. He could see that a few were doing the same on the larboard bow. They at least could see the way the battle was going and were taking their chances in the water rather than suffering imprisonment. It was a good decision; the shore was no more than fifty yards away, nothing for a moderate swimmer. He saw one man leap over the side clutching a hand-spike to keep him afloat.

'Mister Pontneuf! The cutter's ours, secure any of the enemy left on deck and let's get underway.'

Then, in an instant it appeared that the situation had changed. With a great roar a horde of men burst onto the deck from the main hatch. Gresham clutched his sword and was about to give the orders to face this new threat when he recognised the man at their head. It was Roscoe, and his followers looked too much like British sailors for there to be any kind of mistake.

'Mister Roscoe,' he bellowed, 'set the jib and staysail. When her head has cast to the south, we'll cut the cable and be on our way. Where's the axeman?'

'Here, sir, I've just been helping the marines.'

'Very well, get forward and stand by at my word. You're to take no part in setting the sails, you understand? Your only task is to cut that cable when I give the word.'

'Aye-aye sir.'

The bosun's mate grinned in the dark. Those were the very orders that he'd been given back on *Dartmouth's* deck. He'd disobeyed them to make the breach in the boarding net, and again to carve a path through the Frenchmen at the bow, but he knew very well he'd be more rewarded than punished for his transgression.

The marines were rounding up the prisoners, separating the badly wounded and pushing the two or three bodies into the scuppers, out of the way.

It took no time for the staysail to be hoisted and, with half a dozen seamen bodily hauling the clew out to starboard, the head started to cast to larboard, away from the battery. The cutter was essentially sailing against its anchor cable and its stern was turning reluctantly to the east, wavering indecisively.

'Are you ready with the main, Mister Roscoe?'

'Aye-aye sir.'

If he was unsure of his status now that his ship was recaptured – was he still its commander? – he wisely chose to leave that argument for another time.

'Stand by forrard!'

Now they were beam on to the light breeze and in another few seconds the bows would start to swing back to starboard. Gresham leaped onto the skylight and heard a tinkle of glass as his boot shattered one of the small square panes.

'Cut the cable!'

The axe flashed just once – a cutter's cable was an insubstantial thing for a strong seaman with a sharp axe – and with a jerk the cutter came free. Now the bows paid off quickly.

'Let draw! Staysail sheet to starboard, hoist the main, hoist the jib.'

Now the cutter was sailing freely with the wind fine on the larboard quarter.

'Boats are towing astern, sir,' said Souter.

He'd forgotten about the boats. Thank God for a good coxswain.

'Very well, take the helm. You remember the way out?'

'Aye, sir, I do. We'll need to gybe in a moment.'

Gresham looked at the dim shape of the shore and tried to recall the chart that was in his pocket; he didn't dare show a light.

'We'll hold on. Shave Careenage Point as close as you dare, it's deep water right up to the rocks. I want to get out of range of those guns, they'll know how to point at the entrance for sure, even at night.'

Gresham looked up at the mainsail. It was already drawing well, and their speed was increasing as they came into the clearer air beyond the little inlet. The cutter would be visible now, with her sails gleaming in the starlight, and he wanted to be away.

Boom, boom!

Two guns, just as the privateer had said; all the rest must be facing east to cover the approach to the main commercial anchorage.

The cutter moved faster and faster as she found the wind blowing down from the head of the Careenage. The whole bay formed a natural funnel and while it was light airs out at sea, here between the two arms of the bay, a respectable breeze was blowing.

'Set the tops'l, Mister Roscoe.'

A half dozen men ran up the shrouds. They knew the urgency to get that big square sail drawing.

Boom, boom!

There was a crash from aloft. Gresham staggered as the tops'l yard came crashing to the deck. He saw a man fall and smash into the deck just forward of the mast and another fell clear over the side with a long wail. There was nothing he could do; it would be madness to turn back to pick him up. In any case, if he could swim to the shore he'd be exchanged in no time.

But that was the last shot that came near them. By the time the gunners had reloaded, the cutter had gybed and was around Careenage Point heading out to sea with the strengthening trade wind at its stern.

***

CHAPTER NINE

A Mystery Ship

Thursday, Twelfth of February 1761.
Dartmouth, at Sea. Off St. Lucia.

The lookout on the Morne Dupré would have plenty to report this morning. Carlisle had brought *Dartmouth*, *Kite* and *Mont Saint-Michel* close to the harbour entrance, to flaunt the prize and the recovered cutter in the face of the French islanders. They were sailing slowly nor'west in line ahead with the captured privateer between the two men-o'-war, and with *Dartmouth's* vast Sunday-best ensign flying from its staff.

The carpenter and his crew were hard at work cutting down a spare t'gallant to replace *Kite's* tops'l yard. They'd spent the previous night repairing the privateer's shattered rudder, but none of them minded in the slightest. It was a cheerful sound of adze and saw and it lent a make-and-mend atmosphere to the morning.

It had been a difficult interview with Roscoe. The man was clearly apprehensive, and he knew that the commodore would act on Captain Carlisle's recommendation when deciding whether the temporary loss of *Kite* required a court martial to be convened. Few captains came out with their reputation intact. Roscoe was inclined to blame Carlisle for the fiasco, although he was wise enough to do no more than hint at it, and he was sullen and not entirely co-operative.

Simmonds, however, had pointed out that as Carlisle had been detached on independent service by the commander-in-chief, he could hold a local board of enquiry that very day and let the members decide whether to recommend that the case should be taken further. It smacked of skulduggery, of course. Carlisle had been on board *Kite* when her colours were hauled down, in fact he had all but given the order to do so, and the board of inquiry – three members would be sufficient – must necessarily be made up from his own officers. The board's verdict was easy to predict, and it would all be transparent to Commodore Douglas; he must have read many such reports, each with its own degree of veracity.

Nevertheless, the commander-in-chief also had an incentive to suppress the details of the loss of one of his cutters, however quickly it was recaptured. After all, it was his command, and he held the ultimate responsibility. In any case, taken as a whole, the net result of the affair was the capture of a dangerous – and valuable – privateer for the loss of only two men killed, two injured, and one missing with the probability that he had swum ashore and been captured. And of course, Douglas would take the flag officer's share of the prize money for the privateer.

Roscoe may well be apprehensive, but Carlisle was hopeful that his carefully worded covering letter for the board of enquiry would satisfy the commander-in-chief, and Roscoe's shame at hauling down his colours would be local and short-lived. If an account of it ever crossed their Lordship's desks, they would pay scant attention to the doings of a tiny cutter in the faraway Leeward Islands.

Simmonds had gone so far as to draft the outline of the letter before the board had even been convened, and Carlisle was reading it now. It was a minor masterpiece of official writing that almost – *almost* – obeyed the rules for evidence. It stated the truth and it stated nothing but the truth, but it fell somewhat short of the whole truth. And yet it was sufficient to bury the matter. Carlisle was content, and when Enrico brought *Mont Saint-Michel* into English harbour – he would be there on Saturday – the blue ensign would be flying proudly above the Bourbon white, visible proof of a victory. It would be strange indeed if anyone inquired very deeply into the loss and subsequent recapture of a hired cutter.

***

Carlisle's Duty

Carlisle leaned back and considered taking a nap. He'd been on deck all night, conscious that his reputation and perhaps his career depended upon the cutting-out expedition. It had been emotional agony. Having sent the longboat and yawl away, he could do nothing more to influence events, and his role was that of a mere bystander. He was just about to call for Walker to send a message to the officer of the watch that he wasn't to be disturbed when a knock at the door heralded the arrival of Gresham. He sat upright, trying to look like as though the thought of a few moments of sleep had not even occurred to him.

Gresham edged his way into the cabin. Unless both doors were opened, his shoulders were too broad for him to enter without taking a diagonal approach. Behind him came the lesser shape of Midshipman Harley, the rather disreputable young officer from *Kite*. He'd fallen down a hatch when the cutter was taken by the privateer, and he was on board *Dartmouth* now so that the surgeon could keep an eye on him as there was a question about whether his ankle was broken or simply twisted. He was walking without the aid of a stick so in Carlisle's opinion he couldn't have been too badly injured.

Carlisle tried to keep the look of distaste from his face. Harley was the embodiment of all that was wrong with *Kite* and the other two cutters under his command. He was dirty, unkept and as far as Carlisle could tell the cutter's men had no regard for him as either a gentleman or a potential commissioned officer. He was being unfair, and he knew it. Thirty men were crammed into *Kite's* fifty-six foot of length and twenty-two of beam, along with six guns, an allowance of powder and shot and stores for two months. The midshipman's berth was little more than a canvas-screened apartment between the bread room and the bosun's store without enough space to dress standing up, and none at all to store clothes so that they would emerge in a fit state to be seen in polite company. There was no real segregation from the seamen, and all hands, from the captain down, suffered the same atrocious conditions. It was no wonder that desertion from smaller ships was at a far higher rate than the larger frigates and ships-of-the-line. Nevertheless, he believed that they could do more to maintain officer-like standards.

'Mister Gresham, Mister Harley, please take a seat.'

The midshipman turned awkwardly and dropped into the chair, apparently unable to support himself once his knees had bent. Perhaps he really was injured.

'Mister Harley has something to report, sir. He was allowed on the deck of *Kite* during the day, while she was in the Careenage, on account of his injury.'

There was something in Gresham's tone that said that he too was sceptical.

Carlisle turned towards Harley who seemed suddenly tongue-tied. He had inquired about most of the officers and gentlemen in his little squadron and he knew something of Harley's situation. He was Antiguan born and bred and his father had owned a smallish plantation on the northern coast, which at his early death from yellow fever was found to be on the verge of bankruptcy. His mother was under the necessity of finding a new husband before her remaining funds ran out, and not knowing what else to do with an inconvenient fifteen-year-old son, had appealed to every naval person she knew to find a berth for him. Commodore Douglas had taken pity on her and sent him to *Kite*, much against Roscoe's wishes, in the rank of midshipman, for which he was in no sense qualified. There he had languished for five months, friendless and without any official notice taken of his existence. It was little wonder that he was overawed at being in the same room as a post-captain and the first lieutenant of a fourth rate.

'Well, Mister Harley?'

Harley gulped and his Adam's apple made an astonishing vertical excursion along the length his throat.

'I… I was on deck all day yesterday, sir…'

Good God, was it only yesterday? Carlisle did a swift

mental calculation: *Kite* had been taken on Tuesday and recaptured on Wednesday night. It was only forty-eight hours since he'd allowed Roscoe to haul down his flag.

'One moment,' Carlisle interrupted. 'Why were you allowed on deck when everyone else was confined below?'

He knew the answer of course, but he wanted to hear the midshipman's version of events.

'It was my leg, sir. Captain Roscoe represented that it was in danger if I was confined below, and the prize master allowed me to sit by the taffrail under guard, just until it got dark.'

Carlisle nodded; it was a normal human reaction from the Frenchman. After all, what danger could one limping midshipman pose in the safety of the Careenage, under the guns of a battery?

'Were you the only one allowed on deck?'

'Yes, sir.'

Harley was evidently unsure whether this line of questioning was leading him towards some sort of censure.

'Very well, carry on.'

'I was able to get a good look around, sir. I could see part of the battery to the east of the cove, and I saw some people that looked like customs officers or perhaps prize agents come aboard. They had lawyer looks about them. They and the prize master were disagreeing, as far as I could tell, sir. They wanted him to shift into the harbour the other side of the point, but he refused and turned them off the deck, sir.'

If Harley imagined that this was valuable information, he was mistaken. Carlisle was about to bring the interview to an end when Gresham intervened. He dug the midshipman in the ribs, quite savagely.

'Now, Mister Harley, tell the captain what I told you to tell him, he's not interested in tittle-tattle.'

'Well, sir,' he replied, his Adam's apple performing another feat of gymnastics, 'there were three other ships in the cove…'

'The captain knows about the luggers, Harley. Get to the point!'

He gulped again, then became surprisingly lucid, as though, after some circumlocutions, he'd arrived at a subject that he felt confident in addressing.

'There was a ship at anchor, sir, she had the look of a privateer or a slaver, but I could see she wasn't either because she had a regular merchantman's crew and she was in ballast, awaiting a cargo it seemed. I saw none embarked while I was there, although there were some big butts and a few hogsheads being rolled onto the little sandy beach at the head of the cove.'

Harley was warming to his topic, and he'd even forgotten to wince when he moved in his chair.

'Thing is, sir, her rig was raked a little too sharply to be a Frenchman. I've seen them all at St. John's and I know a French West Indiaman when I see one. This one was too flash, sir, too flash by far. I'd say she was a Yankee...'

Harley's report came to a stammering pause as he realised what he'd just said, and all the confidence drained from him. He glanced at Gresham but found no help there. Carlisle's frown turned to a thin smile, and he nearly laughed out loud; he knew exactly what had tripped up the midshipman. He'd first heard the word *Yankee* when he'd been at the siege of Louisbourg two years before. By the time of the siege of Quebec in 'fifty-nine it had become a commonplace. It was seen as an insult in some quarters although nobody could really state the origins of the word. He'd heard General Wolfe use it often enough and he certainly hadn't meant it to convey any judgement on his American soldiers. It was one of those unfortunate nicknames that was fated to stick, and no New England sensitivities would move it an inch further towards its demise.

'Never fear, Mister Harley. I'm no Yankee, being raised in Virginia, in the southern colonies, but you need to be sure of your audience before you use loose terms like that. I assume you mean the ship looked like a New Englander?'

Harley gulped and shuffled in his chair.

'Y...yes sir. It looked like a Massachusetts ship or a Rhode Islander, sir, begging your pardon, sir, like them that used to go privateering before the trade dried up. And her crew weren't dressed like Frenchmen, they looked like regular New England sailors.'

Carlisle studied the young man. Fifteen, that was his age if his mother hadn't lied, which was quite possible in her desperation to provide for an awkward child. In any case he was too young and had too little time on ships' books to be a midshipman. He'd lived near St. John's all his life so he must have memories of French ships before the war as well as British and New England ships in the triangular trade between New England, the Guinea coast and the Leeward Islands. He'd have seen many of them turn to privateering as a more lucrative enterprise and he'd have seen the gradual demise of that occupation as the French commerce was swept from the seas. He could be relied upon to know his ships.

'A prize, perhaps, Mister Harley?'

The midshipman shook his head.

'I don't think so, sir. There were no guards on the hatches and the men all worked as though they were a regular crew. I thought that I may have heard someone shout in English, but they were to leeward at half a cable, sir, so I can't be certain.'

'Did you see the ship's name?'

'No, sir, there was no name on the transom, but I could swear she wasn't French.'

New England ships had adopted a rather conceited style of exaggerating the angle of their masts. Most ships afloat had a modest rake towards the stern and past a certain point there was no advantage in increasing it. It was showmanship, nothing more, a statement that they were so prosperous that they could afford to prettify their ships, against all nautical sense. Carlisle had often laughed when he'd seen them. However in this case it was a reliable way of identifying a Massachusetts or Rhode Island ship, and Harley's description seemed to rule out its being a prize. He realised that he was staring at the young man, who was looking increasingly alarmed. There was little more to be gained by quizzing the midshipman and Carlisle dismissed him, watching with amusement as he again exaggerated his injury and limped out of the cabin in a crab-wise fashion.

***

'What do you think, Mister Gresham?'

'About his injury or the ship, sir?'

Carlisle smiled in return; his first lieutenant's good humour was infectious.

'Well, I caught only a glimpse of her upper masts, because she was behind the cutter when we approached, and I didn't have time to look when we were on *Kite's* deck. Mister Torrance saw her more clearly as he boarded the cutter over the larboard side, and he thought she looked a little odd, but like me he was otherwise occupied. Whittle was pulling stroke in the yawl, and he would have seen her. I can send for him if you like.'

Carlisle smiled. It was hardly likely that Gresham or Torrance or even Nathaniel Whittle had any time for staring at strange ships when they were fighting a French crew on their own deck, then working the cutter out of the anchorage under fire from an enemy battery.

'You can let Whittle sleep in peace. I have no doubt that he would have told me already if he'd seen anything suspicious.'

'That's for certain, sir.'

Gresham knew all about Whittle and his subversive ways.

'I would have said that she was a schooner, with her rake and her bare upper poles, in fact that's in my report, sir. But if her upper yards were struck down, she could easily have been a Yankee – I beg your pardon, sir – a New England merchantman.'

Carlisle ignored the slip. He was determined that he shouldn't show his colonial sensitivity, and in any case, the nickname had no significance to a Virginian.

'Or a New England prize taken some time ago and now sailing as a French privateer, perhaps.'

'Yes, sir, but Harley said she was in ballast, she appeared to be awaiting a cargo, and those butts on shore, they sound like molasses, perhaps. But I can't understand why she wasn't in the commercial port with all the other merchantmen.'

'Then most likely she's a New Englander taken by the French and now waiting for an anchor berth to load a cargo for the next convoy home. Let's waste no more time on it, Mister Gresham. Now, I believe I'll close my eyes for a few minutes, and I advise you to do the same, you must be exhausted after your night.'

***

Carlisle stretched his long limbs on the cushioned locker below the stern windows. Beazley had his orders and Gresham would make it quite clear what would be the fate of any young gentleman that disturbed his captain by skylarking above his head on the poop deck. He could close his eyes until *Kite's* topmast yard was ready to be sent over.

But the Yankee ship was intriguing – there, he was using that word himself – for he was now almost convinced that it had its origins in New England. It could be a prize, of course, particularly as it was anchored in a known privateer lair, and it would hardly be surprising with so many letters of marque being issued by the governor of Martinique. But there was another possibility, one that Carlisle was reluctant to acknowledge. That New England ship could be a smuggler, trading with the enemy in illicit goods, and the butts and hogsheads sounded much like the standard containers for molasses. Unlikely, but a distinct possibility and one that he would have to consider if ever he met the ship at sea.

***

CHAPTER TEN

A Chase

Thursday, Nineteenth of February 1761.
Dartmouth, at Sea. Diamond Rock Nor' by East Two Leagues.

The hills of Martinique were bathed in an orange glow as the last light of the day reflected off the high trade wind clouds. *Dartmouth* was thrashing to windward on the larboard tack with spray drenching the deck as she heeled far over with her lower ports awash.

'This is more like it,' said Gresham, rubbing his hands, 'we haven't had a good tussle to windward for weeks, and it's too damned hot in the day, whatever you may say.'

Enrico's dark Mediterranean face split into a wide grin. He had grown up in a land of baking summers and he found nothing remotely uncomfortable about the climate in the Leeward Islands. But he privately agreed that there was nothing like a hard beat into a stiff nor'easter to lift the spirits.

'What's on the captain's mind?'

A close friendship had developed between the scion of an aristocratic Sardinian dynasty and the bluff sea officer of no notable family, and when nobody was listening, they dropped the formality of Mister Gresham and Mister Angelini.

'He wants to get to windward of the islands before the morning. He has an idea that the commodore's frigates may miss something, a French convoy perhaps, and anyway he's happy that all the harbours are blockaded, so he can roam a bit more freely. That's why we're beating south, so that we can take a single tack to weather Salt Pit Point in the morning watch.'

Enrico nodded but didn't reply; he was busy working through the distances to be run. Yes, they could be to windward of Martinique by sunrise, and he'd served under

Carlisle's Duty

Captain Carlisle too long to ignore his intuition.

'You won't have noticed, but he's much happier since you came back from English Harbour. I think he was worried about the commodore's reaction to that business with *Kite*.'

'He seemed his normal self when I saw him. However, his concern was all for nothing. Mister Douglas barely glanced at the minutes of the investigation. He told me as an aside that he lost cutters at the rate of one a quarter and wasn't inclined to reckon them too closely. They had a job to do and that meant standing into danger as often as not. He'd never had the slightest reaction from their Lordships when he reported one lost. In any case, he was far too delighted with the privateer to worry about a hired cutter, prizes having grown so scarce lately.'

Gresham stole a sideways glance at Enrico. He had wondered why Carlisle had sent the third lieutenant away as prize master, and not himself or Wishart who had been much more closely involved in the capture. But the captain was no fool and he knew how valuable a man like Enrico Angelini could be. Most sea officers had a deep-rooted regard for the nobility and especially exotic, foreign nobility, and Enrico had never lost that impenetrable aura of aristocratic superiority that he'd been born with, not even after three-and-a-half years treading the decks of British men-o'-war and eating salt pork twice a week. Douglas would have found it much easier to interrogate either of the British sea officers regarding *Kite's* loss, if he had been at all inclined to cause trouble.

'The captain made it easy for him, of course,' Enrico continued. 'He didn't send *Kite* back for repairs and nor did he relieve Lieutenant Roscoe, as he may otherwise have done. No, from English Harbour it looked like business as usual but with the delightful addition of a prize. I'm surprised that Captain Carlisle thought anything of it.'

Enrico walked with Gresham for a few more moments even though he'd been relieved by Wishart ten minutes ago and his supper was waiting. Despite telling Gresham that he was surprised, he was really nothing of the sort. He knew his cousin Edward Carlisle rather better than Gresham did, and he knew the devils that pursued him. As an outsider himself, he could understand how Carlisle could never really feel at home in the navy. It wasn't that he was pining for his home in Virginia, it was just that he felt – perhaps unreasonably – that his conduct was always being measured against different standards to his fellows, that his colonial upbringing made him permanently suspect. It verged on paranoia in Enrico's opinion, and he was always surprised at its intensity, though the fact of its existence was easy for him to understand.

'Well, I'll see you for supper no doubt,' said Gresham. 'I just want to have a word with Wishart.'

Enrico tipped his hat in reply and took the steps three at a time on his way down to the wardroom. Gresham turned towards the wheel where he knew he'd find Wishart, but a shout from the masthead stopped him dead.

'Sail ho! Sail five points on the larboard bow, dead to windward, a tops'l maybe.'

He saw Wishart pick up the copper speaking trumpet.

'What do you make of her, Whittle?' Wishart shouted up to the main masthead.

There was a short silence. It was Whittle's way of telling the officer of the watch that if he knew what it was, he would have said so without being asked stupid questions. The silence was just long enough to make the point.

'Dunno, sir, just a tops'l.'

Wishart knew very well what was happening and he fell into the trap every time. His enthusiasm was to blame; it carried him away to the point of appearing foolish. He should have merely acknowledged the lookout's report and waited for supplementary information. He might have considered having a bosun's mate put the lookout into his right mind at the end of his trick at the masthead, but Whittle was different, and it would be a bold officer who

Carlisle's Duty

disciplined him. Like the other officers, Wishart just had to put up with Whittle's liberties for the sake of harmony. And in any case, Whittle was a damned good seaman and the ship's undisputed champion lookout.

'Mister Young. My compliments to the captain and we have a strange sail right in the eye of the wind, between the two islands.'

Horace Young hurried away to the great cabin. This also was a piece of theatre because the captain would certainly have heard Whittle's report through the cabin skylight, and he knew just where his ship lay in relation to the islands and therefore where the strange sail must be.

Carlisle waited for the midshipman's report before walking unhurriedly onto the quarterdeck.

'Anything more, Mister Wishart?'

'No, sir. I had a look at the chart and with the westerly we had until the first dog, I reckon she must have left St. Lucia, perhaps from the Careenage, and be trying to beat up through the gap, like we are.'

Carlisle nodded. He'd made the same deduction. But what concerned him was why a vessel large enough to be carrying a square tops'l – it couldn't therefore be a little local boat – would want to beat to windward when all of the useful ports lay on the leeward side of the islands. Could it be a lone French West Indiaman heading out across the Atlantic? If so, her captain was very brave or extremely foolish to try to get past the string of frigates that Douglas had strewn to windward of the remaining French islands.

'Deck there, it's a ship sir, sailing hard on the wind, starboard tack. I can see all three tops'ls now.'

Carlisle picked up the traverse board and the slate to remind himself of the weather during the day. As he thought, the wind had been more nor'easterly than easterly. That ship couldn't have weathered Salt Pit Point in a single board, it must have been forced further to the west than it had intended and was holding on against the chance that the wind would veer a few points.

'She's going about, sir,' shouted Whittle from far aloft, with just the first hint of excitement in his voice. Nothing invigorated the hunter more than a fleeing prey.

'The chart, if you please, Mister Wishart.'

Charts would have had a short life indeed if they had been routinely kept on the wind and spray-soaked quarterdeck. No sailing master would have allowed it, and because they were normally his personal property they were kept in his cabin. Midshipman Young in his zeal to fetch the chart collided with Beazley who had heard the commotion and was coming onto the quarterdeck, chart in hand.

'What does she bear, Mister Wishart?'

'I can't see her from the deck sir, but if the lookout's right, then she bears nor'east by east.'

Carlisle made a prick in the chart with his dividers while Beazley scowled at this wanton vandalism. He never, ever pricked a chart and rarely made even the softest pencil mark. Charts at two shillings each weren't to be pricked and prodded, they were rather to be cosseted and only brought on deck under the most benign conditions.

'Why didn't he just bear away for one of those little places on the south side of Martinique? What's that ship's master thinking of Mister Beazley?'

The sailing master scratched his head and studied the chart, covertly rubbing the back of a fingernail over the tiny hole that his captain had made. There were plenty of anchorages in the lee of Salt Pit Point, some of them covered by batteries and most of them too shallow for *Dartmouth* to follow. That would have been the obvious refuge for a French West Indiaman on a lone, unescorted passage. Carlisle could see that the ship would have been safe before *Dartmouth* could catch her.

'Maybe he didn't see us, sir, perhaps he tacked to weather the point.'

Beazley pointed his finger at the south-eastern extremity of Martinique. *Les Salines* on this French chart, Salt Pit Point as generations of English seafarers knew it.

Carlisle's Duty

'Wind's veered a little in the last glass, sir,' said Wishart.

Carlisle looked at the dog-vane and then at the compass in the binnacle. Wishart was right, the trade wind was more easterly now. If the chase's master had held his course, he'd have weathered the point.

'He's taking a risk, sir, hoping that we'll lose sight of him tonight,' said Gresham.

'Full moon rises just after sunset,' Beazley added with a wise nod of the head and a glance at the first lieutenant.

Gresham smiled ruefully. There'd be little chance of the chase escaping them in that case. By the last dog watch they'd be close enough to stay in touch by the light of the moon.

'Well, his behaviour's odd, but it's a mystery that can best be solved by boarding. Mister Wishart, I want every ounce that you can squeeze out of her, if you please. I'm sure Mister Beazley will stay on deck to help you.'

***

The sun dipped inexorably towards the horizon as the two ships beat against the steady easterly wind, further and further into the Atlantic. *Dartmouth* was barely the faster, and it was only after two hours that the chase's tops'ls became visible from the quarterdeck.

'Odd, don't you think,' said Wishart as he stared forward into the stiff breeze. 'I would say that our friend over there isn't trying too hard to escape. Look, he's rigged for t'gallants but hasn't set them. He surely must have seen us. Ah, he's going about now, there's no chance at all for him on that tack. Mister Young, my compliments to the captain and please inform him that the chase has tacked.'

'He's just planning to weather the point, Mister Wishart.'

Beazley was still on deck, watching the luffs and growling at the steersman.

'He looks very much like a man going about his lawful occasions.'

Wishart sniffed. There were no lawful occasions in this sea, not after five years of war. The master of even a neutral ship would know that his cargo was liable to be impounded unless he could prove that he wasn't trading with the enemy.

Carlisle came on deck and cast a glance to the west. They had perhaps half an hour of daylight left, then an hour of twilight, but he knew that the moon would rise before it was fully dark.

'Pass the word for the first lieutenant.'

'Here, sir,' said Gresham hurrying up the ladder.

Horace Young had sent a boy to tell him that the captain was coming on deck, and with the light fast fading it was odds on that he'd be called to make plans for the night.

'Unless our friend over there comes to his senses, we'll be alongside him during the middle watch. There'll be a swell running, you can feel it already, so have the yawl and cutter made ready for a boarding.'

'Aye-aye sir,' Gresham replied as he scrutinised the chase.

It was the first time he'd had sight of it as he hadn't cared to make the climb to the maintop. There was something familiar about it, he had a sense that he'd seen it before. His conviction formed slowly but surely.

'Look at the rake of that main t'gallant and topmast. I do believe that's the ship that was anchored near *Kite* in the Careenage. There can't be many of that sort in the Leeward Islands. She's a New Englander, in any case. What do you think, Mister Wishart?'

Carlisle looked sharply at Wishart as he trained his telescope at the tiny white dots on the horizon. He was frustrated at having to rely on others for long-distance sightings, but he knew that he wouldn't be able to see anything worthwhile, telescope or not. His eyesight had been deteriorating for years and he'd already decided to seek a medical opinion when he was next in London, or perhaps Philadelphia.

'Aye, that's a New Englander all right, although whether it's the same one I can't say, not having been in the boats that night.'

Carlisle's Duty

'Deck ho! Coming down to report, sir.'

Whittle slid down the main backstay and landed lightly on the quarterdeck. He knuckled his forehead to Carlisle and without further ceremony started speaking, ignoring the dangerous look in Gresham's eye at this disrespectful behaviour.

'It's that ship we saw when we cut out *Kite*, sir. The same rake on the masts and she has no real foretop, just a sort of platform over her cross-trees. I'd know her anywhere, sir.'

'Very well, thank you Whittle.'

Carlisle chose not to question the able seaman. Unlike most of the deck hands, Whittle wasn't at all reticent in front of officers and he would surely have said all there was to say.

Whittle grinned and ran back to the shrouds for his long climb up to his perch.

'Well, well, there's a tale to be told here but we won't hear it until we catch yonder ship. I do believe you could pay off a point or two now Mister Beazley, and let's see how we do then.'

***

The fifty-gun ships had never done well sailing on a bowline, their hulls were too short for their displacement, and they carried their main deck guns too high. They heeled sharply and pitched extravagantly in the slightest of seas. But like many an unweatherly broad-beamed heavyweight, with the wind two points free *Dartmouth* added a good knot and a half to her speed. At four bells in the middle watch the chase was so close that it would have been positively rude for its master to ignore the great two decker that was illuminated by the silvery light of the full moon. The chase hove-to and lay plunging up and down in the long Atlantic swell. She was fully laden, that much was clear, and that accounted for the ease with which *Dartmouth* had caught her. One look at that slim hull and those tall masts told the story of a fast ship that could outsail a fourth rate on any point of sailing, were it not for the cargo.

'She's not French, that's for sure,' said Gresham as the yawl and the cutter were hauled alongside. 'My bet is that Whittle has it right, she's that New Englander from the Careenage. I must say, I admire his confidence, although how he thinks he can explain trading with the enemy is beyond me.'

Carlisle pursed his lips. He knew that the whole question of trading in wartime was far more complex than his first lieutenant imagined.

'If he's anything other than French, bring him back on board, Mister Gresham. If he doesn't care for a boat trip you may insist and bundle him down into the yawl in a cargo net if need be. If he's French, then he's a prize and hurrah for our good fortune.'

'Aye-aye sir.'

Gresham grinned as he swung his leg over the gunwale to climb down into the boat.

***

CHAPTER ELEVEN

An Informer

Friday, Twentieth of February 1761.
Dartmouth, at Sea. Salt Pit Point Nor'west Three Leagues.

'Mister Kendrick, sir, master of the *Hope*, and Mister Cranston, supernumerary.'

The two men that Simmonds ushered in were entirely different. Kendrick was tall, lean and weather-beaten and dressed in the normal brown and grey of a merchant master. Cranston was shorter, somewhat stout and wore a blue suit with breeches and white stockings, a most unusual outfit for a merchantman at sea.

'Mister Gresham sends his respects, sir, and he thought it best that he stays in *Hope* for the time being.'

Carlisle nodded briefly. Gresham would be rummaging the merchantman while its master and this curious passenger were being interviewed. It would be a cursory inspection, but it may throw up something to pin the ship to St. Lucia. He stood to receive his visitor. He didn't quite know what he expected, apprehension or perhaps righteous defiance, but neither Kendrick nor Cranston showed any of these emotions. Kendrick looked like a man without a care in the world with perhaps a trace of insolence, while Cranston appeared supremely self-confident, a man with right on his side and no thought that he may be suspected of wrongdoing. Carlisle could detect no hint of a guilty conscience, nothing that suggested a defensive position. Neither spoke but they took the offered seats and when Simmonds settled himself with his pen and ink in the corner of the cabin – a clear indication that this was more than a routine discussion – neither so much as glanced in that direction.

'I gather you are the master of *Hope*, Mister Kendrick, but may I ask what your position is, Mister Cranston?'

Cranston looked surprised at the sound of Carlisle's voice, then quickly mastered his emotions.

'I am the owner's representative, Captain Carlisle, and I'm sailing on this voyage because it's a new venture for the company.'

Carlisle looked for some sort of nervousness but saw nothing but confidence. It was just possible that they had a legitimate reason for sailing these waters and he must act on that assumption until it could be proved incorrect.

'Well, you are welcome aboard, Mister Kendrick and Mister Cranston. I see you've brought your papers.'

Kendrick opened the leather satchel and brought out a thick sheaf of documents that he placed carefully on the table, still piled one atop of the other, with no attempt to offer them for inspection.

Carlisle barely glanced at them. If it was necessary, he'd have Simmonds and one of the sea officers read through them. For now he just wanted to know who and what he was dealing with. Kendrick still hadn't uttered a word. Carlisle was starting to feel that he was being slighted. He looked hard at Kendrick, but the man didn't even flinch.

'Perhaps we could start with you telling me where you are bound, what cargo and where loaded.'

Carlisle spoke in a firm voice to cover any hint of sarcasm. It had been the invariable rule when meeting merchant masters at sea that they would start with the time-honoured formula: what ship, what cargo, where loaded, where bound.

'Well, captain, it appears that we are countrymen at the very least,' Kendrick said at last. Then without waiting for any comment, 'my ship's from Providence, Obadiah Brown & Company, and we took on a load of molasses at an anchorage on the west coast of Tobago. I'm on passage back to Narragansett Bay now.'

Carlisle turned over the first page of the cargo manifest and saw the word Tobago clear as a bell. It was obfuscation of course. Tobago had been declared a neutral island at the end of the last war, and all the European colonial nations, Britain, France, Spain, the Netherlands and Portugal had left it to its own governance. Sure, there were sugar fields on the island although it was doubtful whether there was enough crop to produce a ship load of the molasses by-product. With no proper customs houses, nor any officials of any nature, it would be hard to prove that Kendrick had not taken on his cargo at Tobago.

'Then you seem to be missing your course for New England, Mister Kendrick.'

Kendrick shrugged. The wrinkles around his eyes betrayed the ghost of a smile.

'We had to run for a day and a half before a storm of wind, just south of Barbados, and that took us into the Caribbean between St. Vincent and St. Lucia, and I didn't fancy beating back that way. I decided to risk the leeward side of St. Lucia, but the French are just too active in Martinique, being their navy's main haven, so I rounded the Cape and now I'm beating through into the Atlantic for a straight run home. I'd appreciate if you could let me go on my way now, Captain, as my luck could run out at any time, being so close to Fort Royal.'

Carlisle noticed that Kendrick's stare had hardly wavered the whole time he'd been speaking. It was a plausible story as far as it went, but wouldn't a merchant master ask to be escorted past Martinique and perhaps even past Dominica? *Hope* was in mortal danger from privateers until she had cleared to the north of the French islands, and although the risk diminished as the latitude increased, the French were still active right past the Bahamas and the southern American colonies. Most captains with a full cargo would make for English Harbour and pick up a north-bound convoy rather than run the gauntlet of the hungry French privateers.

He was certain that he was being lied to, and that Gresham and Wishart had correctly remembered the ship that had been at anchor in the Careenage. Now he regretted sending Midshipman Harley back to *Kite*; he may have been able to identify Kendrick and Cranston. He looked again at the documents. Given time he was sure that he could find a discrepancy that would allow him to take Kendrick and his ship back to English Harbour for a proper rummage of the holds and scrutiny of the documents. The silence in the cabin was starting to grow oppressive when he heard a boat coming alongside and the sounds of someone hurrying up the ship's side, then Walker came into the cabin.

'Begging your pardon, sir, but Mister Gresham has returned in the yawl and is asking if he may have a word on the quarterdeck.'

Carlisle looked again at Kendrick. For the first time the impassive Rhode Islander looked uncomfortable.

'Mister Simmonds, please entertain our guests. I'll be back in a few minutes, I expect.'

***

'Mister Gresham, you have something to report?'

'I do sir. I had a quick look in his hold; there's a top tier of hogsheads and two lower tiers of butts. It's molasses, like the mate told me, and it looks like a full load. You can see she's deep in the water.'

'That's just what the master told me; he claims that he loaded his cargo at Tobago.'

'The mate gave me the same story, sir, a little place on the west coast of Tobago, he didn't know the name. Thing is, all the markings that I could see are in French, burned deep around the head.'

'The locals in Tobago speak French, I understand,' said Carlisle interrupting, 'and Spanish and a little English. A hogshead or a butt from Tobago could have any markings at all. I doubt whether there are many coopers in the place, and they probably use old ones that have done the rounds of the islands.'

'But these are all new, sir,' Gresham looked eager, like a hound on a scent, 'so new that the staves haven't taken up yet, that's how I could taste the molasses so easily, it was seeping out all over the place. New hogsheads for sure though I couldn't get at the butts. Those I saw, I'd swear they were made by Frenchmen. They've got that funny rounded chime, not like the English chamfer.'

Carlisle stared abstractedly at the New England ship. The sun was just starting to rise, bathing the scene in the cheerful light of a new tropical day. *Hope* was hove-to quite peacefully, wallowing on the Atlantic swell with the weed not yet grown on the half fathom of clean planking below the waterline, that showed how deeply she was laden. He could see his boarding party chatting to the crew, waiting for Gresham to return. He was certain now that Kendrick was smuggling Molasses from St. Lucia to Rhode Island to feed the colony's rum distilleries, the problem was in proving it. He could be personally liable for the owners' losses if he took *Hope* into English Harbour, and the ship was found to be innocent. And he could guess what arguments Kendrick and Cranston would make, and how difficult they would be to refute. Cranston had the nasty look of a lawyer about him, or at least a man who dealt in legalities. A small anchorage on Tobago was the perfect bogus loading port, the island had little in the way of officialdom and almost no regular contact with the English islands. If Kendrick and his crew held to their story – and New England ships were notoriously clannish – it was quite likely that the vice-admiralty court at St. John's would dismiss the case out of hand. He needed something more, and the testimony of the cutting-out party – a possible sighting on a dark night with the distraction of an opposed boarding – would be torn to shreds. He needed solid evidence to bring *Hope* into English Harbour.

'The cutter's coming back, sir,' reported the mate of the watch.

Carlisle could see that for himself. The boat was moving fast through the water, faster than would be normal for a routine pull between two ships at sea. He could see that the crew were hauling hard at the oars and the coxswain was standing in the stern sheets to urge them on.

'What the devil…?' Gresham's brow looked like thunder. 'I told Mister Torrance to keep the cutter there until I come back.'

The cutter bumped alongside. Carlisle didn't join his officers in looking curiously over the side, but paced the deck, deep in thought.

'Whittle, with one of the New Englanders, it looks like.' Gresham was leaning over the gunwale, examining the boat's passenger. 'Perhaps we have a volunteer.'

He rubbed his hands. Every first lieutenant longed for volunteers, particularly prime seamen with a few years of deep-sea experience. He'd have pressed a few of the Yankee crew if it had been allowed, but all King's officers knew that they couldn't press hands from merchantmen at sea, not until they were in pilotage waters and could work their way to their destination with a short-handed crew.

Carlisle had a moment to wonder. A volunteer wouldn't account for the tearing hurry to get back to *Dartmouth*, nor would Whittle have needed to accompany the volunteer, the coxswain of the boat could have done that. A volunteer, or something else, perhaps?

Whittle strode straight past the gathered officers, pulling the nervous-looking seaman in his wake. He knuckled his forehead and prodded his new friend to do the same. He was clearly enjoying himself, being the centre of attention with, for once, an honourable cause.

'Matthew Dumble, sir, cooper from Hampton, volunteer for the King's service,' he declared, officiously.

Whittle was beaming in pleasure, more so than was reasonable for the acquisition of a single colonial cooper.

'He has something to tell you, sir, if we could be private-like.'

Carlisle looked keenly at the man in front of him. He was entirely unremarkable and would have passed without notice on the deck of any British ship or in any seaport under King George's rule. Yet that brief introduction had revealed that there was something odd about him. He was a Virginian on a New England ship, and that was unusual enough to warrant investigation. Most New England ships were cosy, almost family affairs, with the men coming from the same colony and in most cases from the same town. It wasn't unknown for a ship's crew to come entirely from a single family. A Virginian would be seen as an interloper, an outsider with a different perspective on the world, with odd habits and with different loyalties. As a Virginian himself he could imagine how Dumble might feel uncomfortable in a Providence ship.

'To the poop deck, then. Mister Gresham, please join us.'

***

The wind was keener here on the highest deck of the ship and Dumble's long hair flew to leeward in streamers when he took off his cap. Carlisle moved to the leeward side so that their conversation wouldn't be heard in the great cabin, where Kendrick and Cranston were awaiting his return.

'You wish to volunteer, Dumble, is that correct?'

'Aye, sir, I do.'

Carlisle studied him for any signs of subterfuge. He looked troubled, frightened even, but not dishonest.

'You'll know that it's unusual for men to volunteer from merchantmen in the middle of a voyage, you'll be lucky if you ever get paid for your time so far, and a note-in-hand from the master, well, you perhaps know the chances of you ever redeeming it. So why? Why do you want to leave *Hope*?'

Dumble shuffled nervously then straightened up.

'It's like this, your honour.'

He looked swiftly around to see who was listening. Apparently satisfied, he continued.

'I was paid off from my last ship in Newport and spent weeks and weeks looking for a way to get back to Virginia without having to pay my passage. I was down to my last few coins when I heard that John Brown – he's from

Providence across the bay – was looking for a cooper for a run to the West Indies. So I signed on, it was that or begging on the waterfront, and those northern winters are bitter cold, sir, deadly. But they treated me bad, not being from Providence and not even from New England, and after we'd been a week on passage, I heard that it was a smuggling trip!'

He looked wide-eyed at Carlisle, as though he was telling him something new.

'A smuggling trip, I say. Molasses from the French islands, cheaper than the British islands and no tax to pay if they slip quietly back into Narragansett Bay when the customs men aren't looking. Well, I didn't like it, not so much the smuggling but the dealings with the French. And it went against the grain to sail bold as brass into a French harbour. But I decided to play along and at least I'd have enough to buy a passage home from Providence or maybe get lucky and sign on for a coasting trip.'

Dumble was warming to his story and all his awe at being in front of a post-captain had evaporated.

'Well, sir, we picked up our cargo at St. Lucia. Horrible, unseasoned staves and French-built butts and hogsheads at that. I spent a week just trying to tighten them up before we brought them aboard, and when they started to weep, what with the movement of the ship at anchor and all, Mister Kendrick and that man of business blamed me! Said they'd dock the value of the lost molasses from my pay. Then the others started to make game of me, and one thing and another, by the time we left the Careenage yesterday I was right fed up with the whole parcel of them. When we were boarded, I saw Nat Whittle and as soon as he opened his mouth, I knew right away that he was from Virginia, but bided my time until Kendrick had gone. And here I am happy to serve and looking for the volunteer's bounty, your honour.'

Carlisle studied Dumble for a few more moments. He appeared genuine and his testimony would probably sway the court in Antigua. It was almost too good to be true.

Carlisle's Duty

'I've heard of you, your honour, from my mates that hail from Williamsburg. I reckon you'll treat me fair, not like those damned Yankees, you being an Old Dominion man yourself.'

'Well, Matthew Dumble, will you tell this story to a vice-admiralty court in Antigua? You'll be on your oath, mind.'

Dumble grinned. Along with his way of speech, it was a good sign that he was no New Englander; they took their oaths seriously to the east of the Hudson Valley. That wasn't to say that they were any more truthful, just that an oath had an old testament sound that struck a chord with those dour Calvinists, and they tended to look solemn and church-like whenever it was invoked.

'That I will, sir, and with pleasure, if you'll take me on as a cooper's mate.'

The man was bargaining now. *Dartmouth* already had a cooper and a cooper's mate, and the ship's establishment didn't call for a second mate. However, the coopers came under the direct control of the purser and Carlisle knew very well that any nip-cheese worth his salt could work the books to hide this minor irregularity. In any case, if Dumble proved incompetent as a cooper, he could always be rated ordinary once *Hope's* case was settled.

'In that case, Whittle can take you to his mess and I'll have the purser sign you on and give you a chit for your bounty. My clerk will make sure that the agent in Providence gets your pay to date from Obadiah Brown's company; you're entitled to that for volunteering for the King's service.'

***

When the two had gone, Carlisle thought for a moment. He had enough evidence to bring *Hope* into English Harbour. He knew that the court had a brisk way of business, and he guessed that there'd be little sympathy for a New Englander who was attempting to break the islands' monopoly on supplying sugar and molasses to the American colonies. He could send her in with one of the sloops, but he instantly rejected that idea. He may have to appear in person before the court and there was no urgent need for a fourth rate to be on station, not with the French so inactive. And he didn't like the thought of Cranston stating his case before the court without being there to refute the lies that he knew would be told.

'I'll keep Kendrick and Cranston here, Mister Gresham, so that they can't cook up any more stories with the crew. Take command of *Hope*; don't let them know anything except that they're being brought in for rummaging. I'll take the leeward route to English Harbour and speak to *Rabbit* and *Falcon* as we pass by. The longboat can reach across to the Careenage to let Roscoe know; you can choose either of the mates to command her. Stay under *Dartmouth's* lee and follow me into English Harbour.'

***

CHAPTER TWELVE

Salutary Neglect

Saturday, Twenty-First of February 1761.
Dartmouth, at Sea. East of Guadeloupe.

Dartmouth was a happy ship as it reached north towards Antigua with a fair wind and a flowing sheet. Even the victualling accounts didn't seem too impenetrable on this finest of Caribbean days. And for once the purser was cheerful, having an additional cooper's mate over and above the establishment, in the certain knowledge that his captain would collude in any mild dishonesty that was required to hide the fact from the navy board. A purser's ability to make a profit, Carlisle knew, was largely governed by his ability to control wastage in the ship's victuals, and the cooper and his mates were vital allies in that campaign. With an extra cooper's mate, the routine of tightening up the casks – a judicious tap with the hoop driver normally did the trick – could be done more frequently and the vast range of firkins, barrels, hogsheads, butts, puncheons and the rest of the cooper's litany of cask sizes could be rendered that much less porous. Still, Carlisle found this twice-monthly ritual with the books tiresome, particularly as he knew from bitter experience that any errors would come back to haunt him when *Dartmouth* was eventually paid off.

'Expended over and above the normal issue when the longboat was sent away last week, sir. The men had their ration and then the remainder was lost when the longboat grappled with that privateer.'

Carlisle knew that the purser was stretching a point, he could tell by his smug look. The shortfall in rum had other more mundane causes such as seepage and drippage, and the purser could write off a certain amount under those headings. Nevertheless, the longboat being sent away, and the first lieutenant demanding that the men have their rum ration with their *al fresco* dinner, had given him an opportunity to create a little leeway in his accounts, *a little slack in his pocket* as he put it, just in case of future contingencies, of course.

'Perhaps the next time this happens you could ensure that only enough spirit is passed down into the boat to satisfy the immediate need…'

Carlisle was tired of this continual sparring with the purser, and he was annoyed that Gresham had allowed the rum to be taken away in the boat; the men could perfectly well have been served their spirits in the dog watches when the longboat was back in tow. He sighed heavily. Walker's interruption was not entirely unwelcome.

'Beg your pardon, sir, but you told me to let you know a few minutes before eight bells. And Mister Cranston has asked for the favour of a meeting with you.'

Carlisle wasn't going to be rushed and he wasn't going to miss the noon sight, not for any damned owner's representative. Whenever he could he made a point of watching the young gentlemen take the noon sight, and there were a great number of them to be watched, not just the midshipmen but also the more promising of the youngsters who gloried in the euphemism of captain's servant. Beazley wasn't always available and while the useless schoolmaster that had been foisted upon him could oversee the calculations, he had never learned the mechanics of actually taking the sight. The master had forbidden him to touch a quadrant again when he saw him drop one on the deck, having chosen not to loop the lanyard around his neck before taking the instrument from its box. Of all the deadly sins that kept Beazley awake at night – and there were a great many – the dropping of a quadrant was far and away the most heinous.

The noon sight didn't take long, and it always put Carlisle in a good humour, particularly in these latitudes where it was a positive pleasure to be on deck. He was almost whistling as he passed the wheel on his way back to the great cabin.

'I'll see Mister Cranston now. Pass the word for Mister Simmonds, if you please.'

***

Cranston had lost some of his self-assurance, but he still had that arrogance that seemed to be an essential part of his character. Carlisle had seen it before in New Englanders. It came with their non-conformist religious practices and their undoubted success in growing a colony based on trade rather than agriculture. They were so different from his own people in Virginia, and to him they were as foreign as he had once considered Englishmen to be.

'What can I do for you, Mister Cranston,' he asked once they were settled and had accepted the coffee that Walker offered.

'I'm interested to know what your intentions are, Captain. Your officer – Mister Wishart, I believe – told me that our ship was being taken into English Harbour for the cargo to be investigated, but I've heard nothing more. I would have hoped that I might hear your point of view.'

Carlisle's gaze gave nothing away. He had deliberately avoided meeting either Cranston or Kendrick after he had decided to seize their ship and had resolved to have nothing to do with them until they met at the vice-admiralty court, if indeed he or they were called at all. However, they were messing in the wardroom, and it would have been unusual if they hadn't heard the elements of the case from his officers. It was only the glory of this beautiful day with his ship on its favourite point of sailing that had persuaded him to relent.

'It appears fairly clear, Mister Cranston. You've been trading with the enemy, and furthermore you must have been intending to bring your cargo into Providence without the usual formality of paying the customs dues. That's two separate charges, although the first is quite sufficient, I believe. There's a vice-admiralty court in English harbour; they're legally competent to handle cases such as this, and that is where we are bound.'

A heavy silence fell upon the cabin as Cranston digested this speech. Carlisle could see that he was choosing his next words with care.

'May I ask what evidence you'll bring to prove these accusations, sir?'

Carlisle considered for a moment. Cranston must have seen Dumble in the thirty-odd hours he'd been on board *Dartmouth*; he was everywhere, glorying in his elevated status as second cooper's mate of a ship-of-the-line, and inclined to be voluble about his treatment in the Yankee ship. And the purser, a garrulous man, would have let the whole wardroom know of his good luck. Cranston would have guessed that Dumble had spilled the beans, and that his testimony would be convincing. He must be bitterly regretting Kendrick's treatment of the Virginian, if Dumble's account of his time on board *Hope* was true. The evidence was indeed compelling. Still, there was no value in showing his hand and it may prejudice the trial in some way if he did.

'You may not, Mister Cranston. You'd be better advised to consider any mitigation that may be applicable.'

Carlisle knew that he sounded pompous, but this was a matter not only of the law, but of his own financial security. The damages for unlawfully detaining a laden ship could be crippling.

'That's unfortunate, sir, because you may be causing yourself a good deal of trouble that can be avoided here and now, if we can talk freely about the matter.'

'Indeed? You may speak as freely as you like, Mister Cranston, but you'll understand if I reserve my own position.'

Carlisle sat back in his chair. He didn't really want to hear whatever Cranston had to say, but it seemed unnecessary to throw him out of the cabin. The evidence was overwhelming, but he may yet hear something to further strengthen his case.

Carlisle's Duty

'You have heard of the policy – I won't call it so much as a rule – of *wise and salutary neglect?*'

Carlisle didn't reply. He'd heard of it, of course, but there was no need to be brought into a dialogue.

'We'll, let me review the situation. During the peace, the tax on sugar and molasses brought into the American colonies was found impossible to collect, and it cost more to enforce the law than could be gained from the revenue. The British government, together with the colonial authorities, quietly agreed to turn a blind eye – *wise and salutary neglect* it was called in parliament, I understand – and that situation continued through to the start of the present war. All parties were happy with the situation and friction between parliament and the colonies was minimised, at least as far as the sugar and molasses trade was concerned.'

Carlisle was well aware of the way that the tax was avoided. He'd been involved in the attempted enforcement himself when he served in the sloop *Wolf* in 'thirty-nine and 'forty and had experienced at first hand the futility of trying to enforce a customs blockade on a coast thousands of miles long, in the face of an uncooperative population.

'Set aside the greater matter of the sugar and let us consider the molasses trade alone. The policy was beneficial in the extreme. The rum distilleries in Rhode Island had their cheap imports of molasses from the French islands while the British islands didn't suffer unduly having a ready market for as much as they could produce. The British government and His Majesty's navy and customs officers were freed from the impossible task of enforcing the tax and could concentrate on more important matters.'

Carlisle still showed no sign of whether this was all news to him.

'Of course, when war came with France, the trade stopped and the Brown company, like many others, turned to privateering. That was also a profitable business until last year when nary a French merchantman could be found without half of King Louis' navy escorting it.'

Carlisle could see and even sympathise with Cranston's position. He knew how vital these imports were to the New England colonies, but that was not the issue, and he wasn't going to allow it to taint the case.

'Now, you can perceive why the molasses trade looked so promising again. There was just the small matter of the war with the French. But you see, Captain Carlisle, there is no more war with the French in the American colonies. Thanks to the might of the King's arms, they're gone, all bar a few holdouts that are of no consequence. We colonials,' he smiled ingratiatingly, intending to show that he included Carlisle as a fellow colonial, 'have no more quarrel with them. My employers take the position that the war with France is over, and we should revert to the same situation as in 'fifty-five, *ante bellum*, trading openly with the French islands.'

Was this an admission of guilt? Carlisle could hardly hope for so much.

'However, you can perhaps see why we chose to state that we loaded our cargo at Tobago. We hoped that it would prevent our voyage being unduly interrupted in the case of meeting a King's ship. You can see how successful we were,' he shrugged his shoulders and swept his hand in a motion that was intended to show the absurdity of his position, 'but it's hardly a matter for the vice-admiralty court. In fact, I can imagine them being rather irritated at the waste of their time. We would of course have stated the true source of our cargo before landing it at Providence, so the charge of smuggling won't stand.'

Carlisle had schooled himself over many years to remain impassive during meetings like this. On board his ship he had extraordinary powers and the men who came before him to tell some tale to mitigate their misdemeanours could be encouraged to dig themselves deeper by his silence and his unreadable expression. But this fellow Cranston was struck from a different mould, and he gave back as good as he took in the way of stoicism.

Carlisle's Duty

'Now, my position, and the position of my employers and almost certainly the position of the Rhode Island customs officers, is that *Hope* wasn't trading with the enemy, for the simple reason that the French are no longer a threat to the colony, and she was no more smuggling than Mister Brown's ships were six years ago. It may be of interest to you to know that Mister John Brown, the junior partner in the company, is a member of the vice-admiralty court at Newport and in a position to understand these matters. What I have just told you is the situation as he saw it before we left Providence and that is why I feel so confident in advising you.'

Cranston stopped abruptly and gazed at the sea through the great stern windows.

'You have a remarkably fine view from here, Captain.'

Carlisle studied the man who sat opposite him. He knew something of the Obadiah Brown company. It was a family business and had grown through judicious and successful trading. Cranston was giving nothing away when he admitted that their ships smuggled molasses between the wars, it was a commonplace and neither the navy nor the customs officers interfered with it. His point about trading with the enemy was less persuasive. Cranston was certainly a man of parts. He was playing his hand with skill, a fighting retreat that contested every barricade. This was the first line of defence, the attempt to persuade his captor that it wasn't worth the risk to bring *Hope* to the vice-admiralty court.

'We can still end this without any further trouble, Captain Carlisle. If you'll return me and Captain Kendrick to our ship and allow us to continue our passage to Providence, we'll say no more of the matter. Once we're in English Harbour it will be too late; other powers will decide how this will end and we may both live to regret it.'

Cranston had clearly said his piece. Carlisle was tempted to dismiss him without another word but there was something about the man that angered him, and he wanted to prick that bubble of self-assuredness.

'Mister Cranston. It seems to me that you are missing one very important point. Rhode Island and all the other colonies, my own included as I'm sure you know that I'm a Virginian, owe our unquestioned allegiance to King George. The King and all his subjects, including those in the colonies, are at war with France and will remain in that situation until he and his government decide otherwise. It is not for you, nor even for I as a King's officer, to decide when the state of war is ended. Setting aside the matter of smuggling for now, and the court may not be so accommodating, I note that you have admitted that your ship has been trading in a French port.'

Carlisle inclined his head towards Simmonds. The implication was obvious; the clerk's notes of the conversation could be used in evidence.

'The position is quite clear; my duty to the King can only be discharged by bringing you in to English Harbour and laying the case before the vice-admiralty court. That is what I intend to do. These are serious charges that can be levelled at everyone involved in the enterprise: yourself, Mister Kendrick and Mister Brown and his partners. As I said before, you'd be better advised to consider any mitigation for your actions, rather than contest the points of law, which as far as I can see lie wholly against you. Now, if you'll excuse me, I have other matters to concern me. Mister Simmonds will see you out of the cabin.'

Carlisle turned away and heard Cranston walking stiffly out of the cabin.

***

Duty. He'd used that word without a thought. He'd flung it at Cranston almost casually, and yet it was the nub of the matter. There was no prize money or any other financial incentive in bringing in a British ship, not in time of war, and it was only his duty that motivated him. That was so, wasn't it?

Carlisle was walking the poop deck again, striding hard and fast, trying to clear his head after that distasteful

Carlisle's Duty

interview.

And yet duty didn't say it all; but if not duty and duty alone, then what?

Every subject's duty is the king's; but every subject's soul is his own.

Those were the words that Shakespeare put into King Harry's mouth, before Agincourt. Was he guilty of letting his own personal affairs – his pride – intrude on the King's business? Every move he made, every decision he took, it seemed to him, was subject to scrutiny by his peers, who were watching keenly for any quirks that could be attributed to his colonial upbringing. In his mind, his loyalty was perpetually being questioned and as he analysed this latest act, it became clear that the need to be more rigorous than his fellows in colonial administration matters had led him down what was, quite probably, a foolish path.

What would the other post-captains on the station do in this situation? He could imagine. They'd have accepted the glib narrative of a trading voyage to Tobago, they'd have welcomed the volunteer cooper with open arms and then told him to keep his opinions to himself. The incident would have been nothing more than a line in the master's log and it wouldn't even have been mentioned in the captain's. Kendrick and Cranston would have continued their voyage unhindered, and the incident would have been forgotten by the morning.

Carlisle stopped at the taffrail and stared at the ship's wake, stretching in silver-rimmed ridges far astern to eventually be lost in the hungry ocean.

His duty, yes, but also his damned personal pride. And for that he'd imperilled his own wealth. He didn't dare to calculate the worst damages that could be awarded to Obadiah Brown & Company, and they would all fall upon his head. It was a gamble with no tangible prize but the possibility of a ruinous forfeit. A fool's wager.

And yet he still had the opportunity to withdraw his stake and leave the table. With a few brief orders he could send Kendrick and Cranston back to *Hope*, retrieve his own men and send the New Englanders on their way. There would be a few rumours, of course, but he doubted very much whether anyone would give them any credence. Perhaps the commodore would guess that something had occurred – he was no fool, not like Carlisle – but he had better things to do than to chase down an incident with a colonial ship that may or may not have happened.

For a moment he was tempted. He actually paused in his stride and turned towards the poop deck rail. It would be so easy…

And then he thought of the mental torment he would endure. His officers knew, and they would guess the reason if he gave those orders. Probably Enrico would make his case in the wardroom, he was certainly clever enough to divine his captain's reasoning. But that was intolerable. He'd have to live with knowing that he'd done less than his duty, and with knowing that his officers were aware of every detail of his dilemma. No, it wouldn't do. He set his face in a determined expression and walked steadily down the ladder to the quarterdeck, frightening the life out of every man who saw him.

He'd fulfil his duty to his King, and to the navy that in spite of everything, he loved. But he still had that lingering feeling that there was more. What about his duty to his family, to himself, indeed? His fool's wager could yet put his fortune in jeopardy, and for that he would be tried at the court of his own conscience.

***

CHAPTER THIRTEEN

Pandora's Box

Wednesday, Twenty-Fifth of February 1761.
Dartmouth, at English Harbour, Antigua.

Freeman's Bay sparkled in the last of the evening sunshine. The wind had dropped to the merest whisper and the wake from the yawl that was speeding from the King's Yard towards *Dartmouth* left long dark furrows that glinted orange on the crests and the deepest indigo in the shadowed troughs. The Rhode Island merchantman *Hope* was just out of sight from the windows of the great cabin as she lay to her anchor on the fourth rate's starboard bow. Carlisle wished he was able to sit in awful majesty, perhaps writing a letter to his wife, but with so much at stake he couldn't refrain from watching the yawl until it disappeared from sight, making for the larboard main chains.

The vice-admiralty court had met today to consider *Hope's* case. It was expected that they would take two days, possibly even three, but the first day's deliberations might give some sort of indication of the eventual verdict. Simmonds had spent the day waiting outside the court's chambers in St. John's and he would have had a hard twelve-mile carriage ride across the island to bring the news to his captain. Carlisle felt the bump as the yawl hooked onto the chains and he heard the sounds of someone climbing over the gunwale. He composed himself, hoping to look like a man to whom the news – whatever it was – held little importance.

A brief tap at the door – he knew Simmonds' knock by now – and his clerk strode hastily into the cabin. He looked very grave, and Carlisle set his face in an impassive mask, prepared for the worst.

'I came as fast as I could, sir. You'll be the first in English Harbour to hear the news. They've passed the case on to the court at Newport! *Hope* is still impounded, and the marshal will fix a new writ to its mast tomorrow. The court expressed the wish that Commodore Douglas would send her north under naval escort. They noted that the flagship was at English Harbour and that a swift decision could be made to send *Hope* away without delay. The letter was being drafted as I left the court and it's expected to reach the commodore tomorrow.'

Carlisle tried to make sense of Simmonds' breathless report, but it was almost too much. Of all the possible verdicts, this was the one that he had not even dreamed of. It was better than having the court find against him, but it meant that the case would drag on for another month or so, at least. That was inconvenient but it didn't account for his clerk's long face. After all, the court's decision was tantamount to an acceptance that there was a case to be answered.

'You'll recall, sir, that one of the partners in the company is a member of the Newport vice-admiralty court. Mister John Brown if I remember correctly.'

Carlisle did remember. Cranston had dropped it into his monologue almost as an aside and Carlisle hadn't given it any weight at all. But now it was of the greatest significance. The court must certainly exclude John Brown from deliberations where he was so personally involved, but no Newport court could possibly be unmoved by the ownership of the vessel in question. Carlisle pulled himself together.

'They took all day to decide that?' he asked, incredulously.

'No, sir. They considered two other cases first and didn't come to ours until two o'clock. By then the time for dinner was pressing and after a few comments from the chair they unanimously agreed that the Crown had made a case but that it was beyond their competence. It was Mister Cranston's written submission that swayed them. I had the impression that he had made the points of law and custom

Carlisle's Duty

appear so obscure that they feared they would take a week of deliberations to come to a decision, and then they'd be mired in appeals for months or years to come. With dinner approaching they took the easy way out. I fear that the commodore won't like it, sir.'

'He most certainly won't. He'll have to send a sloop, or a frigate and he can ill-afford either of those.'

Carlisle drummed his fingers on the table. The commodore must be told before he received the letter. Should he do it now, at this hour of the evening, or should he wait for the morning? It would certainly affect the squadron's disposition, and who knew what plans Sir James was making at this moment.

'I must tell the commodore. You'll come with me, Mister Simmonds, in case he wants to question you.'

'I'll have a boat sent to request a call, sir…'

'No time for that, Simmonds. We must tell him before he hears of it from other sources. The yawl will do, they'll hardly have stowed their oars.'

Simmonds suppressed a heavy sigh. Carlisle was the only captain in the squadron capable of inviting himself to call on the commander-in-chief without warning, and the only one who would do so in the humble yawl, without his own boat's crew being called away.

***

Dublin was anchored a bare half cable from *Dartmouth* and the flagship's officer of the watch was taken by surprise when the yawl shot towards his ship's side in the gathering gloom. A post-captain was the last person that he expected, and Carlisle had to wait in the boat while a side party was assembled. Sometimes he was exasperated by the navy's obsessive insistence on the forms of ceremony, particularly when they delayed him on important business, even though he knew how important it was to maintain the dignity of rank. He was almost stamping with frustration as he went up the side to the sound of the bosuns' calls.

'Sir James will see you now, sir.'

The grave secretary led the way to the great cabin. This was one of the old seventy-gun third rates that were rapidly being superseded by the seventy-fours, and Carlisle was very familiar with the layout. Nevertheless the majesty of a commander-in-chief – even one who at least in theory could revert to his substantive rank of post-captain at the stroke of the admiralty secretary's pen – required that he be escorted.

'Ah Carlisle, to what do I owe this unexpected pleasure, and so late in the evening?'

Carlisle was oblivious to the hinted rebuke; his mind was completely taken up with the urgency of his business.

'I beg your pardon, Sir James, but there's news from the vice-admiralty court. Mister Simmonds has come in haste from St. John's.'

Simmonds bowed and Douglas smiled a wintry greeting.

'I suppose you'd better take a seat then Carlisle and tell me what has so moved you.'

Carlisle paused to compose himself.

'They've passed the case on to Newport, sir. The merchantman is still impounded, and they've resolved to apply to you for an escort to take her north.'

'Ah, I see.'

Douglas exchanged a glance with his secretary, a knowing glance, it seemed to Carlisle.

'I'm hardly surprised, having seen the argument that the owner's representative was intent on making. What did you say?' he asked his secretary, '*a perfect example of muddied legal waters*, wasn't that it?'

The secretary nodded slowly and laid down his pen.

'His plan was quite clear, sir. He gave the court a problem that appeared so complex, given all the pre-war precedents, that they would despair of ever finding a way through. They'll have been glad to pass it on.'

Carlisle pursed his lips. Why couldn't he have been told that? But then, it would have made no difference once the ship was in English Harbour and under the vice-admiralty marshal's custody. Pandora's box had been opened and no mortal force could close it before every single evil had come forth.

'You are sure of the contents of this letter, Mister Simmonds?'

'Yes, sir. I saw it being drafted from the rough notes. It will be sent here tomorrow.'

'I thought you should hear before someone else tells you, sir. Gossip has swift wings, as they say,' Carlisle added.

'Swift indeed, Carlisle, and thank you for letting me know. I expect I should comply with the court's request, what do you think?' he asked the secretary.

'Oh, all things considered, Sir James, it would be highly advisable. They're largely planters on the court after all and we have enough difficulty with them as things stand.'

Carlisle wasn't surprised. The planters must be appeased of course, but a commander-in-chief also needed to maintain harmonious relations with the vice-admiralty courts in his region, otherwise he'd soon find that his prizes started to be released and his operations against French commerce became enmeshed in legal debate.

Douglas paused and stared at the blackness outside the windows. The tropical night had fallen with its usual abruptness and Freeman's Bay and English Harbour beyond were erased as though they had never been. His servant should have rigged the curtains by now, but presumably he didn't want to disturb the meeting.

'Do you have that list to hand?'

'The squadron summary Sir James? Here it is.'

He scanned the paper for a few moments. Despite the secretary's opinion – his very strong advice – he could of course refuse to escort the merchantman to New England, but that would cause all sorts of complications, particularly if the eventual decision involved damages against the Crown as well as personal damages against Carlisle. The charges would increase with every day that *Hope* was delayed at English Harbour.

'Well, assuming this request comes tomorrow, I can't send a schooner or cutter on an errand such as this, not that I have any available in any case. The frigates are all engaged to windward or watching the French islands and you have most of my sloops, Carlisle. I must keep the battle squadron intact in case the French send an expedition this way, which leaves only *Dartmouth*.'

He gazed sightlessly out of the window, watching the pinpricks of light moving through the dark night.

'Unless something more suitable comes up before tomorrow, I regret that you'll have to sail north and remain at Newport until the case is heard. I'll bring one of the frigates in to look after your flock until you return.'

Carlisle looked stunned. It was a day of surprises, but he knew that if he had spent a little time in thought, the commodore's decision could have been foretold. It was bad news of course. He would lose the command of his little squadron and however much the commodore might plan that he should regain it when the case was over, he knew how fast circumstances changed. It was a consequence of command of a fourth rate; he was condemned to be the commander-in-chief's spare ship, ready to be sent away on any odd errands rather than deplete the line-of-battle or its eyes and ears, the frigates and sloops.

'In fact, there are a half dozen merchantmen waiting for an escort at St. John's, so if you sail on – what shall we say – Saturday? You should have quite a respectable convoy.'

Douglas brightened at the thought. He had been pondering how he could spare a man-o'-war for escort duties, and now the answer was thrust upon him. It was Carlisle's misfortune but then the whole sorry business was his fault. If he could only have looked the other way, none of this would be happening. He put it down to Carlisle being a colonial; he didn't feel that he could give an inch where American commercial interests were concerned.

'If you meet Lord Colville, he will no doubt have a convoy for you to bring back once this is all over. Mind that it's a convoy direct for the Islands though. I know how those runs down through the colonies can be interminable and they'll ask you to wait for more trade at every port.'

Douglas paused for a moment in thought. Perhaps he was recalling that Carlisle's home was in Williamsburg, close to one of those ports that could so delay a convoy. Well, it was in the nature of things that once he had sent *Dartmouth* north, he could no longer exercise strict control over Carlisle's movements. It was generally agreed that although a commander-in-chief couldn't direct the movements of a ship from another station, a captain should comply with his wishes unless it directly contravened his original orders.

'General Amherst has been warned that he'll need to send some men this way, to take St. Lucia and Dominica from the French, perhaps as early as June, so you may be required to convoy the army. We'll see. These grand ideas come and go, and you'll recall that we should have taken Martinique last year, but there it is, still a haven for privateers and a refuge for the French navy when they pass this way. Still, Amherst will no doubt have a lot of underemployed regiments on his hands, with the French mostly chased out of Canada, but we know all about that of course.'

Carlisle nodded. He'd been at the fall of Quebec, as had Douglas, although the commodore had done rather better out of the expedition, with a knighthood for his pains.

'St. Lucia or Dominica, one or the other but not both, that's my guess, but either of them will be a boon. Well, I can't foretell what needs Colville will have and he'll be within his rights to send you where he likes so long as it's generally south. I'll have to leave it to you. In any case, I hope you can return in May, at the latest. I'll need every ship I can find to keep the French navy away from whichever island is chosen next, if they should venture this side of the Atlantic. I don't expect to see you for a few months, so God speed and have a prosperous voyage.'

***

The letter arrived at the flagship at ten o'clock the next morning and by twelve Carlisle had received his orders from the commander-in-chief to take a convoy north in two days' time. There was a mad scramble to prepare the orders for the merchantmen: sailing time and rendezvous off St. John's, signals for use by day and by night, action to be taken in case of separation and the usual injunctions to resist the temptation to reduce canvas at night unless so ordered. Much of it could be copied from previous convoy orders that Carlisle had used, but it still took time to adapt it for this particular occasion.

The intense activity was a blessing; it prevented Carlisle spending too much time in gloomy pondering on the case that was to be tried at Newport. It wasn't only the convoy that had to be prepared, but *Dartmouth* had to be victualled for three months, the minimum for a ship on this side of the Atlantic, and there was powder and shot to be embarked, bosun's stores to be replenished and the longboat's repairs to be completed.

Dartmouth and *Hope* weighed anchor on Friday evening and a favourable land breeze wafted them out to sea. Carlisle could see Cranston and Kendrick on the merchantman's quarterdeck, and they appeared to spend a lot of time talking and pointing at *Dartmouth*. What were they saying? Were they laughing at their imminent triumph? It was quite clear to Carlisle that a Newport court would find in favour of the Rhode Island ship, even if it meant giving a nod to trading with the enemy. The matter of smuggling would hardly come into the deliberations and even if the decision was appealed, the superior court was in London, and it would take months for a verdict to be overturned. And realistically, an appeal would be unlikely to succeed. The government had no appetite for a fight with the colonies, and the arguments about custom and practice and salutary neglect would sound very cogent to men who didn't have to implement the government's policy on the high seas.

The big question for him was what it would cost him

personally. If damages were awarded against him in person, rather than against the Crown, he could appeal against the verdict. It would certainly go on for months and probably years before he'd have to reach into his pocket, and by then perhaps he could contrive to take a prize or two. God send him an uncomplicated French West Indiamen!

***

It was a simple passage west-about around the island, with the blessed trade wind never before the beam, and on Saturday morning they met the merchantmen streaming out of St. John's. By two bells in the afternoon they were abreast of Barbuda and by sunset the convoy was running to the nor'west. A fair wind and a well-behaved convoy, it should have been idyllic, but Carlisle was a troubled man as the leagues and leagues of blue water flowed beneath *Dartmouth's* keel.

He couldn't get out of his mind that what was left in Pandora's box after all the evils had fled into the world and the lid was closed, was *hope*. If ever there was a bad omen…

***

CHAPTER FOURTEEN

The Tempter

Tuesday, Seventeenth of March 1761.
Dartmouth, at Sea. Cape Henry West Seven Leagues.

It had been a fast passage and for once the merchantmen obeyed Carlisle's orders, kept together and flew their tops'ls from one noon observation to the next. A French privateer, a big, ship-rigged beast that could aspire to overpower anything less than one of the newer sloops, followed them as they ran past the Bahamas. But its only achievement was to instil a profound sense of self-preservation in the convoy and to encourage the merchantmen to close ranks so tightly that they could hail one another from their decks without any great effort. It was easy to keep the Frenchman at bay; all Carlisle had to do was to position *Dartmouth* between the convoy and the privateer, and even at night the moon and the stars combined to reveal the enemy wherever he should probe for a weakness.

Nevertheless they were followed all the way to Savannah where two of the ships were bound, and the convoy had to lie-to until they were safely into the river. If there had been two privateers it would have been a different matter, and one slow old fourth rate, despite her overwhelming weight of broadside, would have been hard pressed to keep them both at arm's length. After Savannah the Frenchman gave up and turned south, hoping for some easier prey.

Savannah, then Charleston where three of the convoy departed, then a wide sweep past Cape Hatteras where the bones of many an imprudent ship lay washed by the waves, buried deeper and deeper into the sand with each tide, and on to Cape Henry where another four were to leave for the Chesapeake.

Carlisle's Duty

'Make the signal for the Chesapeake ships to part company, Mister Wishart.'

'Aye-aye sir.'

Wishart tipped his hat and the midshipman of the watch – keen for his captain to notice his zeal – ran up the ladder to the poop deck where the signal locker sat beneath the taffrail.

The Virginia coast could be felt rather than seen, but Beazley was confident that the nearest land was seven leagues or so under their lee. He'd had a noon sight only an hour before and he'd kept a good dead reckoning since they left Charleston. He'd shouted his estimated position across to each of the ships that were bound for the Chesapeake, and already they were edging away to leeward in anticipation of Carlisle's signal, *warming the bell* or *flogging the glass* in the old sea expressions. They'd be between the capes before sunset and if they were sensible and anchored at Hampton, they'd be safe for the night. In any case they were no longer Carlisle's responsibility. He had to take the remainder of the convoy to Sandy Hook and then just *Dartmouth* and *Hope* would continue to Narragansett Bay.

He looked longingly to the west. If only they'd had a storm along the way, lost a few spars or sprung a leak – nothing serious of course but enough to justify him calling at Hampton for repairs – he could be home tomorrow where his wife and child waited for him. It had been five months since he last saw them, five long months of separation. It was nothing, of course. Sea officers could spend years away from their family and he'd been lucky that *Dartmouth* hadn't been sent to the East Indies or been kept in the Mediterranean. It was the fate of fourth rates to be shuffled from place to place in time of war. The decision process that had taken Commodore Douglas no more than a minute or two was typical of the way that these smallest ships-of-the-line were perceived, and he knew that as long as he was in command there'd be little stability in his employment. However, he had to acknowledge the other reason. Even commanders-in-chief had human feelings and Douglas knew Carlisle's domestic situation very well. It wasn't a crucial factor in the commander-in-chief's deliberations, but all other things being equal he'd send *Dartmouth* on the convoying missions in the expectation that there would be a returning convoy to be mustered at Hampton, and that would take a week or so, allowing Carlisle to see his family.

Carlisle watched the Chesapeake ships square away to the west, racing each other for the last few leagues to home. He walked up onto the poop deck and cast a last glance around the horizon, just in case, and with a sigh turned back to the ladder.

'No leaks, Mister Beazley? No sprung topmasts, we have enough wood and water to make Newport?'

'None at all, sir,' the master replied with a grin, 'the ship's hale and hearty and well found, I regret to report.'

The whole quarterdeck joined in the joke. It was well known that the captain yearned for an excuse to follow the Chesapeake ships and drop anchor off Hampton. But it was not to be, not this time.

'Sandy Hook then, Mister Beazley, and we'll discharge our last followers. When do you estimate our arrival?'

'Friday morning, if the wind doesn't back, sir. We'll be a point or two free and even those old tubs,' he motioned towards the convoy to windward, 'can make their four or five knots. Aye, Friday morning, I'd say.'

'Very well, let's try to push the pace a little. They'll all be keen to see the East River so shake out the t'gallants and let's see how fast they can sail when they want to. I'll be in my cabin. Mister Angelini and Mister Simmonds will be joining me for dinner.'

***

Carlisle's dinners at sea were generally quiet affairs. Some captains that he knew kept a grand table and their dinners were often riotous, accompanied by music and half a dozen removes, but his were more modest and in any case,

Carlisle's Duty

Dartmouth could boast nothing more than the marine buglers and drummers and a decrepit old Northumbrian seaman who played a whining fiddle to encourage the men at the capstan. The old man also played an excruciating set of smallpipes – a Northumberland tradition, it seemed – if he wasn't prevented in time. None of those would add to the ambience of the captain's table.

'I wonder that our prize hasn't taken the opportunity to melt away one of these dark nights,' said Enrico as the cheese was served. 'These past three have been thick enough.'

Carlisle had noticed a different quality in his cousin's English in the past few months. It had become less accented, and he used more contractions; even his idioms were starting to make sense, to the dismay of the midshipmen and youngsters who were bitterly disappointed when a whole watch went by without some hilarious malapropisms. He could pass as English now and in the melting pot of the navy he no longer appeared very exotic at all.

'Oh, he won't try anything foolish, you can be sure of that,' Simmonds replied. 'He'd forfeit any chance of being exonerated by the court. There are many things that they'll give a nod and a wink to, but they won't ignore an open defiance of a court injunction, with the writ nailed to the mainmast by the deputy marshal himself. No, he'll follow us to Newport meek as a lamb…'

'Particularly as he can be almost certain of the outcome. What do you think, Mister Simmonds?'

Simmonds lay down his cheese knife and thought for a moment. He was close to his captain, they spent a good part of every day in each other's company, but Carlisle hadn't raised the subject of the forthcoming hearing since the day that the St. John's court had passed the case on. It was unlike Carlisle to interrupt his dinner guests, and that was perhaps a measure of the strain he must be feeling.

'I spoke to a few people before we left English Harbour,

sir. I had expected a variety of opinions and in particular I'd expected the planters to want *Hope's* master and owners prosecuted. After all, the New Englander would be undercutting the planters' own trade in molasses. However, it appears that I was mistaken. In fact, they have a quite different attitude to the whole question of the French sugar islands. Please stop me if you've heard all this, sir.'

Carlisle waved his hand for Simmonds to continue. In fact, he knew most of the arguments regarding trade in the West Indies, but it was always useful to get another viewpoint.

'Well, for a start they don't see the French Islands as competitors at all. When peace comes and the trade goes back to normal, their businesses will be protected by the navigation acts, the molasses act, the sugar act and all the precedents that stem from the cases that have come to trial. Their greatest concern is flooding the market and depressing prices, and if Guadeloupe, Martinique, St. Lucia and the others are brought into the British sphere, then there'll be a glut of produce in Britain and the colonies. So in fact, as far as this war goes, they'd rather it was all over, and the French have their islands returned.'

'But they must detest the smuggling,' Carlisle countered, 'surely it increases the supply to the colonies.'

'Not really. It's such a small amount compared with the quantity of sugar and molasses that they ship abroad. They rather see it as stimulating demand. Mostly it's just molasses in any case and they're not too concerned about it. Anyway, with all the parliamentary seats that the planters control, they feel that they can turn the smuggling on and off at will, just by pressing for more or less enforcement. The American colonies don't have that representation, so the planters hold all the cards. There's another point too. The planters use smugglers themselves when they feel they need to unload a glut, when there's been a big harvest, and they wouldn't want to see the business die off. I confess that I didn't follow the logic of all the arguments, but it was clear that a bit of smuggling was seen as no bad thing, even if the French should profit by it.'

'Ah, and that agrees with something I heard when we were in Virginia last year. There was a feeling that the Jamaica and Leeward Islands planters have preferential treatment over the colonies, and it's all to do with that representation in parliament that you're speaking about. I've been hearing that kind of talk all my life, but it's grown louder recently.'

'I didn't know that Jamaica and Antigua sent representatives to parliament,' said Enrico. 'I thought it was only the English and Scottish boroughs.'

Carlisle smiled. It wasn't surprising that Enrico didn't understand the subtleties of the British parliamentary system; few native Englishmen did.

'They don't, Mister Angelini. But so many members have interests in the sugar islands, indeed a few are plantation owners themselves, that they form a considerable voting alliance in the House. It's well known, and it's factored into the calculations for most divisions. Even if the vote doesn't directly affect the islands, there'll be a network of interest that will include those members, and the government must take notice. Make no mistake, the sugar interest commands a great deal of power, far more than Virginia tobacco or New England timber or rum. It's a real challenge for the American colonies, to find a way of being represented.'

'Nevertheless, why is it that the West Indies should have such representation while Virginia does not? They both produce luxuries, sugar and tobacco, what is the difference?'

'Oh, as for that, a Virginian, or anyone from the American colonies, has generally broken his ties to the mother country and has made the New World his home. The planters, on the other hand, only see themselves as temporary residents in the Islands, and to a man they plan to return to Britain when they've made their fortune. That gives them an incentive to remain in touch with affairs in parliament, while we Americans have created a sort of government of our own in each colony. It makes for very different ways of looking at the world, I can assure you, and it's the root cause of the lack of representation.'

The conversation subsided as the three men thought about the implications. The sound of the ship's pumps filtered through into the cabin, the monotonous clank, clank that happened at the start of every watch. Many officers used it as a way of shaking the sleep from the more idle members of their watch, but it had a serious purpose as every wooden ship gained water at a greater or lesser rate. *Dartmouth* was one of the lucky ones that made no more than a few inches each watch, a quantity that could be expelled in ten minutes at most.

'It'll become an issue, I dare say, as the colonies realise that the French aren't a threat any longer. In fact, I found Mister Cranston's arguments quite persuasive,' Simmonds said.

'Well, on a more cheerful note, it does appear that I bought my house in Williamsburg at just the right time. The building boom has already started in Newport, no doubt we'll witness it ourselves, and it's starting to spread south. People are confident now, and with a huge continent in front and the Atlantic highway at our backs, we colonials can see a great future for the continent.'

Simmonds looked to the window to hide his smile. It was one of the few times that he had heard his captain refer to himself as a colonial. Normally, it was a sore point for Carlisle, and he was careful to associate himself more with the home country than with Virginia or the wider American world. It appeared that Cranston's monologue had affected him more than he would like to admit.

'Then you'd describe the American colonies as a land of opportunity, sir?' Enrico asked.

'I may perhaps be biased, what do you think Mister Simmonds?'

Simmonds stared at his plate for a moment. He knew

that his captain valued his opinion, and this was a subject that cut straight to Carlisle's heart. Furthermore, Enrico was his close friend, and he knew a great deal about his situation and why he may be asking questions like this.

'I think,' he answered cautiously, 'that with the French gone and the population in an optimistic mood, there's little to prevent the colonies expanding and drawing in more people, and not just from England and Scotland. Europe is becoming crowded, and its institutions are set in their ways; decayed, you could perhaps say. An ambitious man can make much of himself in the New World. If I may take the liberty of addressing your situation, Mister Angelini…'

Enrico bowed.

'A man of your intelligence and knowledge of the world could do very well in the Americas. Oh, I don't doubt that your family situation will always find you well provided for in Sardinia and if the plans for a new navy come to fruition, you will be well placed, but I wouldn't rule out America, not if I were in your position.'

Enrico smiled at that. He was by no means sure that his membership of the Angelini family was an asset in Sardinia. When he'd last visited – was it only last year? – he'd detected a definite decline in the family fortunes, and he felt like an outsider.

'Well, gentlemen, one thing's for sure. The Americas are British and will remain so. We all can come and go as our fancy takes us. On that note it's perhaps an appropriate time for a toast. Fill the glasses now, Walker, and no short measures.'

'Gentlemen, I give you King George, may his reign be long, and may he be honoured on both sides of the Atlantic as long as the empire shall last!'

***

The knock at the door exactly coincided with the last drops of the Captain's good claret leaving the glasses.

'Mister Gresham's compliments, sir, and he begs to report that that ship's making water, sir. A foot or so in the past hour. Watch on deck are clearing it sir, and Chips is rummaging in the hold, sir.'

Carlisle looked sharply at the midshipman. Was this a joke? If so, it was most unlike any of his officers and it would go hard with the instigator. No, of course not, nobody would be so foolish, would they?

'Tell Mister Gresham I'll be on deck immediately.'

The midshipman ran from the cabin, conscious that in some way he had stirred up the captain's suspicions, as Carlisle flung down his napkin and rose from his chair to end the dinner.

The officers on deck all looked studiously at the sails, the helm and the far horizon when Carlisle marched out of the cabin. All except the first lieutenant on whose broad shoulders the storm – if there was to be such a thing – would naturally break.

'I trust I'm not being made game of Mister Gresham.'

'Oh no, sir, nothing of the sort, the leak is real enough. Ah, here's Chips now.'

'In the hold, sir, right below number five gun of the main deck, a foot above the orlop. It's in the wing beside my store, so it's handy to get at from inside, maybe three feet below the waterline. A butt's started, sir, at the forward end of the plank.'

A butt! That meant that the joint where two plank ends were fastened at a frame had sprung free. The treenails must have pulled through or rotted or snapped. It was common enough and the unexplained losses of ships on passage were generally attributed to sprung butt ends. The edge of the plank would be scooping in water through the gap, and the faster the ship sailed, the greater the flow. At least it was on the starboard side so the leak wouldn't be too far underwater. Unless the wind shifted, they should be able to make Narragansett Bay on this tack.

'What can you do, Chips?'

The carpenter scratched his head.

'Well, sir,' he said slowly, 'we need to be hauled over to

Carlisle's Duty

get at it to make a proper job. If the nails at the next frame hold, I can stuff it with rags and pitch and build a cofferdam over it, there's a rider right there that'll take the nails. That'll take me an hour or two, my mates are on it already.'

'If the next frame holds, will the leak increase?'

'No, I don't think so, sir, not unless the weather turns nasty.'

'Very well, get to it and let me know when you have it under control.'

The carpenter hurried away leaving wet footprints on the quarterdeck.

'Mister Beazley. You told me we'd be at Sandy Hook on Friday. When do you expect to be at Newport if we touch and go at Sandy Hook?'

'The wind will doubtless be heading us abreast Long Island, sir, and we'll need to make a board to the south. Sunday, if all goes well.'

Carlisle nodded. He could hear the pumps again, or was that the voice of the Tempter? The damage was sufficient excuse to make for the nearest port. Ships had foundered because of a single sprung butt, and nobody would question his decision for a moment. Chesapeake Bay was still under his lee and with only the heavily trafficked coast of New Jersey to pass, his charges for Sandy Hook could easily make their own way. He could signal for *Hope* to follow him, and he could be at anchor before dark and home tomorrow. And yet, in his heart he knew that it wasn't right. He had his duty to consider and the sooner he got this business over with the better. Newport had all the facilities to half-careen the ship so that the carpenter could repair the sprung butt. The watch on deck had some sweating to do to keep the ship afloat in the meantime, but it would do them no harm. He looked up at the commissioning pennant streaming bravely towards the Virginian coast, then with a resolute turn of his body he walked past the quartermaster towards his cabin.

'Let me know if anything changes, Mister Gresham.'

With a surprisingly light heart, Carlisle stretched out on the cushions below the stern window and watched the endless sea churning in *Dartmouth's* wake, satisfied that he'd resisted the worst of temptations.

***

CHAPTER FIFTEEN

Colonial Interests

Sunday, Twenty-Second of March 1761.
Dartmouth, at Sea. Off Point Judith.

'It looks bitter cold over there,' said Gresham, thrusting his chin to the west where Block Island's snow-covered outline was just becoming visible.

The first lieutenant's bulk was made even greater this morning by the odd assortment of woollen garments that he was wearing under his oilskin, and his hands were thrust deep inside the outer garment so that only his head and his tricorn hat were available for pointing.

'I went ashore there once, a few years back, to see a man about a cargo that had to be paid for,' Beazley replied, 'and a more desolate place you couldn't find this side of the Greenland Sea. Of course, the weather blew up and I couldn't get off the damned island for two weeks, and then only at the risk of my life in the most ill-found fishing yawl that you ever saw. It makes me shudder when I think of it.'

He turned his back on Block Island and scowled at the innocent steersman.

'Beg pardon, sir,' said a midshipman who had just slid down the ladder from the poop, '*Hope* is closing us on the lee quarter.'

Gresham thrust his head over the larboard gunwale and looked astern. The merchantman was moving up as though to speak to her escort. With *Dartmouth* under reduced sail, *Hope* was moving through the water at least a knot faster.

'What the devil does he want now,' Gresham muttered.

He shouted over his shoulder at the midshipman.

'My compliments to the captain and it would appear that *Hope* wants to speak to us.'

'I'm here, Mister Gresham.'

Carlisle had come noiselessly from his cabin, his footsteps muffled by the thin layer of late winter snow that covered the quarterdeck.

'Brail up the main tops'l and let her draw alongside.'

There is a strange quality to ships sailing through snow. All the usual sounds are deadened, and the eye is deceived; distances appear greater than they are, and the fine detail is lost in the swirl of white flakes. *Hope* was in fact very close indeed and in ten minutes she was tucked under *Dartmouth's* lee at easy hailing distance.

'Captain Carlisle, good morning to you!'

That was Kendrick, easily distinguishable by his height, with Cranston standing at his shoulder, like his conscience.

'Good morning, Mister Kendrick.'

He refused to use the title *captain* for the merchant master. It was becoming almost normal to do so, the Honourable East India Company having made it fashionable, but Carlisle clung to the distinction between a merchant master and the captain of a King's ship.

'Do you intend to take a pilot, sir?'

Kendrick's voice came loud and clear through the falling snow despite his disadvantage of shouting against the breeze.

Now what was all that about? Carlisle looked at Beazley who shrugged.

'Yes. I'll heave-to off Point Judith, just follow my movements.'

Carlisle saw a swift exchange of words between Kendrick and Cranston. A question from Kendrick and an answering nod from the man of business. It had been quite clear from the first meeting that Kendrick deferred to Cranston in any matters not directly concerned with working the ship, but that relationship appeared to have extended into matters of navigation.

Carlisle's Duty

'I'm a Narragansett Bay pilot,' Kendrick shouted, 'if you follow me, I can lead you right into the Newport anchorage. There'll be no waiting off Point Judith and no fees.'

Carlisle could see out of the corner of his eye that Beazley was emphatically shaking his head. He didn't need the master to tell him that it was inadvisable in the extreme. With no contract of pilotage, Kendrick could shake off any blame if *Dartmouth* should have a mishap in the difficult waters of the bay. And of course it was entirely possible that Kendrick would deliberately put *Dartmouth* aground. The two-decker needed at least a fathom more water to float than the merchantman and there were any number of places on the approach to Newport where *Hope* could sail happily over a shoal that would rip the bottom out of *Dartmouth*. And there were those dreadful Dumplings across the water from Newport, a group of tide-washed rocks just waiting for an unwary ship in thick weather. Of course, it was outrageous to even think such a thing about a respectable merchant master, but with Cranston pulling the strings like some sort of sinister puppeteer at a county fair, Carlisle was taking no chances.

'Thank you, Mister Kendrick, but I'll take a Point Judith pilot. You may do so or not, as you wish. In any case, follow my motions and stay astern of me until we are past Brenton's Point. You may berth wherever you like inside Goat Island. Remember that you are impounded and cannot touch your cargo until the court permits.'

He saw Kendrick shrug his shoulders and turn back to Cranston who gave a short laugh and turned away, presumably to seek the warmth below decks. Then Kendrick was occupied in taking the way off his ship to drop back astern of *Dartmouth*, and he didn't give Carlisle another glance.

Did they really think he would comply with that suggestion? Probably it was some sort of manoeuvre to influence the coming court case, an example of how they had attempted to be helpful to the King's ship but were rebuffed. The incident strangely upset Carlisle's equanimity – he felt that he had come off second best – and he stomped up to the poop deck with never a word to Gresham or Beazley.

***

It was an easy broad reach past Block Island and soon they were staring into the still-falling snow to catch a sight of the low spit of land that formed Point Judith.

'I can see it now, sir,' said Beazley.

Carlisle peered into the white screen that seemed to start at the end of the jib boom, but he couldn't see anything at all. For all he could tell they might be far out in the ocean, but for the leadsman who had been steadily reporting fifteen or eighteen fathoms for the past hour.

'Three miles, I reckon,' Beazley added. 'We're right in the approach to the East Channel. We should heave-to here, sir.'

Carlisle looked doubtfully to the west. He'd just persuaded himself that he could at last see the point of land, a ghostly vision of solid white that came and went in the flurries.

'Will they see us from the shore?'

'Aye, they'll see us, I'll heave-to now, if you please, sir.'

'Very well. And a gun to leeward just to be sure that *Hope* sees what we are doing and to wake up the pilots.'

Carlisle strode up to the poop deck to watch *Hope*. He jumped as the quarterdeck six-pounder fired its half-charge of powder.

The snow was easing now, and suddenly Point Judith was plainly visible. He saw a small cutter shoot out from the harbour to the west of the point, its dark lugsail looking like a square block against the snow. In twenty minutes it was alongside, and a stout Rhode Island pilot climbed over the gunwale. Carlisle looked over the poop rail to see Beazley talking to him. Simmonds was there and they disappeared below the poop deck presumably to sign the agreement in the shelter and relative warmth.

'I can see the tower on the Beavertail now, sir,' said Gresham.

Carlisle moved to the larboard side and looked past the masts and the rigging. There was the dull orange glow of the fire on top of the low stone tower. It was a primitive affair and it had none of the modern sophistication of lenses and reflectors. On a day like this, when the flame was barely visible at three miles, it was easy to see how ships still met their end on the Beavertail's cruel black rocks.

'Make sail when you're ready, Mister Beazley.'

The southerly breeze pushed them slowly towards the East Passage. Soon the Beavertail light was abeam to larboard, then they were into the true narrows where the passage was less than a mile wide but still twenty fathoms deep. As they passed Castle Hill, the snow stopped and a few minutes later the watery spring sunshine brought the whole of the enclosing coast into view. It was a strangely colourless landscape with all the greens and browns blanketed by snow leaving only white and shades of grey.

'There's an anchorage off the middle of Goat Island, Captain, will that suit you?'

The pilot was gruff and uncommunicative. Word of *Dartmouth's* errand had preceded them and if this Rhode Islander's attitude was any indication, they couldn't expect a warm welcome in Newport.

Carlisle merely nodded. *Dartmouth* drew too much water to safely swing to an anchor inside Goat Island, and in any case, if he wanted to be inside, they would need to be towed around Benton's point as the wind was dead foul to clear the south end of the island. The master and Chips had decided that they could get at the sprung butt end by shifting all the guns across to the larboard side; there was no need to haul her down against a hulk with all the attendant trouble of bringing the topmasts on deck and landing the guns and stores. It was a matter of a day or two's work if the weather held, and they could do that at the anchorage off the island, without any help from the shore.

He watched as *Hope* launched her own boat and inched painfully south, around the southern point of the island and out of his view. It seemed strange to lose sight of her after all this time. The merchantman had been under his wing for over a month and Carlisle had become used to confirming that she was still there whenever he came on deck.

***

'So that's what *Hope* has been up to! I had wondered when I heard that Joseph Kendrick had taken her off to the islands, with John Brown's man of business on board. Some skulduggery, it was obvious, but smuggling French molasses while the country's at war, that's a bit rich even for the Browns!'

The chief customs officer warmed his hands in front of the fire and gazed in perfect awe at the King's officer who had brought a Brown ship back to its natal lair to be judged. It was like Daniel walking into the lion's den of his own free will.

'The court's sitting in two days as it happens. They won't be on your side, you know, but I'll be able to make the Crown's case and with none of the Brown clan in attendance – I can at least make sure of that – there's perhaps a chance of conviction. They have to be careful you know. If they are too obviously partial, they'll all lose their places on the court, and that's not only a dead financial loss of their stipend, but they won't be able to influence any future cases. I've been moving to change the balance of the court for some time, but the governor disagrees. Or more accurately, the governor doesn't feel that he can make so many political enemies all in one stroke. Did you have any trouble getting here?'

'Just a few shouts and jeers, but no actual missiles, thank you, Mister Jarrow.'

If he had needed any confirmation of the town's mood, he need only have seen the mob that surrounded *Hope's* boat, raising loud huzzahs and hollering their support as Kendrick and Cranston came ashore. A few of the more respectable Newport townsfolk looked less happy to hear that a Rhode Islander had been brought in by the navy, but then, it was a Providence ship, and they did things differently over the water. The mob had largely dispersed when his own boat landed at the Long Wharf, just to landward of the drawbridge, but a few had spotted him and followed him to the customs house. One or two were still lounging about on the street but Souter and the boat's crew deterred them from coming too close.

'Will I be called, do you think?'

'Oh no, Captain, that would be most unusual. As I understand it, the case isn't likely to be defended on the basis of the facts, but on the question of whether a Rhode Island ship should be deemed to be trading with the enemy – and smuggling of course – when engaged in an activity that has been winked at for decades. You see, the vice admiralty court deals more in practicalities than in legal niceties, until it comes to sharing prize money. It would harm our case for you to appear in person. I can see the broadsheets now, David and Goliath! with you cast as the wicked Philistine giant tormenting the righteous David; these people thrive on that sort of story. No, I'll make the Crown's case. I know all the most persuasive arguments but, in the end, it will be decided by men who have the colony's interests at heart, not the Crown's, and in cases such as this they are by no means the same thing.'

Carlisle spent an hour with Jarrow. By the time he left, there were no loungers remaining on Thames Street and he was able to walk the short distance back to his boat without any trouble. His mind was only partly on the case, for all around him he could see the fruits of the French eviction from the continent: the town was in the grip of a post-war building frenzy. The French may still be pressing Britain's allies in Europe and threatening the King's Hanover domains, and French privateers may still be menacing British commerce on all the seas of the world, but here in the heart of New England, the solid merchants and shipowners had no doubts about the future of the American colonies. Their money followed their sentiments in a building boom, a great release of pent-up demand for goods and services, and a growing resentment that they were being held back by affairs that were no longer any of their business. It was exhilarating in a way, all this energy, all this faith in the future. He wondered how much of it was spreading south to his own home. But mostly he wondered what verdict the court would arrive at in two days' time. He knew that he faced a potential ravaging of his own hard-won fortune if the Browns were awarded damages. It could be argued that he'd delayed *Hope's* return by as much as two weeks and there could be punitive damages too. He tried to calculate a worst case, but the numbers eluded and depressed him. Well, he would just have to wait for the verdict.

***

It was Simmonds who brought the news, as he had back in English Harbour. Carlisle had sent his clerk to assist the chief customs officer in case there was any question of the facts of the affair. He heard the boat come alongside, just like at English Harbour, he heard Simmonds come over the side – there was no ceremonial for a captain's clerk – and heard his knock. The cabin door opened without any invitation and Simmonds walked in. Carlisle tried to read the verdict in his face but found it impossible.

'You are come from the vice-admiralty court, Mister Simmonds?'

Carlisle knew that it was a mere hollow gesture, but to his dying breath he would give the impression of being a man supremely unconcerned with such trivialities as a court judgement.

'Yes, sir. The judgement was read a half hour ago. They found in favour of Obadiah Brown & Company, of course, but there are no damages!'

Carlisle let out a long breath. He was professionally disappointed but not at all surprised that *Hope* and her cargo had been released, but the lack of damages; that was personally important. Over the past two days his imagination had conjured up the most extreme examples of punitive fines. In his nightmares he lost his house, was thrown into the Marshalsea for debt and his wife left him in disgust and disappointment. But none of that would now come to pass and his relief was plain to see.

'Mister Jarrow performed magnificently, sir. He didn't fight the points that he knew were already lost, and he didn't press for the forfeiture of the ship or the cargo, he just kept hammering away at the incontrovertible fact of trading with the enemy and hinted that any talk of damages would compel him to raise that point in a criminal court. The Browns were forced into a corner. If they insisted on damages, they risked losing the whole case and, in the end, they accepted the restitution of the ship and cargo as is. I'll have a transcript of the proceedings tomorrow, sir.'

Carlisle stood and looked at Newport Harbour out of his stern windows. The constant stream of boats running backwards and forwards between the anchored ships and the town gradually soothed his racing heart. One part of him was glad that the Browns had won the case; all this urgent endeavour, all this frantic growth, depended on the colonies' ability to trade. The day would come when they could look inland for their prosperity, he was sure, but for now the sea was their lifeblood and if they couldn't trade freely, they would wither and fail. He had a strong feeling that his work at sea was done, that the French threat had been defeated, and that now he should be part of this great mission to expand the King's territories in America. It took an almost physical effort to drag his eyes away from the harbour and his thoughts back to the present.

'Very well, Mister Simmonds. Thank you for your assistance. What was your feeling of the mood in the town?'

'I think euphoric is an appropriate word, sir. There was no threat to my person when I left the court; on the contrary they cheered me and Mister Jarrow. There appears to be a strong sense that justice has been done, at least justice as they see it. Although how the navigation acts will ever be enforced again is beyond my imagination.'

Carlisle nodded slowly in agreement. By their lights the verdict was correct, and colonial rights had been upheld. It was a narrow view that excluded the interests of the mother country, but it was a fair reflection of the situation as seen from New England.

'Then would you be kind enough to send a note to Mister Jarrow to ask if I may call on him tomorrow?'

***

Carlisle's meeting with Jarrow was short. There was little to be discussed after he'd given his heartfelt thanks for the customs officer's defence of the case.

'I fear that a difficult precedent has been set, Mister Jarrow.'

'Oh, it's nothing new, and hardly a precedent, Captain Carlisle. In fact, the judgement doesn't explicitly challenge the molasses and sugar acts, it cleverly avoids addressing them at all. Sure, it's one more *implied* precedent, but it can't be admitted in any future case. The truth is that I have never been able to collect customs dues on the islands' produce, whether British or French, and I don't try. My one wish is that I'm never required to do so. You've seen the passions it generates in the lowliest of people, even when they won't personally profit by the evasion. You can perhaps imagine how the traders feel about it.'

Jarrow reached for a folded letter from his desk and offered it to Carlisle.

'This will perhaps amuse you. You've been invited to dine with Mister John Brown – he's the youngest of the partners – at the King's Arms, just a few steps from here.'

Carlisle stared at the letter as Jarrow eyed him with a hint of an amused smile. It was in all respects a proper correspondence between a successful business partner and the captain of a King's ship, and it made no reference at all to the recent case or its outcome. To one who hadn't lived through the past month of uncertainty it would appear entirely innocent. Carlisle was clearly not such a person.

'Do you care to accept, sir?'

'I find I must ask your advice, Mister Jarrow. What's behind this, what does Mister Brown expect to gain from meeting me?'

Jarrow poured himself another glass of wine and offered to fill Carlisle's glass, but he held his hand over it.

'Mister Brown is perhaps trying to build bridges, Captain. After sober reflection, he's probably mightily relieved that he wasn't awarded damages; that would have put him on adversarial terms with every King's officer that sails these waters. He may wish that the taxes were gone to the devil, but he certainly doesn't wish the navy gone, not while the French privateers are still at large. He'll be trying to win your friendship, or at least to reduce your enmity. You asked for my advice. I would say you should accept the invitation and enjoy his hospitality. You can hardly lose by it, and I strongly suspect you'll win the hearts of the mob if they see you strolling arm in arm with John Brown. You'll have noticed that I haven't been invited. I wouldn't accept in any case; it would only prejudice my judgement when I next have to bring the Browns to account, and you can be sure that it won't be too far in the future.'

***

CHAPTER SIXTEEN

Trade's Increase

Wednesday, Twenty-Fifth of March 1761.
The King's Head, Thames Street, Newport, Rhode Island.

The King's Head was one of the first buildings to be started when the news of Quebec's fall in 'fifty-nine reached New England and it had only recently been completed. It smelled of newly worked oak beams, cedar shingles, fresh paint and prosperity, and by the welcome that Carlisle received, it already aspired to be the meeting place of choice for Newport's leading men. The proprietor and his wife showed Carlisle to a private room on the upper floor with a view over the busy Thames Street and out to Goat Island, with the harbour and the wooded expanse of Conanicut Island beyond.

Jarrow had described John Brown, but nothing could have prepared him for the sheer energy of the short stocky man who greeted him. Carlisle was immediately reminded of a prize fighter that he had once met in London, before a match on which he'd placed a substantial wager, but Brown combined his physical presence with the self-assurance that came with the knowledge that he needed no man to be his patron.

'Captain Carlisle!' Brown advanced a pace towards his guest. 'What an immense pleasure to meet you at last, and it's so good of you to come at such short notice.'

Brown's face wore a wide, open smile and his obvious good humour was infectious. Carlisle had already decided that he would hold no grudge for the outcome of the case, not unless he suffered any insult from Brown.

'The pleasure is all mine, Mister Brown.'

There was another man in the room, one who was clearly waiting to be introduced. A seaman by the look of him, Carlisle decided. He appeared thirty or thereabouts, taller than Brown and he wore a good blue broadcloth suit with scrupulously clean linen at his throat and cuff, as though he had dressed carefully for this dinner. A plain merchant captain, perhaps, and yet there was something about him; Carlisle was reminded of the sailing master who had guided Saunders' fleet up the Saint Lawrence to Quebec. Not in his looks, but in his bearing. This man was very like James Cook; he had that same air of competence and that same enigmatic expression that suggested that he was only lingering in this humble guise for a while and that his future held wider horizons.

'May I introduce Mister Abraham Whipple?' Brown waved the other man forward. 'Captain Whipple commands the privateer *Gamecock,* refitting at Providence, the only one of my interests that continues to find prizes for me after you King's officers cleared the seas of French commerce.'

'I'm very pleased to meet you, Captain Whipple,' Carlisle said, and he meant it.

Now, why had he given Whipple the title of *captain*, when he had steadfastly withheld that distinction from Kendrick? Still, it had been said now and perhaps it would do no harm. He could see that Whipple had noticed though, and a layer of reserve was stripped from him.

'It seems to me that I've heard of *Gamecock*,' Carlisle continued, thinking rapidly. 'Ah yes, she's famous for taking twenty or so prizes in one cruise last year, were you commanding her then, Captain Whipple?'

'Twenty-three, to be exact,' Brown exclaimed before Whipple could open his mouth, 'and yes, Captain Whipple was in command.' He looked at his associate with pure affection.

Carlisle did a rapid reappraisal. He knew that a typical privateer captain's share was around ten percent of the condemned value of the prize and its cargo. Whipple would have made himself a wealthy man as well as considerably increasing his investors' fortunes. With John Brown on the Newport vice-admiralty court, with a successful captain such as Whipple to bring in the prizes, and sufficient capital or credit to pay their share of outfitting the expeditions, the company was sitting on a self-perpetuating goldmine. It must have come as an unpleasant shock when the French effectively stopped sending their merchantmen to sea, at least not without a strong escort, at the end of 'fifty-nine. It was no wonder that John Brown was looking for new uses for his ships and was prepared to pioneer new markets, even those that sailed as close to the wind as *Hope's* cruise.

'Yes, sir. I've had the honour to command *Gamecock* for a few years now, and we did take a fair number of prizes in 'fifty-nine. The exact number is open to interpretation as some were re-taken, some strayed and one foundered soon after she struck, but twenty-three is a good number for the broadsheets.'

Whipple's smile had a trace of embarrassment, as in one whose exploits are being lauded beyond their merits.

'Sadly last year was something of a disappointment, but I don't need to tell you about the situation that the French find themselves in.'

'Well, I regret that I can't offer you gentlemen much hope where the French are concerned, but you should know that they're putting a lot of pressure on Spain to join the war on their side, and if that happens you may have a second season of harvests in the privateering line. I wouldn't lay up my guns just yet.'

That attracted their interest, and it started a lively conversation about the prospects for the next few years. Carlisle couldn't remember when he had enjoyed a dinner so much. His hosts were genial and intelligent and clearly had a deep personal interest in the American colonies. And yet it was only towards the end that Brown referred to Carlisle's own situation.

'Of course, the health of the British colonies must be of personal interest to you, Captain Carlisle. You're quite famous in these parts, you know, as one of the few colonial post-captains. Oh, I do trust that you take that in the spirit that it was intended.'

It was the first time that Carlisle had seen Brown unsure of himself. It was quite possible that his guest may be offended by the being named as a colonial and in fact he had heard it used as an insult throughout his naval career, although less so as he rose up the seniority list.

'I'm perfectly comfortable with being a colonial,' Carlisle replied, and at a certain level he spoke the plain truth. 'I had hardly ever left Virginia before I joined my first ship and I'm quite attached to my hometown.'

'I had heard that you've recently purchased a property in Williamsburg,' Whipple added, 'just beside the governor's palace, I'm told.'

'You know Williamsburg?'

'Certainly, sir. Before the war I sailed down that way, mostly carrying rum and bringing back tobacco. I believe I can even see the very house in my mind's eye, if my information is correct, between the church and the palace, beside Mister Wythe's home.'

Carlisle nodded and smiled. It was good to hear that even this far from Virginia, a more-or-less randomly met stranger could pinpoint his house. It made his new home somehow more substantial, less ordinary.

'The very same, although I can claim no credit for choosing it. My wife was resolved to have it before ever I was aware that it was for sale.'

'Ah, we all labour under the difficulties of a sailor's life, sir.'

'Well, I don't envy you seafaring gentlemen. I find enough to occupy myself on land now that the French have been thrown out, for which I must thank you sir.'

Brown bowed to Carlisle, who raised his glass in reply.

'And I've no doubt that the opportunities will only increase. I heard that the population of these colonies exceeds two million – an extraordinary number – and that it's been doubling every thirty years. The lands beyond the Ohio are open to us now and all of those thousand leagues to the far Pacific. How long, I wonder, before we are a greater number than those in the islands of Britain? By simple mathematics, in fifty years we'll equal the present population of England and Wales and Scotland, and even if you allow them a modest rate of increase, we'll exceed them in a hundred years or so.'

Carlisle was unsure what Brown was proposing and he did no more than incline his head.

'The beauty of this continent is that there is so much space, enough for everyone to live well. Of course, the King will always be in London, and we'll always be loyal subjects, but there must come a time when the relationship is more one of equal partners, don't you think?'

Carlisle considered whether he should object to Brown's argument. It wasn't exactly disloyal, but this talk of an equal partnership sat uneasily on his mind. Whipple saved him from breaking the friendly atmosphere.

'You'll be calling in Williamsburg on your way back to Antigua, no doubt, sir.'

Brown flashed Whipple an angry glance, but it faded in a moment as he realised that he'd been prevented from further committing himself in front of a King's officer. Among the people that he normally met, it was quite usual to refer to a future change in the relationship with Britain, but for a King's officer to acknowledge it was another thing altogether.

'Oh, I wish it were that easy. My time is not my own and the commander-in-chief at English Harbour wants me back as soon as ever I can contrive it. You know the tyranny of the logbook and I imagine you have to satisfy your owners and investors as I have to satisfy their Lordships. It's well known that my home is in Virginia and if one of those clerks at the admiralty should see that I entered the Chesapeake without a good reason, the doom-laden skies of Whitehall will fall about my head and my accounts won't clear until long after I'm in my grave. I was sorely tempted on the way north, with an almost plausible excuse of a sprung butt-end, but no doubt you heard about that.'

Brown nodded sagely. Kendrick would have told him, and both he and Whipple had seen *Dartmouth* being heeled for the repair. It was the nearest they came to acknowledging the incident with *Hope*.

'Then you need a convoy for Hampton,' said Whipple. 'There's at least half a dozen sail waiting in the road there, can't you gather them up?'

Carlisle glanced out of the window. The anchorage inside Goat Island was crowded with brigs and schooners and there were a number of deep-laden merchant ships lying beyond the island near *Dartmouth*.

'Sadly not even that is in my gift. Lord Colville commands from Halifax, and he'll order a convoy when he feels the time is right. I would be rightly censured for taking any such action.'

'Well, I hope you find the occasion to visit your family, Captain, and in the near future too. Meanwhile, I would like to propose a toast…'

The three men pushed back their chairs and stood.

'…to the navy, may it continue to rid the seas of the King's enemies.'

Carlisle sipped from his glass as he thought of an appropriate response.

'I'll add to that, if I may. To trade's increase and to colonial prosperity.'

Boom!

The windows of the tavern rattled to the concussion from a light gun, a six-pounder perhaps, but its report had a peculiarly elongated sound.

Another, then a whole series at regular intervals, as though the gunner was marching six paces between each.

The door burst open, and Souter stood there with a worried looking innkeeper peeping over his shoulder.

'*Dartmouth's* firing a salute, sir, and I can see a man-o'-war's tops'ls coming through the passage, flying a broad pennant, I believe. There's a snow-sloop astern of her.'

***

Alexander Colville – Lord Colville – was looking older than when Carlisle had last seen him on the Saint Lawrence in 'fifty-nine. He'd spent another two winters at Halifax since then, and the cold and damp seemed to have seeped into his skin. It was widely assumed in the service that he clung onto the American command in an effort to gather enough funds to restore his family fortunes and redeem the mortgages on his Scottish lands. The pickings weren't rich now that the French had capitulated at Montreal, but it was better than striking his broad pennant and taking command of a third rate, doomed to rot in the line of battle with never a prize to be taken nor the occasional two percent freightage to be claimed. He was in a desperate battle to accumulate cash before the end of the war brought his inevitable unemployment and half pay. For all his noble lineage, Carlisle guessed that Alexander Colville was in a worse financial position than the lowly post-captain who sat before him.

'Well, I'm still here, Carlisle, and still haunting *Northumberland's* decks, but I must say I'm surprised to see *Dartmouth* on my station. I've heard nothing from Sir James on the matter. It was a good effort, by the way, to fire a salute with your decks at such a ridiculous angle.'

There was no hint of censure. Colville and Carlisle were old friends from the North American campaigns, and Colville was well aware that there must be a good reason for Carlisle to have strayed so far from the Leeward Islands.

'Well, My Lord, as for the guns, I confess I was dining ashore while my carpenter was repairing a sprung plank, but I expect my gunner kept the quarterdeck six-pounders clear for just such a contingency; he'd have dropped dead from sheer exasperation if he'd missed the chance for a salute. He'll have fired on the downward slope, as it were.'

'Then that accounts for the strange sound. You'd have been excused for not saluting at all, what with my unannounced arrival, but I'm glad you did. It does no harm to let these New Englanders know that the navy has business in these parts. But what brings you here?'

Carlisle told the whole story from the sighting of *Hope* at St. Lucia to the verdict of the vice-admiralty court. He said nothing about being taken prisoner by a French privateer. One day he would be able to laugh at it, but for now the memory was too raw.

'I just need to complete my wood and water and take on fresh provisions and a few of these good Rhode Island hogs, and with your permission, sir, I'll be away for English Harbour.'

'Well, I'm glad to hear that you weren't cast into damages, but it just goes to show how careful you must be. Even with the letter of the law on your side, you always have to consider local interests, although I'll agree that this was a particularly egregious case. I'll speak to Jarrow later; it will be interesting to hear his view of the case, and whether the Admiralty will appeal against the verdict. It'll be a question of whether Pitt has the stomach for a fight with the colonies. My guess is that he'll leave things as they stand until this war's over, then he'll address the question of the navigation acts and taxation. God knows, the treasury will need every penny it can raise. The victualling agent has looked after you properly?'

'He has, sir. The hogs were being driven to the jetty as I came off. It was all my coxswain could do to stop them being herded into my boat.'

Colville laughed at that. He knew how difficult it was to persuade civilians, particularly colonial civilians, of the awful majesty and dignity of a post-captain. He paused for a moment and stared abstractedly at his desk.

'You bought a place in Williamsburg recently, if I remember rightly.'

Carlisle nodded cautiously.

'Well, perhaps we can do better than a straight run back to English Harbour.'

Colville smiled conspiratorially and came close to winking.

'You see, I'm short of cruisers as always and there's a vast flotilla of ships out there,' he swung his hands to the stern windows where a crowd of tall masts blocked the view, 'mostly bound for the Chesapeake but some for Antigua and Jamaica. I'll be sending Everitt in *Stirling Castle* and three of the line and all the frigates that I can spare to carry General Rollo's army to St. Lucia and Dominica, but they can't take a convoy, not to the Chesapeake and the southern colonies, and that leaves me desperately short. I'd planned to bring one of my frigates down in a week or so, but if it's on your way, I can't imagine that Sir James will object if I give you the job. You can gather up any others for the Leeward Islands and Jamaica at Hampton. That will take a week or ten days, and you can see that delightful wife of yours.'

Carlisle tried not to let his joy show, but Colville knew him too well, and in any case, the commodore had heard the extravagant tales about his wife's beauty and amiability. It would certainly take a week to send the word throughout the Chesapeake Bay area and for any ships that were bound for the islands to complete their loading and work down the rivers and creeks to Hampton. He knew what would happen. One or two would arrive at the stated time with notes from their friends and from whatever colonial official they could find, asking that the convoy wait just another day or two for a few more ships, and that day or two would extend to another week and then another. Nobody wanted to risk the French privateers on a lone passage.

'You'll need a sloop to guard that unruly mob, you can take *Shark*. Preston Warner has her now. He's a good commander though a trifle old for his rank.'

'I had *Shark* for a convoy back in 'fifty-eight, sir. John Anderson had her then.'

Carlisle's Duty

Carlisle's meaning was clear. A lot had changed in three years and a snow-sloop of eight guns was a relic. Warner would find most French privateers a handful and he'd have to be forever on his guard in case he became the prey. It was better than nothing but not by a great margin.

'Well, it's all I have,' Colville said with an air of finality, riding over Carlisle's unspoken objection. 'That's agreed then. I'll send a letter to Sir James explaining why you're late returning; I'm sure he'll concur that it was too good an opportunity to miss. You can sail on Saturday.'

***

CHAPTER SEVENTEEN

A Falling Glass

Saturday, Twenty-Eighth of March 1761.
Dartmouth, at Sea. Block Island NW 3 Leagues.

'Here comes the first one, sir.'

There was a hint of spring in the air and Gresham was enjoying the fresh breeze with its promise of warmer weather to come. In this clear morning air he could see the hills of Block Island standing stark and grey just nine miles to the nor'west.

'Let's hope they can at least find the rendezvous,' Carlisle replied with his eye to the telescope. 'It's further offshore than I would have liked but with this stiff nor'easterly I couldn't risk having them all milling around off Point Judith, not with Block Island under their lee.'

Gresham nodded in agreement. He could easily recognise when his captain was in a good mood because he explained his decisions rather than leaving his officers guessing. It would only take one of the merchantmen to fall upon another and two or three of them could be wrecked before their very eyes. Mustering a convoy was always a ragged business and it was best done where there was room for errors to be made without them becoming tragedies.

'There's the second one, and the third. They're coming thick and fast now.'

Even in this clear weather the ships of the convoy couldn't be seen at more than ten miles, and they had six leagues to run from the Beavertail Light to the rendezvous. Their tops'ls popped up in ones and twos until the northern horizon was a mass of white squares, all growing larger as the soldier's wind brought them swiftly down to *Dartmouth*. There should be fifteen of them, mostly snows and ships, but Gresham could only count fourteen. That wasn't unusual; inevitably at least one of them would find themselves unable to sail and that would be that. There was no waiting for them, not with fourteen other merchantmen eager to make their passage.

'Brail up, Mister Beazley, we'll take station to windward,' Carlisle said as the first of the ships came abreast. 'Make the signal to proceed to the sou'west.'

The lead ship was a fairly new timber carrier, specially adapted to take the huge baulks of oak and pine that the master shipwright at English Harbour had demanded. Her master was an old friend of Beazley's who attested to his navigational ability. That was essential because that ship would lead the whole convoy to its landfall off Cape Henry, while *Dartmouth* took a position where it could best defend it from any French commerce raiders. If the wind had been more northerly then Carlisle would have been happy to lead, but with a dead run to the sou'west, his proper station was astern.

It was a noble sight that always brought a smile to Carlisle's face. Here was the physical evidence of Britain's mastery of the waves. No French convoy could run from one of their Atlantic ports to another without an escort that was capable of defending against an attack by a squadron of British men-o'-war. They were forced to send most of their commerce by inland waterways or by road at vastly greater expense and inconvenience. Here, off the coast of America, the threat was from a roving privateer, and *Dartmouth* and *Shark* could easily see off such an attack.

The timber carrier had reduced sail so that the laggards could catch up and now they were starting to sort themselves into their chosen positions, each vessel keeping a safe distance from its fellows ahead, astern and on each beam. Carlisle gazed contentedly at the crystal-clear sky and the ships.

'What do you make of this wind, Mister Beazley?'

The sailing master studied the horizon to the nor'west, gnawing at the knuckle of his thumb.

'Come on, surely you can't say anything against this

prosperous breeze. The horizon's clear all round.'

Carlisle swept his arm from east through north to the west.

'It's clear now, sir, but that's the problem. It's been clear for three days, wonderful weather to haul the old ship down and fix that butt end, but it can't last. It'll head us before tomorrow, I reckon.'

Carlisle smiled, but he had the greatest respect for Beazley's ability to guess the weather a day or so ahead. And there was something in what he said. He'd heard the theories about the balance of the elements and how that balance had to be restored when it was shaken out of equilibrium. That was what caused the changes in wind, or so it was reckoned. The problem was that nobody had yet managed to make any rational sense of it. The theory was all very well, but it lacked a practical application. The best that he could do was to listen to his experienced sailing master. If the wind held – if Beazley's prediction proved false – they would be at anchor at Hampton on Wednesday, or perhaps even Tuesday evening. But if Beazley was right, they'd be lucky if it didn't take them a week longer.

'Let me know if you see a sign of change, Mister Wishart, or if the convoy starts to scatter. I'll be in my cabin.'

***

'Beg pardon, sir.'

Beazley's disembodied head appeared round the cabin door, as if to deny that he was really disturbing his captain so soon after he had left the quarterdeck.

'What with you being so busy in Newport I didn't have a chance to show you my new machine.'

'Do come in, Master, what sort of machine would it be?'

Beazley shuffled from one foot to another, as though he was embarrassed.

'It's a weather-glass, sir, I'm trying it to determine if it has any application at sea.'

Carlisle suppressed a smile. Weather-glasses had been used on land for nearly a century and their principle was well known, and well contested. They'd had a certain amount of success in predicting wind and rain and he knew that in some places they were used to decide when to hire the casual men at harvest time. He'd heard of a case of rioting among farm labourers in Suffolk who feared that they'd lose their customary slack time when they were hired before an unexpected turn in the weather made it impossible to get the crops in. Most people, however, argued that the weather-glass only told you what anyone who worked the land could have guessed. They were a scientific toy and little else, in Carlisle's opinion, but he knew how diligently his sailing master tried to advance the art of navigation, and he didn't want to discourage him.

'Well, bring it in, Mister Beazley, let's have a look at it.'

Beazley ushered in a master's mate and a midshipman who were carrying the instrument with infinite care. They propped it against the cabin partition, wedging it between two frames of the panelling. Despite his scepticism, Carlisle rose to examine it.

'I bought it from an instrument maker on the corner of Ann and Spring streets in Newport. He'd received it in payment of a debt from a man who brought it over from London. You can see the maker's marks although they've been rubbed too much to make out the name, but the workshop is on Cornhill, by the Exchange. It's not intended for the sea, it'll hardly take any knocks, but I'm hoping it will prove useful…'

Beazley was evidently nervous about showing the instrument to his captain, he was talking almost at random and making anxious gestures with his fingers. Weather-glasses had been the subject of a deal of mockery over the past few years and were generally put into the same category as mechanical timepieces, useful on land but with no prospect of any real utility at sea. The problem was in the movement of a ship and in the extreme changes of temperature. That and the salt air and moisture quickly destroyed any hope of accuracy and generally ended in an expensive crash when the instruments succumbed to a hard lee roll.

Carlisle had seen a few weather-glasses in England, but he'd never known of one to survive an Atlantic crossing. This one must have been kept in its own box, well packed with straw, because the tall, delicate glass tube was still intact, and it glinted in the meagre sunshine that crept into the cabin through the great stern windows.

'Is that quicksilver?'

'It is sir, it's the only liquid – if I may call it such – that is heavy enough to make a usable weather-glass. Water or spirits of wine or anything else of that nature would need a column many yards long.'

Carlisle nodded. He knew that much about these instruments. Even so, the glass tube was nearly a yard from tip to toe and the slightest knock would undo it.

'I understand that for normal use the quicksilver only advances and retreats in the top few inches of the tube,' Beazley continued, 'so the greater part can be hidden for day-to-day purposes. The cooper has promised to build a long case that will extend to within six inches of the top and when that's done I'll ask the armourer to make a little copper cage for the rest of the glass, so that I can still read the height of the quicksilver against the scale.'

Carlisle studied the top closely. A paper scale was glued behind the glass tube, and it was labelled *Calm, Rain, Wind*, from the top down. The maker of this glass hadn't bothered to add a scale of inches, so it was intended perhaps for agricultural use rather than as a scientific instrument. The head of the column of quicksilver was convex, making a neatly rounded top, like a shining penny bun in miniature. Carlisle crouched to bring his eye level with the scale.

'The quicksilver is very low, Mister Beazley, and it appears to suggest that we're in for a blow. Am I reading it correctly?'

Beazley looked embarrassed. He wasn't ready to defend his instrument, nor had he sufficient confidence to state to

Carlisle's Duty

his captain that the weather was about to turn nasty. He waved the two glass-carriers out of the cabin.

'I must say that I haven't yet mastered the principles, sir, but the theorists claim that when a wind blows parallel to a surface, its weight against the surface will be reduced. We see that every day in the way that a stays'l lifts when the ship's pointing too high. If the weight is lessened then the amount of quicksilver that it can support is necessarily reduced, and the level in the glass falls. At least that's the theory,' Beazley added, 'but I haven't yet seen it proved at sea.'

'But do you see the flaw in the theory, Mister Beazley? If we take it at its face value, the quicksilver will only react when a gale of wind is actually blowing, and we'll be able to see that for ourselves. It'll be useless as a tool for predicting the wind, although perhaps a comfort to know that the gale has a theoretical as well as a physical existence.'

Carlisle strode to the stern window to hide his smile. There was a fresh breeze blowing but nothing more, and a glance to windward gave no hint of a change. Beazley looked uncomfortable and absent-mindedly stroked the long glass tube. He was evidently attached to his weather-glass and Carlisle knew that he'd be foolish to mock his excellent sailing master.

'How does it predict rain?'

'In a similar manner, sir. It's well known that when the weight of the atmosphere is diminished, we can expect rain, and that same reduction in weight causes the quicksilver to fall. But we already know that wind brings rain, so it may be that the rain label is superfluous.'

'And when it suggests a calm, Mister Beazley?'

'Well, it appears that the reverse is true and when the wind subsides the weight of the air will increase, and the glass will rise. I do take your point that the theory suggests a tool that tells you what is happening rather than one that predicts the weather, but many eminent philosophers vouch for its use in that manner. I know that a paper was presented at the Royal Society only a few months ago; it caused quite a stir. I don't stand by its utility sir, not yet, but I do intend to record its predictions and attempt to correlate it to the weather that we experience in the following day. It can do no harm…'

Carlisle took another look at the instrument. He was instinctively in favour of anything that could advance the art of navigation, and if the weather-glass should prove itself, then it would be an undoubted step forward.

'Well, I commend you for this, Master. If we had a way of deciding what the weather will be, we could save ourselves a lot of hard knocks, aye and many a man would live who may otherwise perish. I'll be glad to know what conclusions you come to. But for now, we must look out for squalls, it seems.'

***

It would have been too easy to make game of the sailing master as he paced the poop deck casting anxious, furtive glances astern. All through that afternoon and first dog watch he kept the deck while the convoy bowled along under billowing tops'ls without a care in the world. He came down at last and ate a silent and disappointed supper, watched by the other members of the wardroom who knew exactly why he had kept his lonely vigil. At intervals he excused himself, but everyone knew that he was going to commune with his weather-glass in his cabin, like a hermit adoring a graven image or an icon of a saint in his lonely cave.

At eight bells, just as the silence was becoming oppressive, Wishart came into the wardroom shaking drops of rain from his oilskin.

'Wind's freshening, and it's backed two points already. Old Eli says it'll blow hard before the middle watch, what with the stars being gobbled up – his words not mine – from the north.'

They could hardly resist it, every pair of eyes swivelled towards Beazley.

'Have I suddenly become a subject of interest, gentlemen?' he cried in mock anger. 'What can it be? Is it perhaps that you have never seen a theory proven? Oh, ye naysayers!'

With a shake of Wishart's hand Beazley strode out of the wardroom, followed by a chorus of huzzahs. They all loved the sailing master and his enthusiasms, some of which were even useful.

Carlisle was already on deck when Beazley arrived, having spent a few moments studying his instrument where it had been safely secured in his cabin.

'Well, here's your blow, Mister Beazley. What does the instrument say now?'

'Aye, freshening and backing, sir…'

Old Eli nodded his whiskered head and grinned through his beard.

'…and I would say that we're in for a two-day blow. The glass has fallen even further since you inspected it, sir.'

Carlisle looked forward to where the stars were still shining, then aft into the pitch blackness where the advancing line of cloud had completely obscured the heavens. *Dartmouth* had furled her t'gallants as soon as the convoy was settled on its course and even under tops'ls and courses the two-decker had a distressing habit of creeping up on the merchantmen.

'Mister Angelini. Make the night signal for the convoy to shorten sail.'

His written orders to the convoy masters had necessarily to be brief, but he had insisted on a signal that would warn them that he was shortening sail, a flag signal by day and lights by night.

'And then you may take two reefs in the tops'ls.'

He watched the two blue lights soar up the fore masthead. The nearer ships of the convoy would see it and there was at least some hope that the further ones would. In any case, if they were keeping a watch, they'd see that they were drawing ahead of their fellows. Reducing sail at night in a convoy was always a risk and that was one reason why convoys often shortened sail at sunset, regardless of the weather.

'Now, Mister Beazley, perhaps I may consult the Oracle again?'

***

A hard blow indeed and the wind came stubbornly from the west bringing sharp, cold rain squalls that made a haze over the deck as the drops bounced back from the bare planks. The hoped-for three-day passage stretched into four and then into five as the hapless convoy found itself dead to leeward of its destination. For the first four days the quicksilver lurked low and sullen in the glass, and there were mutterings against the infernal machine, as though it was causing the weather rather than predicting it or merely confirming it. It was the Wednesday forenoon before Carlisle was again invited to the master's cabin.

'It rises, sir,' said Beazley in triumph. 'I made a little pencil mark yesterday and today you can see that it's half an inch higher!'

'I see no easing of the gale though.'

'No, sir, but if the theory proves true the change won't come until *after* the glass has risen, and they say that the quicker the rise the more rapid the change. I don't stand by the instrument, sir, not yet, but let us observe what happens in the next two watches.'

Carlisle nodded grimly. He was heartily sick of this weather that had already delayed his family reunion by three days. In all likelihood his letter would already have reached Williamsburg by road, and for once his arrival would be anticipated. But Chiara could see the weather as well as he could, and she'd know that he would be necessarily delayed.

***

The change, when it came, was dramatic. One moment they were thrashing to windward, fighting for every yard in a vain attempt to avoid being swept out into the Atlantic, and the next moment they were shaking out the reefs under a warm spring sun and cursing the merchantmen who were agonisingly slow to follow suit. The clouds had gone, swept away to the south, the wind had veered through half the compass, and *Dartmouth* was rolling in the last of the gale's swell.

'Tomorrow forenoon then, sir.'

Beazley rubbed his hands in delight. He knew well enough that one success didn't validate the weather-glass, but at least it was spoken of with respect now, and here was the armourer bearing a handsome polished copper cage on a piece of green baize, as though he were bearing the regal crown up the long aisle of Westminster Abbey.

***

CHAPTER EIGHTEEN

The House on the Green

Sunday, Fifth of April 1761.
The Carlisle House, Williamsburg.

Spring had arrived in Williamsburg and fairy rings of purple crocuses were pushing through the grass under the tall trees on Governor's Green. The wide space was almost empty at this hour, just a few sleepy workmen passed by, hurrying to their businesses and a score of ewes and their lambs cropped the grass, confined within a circle of hurdles. A wizened old shepherd touched his hat as the post-captain and his lady strolled by, pursued by a whooping child still young enough to fall at every uneven patch of ground.

The strolling pair paused to watch as the shepherd shuffled the wicker panels to expose a fresh patch of grass, never letting a single sheep escape as he did so. It was a never-ending task; as fast as the hurdles were moved and their pointed posts pushed into their new positions – chestnut, Carlisle remembered, that was the correct wood for the posts, and willow for the lattice – the sheep munched their way through a new strip of grass and the whole thing had to be started again. Not unlike managing a ship, where every sail change was merely a precursor for the next. It felt so good to be home. Carlisle had owned this fine house for nearly a year, and although this was only his third visit, already he felt that he belonged there.

'Are you listening, Edward?'

Chiara turned her head to look at his profile against the low morning sun.

'Eh? Oh, yes, you were saying that we must call on Barbara and Cranmer.'

Carlisle had developed the skill of being deep in his own thoughts while absorbing enough of his wife's conversation to be able recall the last few sentences with some accuracy.

Carlisle's Duty

In fact, he wasn't quite as good at it as he believed, and Chiara was ready to spring the trap that she'd laid.

'Yes, dear, but perhaps you misheard me. I would like to invite them to our home.'

Carlisle's nod could have meant anything from acknowledging his error to a lofty condescension.

'I speak to them often, of course, but when I told them you were expected they were so eager to see you. I know we said we would have today to ourselves, but could we invite them for supper, do you think? We are free this evening.'

That was partly why they were out at such an early hour on a Sunday, so that they could have some time together before the inevitable round of official calls and friendly visits started. They would have to go to church of course. There was little chance of the vicar imposing a fine on him, even though that statute was still in force, but his standing in the town demanded it and his duty as a King's officer made it even more necessary. Chiara would come, of course, even though she was a Catholic. No Roman mass was said within a couple of hundred miles, and she had become used to the Church of England. Nevertheless, Carlisle had hoped to have the rest of the day free. He'd missed his wife and he was intrigued at his son's development since he'd last seen him six months before. In September little Joshua had been just two years old and had entered that destructive phase of a child's development. Now, miraculously, he could be given a cup without it being dashed to the ground a moment later and he would run to his father when called.

'This evening? Oh well, they have been very kind to you.'

He was attached to his cousin Barbara, and particularly after she and her husband, Cranmer Dexter, had offered the hospitality of their home to Chiara when she was advised to travel no further in her confinement. That arrangement had lasted over a year until he had bought his present house, just a stone's throw from the governor's palace.

'Then we must make the most of our time today. No guests for dinner and no callers after church, is that agreed?'

Carlisle grinned in reply. His wife was a very social person and he had little faith that she would get through a church service without either offering hospitality afterwards or accepting it. Still, they could expect to be alone from early afternoon until early evening.

'I'll have to call on the lieutenant governor tomorrow or Tuesday, you know. We'll see him at church, and he'll think it odd if I don't.'

'Then I'll have the carriage brought to the door at whatever time you name,' Chiara said firmly.

She had very positive views about the correct protocol for a visit to the governor's palace and even though it was but a couple of hundred yards away, she wouldn't countenance her husband walking there. Carlisle had lost that battle long ago and, in any case, he knew that his wife was right. He was a post-captain, and in this colonial town he was a relatively wealthy man, with a certain dignity to maintain. Besides, the war would end one day, and he must look to the future. A man who walked to the governor's palace couldn't expect to be taken seriously.

Joshua was bored of trampling the crocuses and he ran off towards the shepherd. Clearly, they were old friends, and the little boy happily impeded his work, grasping at the chestnut stakes and pulling at the willow bark while his parents walked on.

'Is my father happy in the house? It's a great imposition having your father-in-law live with you while I'm away.'

'Oh, I don't mind at all. He's good company and Joshua adores him. He chases him around all day, never giving the poor man a moment of peace, but he seems to enjoy it. Do you know, he hasn't been to the plantation since you were here last? And I've only seen your brother once since September and then after a quick glance he didn't even look in my direction. But at least he leaves us alone now.'

'Father thinks he's going mad, you know.'

They walked a few steps in silence. Charles had been an irritant ever since Edward and Chiara had settled in

Williamsburg. He had been a danger at one point, but with legal advice and some carefully written letters from a firm of lawyers, the threats to Chiara had ceased.

'He may well be right, and my opinion hasn't changed. Charles is so consumed with jealously that it has unbalanced his mind, and he's alone in that plantation day and night with no company but the workers that he terrorises and the overseer who is as mad as he is. He has nothing except that rotting plantation and even that isn't his, not while your father lives.'

'I'll call on him in a day or two. I'll take Father, if he'll come, but there's no need for you to join me.'

Chiara shivered involuntarily. She was afraid of Charles Carlisle; his mad stare and his obsession with his younger brother's success kept her awake at nights. He was capable of anything, in her opinion, and she'd be happy if she never had to lay eyes on him again.

'As Father pointed out, we need to know how well the plantation is doing. He's been content to let Charles manage the estate, pay the bills and take whatever profits there are, but he's looking to write a new will and for that he needs to know the state of the place. He fears that there may not be enough value for me to take a share without breaking it up and selling it piecemeal.'

'Have you not thought of having a plantation yourself, Edward? All the great men of the town do, you know, even if they rarely visit their land.'

Carlisle shook his head emphatically.

'No, I'll not be a planter. I have a few years to think about the future and now that we're determined to remain here,' he glanced at his wife for confirmation and was gratified by a nod of her head, 'I have at least part of the puzzle solved. I went to sea to get away from the plantation and I've no intention of being drawn back into it. In any case, Father and Charles are likely to live for many years yet and I'll have to find something else to do. What it will be I just cannot tell.'

'Then I'll be content to wait, but don't ask me to meet with Charles!'

'Of course, I'm being selfish. Have you any desire to return to Nice?'

Carlisle didn't look at his wife as he asked that question. He thought he knew the answer but wanted her to confirm it without her husband staring at her.

'I write regularly to the viscountess, you know, every month or so, but she only replies twice a year. It's perhaps only an impression, but I don't believe I would be welcome back into the Angelini family. As you saw last year, they've fallen on hard times and their allegiances have changed. Enrico noticed it and when the head of household had to flee the city it was confirmed. There's no place for me there. When the war is over we may pass through that way, if we travel, but I'm not even sure of my welcome as a visitor. The viscountess is not unlike your brother, in some respects. She's consumed by jealousy, bankrupt from bad management of her finances and inclined to blame those closest to her for her troubles. We were like mother and daughter once, but there's no warmth in her letters now.'

'Enrico won't talk about it. I know he was shaken by the scale of his family's decline, and he was glad to come with me when I left Nice. Of course, he holds a commission in the Sardinian navy now, but I have difficulty imagining him taking his place when he's called.'

'He won't go back.'

Carlisle looked quickly at his wife and caught her sad expression.

'I know my cousin and I know the people who govern Sardinia and advise King Charles Emmanuel. He's been too long away, and he has no personal power base to replace the family's influence. He'll be cast aside in this new navy that they're planning, regardless of whatever promises were made.'

'But you know that the whole reason for him staying in *Dartmouth* was so that he would have the skills and experience to command a frigate. Nobody else in Sardinia will be able to do so.'

Chiara laughed quietly.

'You don't know the Sardinian people well enough, my dear Edward. It doesn't matter how well qualified he is – the ministry of marine is not run by another Lord Anson you know – the best he can expect is to be a sort of adviser to the captain who will obtain his position entirely by influence. He will probably be serving under a colonel of horse and his status will be much like a sailing master. He knows that very well, which is why I believe that dear Enrico will find another direction when he is recalled. Until then he's happy to collect his salary and serve with you.'

Carlisle was shocked at his wife's certainty. Yet, a moment of thought told him that she was probably correct. He should have seen it himself, but living so close to someone, in the confines of a ship at sea, doesn't allow the distance to take a dispassionate view of their circumstances. Enrico was a good lieutenant, even though he held a Sardinian commission rather than one from King George, and Carlisle hadn't expended much energy in thinking beyond that.

'In fact, it wouldn't surprise me if he sought a position here in Williamsburg. We would always offer him a home, wouldn't we Edward, until he could set himself up?'

***

Nobody had ever described Barbara as elegant; she was too tall and her nose, elbows and knees were her most prominent features. She walked as though she were traversing thick mud and her hands seemed to have a life of their own, forever fluttering from one thing to another. She knew these defects and had long ago decided that there was nothing to be done about them, and in her social circle – the middling sort of people who are the lifeblood of most communities – nobody really cared. Yet when she smiled, she could light up a room and her laugh was impossible to ignore, causing a cascading reaction, like a row of toppling bottles, in all who heard her.

Cranmer Dexter was as small and round as his wife was tall and lean. He was born a fusspot and that was how he had remained. He was prosperous, by his own measure, being the owner of two bookselling and printing shops in the Virginian capital. Carlisle had known them both all his life although they hadn't been in his thoughts for a long time until he and Chiara came to Williamsburg two years before. Without children of their own they had thrown themselves into supporting Chiara and little Joshua while Edward was at sea.

'My word, you look in good form Edward. You must be feeding well on that ship of yours, you've gained a pound or two.'

Barbara had never been able prevent whatever was in her mind from issuing forth from her mouth, and she had an uncanny instinct for her cousin's weak spots. Carlisle was a rarity among his peers in that he detested the thought of becoming fat. He would never have said that to anyone but Chiara for fear of being laughed at, but he thought of it every morning when he looked down at his stomach. And he knew it was foolish. An ample girth, after all, was a sign that a man could afford to eat well and that he wasn't burdened by the need for physical work.

Carlisle clenched his teeth and sought for a witty riposte, but none came, and he had to make do with a banal reply.

'And you look delightful as ever, dear cousin; and Cranmer, how do you do, sir?'

Dinner at two o'clock guaranteed that by seven everyone was ready for another substantial meal, and Chiara had given her orders to the cook with that in mind. Black Rod – Carlisle still didn't know Chiara's servant's name – brought in the victuals; there were cheeses and a ham and bread, both rye and wheat, and relishes, and a mighty tureen of soup. Carlisle had bought some decent Madeira and a dozen cases of contraband Bordeaux in Newport and they added a merry accompaniment to the meal. It was a happy little gathering with the candlelight, good plain food, robust wines and the company of close friends.

'Your enterprise is thriving, Cranmer?' Carlisle asked after he had satisfied his immediate hunger.

'It is, it is, although not perhaps along the lines that I had expected. Oh, there's a backlog of books to be bound and sold and I have a steady stream of orders from the palace,' he nodded to where the great building sat in splendour at the head of the green, 'and from the council, but it's the private broadsheets, petitions and circulars that are really driving the business. You'd be amazed at how many of our good citizens feel the need to impose their thoughts and ideas upon their neighbours. I have an order of that sort at least every day, and I've had to take on two apprentices to avoid falling behind. They feed on each other, you know, and everyone wants their copy at once, that very day in many cases!'

'Forgive me, Cranmer, but what did you mean when you said that they feed upon each other? It's an interesting choice of words.'

Carlisle helped himself to another slice of ham. It was one of the luxuries that he was reluctant to go without, but he'd found that Virginia hams rarely lasted longer than three or four months in the humid conditions of a ship at sea, and he'd eaten his last a month ago, when the ghastly signs of its imminent deterioration first started to show.

'Ah, I'll admit that I hadn't anticipated it myself, so how would you know? When a Mister Smith – let us say – chooses to write a pamphlet criticising the way that new buildings are allowed to encroach upon the streets, you can be sure that Mister Jones, who's house caused the offence but who hasn't been named by Mister Smith, will want to refute the argument, and he will want to do so without delay, before Mister Smith's ideas can take root. Of course, when Smith reads the scandalous assertions of Jones, he will want to reply, and so it continues. You'd be amazed at the volume of private argument that is conducted in the public forum.'

Enrico was drawn into this conversation by its sheer novelty. It was so unlike anything that could happen in his Mediterranean home.

'Is it only private people who commission these papers, or do people do so on behalf of the government?'

'Well, that's another matter.'

Cranmer stared at the candle on the table before him, phrasing his reply.

'I have to be careful because I don't want to be seen taking sides. I used the building example because it carried no political assumptions and is merely a dispute between private citizens. However, the truth is that I have a steady flow of orders for pamphlets that criticise the governance of the colony. Most of them do so obliquely, but some are more direct. They concern taxation, mostly, but also the colony's relationship with England and how the views of its citizens are represented. From what I've heard, you'll have witnessed similar issues in New England.'

'Oh, I was hardly involved in that at all. The captain was wholly engaged, and we mere lieutenants just made sure that the ship didn't sink in his absence.'

Carlisle shook himself out of his torpor. The food and the wine and the candlelight had all conspired to make him sleepy. He'd heard every word, and in the back of his mind Cranmer's explanation was being processed, but he hadn't really made any sense of it.

'Yes,' he replied slowly, 'there's a feeling in Rhode Island, and for all I know in the other northern colonies, that the end of the war in this continent should lead to changes. In my private capacity I can sympathise with much of what they are saying but in my public capacity as a King's officer, I must keep clear of those discussions.'

If Carlisle had intended that to be the end of the matter, he had forgotten about Cranmer's complete inability to read the mood of a room.

'I confess that I was at a loss when the first order came my way. I was nervous about offending the lieutenant governor – he's an important customer, after all – but we printers are supposed to maintain a neutral stance and so long as it's legal and within the bounds of common decency, we should hold our noses and take whatever commissions we're offered. If you want another example…'

Poor old Cranmer suffered a sharp nudge to the ankle from his wife's shoe. Barbara may have been somewhat outspoken, but that was a fault that pertained only to her own actions. She kept a close watch on her husband's loquaciousness, and she could tell when he was embarrassing their host.

'Have you heard from Mister Holbrooke, at all,' she asked, 'or the Reverend Chalmers? I can hardly look at the stars without thinking of them and Mister Halley's comet that we watched together. Was that really two years ago? How time flies.'

***

CHAPTER NINETEEN

A Single Shot

Monday, Sixth of April 1761.
The Carlisle Plantation, Jamestown, Virginia.

Carlisle stared in horror at the dreadful scene outside the carriage window. It was far, far worse than he had imagined, and in his anticipation of this day, his mind had plumbed some considerable depths.

'How long has it been like this?'

'Eh?' Joshua had been staring blankly at the fields with an expressionless face. 'Oh for some time now. You didn't come this way last year, did you?' there was a hint of reproach in his voice. 'I told you that Charles was letting the place go to rack and ruin.'

Indeed he had, Carlisle thought as he exchanged horrified glances with Enrico. His father had said many things, but Carlisle was increasingly certain that the old man's mind had started to wander, and he had given little credence to the tales of woe. The senior Joshua was at his happiest when he was playing with his grandson, and it was only with difficulty that he could be brought to discuss the family business. If there had been any sign that the plantation had been brought to this pitiful state, Carlisle told himself that he would have acted sooner. But what could he reasonably have done? His older brother was the heir, and his father, when he moved away from the plantation and into the town, breathed a huge sigh of relief and signed over the management to Charles, in perpetuity.

They passed the fields that by now should look like an eruption of chickenpox, with knee-high mounds – the planters called them *hills* – every three or four feet, but most were bare and flat. Away over the undulating land he could see a party of five or six workers hilling a field, but it was much too late, and the soil wouldn't have enough exposure to the spring rain to make it fit for planting in its due season. If the seedlings weren't in the hills by May, then it would only be by luck or divine providence that the leaves could be harvested before the first week in September. A later harvest risked the crop being ravaged by poor weather or even an early frost, and that meant a low yield and poor quality. It was a depressing scene; what had once been a thriving plantation with a sense of purpose about it had become an object lesson in the consequences of sloth and mismanagement. Even Enrico, with no family background in agriculture, could see that all was not well on the Carlisle plantation.

Another thing occurred to Carlisle; he had seen no slaves, only what he assumed were indentured servants, and not many of those. He'd heard of this before. An adjoining plantation fell on hard times when he was a youngster, and the owner had found it easier to find buyers for his slaves than to sell the indentures of the Englishmen who worked in a sort of voluntary slavery. It was a sure sign of a plantation's decline.

The coach breasted a rise in the ground and suddenly the house and its outbuildings came into view. It had been a beautiful place, in Carlisle memory, with a view down to the James river and well-tended kitchen gardens with full-leafed trees for shade, but now it looked as though it had been ravaged by war. The house clearly hadn't been painted for years and even from this distance he could see that some shingles had started to slip out of place. The cottages for the overseers, the huts for the few remaining indentured servants and the absent slaves and the tobacco sheds and stables all bore an air of neglect.

He felt a tug at his sleeve. His father was pointing out of the window, looking infinitely sad. All that Carlisle could see were the seedbeds that were set aside in the shelter of low hedges to bring on the tobacco plants before they were moved to the fields. It took a moment to see what was wrong: the seedbeds were bare! They should have been planted a month ago and the seedlings should be protected by pine boughs staked down against the wind. He could see only one tiny patch with some meagre coverage, perhaps enough to plant a twentieth part of the land that had been cultivated in the old days.

The state of the fields and the crops was bad enough, but what really struck home was the lack of activity. Between the Carlisle family, the manager and overseers, the indentured men, the slaves and all their family members, the plantation used to be a busy place, but now it looked abandoned, with weeds where once roses grew and straggly trailing vines where the honeysuckle had blossomed in his half-remembered youth.

He recalled the old days when men like Whittle's father had been serving out their period of indenture. They'd been happy days, at least in his memory, and everyone on the plantation had a kind word for the owner's second son. Whittle senior had finished his time a few years ago and now had a small farm a couple of miles north, a tenant on another planter's land.

Carlisle hadn't had any dealings with plantation life for over twenty years, but he knew a financial disaster when he saw one. The plantation would be lucky if it produced a crop at all, and if it did it couldn't possibly cover the costs of the labour and the other overheads. Perhaps that was why there were so few people. After Charles had sold his slaves to keep his creditors at bay, he must have started into the indentures, selling the contracts of those who hadn't already fled. Even the kitchen gardens were untended with rampant weeds where there should be infant maize and squash and cabbages and melons.

***

Carlisle noticed Souter shifting in his seat as the coach rolled to a halt. He had been reluctant to bring his coxswain, but he remembered the last time that he met his brother and had heeded his wife's advice to take precautions. There was nobody to be seen. Carlisle looked at his watch. Eleven o'clock, the exact time that he had stated in the note that he had sent to his brother the day before. Souter held open the coach door and he once again trod the earth where he had been raised. He wasn't in the least sentimental about his old home, but still it felt like a more significant moment than it had two years ago. Perhaps the difference was that he could see an end to the war and a day when he would return to Virginia, at least until their Lordships again required his services.

They stood before the great door with the cool April wind whipping against their coats, unsure what to do next. It was no use waiting for his father to make a move, he was evidently terrified to even approach the house.

'The Devil take it,' Carlisle muttered at last.

He strode to the door and knocked loudly with the cane that he had brought instead of a sword, to ease his brother's mind. He heard the hollow echoes from within as though it was an empty shell. Nothing. It felt devoid of human life. He was contemplating his next move when he heard a noise from the side of the building to his left. A scruffy looking mongrel trotted into sight and froze when it saw the strangers, its teeth bared, its tail tucked and its shoulders low. The bulky figure of his brother Charles followed the dog, leaning heavily on a crutch and holding a pistol loosely in his right hand. Carlisle noticed the hand's tremor and that the pistol was cocked. He sensed rather than heard Souter walk swiftly and silently to the coach.

'Brother Charles! It's been a long time. Are you expecting intruders?'

Carlisle tried to look happy to see his brother, but his gaze kept shifting to the pistol which was still mercifully pointed at the ground. He hoped that Souter was being discreet. The blunderbuss and brace of pistols that he had kept hidden in the coach were for use in extremis only, and for now he could at least pretend that his brother was fearful of robbers and had no more sinister intent on his mind.

Charles opened his mouth, but he evidently had

difficulty speaking. He cleared his throat and tried again.

'Brother Edward,' he croaked, 'in a fine coach indeed and with your shipmates I see.'

Carlisle looked more closely. The left side of his brother's face had fallen, pulling the lower eyelid away from the eye. It looked as though he had suffered an apoplexy, and that would account for the crutch and the difficulty in speaking. He noticed that his brother had entirely ignored their father's presence and indeed Joshua was trying to make himself as inconspicuous as possible.

'You are not well, Charles.'

Carlisle took a step forward but stopped abruptly when he saw the pistol's muzzle raise by an inch. He heard the twin clicks of a brace of pistols being cocked behind him. Had Charles seen Souter? Did he care? They had discussed the contingencies, in a broad sort of way, and he had reluctantly agreed on the circumstances that would cause Souter to intervene. His coxswain would fire before his brother's pistol was levelled; it was just too dangerous to wait for him to squeeze the trigger. At less than ten yards' range even a shaking hand had a chance of hitting its target.

The situation was ridiculous and there was a great danger of it getting out of hand. Carlisle made a downward sweep of his hand behind his back. He didn't look back, but he was sure that Souter would have seen it and lowered his pistols.

'Don't come any closer,' his brother said through gritted teeth. 'I'll not have you take the plantation from under my feet.'

Nobody was moving, it was like one of those tableaux that were becoming popular on the stage, an enactment of a moment in time: Hamlet confronted by his father's ghost, Octavian beholds Caesar's pierced and bloodied body, Guy Fawkes dragged to the scaffold, defiant to the last.

'You are not well, Charles,' Carlisle repeated, 'you should let us help you. We are family after all.'

'Never!'

Charles spat out the word, but the distortion of his

mouth mangled the vee sound. His speech was like a two-year old, Carlisle's son could form his words better than that. He was careful to keep his distance.

'When did your illness start, Brother, have you seen a physician?'

Charles just glowered at him and offered no answer. There was an awkward pause in which he heard the soft sounds of his father crying.

'Won't you let us help you, Charles?'

'I know what you want,' he replied, still slurring his words. 'You plan to take the plantation away from me. Well you'll never do that, not as long as I live, and I plan to be on this earth to laugh over your grave. Be gone and take your foreign kin with you. You're not welcome here and the next time I see you I'll not give you the courtesy of conversation. I'll shoot you on sight like the vermin that you are.'

Carlisle watched his brother's right hand out of the corner of his eye. The pistol was waving wildly but at least the muzzle pointed to the ground. He knew he could end this now. He could take a step forward; Charles would raise the pistol and Souter would shoot him dead on the spot. The risk to himself was not great. Even if Souter should be slow or irresolute – and neither was likely – or if both of his pistols should misfire or both balls miss their target, it was unlikely that he was in danger from his brother's pistol. Charles' shaking had become so pronounced in the few minutes since they arrived that his shot could fly anywhere. He heard the scraping of leather-soled boots; the coachman had evidently come to the same conclusion and decided that it was time to find a less exposed position.

He could end it now and it was a hundred to one that his brother would be stone dead before his pistol reached the horizontal. There'd be no legal problems, he was certain, and no Virginia judge or jury would convict him. The coachman was an independent witness to the events and the whole town knew that there was something rotten at the heart of the Carlisle plantation. He could see a pair of ragged field hands watching with dull eyes, and he was willing to bet that they had no love for their master.

And yet he had no wish to cause his brother harm. They'd never been close, being of very different temperaments, but they were the nearest of kin and if he could help Charles he would do so, despite the hard words that had passed between them.

'Very well, Charles, we will leave now, but I would be grateful if you would reply to the letter that I'll write. I hope that we may be friends again, as brothers should, and I trust that I'll be able to convince you that I have no designs upon the plantation. It's yours by our father's wish and I'll not contest that.'

He could see his brother's rising agitation and he feared for its consequences. Rather than risk a bloody confrontation, he bowed, turned on his heel and walked stiffly to the coach. He saw as though through a mist that Souter was standing at the coach's tail with a cocked pistol in each hand, both pointed at the ground, and with the wicked-looking blunderbuss propped against the wheel. Enrico was poised too, and his right hand was on the sword that his aristocratic upbringing demanded was always at his side, while his left rested in a pocket where he habitually kept a small pistol. Souter's eyes never moved as his captain passed, they were locked upon the pathetic figure of his brother. Carlisle helped his father into his seat; he was hardly in a better case than his brother and his cheeks were wet from tears.

The danger was over now. Carlisle could see that his brother's irrational fears and anger were subsiding as the object of his hatred became less of a physical presence, merging with the coach and the horses into something less real and personal. He waved for Souter to come into the coach, but he shook his head and pointed to the high seat beside the coachman. Carlisle knew he was right. His brother was clearly insane as well as physically impaired and he could change his mind at any moment and decide to fire at the coach. Carlisle was vaguely aware of the state of mind that could cause such an action, even though it meant the perpetrator's certain death. His brother had nothing to lose. That talk of laughing over his grave was merely bluster, and it was quite clear that Charles had little chance of seeing the year out. Nothing to lose and much to gain, in his disordered imagination, by killing the object of his hatred.

The coachman whipped up the horses and the coach took a tight turn in front of the house. Charles didn't move. Carlisle noticed that his pistol hand was steady now, but his body still leaned heavily on the crutch, giving him a menacing lopsided look. He leaned out of the window for a last look at his brother; he had a curious feeling that they wouldn't meet again. Then, as the road turned and the building hid Charles from view, he reached for his father's hand and felt its wetness where the old man had been wiping away his tears.

The rumble of the wheels and the thunder of the horses' hooves drowned the sound of the single pistol shot and the three men inside the coach missed it, but Souter heard the sharp crack from his high perch, and it was he who ordered the coachman to rein in.

***

CHAPTER TWENTY

The Family Property

Friday, Tenth of April 1761.
Bruton Parish Church, Williamsburg.

There's nothing so bleak as a fresh graveside on a cold afternoon. Carlisle waited with bowed head as the pallbearers stepped slowly from the church and the bells tolled their knell for the death of Charles Carlisle. Chiara held fast to his arm, shivering in the knife-like wind, while his father clung to the other arm, sobbing softly all the while.

The committal service was short, and Carlisle wasn't really following it. He threw a handful of earth on the coffin when the vicar looked at him meaningfully, and he clenched his hands in prayer, but it all seemed unreal. He felt no real sadness at his brother's untimely death, the memory of that brief last encounter was all too vivid. He was as sure as he could be that Charles would have committed some mischief if he had lived a few days longer, in fact when his coxswain heard the shot, he had been thinking about what precautions he should take to safeguard his family. Charles' life had been in a downward spiral for years, and all things considered he'd probably taken a rational decision to end it. Carlisle wondered what the vicar would say if he could read his thoughts. Probably he'd be shocked and on Sunday would deliver a sermon on the sin of self-murder and the duty of a family to preserve the life of its members. That was the conventional view of the sanctity of life, but the vicar hadn't stood before that devastated plantation house and seen his brother's madness striving for control of his soul.

Then it was all over. The gravediggers, who had been standing impatiently behind a tree, started to pick up their shovels and rakes; they clearly wanted to get the job finished so that they could go home to a warm fire. Chiara took Joshua firmly by the arm and guided him back towards the house. Edward lingered a moment in the churchyard, wondering what he should be feeling at the death of his brother. Surely this indifference was wrong, and yet – try as he might – he could find no other emotion within himself.

'My condolences, Captain Carlisle.'

The lieutenant governor's brusque approach shook him out of his reverie. Francis Fauquier had attended the funeral out of respect for the younger Carlisle brother, not the deceased elder. Charles' increasingly erratic conduct had been brought to his attention too often in the past few years, and he was glad to hear the last of him.

'Thank you, sir, it's a sad day for the family. And I apologise for not calling on you sooner, but as you can see, my family has demanded all my time.'

'Your father doesn't look too well. He's taken it badly, I suppose.'

Fauquier, in his usual abrupt manner, avoided any comment on the sadness of the brother's passing, or on the absence of the customary call.

'I regret that my father hasn't been himself for a few years now.'

Carlisle hoped to end the conversation, yet he knew that the lieutenant governor was difficult to shake off when he had something to say.

'Have you thought what will become of the plantation? I expect King George will demand your services at sea for a few years yet, and it'll be inconvenient for you to take an active part in the management. Will your father take the house again and rebuild the business?'

Carlisle shook his head.

'There's not the slightest chance of that happening, sir. In fact I find I must apply for an order to allow me to manage my father's affairs; without reference to his wishes, if necessary.'

Fauquier nodded sympathetically as they walked slowly

back towards Duke of Gloucester Street.

'You'll have no difficulty there, Carlisle. If your father isn't able to sign the papers, the court will no doubt declare him incapable and appoint you as his guardian. Everyone knows the situation and none of the other planters want a derelict property on their doorstep. Will you sell?'

Now, was this a casual question or did Fauquier have a less altruistic motive in asking. Lieutenant governors rarely had long tenures and he must be considering his own future. Could he be looking for a property in Virginia? There was a strong feeling that land prices were about to rise in the wake of the French capitulation. Carlisle had seen the building boom in New England with his own eyes, and most informed opinion suggested that the surge of enthusiasm would reach Virginia before the summer was out. It was unlikely that Fauquier would live on a plantation himself, it was hardly the place for a lieutenant governor nor even a retired one, but as an investment? That was more likely.

'Well, there are a few hurdles to jump yet, sir. My father had already handed over the plantation to my brother, although it's still not clear to me whether Charles actually owned it or merely managed it on my father's behalf. He didn't make a will, which further confuses the issue, and of course my father is still alive. One way or another the plantation's future will be in the hands of the lawyers.'

Fauquier smiled conspiratorially.

'Oh, I really don't see that as a problem. Who acts for you?'

'I've asked George Wythe, but he's out of town and I haven't heard from him.'

'A good choice, Carlisle. Mister Wythe has a finger in every committee and on every court, being a burgess.'

Carlisle knew that very well. Apart from his long-standing friendship – they had been at school together – he wanted someone on his side who could cut through the tangle of laws and customary practice to bring this to a swift conclusion.

Carlisle's Duty

'But your inclination, Carlisle, what do you want to do? It's still a vast great parcel of land in a prime position, and with a little energy and capital it could be restored to its former productivity. It has essentially lain fallow for the past two years and that will increase its attraction.'

That was just the question that Carlisle had been asking himself: what *did* he wish to do, and so far, the answer had eluded him. A week ago he would have had no hesitation in stating confidently and unequivocally that he wanted nothing to do with the whole ghastly business. But now, with the prospect of losing – no, actively disposing of – the family plantation, he wasn't too sure. He'd grown up on that stretch of land, he'd sailed on the James River, and he'd played in the fields; all that would be lost if he sold up.

'I think, sir, that I need a day or two to consider.'

'And yet your convoy is gathering daily, which is something I wanted to talk to you about, if you don't mind.'

Carlisle inclined his head in a noncommittal gesture. He was slightly irritated by this hurrying along of his decision, although he knew that it was just the way Fauquier spoke. And he had a fair notion of what was coming.

'I've had a representation from Richmond. They have hogs and lumber and Indian corn for Jamaica and the Leeward Islands, but they need another week or so to collect the lighters and barges and bring them down the river. Now, I can't direct you to wait for them, that would be trespassing on the Admiralty's business, but as a lieutenant governor I can represent to you the urgent need for the produce of this colony to be sent abroad without delay, now that spring is decidedly present.'

Carlisle looked at the people hurrying by with their collars turned up against the chill wind and thought of contesting that assertion but held his tongue.

'And the governor of Jamaica wrote to me in the most direct terms regarding the need for timber for the new buildings and hogs to feed his people. I'll be frank. You would be obliging the Old Dominion greatly if you delay your convoy by a week or so.'

Just so, Carlisle thought. It was about the only subject that would cause the lieutenant governor to seek him out, and he hadn't failed to notice the emotive use of Virginia's anachronistic nickname. It dated from the restoration and evoked a time when loyalty to the Crown was not taken for granted. And just as Fauquier guessed – in fact it was probably why he chose this moment to broach the subject – delaying the convoy would solve an immediate family problem. It would give him time to sort out the legal tangle and to decide what to do with the plantation. Commodore Douglas would start to wonder about *Dartmouth's* delay, but he'd have a letter in a week or so and he'd be able to guess the rest. Convoy sailings were notoriously indefinite, and every escort commander was bombarded with petitions, promises, gifts and threats to delay the sailing date.

Fauquier looked briefly annoyed as Carlisle considered the matter, then he remembered that he had no real power to influence Carlisle's decision.

'I apologise, Captain. This is neither the time nor the place to discuss the King's business. Perhaps you could call at the palace tomorrow. Shall we say eleven o'clock? If that's agreeable my secretary will send a note to your home this afternoon.'

***

The callers had all departed, Joshua senior and Joshua junior were both in bed, and Carlisle, Chiara and Enrico had subsided into deep chairs in the drawing room. Black Rod came in and closed the curtains and trimmed the candles.

'Do you wish for any refreshment, your Ladyship?'

Carlisle knew that he should resent the fact that the man never, ever referred questions to him when Chiara was present, despite being his servant at sea for some months and his servant now by dint of the fact that he abided under the Carlisle roof and ate of the Carlisle victuals. He'd been the Angelini family's master of household for all of Chiara's life. Since he had crossed swords with the viscountess, and could no longer return to Nice, he had become a permanent fixture in the Williamsburg house. Nothing would curb his devotion to Chiara and no power on earth would prevent him calling her by her honorary title, however absurd it may appear in the colonies.

Chiara looked at Edward and Enrico for confirmation.

'No, I think that will be all, thank you.'

'In that case and with your permission I will retire, your Ladyship.'

The room had sprung into life with the trimming of the candles, and the rejuvenated flames cast crisp shadows on the walls and deepened the intensity of the dark corners. Some of the somnolence of the room had been lost and it stirred the occupants into conversation.

Carlisle looked from Chiara to Enrico.

'Do you know his real name? Black Rod was of course the name he was given by George Holbrooke, more in jest than anything else, and this Rodrigo Black that he used when he signed on *Dartmouth's* books is obviously nonsense. I'm surprised at myself for colluding in such a falsehood on an important document.'

Chiara and Enrico exchanged glances. Sometimes Carlisle was convinced that they had secrets that he wasn't privy to, things buried deep in the Angelini family's past. And yet, in this case, he wasn't sure that they knew any more than he did.

'If he has a name, it was never used in front of me,' Chiara said, looking sideways at Enrico.

'And I have only heard him referred to as the master of the household, or sometimes just *master*, rather like Mister Beazley, the sailing master,' Enrico added.

'I suppose his age is also a mystery.'

Chiara and Enrico looked blank.

'He's always appeared the same age to me,' Chiara said, 'and I've never thought to ask.'

For the life of him, Carlisle couldn't decide whether they were hiding something. It was their Mediterranean manners, so difficult to penetrate.

'Well, I believe that's one mystery that will never be solved. But for now we have a question that is much more pressing: what to do with the plantation.'

'Is it so pressing, Edward? Can't it just be left to plod along for a while until you are home for a longer spell?'

'I regret not, my dear. There are loans to be serviced, repairs to be made and servants to be fed. My father could be liable at law if he doesn't fulfil at least the minimum that is required of the indentures. As far as I can tell there are about a dozen men – all indentured – and some with families. They have no pay of course but they are entitled to be decently housed and fed, and that has evidently not been the case. If they had any vital force at all they'd abscond and save us a deal of trouble.'

'Then the choice is between selling and investing, sir,' said Enrico. 'What does your father think of the matter?'

Carlisle watched the shadows swaying back and forth as a draught caught the candles. That window sash needed some attention; he'd take a look himself before he called in a carpenter.

'It's his plantation of course. I'm the sole heir now but he should make the decisions during his lifetime. The problem is…'

'The problem is, dear Edward, that your father is in no case to make any decision beyond whether his egg will be boiled or fried at breakfast. It would be sheer torture to demand that he think about the plantation, and I fear that it may do him harm.'

Carlisle looked a little shocked at his wife's blunt assessment but recognised that it needed to be said. He knew that Chiara would look after his father when he sailed away in a week or two, and she deserved to have the legal issues at least on the way to resolution before then.

'Just so, just so. I'll take George Wythe's advice, but I imagine I'll have to apply for an order to make me responsible for all decisions regarding my father, to make him my ward, in effect. That will pave the way for a decision on the plantation. However,' he added, gazing at the candlelight, 'none of that will affect the greater decision, invest or sell, just as Enrico so concisely puts it.'

There was silence for a moment, as each considered the implications.

'Forgive me, sir. This is your private business and I know little of the costs of keeping a Virginia plantation…'

Carlisle nodded for him to continue.

'…I saw the plantation and it appeared to me that it would take a long time to restore its prosperity; years, I would say, rather than months, and it could absorb a very great fortune before it started turning a profit again. I wonder whether you have the funds available, after buying this house.'

Carlisle would certainly have resented that question had it come from anyone other than Chiara's cousin. Enrico was so like a part of the family that Carlisle didn't think twice about replying frankly.

'No, I don't. I would have to borrow to raise enough capital, and my belief is that it would take five or ten years to repay the loan. This year the plantation will produce nothing and will be a dead loss. Next year, with a great deal of effort, it may produce a crop, but it will still need investment. In the year 'sixty-three it may produce a profit but that will all be absorbed in servicing the loans. Ten years is more likely than five, I think. Ten years of solid hard work and stewardship.'

He looked at his wife who slowly and firmly shook her head.

'I perhaps know your mind better than you do, Edward. You have told me that you are no planter, and I believe it to be true; you would grow restless if you were tied to the soil. Whatever you decide to do when this war is over, it should be something that captures your interest, not a farm!'

Carlisle smiled at that. Chiara was right, of course. It was only a surge of sentimentality brought about by his brother's death and the reality of his father's intellectual condition that had made him even consider keeping the plantation. A week ago he wouldn't have even considered it. And his father would never step foot on the place again; he was already haunted by the memory of that dreadful scene when the coach turned back to find Charles' body. His mind was clear now. Make some sense of the plantation's legal position, arrange for a power of attorney over his father's affairs, and put it up for sale before the convoy sails. He was in no doubt that there would be eager buyers and even in its present condition, its location on the river would command a good price.

***

CHAPTER TWENTY-ONE

Borrowed Time

Saturday, Eleventh of April 1761.
The Governor's Palace, Williamsburg.

Carlisle's moral ascendancy over his wife had always rested on shaky foundations. It was partly due to her aristocratic family, but her personality also had a lot to answer for. Now, with his mind in disarray after his brother's funeral and with Chiara's competent management – or was it manipulation? – of three generations of Carlisle men, his defences had been thoroughly breached, and he had no means of resisting the hated carriage ride. He didn't object to dressing with care for a call on the lieutenant governor and the gravity of the occasion wasn't in any way lost upon him, but he still found the carriage ride absurd.

On a morning walk with Chiara, he had surreptitiously counted the two hundred paces from the steps of his own home to the palace gates. Add another thirty for the distance from the gate – which would be opened for his carriage – to the steps of the palace, then adjust for his wife's shorter stride and it came to a mere two hundred yards on a dry, gravelled path. He could walk the distance in less time than it would take to board the carriage and he would hardly be settled in his seat before he had to alight again.

***

'Captain Carlisle, I must apologise for accosting you with business matters at you brother's funeral; it was unforgivable.'

Fauquier didn't look like a man in despair at ever being forgiven, but he did look like one who found himself at a moral disadvantage through yesterday's blunders. Carlisle had often wondered about this concept of moral ascendancy. It was intangible and yet it was vital. Some could gain it with no apparent effort, and some strove all their lives and never achieved it. It was the magic ingredient in the recipe of a man or a woman, the element that won battles and business deals, treaties and marriage settlements and Carlisle knew very well that if he had a moral advantage over the lieutenant governor, it was only temporary.

'I understand that Mister Wythe is expected today, which will no doubt be good news to you.'

Carlisle nodded; he had already heard. Elizabeth Wythe had told Chiara yesterday afternoon. He recognised that this was Fauquier's way of starting a negotiation, handing out gratuitous trifles of information to grease the wheels.

'Then I trust you will be able to clear up your brother's – and your father's – affairs without too much delay. Do be sure to let me know what you decide with regard to the plantation.'

'Mister Wythe hasn't agreed to act for me yet, sir, and I'm reserving any decisions until I've heard his advice, if he's willing to give it.'

He really didn't want to discuss the fate of the plantation today. He'd taken his deliberations as far as they would go without professional advice, and he was wary of being compromised by the lieutenant governor's eagerness.

'Just so, Carlisle, just so. Incidentally, I had the pleasure of meeting your cousin by marriage, Mister Angelini, who I understand is at least technically in the Sardinian service. A fine young man indeed. He'll be a loss to the navy when he's recalled.'

Carlisle hid his irritation. For some reason Fauquier's interest in Enrico disturbed him, it was family business not government business, but he merely bowed and didn't pursue the subject.

'Now, about your convoy. How many vessels have gathered at Hampton so far, if I may ask?'

'Eight, sir, three for St. John's and five for Kingston and various ports on Jamaica. I had a note from my first lieutenant yesterday, and he expects three more from the Delaware before we sail on Wednesday of next week.'

Fauquier picked up a sheet of paper on his desk and studied it for a moment.

'Little do I know of naval affairs, but isn't that small for a convoy protected by a ship-of-the-line and a sloop-of-war? There are another eight or so at Hampton waiting for their cargoes to come down from half a dozen places on the James as far as Richmond. The lighters will start moving today but the ships still need to be fitted out and loaded, and that will take a week. If you don't take them, they'll be forced to wait at least another month. Some of them may decide to risk an unescorted passage.'

Gentle leverage, Carlisle understood. Fauquier was hinting that part of the blame would fall on his shoulders if any of the stray merchantmen were taken by French commerce raiders.

'Small or large, sir, Lord Colville requested me to wait ten days then proceed with the convoy to the Leeward Islands. If any of the owners decide to send their ships without escort, then upon their heads be it, but I would advise strongly against it. The French navy may be confined to port, but the privateers are not.'

'Yes, yes, but as I understand it, Lord Colville can only request, not order a ship belonging to the Leeward Islands, and Sir James at Antigua has given you no particular time for your return, isn't that so?'

Carlisle was playing his own game. He dearly wanted to wait for those Richmond ships. The delay would give him another week with his wife and son, and in that time, he could hope that the court would award him a power of attorney over his father. That would allow him to instruct George Wythe, or another attorney if George declined. It would solve so many domestic problems, but he still had to balance his commitments to the navy and cover himself in case Commodore Douglas should consider that he had committed the cardinal sin of lingering in port. There was another point too; if he agreed too readily to Fauquier's request, the lieutenant governor would conclude that he owed Carlisle nothing for this favour, in fact he may consider that Carlisle owed him a debt. There was no knowing when he may need Fauquier to feel obliged to him, but it was nevertheless a bankable asset in his dealings in the colony.

'*If* I can agree to this request, sir, and I say *if*, how sure can we be certain that these Richmond cargoes will be at Hampton and loaded by a week from Wednesday?'

Privately, Carlisle was convinced that it would take longer than a week, but he was building that extra time into his calculations. It was a rare convoy that sailed on time.

Fauquier picked up the letter again and handed it to Carlisle.

'See for yourself, Carlisle. This is signed by a dozen of the prominent men in Richmond, and they all assure me that the cargoes will be running downstream within a day or two.'

Carlisle read the letter. Just as he expected, the estimate of the time it would take to load the barges and lighters, work them downstream through the shallow James River and load them into ships at Hampton was wildly optimistic. If he agreed with this, he would be lucky to sail by the twenty-seventh, and early May was a distinct possibility. This was a Godsend, and he was sure that he could answer any criticism from Sir James. After all, he'd been *requested* to divert to Hampton by a commander-in-chief and he'd been *requested* to stay longer by the King's own representative in the colony. Sir James would surely suspect an ulterior motive, but he wouldn't be able to do anything about it.

'Then I agree, sir. However, I must ask you for a written request that I delay the convoy's sailing date and I must insist on the right to sail on Wednesday the twenty-second, whether or not the Richmond cargoes have been loaded.'

Fauquier smiled and held out his hand.

'Then that's settled. You'll have your letter this afternoon. Now, I feel that I've trespassed too much already, but if you would care to send one of your officers to Richmond, I think you will find that the loading will be expedited.'

The lieutenant governor wasn't fooled at all by Carlisle's manoeuvering. Once the Richmond cargoes had been agreed, *Dartmouth* would find it impossible to argue a case for sailing even if the lighters hadn't yet left their wharves far up the James River. Like it or not, his time at Williamsburg was to be limited not by naval orders, nor by his own inclination, but by the speed that the cargoes could come down from Richmond.

***

Carlisle was surprised to see the familiar figure of his second lieutenant at his front door when he alighted from the carriage.

'Mister Wishart, what a pleasure it is to see you, but how did you arrive so early? The Hampton coach can't be here yet.'

He could see that his lieutenant was burning to make a comment on his two-hundred-yard carriage ride but didn't dare.

'The longboat, sir. Davies swore that he could find Archer's Hope Creek again – even after two years – and bring us up to Princess Anne's Port, and he was as good as his word. I left an hour before sunrise and this southerly wind with a flooding tide brought the boat up the river at a furious pace.'

A host of memories came back to Carlisle. Two years ago – no, more than that, his son was two-and-a-half – he'd taken *Medina's* longboat on that same route to reach Williamsburg on the very day that Joshua was born. He remembered the crew singing as they pulled along the creek in the fading light of the evening – *Queen Anne commands and we'll obey, over the hills and far away* – and he remembered the deep joy at discovering that he had a son.

'Well, an epic voyage, I doubt that it's ever been achieved so quickly. You have messages, I gather?'

'Yes, sir.'

He handed over a package of letters, wrapped, weighted and sealed as though for an ocean voyage and not a gentle trip up the river.

'The carpenter sends his compliments and requests to haul the ship over and take a look at that butt-end again, just to be sure.'

'What does Mister Gresham say, and Mister Beazley?'

'They agree, sir. There's a letter from the first lieutenant in that bundle, sir.'

'Very well, anything else of importance?'

'One man in irons for drunk on shore, sir, but otherwise all is well.'

Carlisle knew he was lucky. He'd given shore leave by watches and the men would have been spending freely in Hampton. One case of drunkenness was nothing and it could have been far worse. He knew that he'd be lucky to sail from here without losing a handful of men to desertion. It was a balance; he could have denied the men any shore leave and stored up the discontent for later, or he could give leave, accepting a small wastage of his manpower. If they were going to run, they would leave it until the last few days before sailing, to reduce the opportunity for a party from the ship to hunt them down. Once *Dartmouth* sailed, they had little to fear from the colonial authorities who were glad to see more able-bodied men. He was comforted by the knowledge that it was generally the disaffected men who deserted, the ones who wouldn't throw their weight behind a rope nor be at the front of a boarding party.

'Then you come just in time, Mister Wishart. Stay to dine with me and then you and Mister Angelini can take a coach up the river as far as Richmond and meet the merchants there. I'll explain over dinner, but first I have another call to make.'

***

George Wythe looked as strange in his thirties as Carlisle remembered him as a boy. A high forehead with a hairline that barely crested the summit of his head, an austere, pale face and penetrating eyes. He'd been mocked for it as a child, but his parents were wealthy, and the young Wythe just shrugged it off. He was probably the gentlest man that Carlisle had ever met, and he could calm the most heated of discussions merely by his presence. Perhaps that was why he had risen so far in the government of the colony and why he had been chosen to be a burgess. But how on earth he had managed to capture the heart of such a beauty as Elizabeth Toliver was a mystery that nobody had yet explained satisfactorily.

The southerly breeze that had wafted Wishart up the James river at such a remarkable speed had hurried away yesterday's cold weather and fulfilled the promise of spring in Williamsburg. Carlisle and Wythe took their coffee in the yard behind the attorney's house, just a few steps from Carlisle's own.

'I gather your father is in no state to agree or disagree?'

Carlisle shook his head.

'He won't understand what's being asked of him. I hope that his condition will improve but I see no sign of it yet.'

'Then I don't see any difficulty at all with the power of attorney. If I may meet your father, then I can endorse the paper as attorney for both you and he with an easy conscience. He will not have to sign anything or even know that it's happening. The only challenge that I can imagine is if some natural child of your brother's should emerge, or if you should ever cast your father out onto the parish. I gather neither of those events is likely.'

Carlisle smiled at the thought.

'Not in the least. Chiara would never let me put my father out of the door, even if I should wish to do so, and nobody has ever heard of my brother having anything at all to do with a woman. No such person has been seen at the plantation since my mother died.'

'I'll have the power of attorney drawn up next week and I'll have a man look over the plantation and give an appraisal of its value. I'm sure you'll have no difficulty selling it. We can worry about the indentures when we have a buyer; he may want to take them on which will ease matters considerably. Meanwhile you'll have to spend a little to keep the place habitable and to look after the workers.'

'Yes, I'd expected that.'

'I gather you've dismissed the manager.'

'I have. He's been siphoning money from the plantation for years although it will be impossible to prove, with no ledgers worth their name.'

'Well, I may be able to look into that for you also, although, as you say, it could be difficult and there's that old adage that we should consider about taking blood from a stone. Meanwhile, my advice would be to offer the head overseer a bonus if he can maintain the place as it is until a sale is completed. You'll find that's money well spent. If he accepts, I can draw up something that only commits you to pay if he does as he promises.'

Carlisle was beginning to relax for the first time since that terrible day when his brother shot himself. If all went well, he'd be able to sail to Antigua having done everything he needed to do, leaving the rest in Wythe's hands. Of course, the attorney's fee would be substantial, but then it was his father's money, not his. With a bit of luck they'd be rid of the plantation before he next came home, whenever that would be.

'Will you dine with me, George? You and Elizabeth?'

'I regret not, Edward. As you see I'm newly returned and have a great number of matters clamouring for my attention. I'll see you next week with the papers to sign, and all I ask before then is that you speak to the plantation overseer.'

***

It was a cheerful dinner with the weather turning fine and the windows opened for the first time since the last autumn. Carlisle realised that the four of them had been together more-or-less for five years, since he had taken his first frigate, *Fury*, into Villa-Franca way back in 'fifty-six. They had shared adventures, happiness and sorrows and

Carlisle's Duty

they talked without ceasing long into the afternoon. As the shadow of the house lengthened on the green, Chiara excused herself leaving the three men to finish the port.

Carlisle moved his chair closer to the window to catch the last of the daylight.

'I do believe we can address some of King George's business now. You'll leave tomorrow for Richmond. You can hire a carriage in the town, and it will carry you there in two days, easily. There are inns along the way.'

Wishart was studying the map and stepping off distances along the James River. Carlisle saw him and laughed.

'It's a good three days on the river. Even if this wind holds, you'll lose any effect from the tide and you'll be fighting the stream the whole way. No, the longboat can go back to the ship and tell Mister Gresham why you haven't returned, so that he doesn't mark you down as run. Now here's a letter for the merchants. In it, I've stated our sailing date. You must impress upon them the need to have their cargoes loaded in time. They'll swear on the bible that they'll meet the schedule, but it won't mean a thing until I see those ships at short stay in Hampton, ready to sail on the twenty-second. What I need from you is an assessment of their ability to make that date; not what they say they can do, but what it appears to you that they can do. Spend a day in Richmond then hasten back. I'll expect you on Thursday or Friday.'

***

Wishart and Enrico left for the King's Head, where much of the life of the town could be found. Carlisle found that Chiara was busy with little Joshua, and he took the opportunity for a stroll. He took the lanes that ran behind the houses that faced Duke of Gloucester Street. They had a magical quality in the early evening, with rustic bridges over the little streams that tinkled their way towards the great rivers. Best of all, they were relatively untraveled at this time of day, with the workshops and builders' yards closing and the coffee shops and inns not yet in full flow.

This was his town; he knew that now. And more importantly it had become Chiara's town. A year ago he was ambivalent, even though he'd bought a house here, then what had changed? Of course, it was the plantation. That dreadful place had preyed upon his mind, and without his knowing had turned him against his hometown. With the future of the plantation all but settled, he could see Williamsburg and the whole colony from a different perspective. This was his home and now he could hardly wait for the war to end.

***

CHAPTER TWENTY-TWO

Horse Latitudes

Wednesday, Twenty-Ninth of April 1761.
Dartmouth, at Sea. Off Cape Henry.

The wind blew brisk and warm from the west, raising little white topped waves even in the shelter of Hampton Roads, an auspicious wind that would waft the convoy clear through the straits to the rendezvous off Cape Henry. Carlisle made a final count: eleven ships for Jamaica, seven ships and a brig for St. John's. It was a respectable convoy and at least he didn't have to call at any of the ports in the Carolinas or Georgia.

'Weigh anchor, Mister Beazley, and take us to the rendezvous.'

Hampton Roads was a huge expanse of water, but even so it was no place to be manoeuvering a great two-decked ship of the line. Carlisle was taking *Dartmouth* out to the rendezvous, some seven leagues from the anchorage, to await the convoy. *Shark* would bring up the rear and encourage the laggards. It should be simple with this westerly wind. All the merchantmen had to do was win their anchors and set their sails, the wind would do the rest and as long as they were underway by noon, they'd easily make the rendezvous before sunset. That was the theory, but when it met the obstinacy of nineteen self-willed merchant masters, any number of things could happen to delay the gathering. Even now, Carlisle could see a myriad of boats running between the Hampton shore and the ships.

'Look, sir,' said Gresham, 'there's a lighter coming off. They'll never swing a lighter's load aboard in time.'

Carlisle had been watching it for some minutes. It was heading for one of the Jamaica ships and he could see that *Dartmouth's* longboat was speeding towards the errant vessel. Wishart had orders to be firm; the convoy would sail from

Cape Charles by sunset and any laggards would have to shift for themselves. He looked more closely; the lighter wasn't fully loaded, he could see that it was riding high in the water, probably it was just a last few barrels or bales. It was hard to imagine that the ship's master would risk missing the convoy, not with the French privateers still so active.

'Ah, he's hooked on. I can see Mister Wishart going up the side.'

Gresham had little to do while Beazley handled the ship, and he was an eager observer of the proceedings.

'*Shark's* underway, sir,' Enrico reported from his station beside the binnacle.

The eight-gun snow-sloop may be obsolete but at least it was small and nimble, and Hampton Roads held no terrors for Warner. He was to bring up the rear after all the convoy had weighed, while the longboat hurried from ship to ship, chivvying them into some sort of order.

'Anchor's aweigh, sir.'

'Very well, Mister Beazley.'

There was no need to say any more; he'd already told the sailing master to take *Dartmouth* to the rendezvous.

He'd have to leave it to Warner and Wishart now. All his preparations came down to this moment and now there was nothing that he could do to influence events. *Dartmouth* would sail out of the road and – with good fortune – the convoy would follow, one after the other. He'd given them an order in which they were to sail, but he knew that his plan was only a basis for change. Ships would be slow in weighing, some would find their anchor fouled and spend an hour clearing it, some would just decide that they wanted to do things their own way. Warner and Wishart could point and shout, they'd even discharge their swivel guns if the felt they weren't making their point strongly enough, but the merchant masters were lords on their own decks and in the end, they'd do what they wanted.

Dartmouth moved slowly towards Point Comfort under her tops'ls. Carlisle trained his telescope on the land in the hope that he'd see Chiara. She'd insisted on coming to Hampton and she'd slept on board for his last night at anchor. The longboat had taken her ashore in the first grey light of the new day, and Carlisle knew that she wouldn't turn for home until she could no longer see *Dartmouth's* tops'ls. It was over a mile to the Hampton shore; Carlisle wiped the lens of his telescope and looked again. He could just make out two figures standing at the small jetty by the creek. Chiara and Black Rod, he was sure, with the tall dark figure of the head of household standing a few feet to the rear. He even thought he could see a handkerchief being waved, but perhaps that was just his imagination.

'The first merchantman's weighed,' Gresham reported, 'and there's another at short stay.'

Carlisle turned back to the ship's business with a sigh.

***

'We're out of the Drift now, sir. We've made good our true course since last noon.'

Beazley had a look of deep satisfaction. The blessed westerly wind had carried the convoy on its sou'easterly course, and they appeared to have passed through the Atlantic Drift's influence without being set too far to the north of their planned route. He returned his quadrant to its box which a midshipman carried to his cabin, cradled in his arms against the motion of the deck.

'The weather-glass is rising, sir.'

Beazley sounded less confidence than when he had announced the latitude from the noon sight.

'Indeed?'

Carlisle was trying to count the ships that spread in a disordered gaggle to leeward and didn't really want to be interrupted by the master's comments on his pet instrument.

'Fair weather, perhaps, sir.'

Carlisle merely grunted in reply. He was starting to grow

tired – aye, and sceptical – about the master's weather-glass. He'd suffered watch-by-watch reports on the quicksilver's rising and falling and as far as he could tell it told him nothing that he couldn't see out of his own cabin window. The piece of seaweed that old Eli kept nailed to the binnacle was more useful in that it at least responded to the changing moisture in the air an hour or so before a human could detect it, although the cook claimed that he felt it in the stump of his leg even earlier. It was all so much nonsense and if he had more moral courage, he'd order the master to throw the damned thing over the side.

'Fair weather with a northerly wind?'

Beazley shrugged his shoulders.

'I can't tell, sir, although we'll be in the horse latitudes in a day or so.'

Carlisle had never experienced the horrors of the belt of still air between the sou'westerlies of the northern latitudes and the nor'east trade winds that blew above the line. He'd sailed through that region often enough but had suffered no more than a day or so of variable winds and certainly he had been subjected to none of the torments of day after day of flat calm that mariners of old talked about.

'I've been looking through the log for our passage from Newport to Hampton, sir, and I've compared the winds with the readings from the weather-glass. It's not conclusive, not by any means, but I can see a correlation. If we had known what we were looking for we could have anticipated that blow off Long Island.'

'The quicksilver was falling, as I recall.'

'It was, sir,' Beazley brightened at this first sign that Carlisle was open to talking about the instrument, 'and it fell a good four or five hours before the weather turned. If I can only make enough observations of the glass and compare them with the weather a watch or so later, then I might be able to make a table of indications and probable effects.'

Carlisle looked again at the convoy. *Shark* was setting more sail as Warner chased an errant merchantman that was sagging away to leeward, but otherwise all the ships were more-or-less in their stations. The sun was at its zenith, bathing the deck in warmth and light; it had turned into the first truly warm day since they left the islands two months before, and he felt the first stirrings of a better humour.

'Would this be a good time to inspect the instrument again, Mister Beazley?'

The sailing master beamed with pleasure. Really, it was too comical. Carlisle had never become used to the idea that he could set the tone for all of his officers, and by extension the whole company of the ship, merely by his own mood, and yet it was demonstrably so.

***

The weather-glass looked resplendent in its long wooden case and copper cage. Beazley clearly treasured it and the whole assemblage gleamed with beeswax, twinkling polished glass and the reddish colour of polished copper.

'You see, I've made pencil marks to remind me of the previous measurement and I make a note of whether it has risen or fallen at the change of each watch.'

Carlisle was offered a slim notebook with a long line of dates, times and arrows pointing up, down or sideways. He was still unconvinced, but he accepted that in the quest for advancement in navigation, every new idea must be tried. Chiara had a phrase for it that always amused him: *You have to kiss a great number of ugly frogs before you find your handsome prince*. Perhaps it was rendered more elegantly in Italian.

'I saw one in London. Oh, it must have been before this war; it had a paper scale glued beside it, marked off in inches. Have you considered that, Mister Beazley? It would give you a more empirical reading than this simple *rising, falling and steady*.'

Beazley looked lovingly at the glass.

'In fact I have, sir, but I fear disturbing the armourer's cage. You see, there's nowhere to fix it unless the cage is moved, and I'm not sure I could stand to see him bring his great awl and screwdriver so close to the glass again.'

Carlisle didn't immediately answer. It was a specious argument because with the screw holes already drilled the armourer could merely remove the cage and replace it after the paper had been fixed in place. In fact, the armourer's tools were extraordinarily fine; they were used to repair the delicate mechanism of a flintlock as well as to beat a bent trunnion back into shape. He could guess the real reason; Beazley didn't want to spoil the beauty of his instrument by gluing another piece of paper to the wood.

'I have a good piece of ivory in my cabin, Master, it came from a Ceylon elephant's tooth, so it won't yellow like those from the Guinea coast. It's not above an eighth of an inch thick, probably less, and a piece of that with inches and sixteenths scratched into it would make an elegant scale. Mister Angelini has a steady hand, as you know from the landfalls that he's sketched, the surgeon can lend a fine knife, and you have the ink. It could be glued over that paper showing *calm*, *rain* and *wind*, so no more holes are required. You are welcome to it if you wish.'

Beazley's face brightened as Carlisle spoke. A Ceylon ivory scale! That was more in keeping with the dignity of the instrument. He would start a new notebook and transcribe the readings from his deck log and from the weather-glass record into one place. Then he could make real progress.

'Well, back to the here-and-now, Mister Beazley. I see that the quicksilver has risen, it's moving into the region showing calm, as perhaps we should expect in this latitude. So it's predicting that the horse latitudes will live up their name and that we can expect to be becalmed, perhaps later today, is that your understanding?'

Beazley pulled at his chin and looked cautious.

'Perhaps, sir, perhaps, but I don't know that the correlation is as definite as you suggest. But as you say, it's a good point of measurement as we move from one region to another. We can make a similar reading as we pass into the nor'east trades.'

'Then I'll send the ivory to you directly and I'm sure Mister Angelini will understand what needs to be done, when you have explained it to him.'

***

Carlisle could see the torment in Beazley's face every time he came on deck. It was certainly a shocking idea that the sailing master of one of His Majesty's ships-of-the-line should wish to be becalmed when he had a convoy to deliver in wartime, but it was quite clear that he would dearly love to see his instrument prove itself. Beazley paced the deck all through that day as the westerlies hurried the convoy towards Antigua on a beam reach, hideously constant in their speed and direction. Even the sun mocked him as it hid behind the advancing ranks of high, white clouds. The master's mates and the midshipmen skipped out of his way when they saw him coming. They knew the score, and to a man they wished the ship becalmed, if that's what it would take to improve the master's temper.

The dog watches gave no relief and when Beazley eventually turned in, the convoy was still making five knots towards its destination, an outrageous pace for all those fat merchantmen. He dozed fitfully, and consulted his instrument hourly, then half-hourly by the light of the moon that shone through his window. At four bells in the middle watch he fell into an exhausted sleep.

'Mister Beazley, Mister Beazley!'

The midshipman was shaking him urgently, his middle-watch whisper rising almost to a shout as the master resisted all attempts to bring him to consciousness.

'Mister Wishart's compliments, sir, and the wind's backing and dropping. He thought you should know.'

Beazley leapt from his cot. He was a fastidious man and would only appear on deck in his nightshirt for a dire emergency, dismasted on a lee shore or a fire in the sail room perhaps. Nothing less would prevent him donning his coat, not under normal circumstances. But today he almost ran onto the deck, frightening the life out of the ship's boy who was dozing on the gangway.

He should have guessed. The moon's light was altogether too regular, uninterrupted by any passing trade wind clouds, and it shone weakly through a thin, high haze that obscured everything else but the planets and a few of the brightest stars. The sails were already starting to droop, and he felt the first windward lurch as the Atlantic swell took charge of the becalmed ship.

***

Carlisle steadied himself as he brought the midday sun's image down towards the horizon. He read from the quadrant's scale and adjusted mentally for the date: twenty-nine degrees, fifty-eight minutes and thirty seconds northerly latitude. They had hardly moved to the south for the past week and if the master's reckoning was to be believed, they'd drifted somewhat to the east since they had lost the wind, perhaps as much as two hundred miles out into the mid-Atlantic.

The ship's motion was uncomfortable, far worse than beating into a North Sea gale or working down the English Channel with wind against tide. Those motions were at least predictable, but this rolling in an Atlantic swell with never a breath of wind to steady the ship had brought some of the most hardened seamen to the gunwale to feed their dinner to the fish. At least it wasn't hot. Carlisle had never been in the true doldrums; his seafaring hadn't taken him south of the tenth parallel, but he'd heard all about the extreme heat, the dry air, the cloudless skies and the absence of wind. At least in thirty north in May it wasn't unbearable, but in all other respects it was just as the doldrums were described. He could understand how the Spaniards had been forced to throw their horses overboard as they started to run short of drinking water. Men could suffer thirst better than the Spaniard's steeds could, and a horse needed ten times as much fresh water as a man. It must have been a bitter blow, but an easy decision to make as they started calculating their passage time, counting their water butts and praying that the weather would break.

'Well, you have your calm, Mister Beazley, I hope it pleases you.'

The sailing master had become hardened to such accusations over the past few days, but this was the first time his captain had succumbed to the temptation. It was unfair, of course. His instrument could only predict the weather – if indeed it could do that – it could not create it. But he knew the superstitions of his shipmates – he shared most of them – and the old, old fear that the naming of a dread event conjures it into being was perhaps the most deeply ingrained. That would be a real problem if the weather-glass should ever become generally used, the sailing masters would be forever suspect of something not far from witchcraft.

'I recorded a small fall in the glass this morning, sir. That's the first fall since it started rising.'

'Then we can hope,' Carlisle said without conviction.

***

The weather-glass had yet to prove its worth, but still, Carlisle was taking no chances. He'd rowed around the convoy during the first day of calm, before the wind dropped entirely and the merchantmen were still in a reasonably close proximity. It was becoming a lengthy voyage and he had to consider whether all of his charges had enough fresh water to last as far as St. John's, especially those with a cargo of live hogs. He'd suffered a long and uncomfortable day, but he'd felt it his duty to hail each and every vessel. Four weeks of water was the least that any of them reported, and he knew that they could reduce the ration to eke that out to six. There was no immediate problem but that had been a week ago. None of the merchant masters had made the signal to say that they needed his assistance, but still, he didn't want to be surprised by an urgent request for water.

'How long do you think to row around the whole convoy and hail every one of them, Mister Gresham?'

The first lieutenant looked dubiously at the glassy sea. There was barely a ripple upon its face and not enough wind to set a sail, but a long, steady swell was rolling in from the south which would make rowing laborious. The convoy was spread out in two groups over the sullen sea and from van to rear must be about six miles.

'Two crews in the boat, sir, and it'll still take all day. Can I suggest we send the longboat and the yawl? I'll take the longboat and make for the rear and Mister Angelini can take the yawl and cover the closest ones.'

Carlisle laughed and slapped Gresham on the shoulder.

'It's very kind of you, Mister Gresham, but you can look after the ship while I take the further group. I can speak to *Shark* at the same time. I'll have a surgeon's mate in each boat just in case any of them ask for help. Call away the boats now, and perhaps I can be back before the dog watches.'

***

CHAPTER TWENTY-THREE

The Sea Gods

Friday, Fifteenth of May 1761.
Dartmouth, at Sea. Antigua South 250 Leagues.

Carlisle wasn't back before the dog watches; indeed it would have been an impossibility as the smooth sea had given a false impression of the expanse of ocean that the convoy now covered. He was hot and tired and frustrated by his shouted conversations with the merchant masters. They had all seemed to imply that the weather was his fault, one of them had even shaken his fist at the boat but ceased quickly when Souter pushed the tiller over as though to come alongside. The doubled crew of the longboat was substantially larger than the merchantman's crew, and they looked in no mood to take any nonsense.

At least the water was holding out and the hogs weren't dying, and there were no other calls on his services. He'd expected at least one plea for surgeon's mates, but even that wasn't required.

Carlisle climbed wearily over the gunwale and onto the deck. He looked his lieutenant over with disfavour. The yawl had completed its rounds four hours ahead of the longboat and Enrico looked well-fed and relaxed.

'Every one of them has water for at least three weeks, sir. We lanced one boil but that only took a few minutes. They could have done it themselves, but the poor man fancied his chances better with a surgeon's mate.'

'Very well. I expect you've already given a report to Mister Simmonds.'

'I have, sir.'

Enrico was a practiced judge of his captain's moods and was eager to keep the conversation short.

Carlisle looked over the quarterdeck rail to the mainmast where a knife had been plunged deep into the good New

England pine. It hadn't been there when he left; someone had done that while he was away in the boat. It was another old superstation and soon, he knew, the men on deck would start whistling, their last and most dangerous resort to summon up the wind. Everyone knew that a whistled wind couldn't be controlled, and there was no knowing what extremes it could cause. They were too far north for a hurricane at this time of year, perhaps, but when they moved south and May started to give way to June, who knew what would happen. He realised that he was frowning.

Gresham saw what had caught his captain's eye.

'It's Whittle's. I'll have it removed if you wish, sir, but…'

Carlisle knew well enough what that *but* meant. If it was a dangerous measure to thrust a knife into the mainmast, it was doubly dangerous to remove it. The ancient gods of the sea wouldn't be mocked.

***

Whittle's knife stayed in the mainmast, so it wasn't evident whether the sea gods had merely done as they had been requested or whether they indeed resented the implied mockery of the infernal weather-glass. Beazley's instrument may have given the first warning of a change – or it may have been just coincidence – but by the start of the last dog watch it was clear to all hands that change was in the air. The first sign was a thickening of the high haze that had hung over the ship for a week. It thickened and lowered and turned from white to grey. Then the first puffs of wind came from the south – the south, of all places – and *Dartmouth's* rolling was momentarily steadied.

'Make the signal for the convoy to reduce sail, Mister Angelini, and give them a gun in case they're blind. What does your glass say now, Mister Beazley?'

The master scratched his head. He looked puzzled.

'I've never seen it like this before, sir, the quicksilver's dropping like a stone. It's almost off the scale. I'm tempted to take it out of its case and search for a crack in the glass, but I can't see any leakage.'

Carlisle's Duty

'Quicksilver won't seep through the cooper's work, that's a certainty. It's not like water, Mister Beazley, it clings to itself.'

'Indeed, sir. If there's a crack in the glass it could be accumulating in the case and we will never know, not until the glass runs dry. Yet it seems unlikely; I could understand the glass shattering, but not leaking slowly. I haven't sent for the cooper yet, but I'll be damned if I know what it means, unless it's a real blow.'

Carlisle looked up at the slatting sails and away to where the furthest ships of the convoy were barely visible. They still had their sails set in the hope of taking advantage of any puff of wind. Well, if he was any judge, they'd soon have all the wind they wanted, and he didn't need the weather-glass to tell him that.

'We'll furl the courses and take two reefs in the tops'ls, I think, Mister Beazley, and let's get all the stays'ls in, the jib will be quite sufficient forrard.'

Carlisle was watching the southerly horizon. There was something there that didn't look quite right, a line of cloud reaching down to the sea and blotting out the horizon. As he studied it, he realised that it was advancing upon them rapidly. He heard the bosun pipe for all hands on deck; he heard the urgency in the master's voice as he shouted the orders that reduced *Dartmouth's* sail. They could all see what was approaching, and it just felt wrong.

With the sails so reduced, the ship resumed its sickening roll as the wind turned fitful. Nobody was fooled. They could all see that ominous grey line advancing with extraordinary rapidity upon the stationary convoy.

Gresham and the gunner were walking from gun to gun, checking the breechings and tackles as the quarter gunners and gun captains tightened the frapping turns. The bosun was aloft, examining the slings of the yards and the puddening. Everyone seemed to have a job to do and only the most useless of the people were watching idly, gawping uncomprehendingly at their fellows.

'Wait for it…'

Gresham was back on the quarterdeck and all the hands were down from the masts; the grey line was almost upon them. It was an eery situation; the wind had dropped away entirely, not the faintest murmur of a breeze stirred the sails, and yet only a mile away what looked like a furious disturbance of the air was rushing towards them.

'Wait for it…'

A cool breeze drifted in from the south bringing the lightest of refreshing rain, and yet it held an air of menace. The leading steersman wedged his foot against the wooden block in the deck and Eli stowed his seaweed in the binnacle, out of harm's way. The rain turned hard, and the wind heeled the ship to leeward.

'For what we are about to receive…'

Gresham intoned the ancient blasphemy as the squall hit them with unimaginable force. *Dartmouth* heeled so that her gunwales were awash and stayed there, with the force of the wind neither allowing her to right herself nor propelling the great ship forward.

Carlisle and Beazley exchanged glances as they clung to the binnacle.

'Let fly the mizzen sheet,' Beazley shouted.

Slowly, slowly, the bows paid off and *Dartmouth* started to make way. Her gunwales were still awash, but the gun breechings were holding, and nothing had carried away.

'Meet her! Don't let her fall off any further!'

Old Eli was watching the dog-vanes and the main tops'l. He knew that it would be dangerous to let *Dartmouth* pay off the wind so far that it came from her stern. Eight points on the bow would be about right, that would convert some of the wind's fury into forward movement and bring the ship more upright.

The steersmen wrestled the wheel as the rudder strained to bring the ship onto its course.

'West-nor'west,' Beazley shouted as the gunwales at last came clear of the waves.

Carlisle's Duty

Dartmouth was flying across the gale now with a huge white bone in her teeth. Carlisle could see the nearest ship of the convoy, fine on the larboard bow. It was one of the smaller merchantmen and it looked as though it had narrowly escaped being knocked onto its beam ends. Water was gushing in torrents from its scuppers, its mizzen was in tatters, and its bows were turning off the wind, clearly out of control. Carlisle could see the steersman wresting with the wheel and as he watched the master ran to add his weight to try to bring the bows back to the wind.

'Give her a wide berth, Mister Beazley.'

The merchantman was clearly in difficulty, it wasn't inconceivable that she'd founder. In this wind, it meant death for everyone aboard, but there was nothing – absolutely nothing – that *Dartmouth* could do to help. It was a matter of surviving the next hours, then looking to the convoy's safety.

'There goes her fore topmast.'

Gresham clung to a swivel gun crutch as he watched the stricken ship pass by to windward. The loss of the topmast and its sail had done some good, at least. The ship's bows started to swing back into the wind and the risk of an involuntary gybe was over, for the time being.

Dartmouth was reaching fast to the west and as far as Carlisle could see the whole convoy was trying to do the same. He could just make out *Shark's* distinctive masts off in the distance, her main tops'l was shredded but it looked like her spars were intact. That was more than could be said for the merchantmen. Every other one had lost a topmast or a jib-boom, and they made a melancholy sight, each one with its gunwales dipping into the water as they tried desperately to avoid allowing either their bows or stern to pass through the wind.

***

The ferocious squall lasted no more than half an hour, but the gale that followed it blew for a full day, driving the convoy to the west and scattering it so far that when it abated enough for Carlisle to bring *Dartmouth* about, only two ships could be seen on the wide, troubled sea.

'Make the signal for all ships to heave-to, Mister Angelini. These two at least will see it and we'll no doubt pick up a few more as they come down on us.'

The wind had backed a few points and it would have been a hard beat to windward to chase the remains of the convoy. Carlisle paced the poop deck anxiously as he waited to see how many ships were left. He knew that *Dartmouth*, with her greater size, would have travelled further west than the merchantmen, and it could be hours or even days before he saw how many of them had survived the storm.

'Sail ho! Sail to windward, three of them, sir.'

Then there was hope. Carlisle picked up the speaking trumpet. It was Whittle of course at the masthead.

'Is either of them *Shark*?'

'No, sir. They're all three merchantmen. One of them has lost a main topmast.'

'Sing out when you see any more.'

Even with the trumpet it was hard to project his voice that far, but he could see that Whittle had heard him.

One-by-one the rest of the convoy was announced. It was almost dark when at last *Shark* was seen running towards them, close on the heels of the last few merchantmen. Warner had done well to bring the remainder in, shepherding the laggards who otherwise may have been unsure what course to steer. As the sun set over the troubled western horizon, the wind backed sharply and fell to a nothing more than a strong breeze. The blessed nor'east trade wind at last.

***

The convoy made little progress for a week after the storm, what with having to heave-to and lower the boats so that parties of men could be sent to help the merchantmen to repair their damage. Carlisle hadn't seen Gresham, Wishart, Enrico, the bosun or the carpenter for days. They and all the specialists – the armourer, the coopers, the sailmaker and the yeoman of sheets – were scurrying from ship to ship, lending their expert help where it was most needed and distributing water butts to the ships with thirsty hogs. *Dartmouth* had become a ship managed by mates and petty officers and there was a definite youthful feel on the deck, not unlike the sloops that he'd visited during the time that they were blockading the French islands. A master's mate strode the quarterdeck now, his telescope under his arm and a secret grin on his face.

'What of the weather-glass now, Mister Beazley?'

'High and steady, sir. They can say what they like about the storm, but I have some excellent readings.'

'It survived then, and no leaking glass tube, I gather.'

'No leak whatsoever, sir, and the mercury is at a sensible height again. Right in the zone of fair weather.'

Beazley gazed at the sky and the sea in satisfaction. Today was the last day that the repair parties would be away. From tomorrow the merchantmen would have to continue their own repairs because the captain had decreed that they'd stretch away for English Harbour. No more boat work and a full table in the wardroom again. He almost smiled.

***

CHAPTER TWENTY-FOUR

Something's Afoot

Thursday, Fourth of June 1761.
Dartmouth, at Sea. Off English Harbour.

'Captain, sir. The harbour's empty, not a mast nor a hull in sight.'

Carlisle plucked the speaking trumpet from its becket on the binnacle. It snagged; the ring often caught on the hook where it had been bent too far around. For the hundredth time Carlisle swore that he'd have it bent back into shape, but he always forgot. He freed it at the second attempt.

'You're certain, Whittle? Nothing at all?'

The pause before the reply was an eloquent expression of Whittle's exasperation at having his reports questioned. Had it been the second or third lieutenants addressing him he'd have let the silence last five or ten seconds, for a midshipman or master's mate he wouldn't have answered at all, but it being the captain the pause was only momentary; enough and no more.

Whittle had an excellent view from the main t'gallant masthead. He could see over the Halfmoon Battery to Freeman's Bay and right over the two spits of land that guarded the entrance to the harbour.

'I'm certain, sir. The bay and the harbour are deserted.'

'The careening wharf and the King's Yard, what do you see?'

'Just a few people walking around sir, like it was a Sunday or a make-and-mend.'

Carlisle returned the speaking trumpet and stood pondering his next move.

'Something's afoot, sir.'

Gresham was systematically quartering the shoreline with his telescope and the truth of Whittle's report was starting to become evident.

Carlisle's Duty

'Something's certainly afoot, Mister Gresham.'

Carlisle narrowly avoiding the sin of facetiousness. He made a quick sweep with his telescope then closed it with a snap.

'Belay the entry and the anchoring, Mister Beazley, bring the ship to, if you please.'

'Mister Gresham, I'll have the longboat alongside with my own crew in ten minutes. I hope not to be long ashore, but I'll send the longboat back if I'm detained. Meanwhile keep the ship to windward and watch for signals. I do believe the commodore has sailed for St. Lucia or Dominica.'

Carlisle heard the word being passed for his boat's crew. That would cause a scramble as they were spread around the ship at their stations for anchoring and they'd have to run below to their chests and seabags and quickly dress in the blue and white clothing that Carlisle preferred, and indeed had supplied out of his own money. He had no idea who he'd be reporting to, but it was best to be prepared. One thing was certain: Sir James wouldn't willingly allow his squadron to sail, either for exercises or for operations against the enemy, without personally flying his pennant in his flagship, *Dublin*. Not the commander-in-chief then, but whom?

There was need for him to shift his uniform, he was already dressed to meet the commodore and he'd taken particular care this morning, because he was by no means certain how Sir James would take the news that he'd spent three weeks at anchor in Hampton Roads. Oh, he had a good tale to tell backed up by Lord Colville's written request and Fauquier's letter suggesting that he delay for the Richmond cargoes, but the fact remained that he had spent more time with his family than any other captain on the Leeward Islands Squadron had achieved since their ships had sailed from England. He'd been a long time off his rightful station, and if Sir James wanted to make an example of one of his captains, this would be an ideal opportunity.

Of course, the calms in the Horse Latitudes and the ferocious storm hadn't helped. The convoy had limped south, fishing masts and spars, splicing halyards and sheets and mending sails as they went. It was a sorry collection of merchantmen that had continued to St. John's under *Shark's* care as *Dartmouth* hauled her wind to the eastern side of Antigua and so to English Harbour. Letters from commanders-in-chief and lieutenant governors, storms in the Atlantic; it all sounded a bit weak when set against the expectation that he would be back in May.

***

The longboat dropped its sails with Fort Berkley astern and the crew pulled long and dry into the King's yard. It was an eery feeling to see the harbour so empty. This was the chief naval base in the Leeward Islands and there were always a few vessels being repaired or just waiting for orders, even when the battle squadron was at sea. Something momentous must have caused the commodore to sail away with every ship he could muster, and Carlisle had a good idea what that was.

As the longboat rounded the blunt end of the King's Yard, Carlisle could see a black-coated figure standing on the wharf, evidently waiting for him. As he drew closer, he recognised the figure as the commodore's secretary, leaning heavily on two canes, with a pair of fussy servants flitting around him like moths around a candle, ready to catch him if he fell.

'Captain Carlisle, you are come in the nick of time, sir, I believe. Sir James sailed two days ago for Guadeloupe in anticipation of the army's arrival. He was obliged to leave me here. The gout.'

The secretary winced as he touched his leg.

'Good morning, sir.'

Carlisle used the usual greeting as a pause to catch his breath after the climb from the longboat.

'St. Lucia or Dominica?'

The secretary shook his head.

Carlisle's Duty

'Who knows, sir? That's for the council to decide when the army arrives. Their rendezvous is St. Mary's Road in the south of Guadeloupe. It was rumoured that Lord Rollo commands the army, although that's not absolutely clear.'

'Lord Rollo was the last nomination that I heard before I left Virginia, and I'd be surprised if anyone else could have been found since then.'

Now, what was that ghost of a frown on the secretary's face? Had the commodore been speculating that he'd find an excuse to stop at Hampton? It was more than likely, and he'd probably have discussed it with his secretary. He would have to tread carefully.

'I'll leave a copy of my report with you and make a duplicate for the commodore then.'

Well, he may as well get his defence established early.

'You'll find that I was sent to Hampton by Lord Colville and detained there at the request of the lieutenant governor while a convoy was gathered. We suffered a tempest that scattered my ships, but they're all safely brought in, although somewhat ragged, and *Shark* is seeing them safe to St. John's.'

'Sir James will not be surprised to hear it.'

Carlisle bit his tongue. It would do no good to argue with the commander-in-chief's secretary, both the person and the position carried immense power. In any case, that was all the secretary needed to know, the rest was for the commodore's ears, but at least he'd stated his case before rumours started to circulate.

'I trust that Lord Rollo will make the rendezvous; he must have been close to my convoy when the storm appeared.'

'We can only hope, Captain Carlisle. Meanwhile, Sir James left orders for you, sir. You may read them in the master attendant' house, if you please, as I believe they will influence your immediate plans.'

The sealed letter from the commodore was slim, probably only a single sheet. Carlisle leaned over the side of the wharf.

'Wait for me here, Souter.'

He left the secretary hobbling far behind as he strode the fifty yards to the pleasant house at the perimeter of the enclosure, one of a number that had been built for the navy board officers who managed the yard. He was offered a cool drink while he read the letter and he took it with real pleasure, it was a hot day.

The letter had only been sealed; it wasn't wrapped in oilskin nor was it weighted. After the normal salutations, he arrived at the important part:

You are hereby directed and required to complete provisions, wood and water for two months and make all haste to join the squadron under my command in St. Mary's Road at Guadeloupe. If you find that I have sailed from Guadeloupe, you are to enquire ashore to determine my destination and join me there. If you cannot ascertain my destination, you are to search diligently for the squadron at St. Lucia and Dominica before returning to English Harbour to await my return.

Carlisle read the letter again. It was sufficient to a point, but it was silent on the purpose of his re-joining the squadron. Was *Dartmouth* to stand in the line-of-battle? Would he be escorting transports, or bombarding the landing sites?

'I beg your pardon, Captain Carlisle. Sir James asked that I inform you that, notwithstanding the written orders, he expects that you will act as the situation dictates. He is particularly concerned in case a French squadron should arrive when the invasion is in progress. He thought it quite likely, given the season. He expects that if you sight them you will do whatever is required to inform him of their arrival and to prevent their interfering with the invasion or with the transports and supply ships.'

Carlisle stared out of the window at the yard. It was quieter than normal, it appeared that everyone was taking a holiday while the commodore was away, and there was a Sunday feeling about the place, just as Whittle had said. Of course, he understood why Sir James had given the supplementary orders by word of mouth. They were difficult to articulate on paper, particularly in view of the uncertainty of the army's arrival date – of its arrival at all, given the great storm that Carlisle had endured – and of its eventual target. Nevertheless, every captain of a King's ship took a risk when he took any action that deviated from his written orders. Had the commodore lost faith in him? Was he giving him enough rope to hang himself?

'The master attendant will see to any requirements you have before you leave.'

The secretary was in a hurry, probably his gout was causing him excruciating pain. Carlisle had never suffered from it, but he knew of its terrors from other friends and knew that it could lay dormant for hours or days before striking again with no warning. The secretary's face had lost its colour and his legs were trembling.

'Two months? I stored at Hampton from the victualling board agent, and I have enough of all species for two months at least. If that's all, then I'll be away immediately. *Shark* should come in tomorrow after they've seen the convoy into St. John's. Would you give my respects to Captain Warner? He'll be expecting to sail back to Halifax as soon as he's taken on provisions, unless the commodore left any orders to the contrary.'

The secretary shook his head.

'There's no convoy waiting and only the usual dispatches.'

'Then he can sail under my authority. If there's nothing else, I recommend that you rest your legs, sir, and I'll be away for Guadeloupe.'

***

CHAPTER TWENTY-FIVE

A Tactical Decision

Friday, Fifth of June 1761.
Dartmouth, at Sea. La Désirade SW 5 Leagues.

Dartmouth was beating to windward in the teeth of a strong easterly, heeling far over to starboard as she made her offing. This was always the problem with a passage from English Harbour to the south side of Guadeloupe, Carlisle reflected, at some point he would be headed by the wind. He could choose to endure that early in the passage by making a long board out into the Atlantic, or he could postpone the pain by reaching down the long leeward side of the island before beating up inside the Saintes. He'd chosen the former because a French squadron from Brest or one of the other Atlantic ports, or even from the Mediterranean would be to windward of Guadeloupe, not to leeward. In any case he'd always had this feeling that unpleasantness shouldn't be deferred.

Beazley had just finished reckoning the latitude from the noon sight.

'We can put her before the wind at the end of the afternoon watch, sir.'

'You're sure we'll weather La Désirade, Master?'

'I'm certain, sir. We'll pass no closer than four leagues. In any case we'll see it soon.'

In which event, it had been worth making that very long board when they left English Harbour. It meant that they hadn't been at risk of being set down onto La Désirade, and they wouldn't have to tack between the islands at night. As it was, they could heave-to off the north side of Marie Gallant and reach into St. Mary's Road in the first light of dawn. But what would he find there? He'd seen nothing of the ships carrying Lord Rollo's army south; had they arrived before him, or were they limping along somewhere to the north, licking their wounds after the storm? Of course, they may have had fair winds the whole way; sometimes storms such as that could be very localised. Well, he'd find out tomorrow, perhaps.

'Land ho! Land on the starboard bow!'

Carlisle picked up his telescope, but he could see nothing yet. It must be La Désirade, unless the master's reckoning was sadly awry. Beazley was so confident that he didn't even turn to look in that direction; he was busy transcribing weather reports from the deck log to his notebook.

'The quicksilver's steady, sir. Has been all day.'

Carlisle had noticed that the master was much more forward in offering the readings from the weather-glass since the storm. Perhaps he considered it not exactly vindicated but at least no longer classed among the curiosities and toys that were so often sold as navigational instruments. He had sat patiently last evening as the master had gone through the readings, comparing them to the weather that they'd experienced. He had to admit that the instrument appeared – and he wouldn't put it any stronger than that – to be correct more than half the time. That was nothing to set against the generations of experience that made up the weather-divining resources that the navy now used, but it was a start. If it did prove to be able to predict wind and rain and calms, then it would be a useful addition. The master was less sceptical, and all his spare time was taken up with his weather-glass. He'd filled two notebooks already with long columns of figures where he tried different ways of correlating the quicksilver against the observed weather. Well, *Dartmouth* had many more sea days to come, and unless this war came to an unexpected end, Beazley would run out of paper and ink long before he was cast ashore.

***

'We can wear ship at the change of the watch, sir, and reduce sail, if you please.'

Carlisle cast a quick glance around the horizon. La

Désirade was out of sight from the deck and there was nothing to suggest the presence of the great chain of islands that lay to leeward. Tomorrow morning they would find the squadron, unless they had already sailed for whichever island had been selected for conquest, and he'd be under the eye of the commander-in-chief again. He had only hours of freedom from authority left.

'Very well, Mister Beazley. Call the watch a quarter hour early.'

That would even out the pain between the watches. Wearing ship and shortening sail wouldn't take more than half an hour in these conditions.

Carlisle walked up the ladder to the poop deck to enjoy the fresh breeze.

'Sail ho! Sail two points abaft the larboard beam!'

Carlisle recognised Whittle's voice as it came from far overhead. He must have relieved the lookout who had spotted the island. He leaned over the poop deck rail.

'My telescope, if you please.'

It could be almost anything: a British convoy bound for Jamaica, one of the squadron's frigates keeping watch, a lost troop transport even. Or it could be a French man-o'-war, or the scouting frigate for a squadron, as Sir James had feared.

The midshipman who brought his telescope had thoughtfully brought the spare speaking trumpet. Carlisle took it from him and angled it upwards to the main topmast head.

'What do you make of it, Whittle?'

'It's hard to say, sir. Could be a frigate's t'gallants. Same course as us, I think.'

A frigate to windward of the islands and steering south, that was strange in itself. The squadron's cruisers should be further out into the Atlantic or steering for Guadeloupe if they were hurrying back to report. He peered through the telescope but of course saw nothing, the strange sail would be below the horizon from the deck. This sighting was hard to explain away; there were few innocent explanations for a ship to be at that point in the ocean, steering that course.

'Mister Beazley, hold our course for the time being. Is the first lieutenant there?'

Gresham was just coming on deck, buttoning up his waistcoat as he took the steps of the ladder two-at-a-time.

'Mister Gresham. We'll clear for action once both watches are on deck.'

Gresham grinned and rubbed his hands.

'Aye-aye sir. It's the French then?'

'Perhaps, Mister Gresham, perhaps, but whatever it is he's to windward and we should be ready.'

Carlisle took a few turns to the taffrail and back before the next hail.

'Deck there. It's a frigate for sure, and she has a cutter in company. They look like ours, sir.'

Now that was interesting. Were they in contact with an enemy? Carlisle brought the chart of the Leeward Islands to mind. If a French ship was shaping a course to Martinique, to Fort Royal, then she could indeed by a few miles to windward of the frigate.

'Bear up, Mister Beazley, full and by. Let's try to cut off that frigate and schooner. Mister Torrance, take the deck telescope and run up to the masthead. Let me know what you make of them.'

Carlisle looked down at the deck that was now crowded with men. He could see the eager faces. After months and months of dull cruising and escorting, the prospect of action against the enemy was exhilarating.

***

'It's *Spey*, sir, I saw her in English Harbour last year, thirty-two guns, sir. And the cutter's *Mosquito*, I'm almost sure.'

Torrance was breathing heavily from running back down the ratlines and his report came in spasmodic gasps.

'Then that's Frederick Percival,' said Gresham, 'we were shipmates in the last war. He wasn't posted until 'fifty-eight.

Ah, there she is.'

The frigate's tops'ls had just appeared over the horizon. Carlisle took a quick look through the telescope and was just in time to see her bear away and steer sou'west. That made more sense, she was steering for the north of Dominica.

'The frigate's signalling, sir, red square flag at the main topmast head.'

Carlisle could almost feel the excitement that rippled across the deck. A red square at the main; either Clinton, the only admiral of the red, was on board *Spey*, which was ridiculous as he hadn't served at sea since the last war and had effectively retired, or Percival was ordering him to engage the enemy! But Percival was junior to Carlisle. More likely he was trying to say that the enemy was in sight. Only flagships carried a full complement of signalling flags and all others had to make do with a limited set. Percival was trying his best to convey his meaning within the constraints of the signalling system.

Boom!

The sound of *Spey's* signal gun came faintly down to them, borne on the easterly wind.

'She's letting her t'gallants fly, sir.'

Whittle was still at his post, and at present he was the eyes of the ship.

'Beat to quarters, Mister Gresham.'

How many times had he heard that thrilling sound? The beat of the drum, the shouts of the petty officers as the men hurried to their stations, the deep, deep sound of the gun trucks on the wooden decks. And it gave him a few minutes of blessed peace from interruptions as all his officers were involved in bringing the ship to its peak of readiness.

If Percival was running before the enemy, then it certainly wouldn't be a single French frigate. He'd have thrown his ship into the fight long ago. It could of course be a pair of frigates, or it could be a French convoy or a battle squadron. Two frigates seemed unlikely, the French navy was short of ships, and it was difficult to imagine a task that required two of its precious cruisers. A convoy then? It must be well known that Martinique, St. Lucia and Dominica were on Pitt's list for invasion, and a convoy to bring back the sugar crop ran the risk of being overwhelmed by greater events. Then the most likely explanation was a squadron of men-o'-war, sent out to protect France's dwindling footholds in the West Indies. But how many? It would have to be a substantial squadron, perhaps four or more.

'The ship's cleared for action and the men are at their quarters, sir'

'Very well, Mister Gresham.'

'*Spey's* signalling, sir,' shouted Young. 'It's one of the commodore's swallowtail signals. Number six.'

Carlisle was starting to get a feel for Percival; he was striving to make himself understood. Six ships, then a battle squadron, not a convoy. Should he show *Dartmouth* to the enemy, or should he keep himself hidden? What would the French commander make of a single fourth rate appearing between him and his objective? It wasn't like the French navy to deploy its ships away without specific orders and he knew from painful experience that commanders of French squadrons weren't easily distracted. Whether his opponent's orders were to disrupt the invasion or whether there was some other objective, he wouldn't be scared away by *Dartmouth*. And Carlisle desperately wanted to see for himself, before he made his next decision.

'Close *Spey* within hailing distance, Mister Beazley.'

Things were happening fast now. *Spey* and *Mosquito* maintained their course while *Dartmouth* thrashed up to windward to meet them.

'Deck there. Tops'ls in sight, beyond the frigate and the cutter. Two of the line I reckon.'

Carlisle forced himself to wait for another report. A few minutes later Torrance hailed again.

'I can see more now, sir. Maybe five or six, directly astern of the frigate. They're all ships-of-the line sir, not a frigate among them.'

Then it was clear. A French squadron of six ships-of-the-line couldn't defeat the combination of the Leeward Islands Squadron and whatever ships Colville had sent down with the army, but if it was well handled it could cause enough damage to postpone or cancel the landings. Then again, it wasn't at all certain that Lord Rollo had arrived, in which case Douglas had only a bare superiority over the French. Then he had two tasks: the first and by far the most important was to tell Sir James of the approaching menace, and *Mosquito* would be perfectly adequate for that. Then he must do whatever he could to disrupt the French plans.

***

Dartmouth came about handily so that when the manoeuvre was complete, he was two cables off *Spey's* beam. He could see that *Spey*, the faster ship, was angling in to hailing distance. Slowly and with great care the two ships came closer and closer. This was always a dangerous manoeuvre at sea, and with the wind astern and the ships tending to yaw as the swell passed diagonally under their keels, it was more perilous than normal. Carlisle could see Percival standing atop the quarterdeck gunwale, his arm hooked through the aftermost mizzen shroud and a speaking trumpet in his other hand..

'I sighted them this morning, sir. Six of the line, two seventy-fours, three sixty-fours, I think, and a fifty. They're steering for the Saintes Passage.'

It could be Jamaica then, but wouldn't they have taken the Mona Passage and stayed well clear of the Leeward Islands? No, it had to be Guadeloupe. When they sighted Marie Galante, they'd put the wind on their starboard quarter and steer for the St. Mary's Road. If an invasion of the French islands was contemplated then they could bet that the squadron and the army would rendezvous in that wide, sheltered anchorage.

Carlisle took a deep breath and shouted back to the frigate.

'I'll send *Mosquito* to warn the commodore. Follow my movements.'

'Will you engage them?'

Now, that was the question. They couldn't possibly defeat such a strong force, just one of those seventy-fours should be enough to deal with *Dartmouth* and any one of them would make short work of *Spey*. No, that would achieve nothing useful. There was a better way, but he didn't want to reveal his plan in case he should have to change it. He was the senior officer present and Percival was obliged to follow his orders.

'I hope so…'

Dartmouth rose on the swell a few seconds ahead of *Spey* and the ships yawed dangerously close to each other. Carlisle waved to Percival to open the distance. The conversation was over.

Mosquito was easier. The little cutter could sit easily under *Dartmouth's* lee quarter and could come much closer than the big frigate.

'Mister Pence. Make all sail for St. Mary's Road. I hope you'll find the commodore there. Tell him the situation, six of the line steering for the Saintes Passage or for Guadeloupe. I will try to delay them. If the commodore isn't there, make for Dominica, Martinique and St. Lucia until you find him.'

Pence had no questions. He could see the urgency of the matter and he merely raised his hand as he shouted his wishes for *Dartmouth's* success. The cutter hauled its wind and steered for St. Mary's Road.

Carlisle took a look astern. The French had gained on him while he'd been issuing his orders; now they were nearly hull-up to windward. He could see the massive masts of two seventy-fours and the slender spars of smaller ships behind them. They looked magnificent with their sails spread to the steady trade wind. Not for the first time, he was awed by the breath-taking beauty of the French-built third rates.

'Mister Beazley. Bring the ship before the wind, we'll make a board to the north.'

***

It would be a short board and the timing was critical if he wanted to execute his plan. There was no question of throwing *Dartmouth* and *Spey* in front of the oncoming French squadron, they'd be brushed aside before they had a chance of inflicting any serious damage. The French would hardly miss a minute in their run to Guadeloupe. Carlisle had chosen to tack to the north in an attempt to draw the French away from their presumed destination. Of course there was always a possibility that the army had already sailed for its destination – whichever of the French islands had been chosen – but he thought it unlikely.

'Make the signal for line of battle, Mister Young.'

Percival had shown that he could use the limited signals that were available, so he should be able to understand his leader's intention. Sure enough, *Spey* fell off the wind a little to make *Dartmouth's* wake.

There was no reaction from the French squadron, but then he hadn't expected any. Whatever orders they'd been given almost certainly didn't include freelance engagement of stray British cruisers. If they'd been ordered to look for the British invasion force, then that's what they would do, and nothing would distract them.

Carlisle could see the French squadron clearly now. They were sailing in two columns about a mile apart and the lead ship in the starboard columns was flying a commodore's pennant. There was just the slightest extra gap between the centre and the rear, and he was pleased to see that the final two ships were a sixty-four and a fifty; that would make his plan less perilous.

'Mister Beazley. I want to tack so as to pass ahead of the rear two and break their formation.'

That would test the French commander's resolve. Would he press on and leave his rear two ships to fend for themselves? Simple arithmetic would say that a sixty-four and a fifty could make short work of a fifty and a thirty-two, but the French had learned the hard way that mathematics didn't always determine the outcome of a sea fight.

***

Beazley was watching the advancing Frenchmen with a ferocious concentration. Just a minute late in tacking and the plan would fail entirely. He took a bearing of the rear ship of the enemy's starboard column and did some rapid mental calculations.

'We should tack when he's just a point ahead of the beam, sir.'

'Very well, Mister Beazley.'

Carlisle looked astern. *Spey* was following in his wake at two cables. If this worked correctly, they'd be able to pass close ahead of the rear two enemy ships, as he planned. He'd have to leave it up to Percival then. He'd met him once, and he seemed competent enough, but he needed more than competence today, he needed a fighting spirit to match.

'Five minutes, sir.'

'Mister Young, hoist *tack in succession*…'

That at least was one order that could be made by a single flag.

'… and when you've done that, Mister Young, hoist the red square at the main topmast head.'

Engage the enemy.

It was the first time he'd ever hoisted that flag in earnest, the first time he'd had a subordinate ship under his command when he went into action.

'Carry on when you are ready, Mister Beazley.'

***

CHAPTER TWENTY-SIX

Breaking the Line

Friday, Fifth of June 1761.
Dartmouth, at Sea. La Désirade SW 6 Leagues.

'Helm's a-lee, sir.'

Eli stood with his feet wide apart, his whole being concentrating on the wind, the compass and the ship's wheel. He could be said to be a part of the ship at that moment, an indispensable link that connected the sailing master's orders to the man at the wheel, and thence to the rudder. And yet he was no mere contraption of wood and rope, he was an intelligent link, ready to advise and modify, and to take over if Beazley should fall.

The great two decker started to turn into the wind. At first the bows moved swiftly to starboard, then slowed as the way started to come off the ship.

Beazley watched the luffs of the sails and the dog-vanes as closely as Eli, waiting for the right moment.

'Up tacks and sheets.'

The bows were right into the eye of the wind now.

'Mains'l haul.'

This was the most dangerous moment and there was always a chance that the ship would stick in irons, her head seeking the wind, unable to pay off in either direction. But *Dartmouth* responded sweetly and with only the slightest hint of balking – just enough to assert her right to do so – her bows came through the wind and started to pay off on the larboard tack.

'Let go and haul. Helm a-lee, meet her.'

Dartmouth turned from a sluggish lumpen mass back into a fleet-footed machine of war. The sails filled, the tacks and sheets were belayed and coiled and suddenly the French squadron filled the ocean ahead. It was a fearsome sight and Carlisle knew that if he had guessed wrongly – if the French commander was in no hurry and prepared to expend a few hours in fighting – then his fine ship and Percival's *Spey* would inevitably be lost. It was a bad moment, but then Carlisle remembered that they'd have seen *Mosquito* squaring away for Guadeloupe. They could be sure that the little cutter would bring the Leeward Islands Squadron upon them, and that was most certainly not countenanced in the mission that had been conceived in Versailles. He could see that the gap between the centre and the rear of the enemy was somewhat larger than he'd thought; that was all to the good.

'What's his bearing doing, Mister Beazley?'

The master squinted along the compass at the fifty-gun ship at the rear of the starboard column.

'Drawing slowly left, sir. We'll pass a cable ahead.'

Carlisle nodded.

'I'll want to be closer than that, but this will do for now.'

He looked up at the blue sky and the high, white trade wind clouds. There was not the slightest chance of a change before sunset.

'It'll be the larboard battery, Mister Gresham.'

'Larboard battery, aye-aye sir.'

The guns were already run out and the crews looked eager to be started. In this weather they were mostly stripped to the waist. The more prudent of them had wrapped their neckerchiefs around their ears against the noise and he could see that they were all wearing shoes. That was good. Too many men had been immobilised by injuries to the feet that would have been prevented by a good layer of neat's leather, but the men would persist in going into action barefoot, if not corrected.

God, they were coming upon the enemy fast. This was the moment that he hated. He could train his men, he could plan his tactics, he could take every precaution to ensure success but, as he well knew, no plan ever survived contact with the enemy. Once the guns started roaring he'd be improvising.

A quick glance to starboard showed that the leading four ships were ignoring him entirely. He was just within long cannon shot of the two sixty-fours but never a ball came his way. It was the very perfection of the French discipline of the mission: they never put to sea without some good cause, and they rarely deviated from their orders. Sometimes Anson must wish his own admirals would have such self-restraint.

'Can you luff a little, Mister Beazley?'

'Aye, sir, I can.'

He jerked his head at Eli who gave the steersman a nudge. Beazley watched the luff of the mainsail twitch in protest as *Dartmouth's* bows inched into the wind.

'Steady. Thus and no higher.'

Dartmouth eased into her new course with her luffs shivering in dissent. It wouldn't do for any great length of time, and it imperceptibly slowed the ship's pace, but it achieved its objective. Now they'd pass within musket range of the fifty-gun ship.

'Stand by Mister Gresham. Fire when you are ready.'

He realised that he was shouting unnecessarily.

The enemy fourth rate loomed large on the larboard bow. They were coming on without regard for *Dartmouth's* first broadside. This must be the junior captain, not confident in his authority to manoeuvre when in line of battle.

'Fire!'

Gresham's shout was drowned by the immediate roar of the larboard battery. The gunners couldn't miss and the enemy – for now – couldn't reply. It would have been a decisive broadside if there had been only one French ship, but *Dartmouth* had other prey.

Carlisle took a moment to look for damage on the first enemy. The beakhead was shattered, the headrail was splintered and there were shot holes in the jib and foresail, but there was nothing serious, no fore topmast shot away, no gaping holes between wind and water. What he couldn't see was the damage that his broadside would undoubtedly have done on the Frenchman's gundeck, as the twenty-four pound balls hurtled from forward to aft. Yet the Frenchman ploughed on with an almost regal disregard for his enemies. Well, he'd have to leave her to Percival while he took on the sixty-four.

***

'She's coming off the wind, sir,' said Beazley, 'turning towards us.'

Carlisle could see that for himself. The captain of the sixty-four had seen what had happened to his consort and was determined to meet the threat on his own terms, mission or no mission.

'Larboard battery ready, sir.'

'This will be longer range, Mister Gresham.'

'Fire when your guns point, men,' Gresham shouted.

Dartmouth and the third rate were going to pass on opposite tacks. It was the greatest test of gunnery, with the point of aim shifting rapidly from ahead to astern. The crews couldn't possibly train their guns fast enough to keep pace, so they had to fix them dead abeam and fire at the right instant. This was the gun captains' moment.

The larboard side guns fired raggedly as their captains fancied that they were pointing correctly. Some shots went high into the sails and rigging while others struck the hull or ricocheted off the sea. It was just a matter of luck if the ship should be at the right point of its pitch and roll when the target came into view, and when the slow match was thrust into the priming pan.

The French were firing now, and Carlisle felt a concussion as a shot embedded itself in the mainmast. A foot lower and it would have utterly destroyed one of the guns and all its crew. But the French had the same problem with aiming as *Dartmouth* did and with their predilection for aiming high, a far greater proportion of their shot missed anything vital.

The two ships drew apart. Carlisle could spare a glance

for *Spey* and the fifty-gun ship. Percival had put his ship alongside the enemy, and they were battering away at each other under a rising pall of smoke. That was no good, it would take a miracle for a thirty-gun frigate to prevail against a fifty-gun ship in the open ocean, but there was nothing he could do to help, not yet.

'Wear ship, Mister Beazley.'

The sailing master gave him a short questioning look. The guns had ceased for a moment as the French ship was out of range. Carlisle found that he could still think and speak rationally.

'We must keep to leeward of him, to stop him joining the others.'

Beazley nodded and started shouting the orders.

That was the problem with engaging the enemy on opposite tacks, it was rare that a ship could fire more than one ball from each gun before the range opened. But the Frenchman had made an error in bearing away to the north, and now *Dartmouth* could stay between him and his squadron.

Dartmouth started the laborious process of wearing. The sail trimmers were called from the guns and every spare man hauled on a sheet or tack so that the guns could continue to be loaded.

Ah. As he expected, the sixty-four was trying to work around *Dartmouth's* bow and escape to the west. If he'd tacked instead of wearing his enemy would be to leeward of him by now and running fast to join the other four. Now, if the Frenchman bore away to larboard he'd run right into *Dartmouth*, and if he hauled his wind he'd be heading back out into the Atlantic. Got him!

These Frenchmen were all of a single mind, Carlisle thought. This one wanted nothing but to rejoin the squadron. They must have discussed this in the quiet moments during their long passage from Brest or La Rochelle. The commodore would have impressed on them the need to reach Guadeloupe or Martinique intact. It was

Carlisle's Duty

inglorious but then the depleted French navy couldn't afford any heroic gestures. Well, in that case he knew what he should do. He'd test their resolve.

'Put me alongside her, Mister Beazley. Starboard battery, Mister Gresham.'

The word passed along the deck and the men raised a huge cheer.

Beazley brought *Dartmouth* round in a great circle until she was in danger of luffing again, forcing the Frenchman away to the north. They were passing astern of the fifty-gun ship and *Spey*, who were now locked into a broadside match, enveloped in a cloud of their own powder smoke.

'Mister Gresham. Have a boarding party prepared. Mister Pontneuf, your marines will lead.'

***

Gresham's starboard broadside was firing now. The sound of the guns was shattering, and Carlisle found it hard to think. *Dartmouth* was taking punishment and there were dead and dying men beside an overturned gun on the upper deck. But this was the kind of gunnery that his men excelled at. There was no need for accurate training or elevation, the French sixty-four was so close that every shot found its mark. And his men were firing three broadsides for every two of the enemy's. That would even out the imbalance in number and calibre of guns, but it still left the outcome to the roll of a dice.

This was where the superiority of Anson's strategy showed. While the French only sent their ships to sea on specified missions, the British navy were at sea almost regardless of need. Those long months and years on blockade duty and cruising against enemy privateers bore fruit in the consummate seamanship and rapid gunnery that allowed a British fifty-gun ship to tackle a French sixty-four. There was another benefit to keeping the sea: *Dartmouth's* crew had a deep-rooted belief in their superiority over any foreign crew, and Carlisle was about to bring that into play.

'Boarding party's ready, sir.'

Gresham held his drawn sword in his massive fist. His face was already stained by powder smoke and there was a spatter of blood on his shirt.

'Your marines, Mister Pontneuf?'

Pontneuf gave an elegant salute with his sword.

'Ready, sir. I'll join my men if I may.'

Carlisle looked along the deck. The marines were gathered on the fo'c'sle. He could see Sergeant Wilson, his halberd in hand, as he kept them in line even though they were crouching below the level of the gunwale.

Gresham had completely abandoned the larboard battery to provide enough men for the starboard and still have a sizeable force to board the enemy. As soon as the boarders were away the gun crews would follow them whatever Carlisle said. This was the optimum moment. In half an hour his crew would be depleted by injury, and fatigue would set in. If he boarded in the next fifteen minutes, he knew that nothing could stop him.

'Bring her alongside, Mister Beazley.'

The sailing master nodded to Eli who gave a gruff order to the steersman. *Dartmouth's* bow swung steadily to starboard and the gap between the two ships narrowed foot by foot.

The seamen of the boarding party were mustered on the poop deck and the quarterdeck. Carlisle could see a few nervous faces, but most of them looked grimly determined and a few were flinging coarse jests at each other, bolstering their courage for what was to come.

Carlisle winced and felt his bones grind against each other as Gresham shook his hand, then the first lieutenant was gone up the poop deck ladder, shouting at his men to keep their heads down.

***

CHAPTER TWENTY-SEVEN

Cry 'Havoc'

Friday, Fifth of June 1761.
Dartmouth, at Sea. La Désirade SW 6 Leagues.

Closer and closer. The French had realised what *Dartmouth* intended and they were mustering to repel boarders, but the smoke was hindering them. They couldn't see where the attack would be launched, so they were spreading their men across the whole of the upper deck, the fo'c'sle, the quarterdeck and the poop deck. He could see them peering through the boarding nets.

Carlisle blew his whistle. The last of the upper deck guns fired and now he could see the crews reloading. *Dartmouth* edged towards the Frenchman in silence, reserving her fire for the final few yards.

The French were still firing, and he saw one shot plough into a gun carriage, bringing down two men.

Thirty yards, twenty yards. *Dartmouth* rose to the Atlantic swell and suddenly they were alongside. The effect of his next blow on the whistle was like the blast of the trumpets before the walls of Jericho. *Dartmouth's* broadside smashed into her opponent at short range. The lower deck guns fired ball, but every other gun was loaded with grape or canister. They cut massive holes in the boarding nets and brought down defenders in great swathes across their opponent's deck. The swivel guns added their weight from the gunwales and from the tops a rain of grenades fell among the Frenchmen waiting to repel the attack. Grapnels flew into the enemy's rigging and onto the gunwales and far aloft a few gallant topmen ran out on the yards to firmly bind the two ships together.

Carlisle had long ago given up the idea of personally leading his men in boarding. It would have been a fine, heroic gesture, but he knew that he couldn't match the sheer savagery of the likes of Sergeant Wilson and that great brute of a Scots bosun's mate who was pushing his fellows aside in his eagerness to get to grips with the enemy. He would only have hindered them, and he could rely on Gresham and Pontneuf to lead the twin attacks.

The bows touched a few seconds before any other part of the ship, and the marines were first across. He saw Pontneuf scramble across the cathead and through one gap in the netting while Wilson pushed Kemp aside to be first through another. Planks were being thrown across to bridge the gap left by the tumble-home. The bosun's mate swung an axe that was normally used to cut cable; it made short work of boarding netting, and in seconds there were enough holes for the marines to pour through. Bayonets were flashing on the French fo'c'sle before the first of the seamen found their way across.

Carlisle loosened his sword in its scabbard. There were no orders to give. Beazley and Eli knew how to handle the ship, while the boarding parties were beyond his control. He could see the gun crews grabbing whatever weapons were to hand: cutlasses, boarding axes, hand spikes, even rammers and worms, and leaping onto the gunwale. Enrico was at their head, looking cool and collected, every inch the Sardinian nobleman as they fought their way through the opposing gun ports. A stream of men came up from the lower deck, led by Wishart, who had lost his hat, screaming encouragement.

Carlisle drew his sword and threw himself into the jostling mob.

***

At the quarterdeck there was less of a gap between the two gunwales, and Carlisle jumped rather than wait for a space on the planks. He fell forward against the boarding netting, his chest and stomach exposed to any thrusting bayonet or pike, but the first few seamen had cleared a wide space almost to the ship's wheel. There was a solid mass of Frenchmen defending this, the centre of command, with what looked like the opposing captain waving his sword and shouting encouragement. Blue coated French marines fired a volley and a man dropped to the deck. On his left Gresham was leading a rush to the wheel, hacking and slashing at the mass of men before him, while more and more Frenchmen ran onto the deck.

This was the critical moment. Those Frenchmen weren't properly armed and for a few minutes he had the advantage. Carlisle threw himself forward, cutting his way through to the French Captain who was likewise trying to push his way to the front to meet him. In a moment of sheer madness, Carlisle thrust the last of the men aside and advanced to meet his French opponent. Time seemed to stand still, and Carlisle noticed that the man was an accomplished swordsman – he could see by the way that he took his stance – probably far better than Carlisle. He'd heard of these moments, when the madness of the boarding was suspended while the opposing captains circled and lunged as though in a personal duel. He was no mean swordsman himself, but he could see that the French captain outclassed him. Every movement of his feet, the way he held his body in perfect balance, spoke of a man who had been schooled in fencing. This wasn't going to be easy, but there was no question of backing down.

Carlisle stepped forward and lunged, the French captain danced sideways and easily avoided his sword, then came the lightning riposte and Carlisle felt the blade rake across his ribs.

This couldn't last long. He recovered and raised his sword tip to stake everything on a wild, unscientific charge. Then he felt a wind across his head and a dark shape flashed across his vision, smashing into the French captain and bringing him to the deck, with his sword spinning away towards the binnacle. The bosun's mate reached forward to retrieve the massive oak rammer that he had used as a spear.

'He'll no' be botherin' ye again, Cap'n.'

***

All along the deck the Frenchmen were falling, turning away, running from the determined, savage onslaught. The wheel was abandoned and on the fo'c'sle the red coats of the marines outnumbered the Frenchmen. Carlisle looked around for someone in charge. The French captain was moaning on the deck with a servant leaning over him. He looked down at the slash across his own waistcoat. It was bleeding but not badly, and the pain hadn't come yet. He remembered vividly that sensation as the Frenchman's sword raked across each rib, but it didn't feel as though any had been broken.

'Thank you, McAllister, that could have gone badly for me.'

He picked up his opponent's discarded sword and walked slowly and deliberately up to the poop deck, fighting the urge to clutch his wounded chest. He was quite calm now and most of the fighting had stopped. If nobody would come forward to surrender and strike the colours, he'd do it himself. The poop deck had been cleared of the enemy, except for a wounded man who clutched his arm as a British seaman stood menacingly over him. A body was slumped against the flag locker, with a massive hole in its chest, a grapeshot most likely.

Carlisle pushed the bloody remains aside to reach the ensign staff. It was a massive affair and the Frenchman had flown his largest national flag for the occasion, a vast white banner dotted with golden fleur-de-lis; it must have cost a small fortune. He fumbled with the figure-of-eight turns that secured the halliard, but they'd been pulled tight by whoever had hoisted it. He tried again, but the pain in his chest was making his hand tremble. The moment deserved at least one heroic gesture; he tested the edge of the Frenchman's sword and with two slashes, the white of Bourbon dropped from the staff. The strong following breeze caught it and it fell inboard of the taffrail to cover the unknown body.

***

Carlisle was conscious of the cheering on the deck below, but he had no time for that.

'First Lieutenant!' he bellowed, and he almost fell with the pain that it caused him.

Souter came bounding up the steps.

'It's all over on the deck, sir. Mister Gresham's forrard, I've sent a runner for him. Are you hurt, sir?' he asked, suddenly seeing the blood seeping through his captain's hand where it clutched his chest.

'Don't worry about that, Souter. What's happening to *Spey*?'

Souter jumped onto the mizzen shrouds and tried to peer through the powder smoke.

'They're at it hammer and tongs, sir, Their ensigns are still flying but it looks like *Spey's* main yard's been shot through in the slings.'

'A famous victory, sir, my congratulations.'

Gresham's coat was torn, his hat had long since gone and every inch of his skin was stained with powder smoke, yet his broad white smile spoke volumes. A fourth rate had taken an enemy third rate, a famous victory for sure.

'Indeed, Mister Gresham, indeed. But now we have to concern ourselves with *Spey*. Get the Frenchmen below and batten the hatches. Keep all the marines and forty seamen and make for St. Mary's Road. Send all the others back to *Dartmouth*. I want to be away in five minutes.'

***

Ah, he could see better now that the French sixty-four had dropped astern. The fifty-gun ship and the British frigate were still exchanging broadsides, about half a cable apart. They both had their tops'ls set and they'd drawn ahead of *Dartmouth* and her opponent.

'Put me alongside her, Mister Beazley. I don't intend to board; we'll just batter her into submission.'

Another cheer. They'd been happy enough tackling a sixty-four, but they knew that *Spey* would inevitably be beaten by her larger opponent. Now it would be two against one, and they liked those odds.

'Starboard battery ready, sir,' said Wishart, delighted to be talking the role of second-in-command at such a historic moment.

'The other four are almost hull-down now, sir.'

Enrico looked as though he'd just been for a morning stroll. He was untouched by the battle, and alone among the officers who had boarded the enemy, his hat was still perched on his head. Untouched, but Carlisle had seen with his own eyes how the Sardinian lieutenant had fought his way onto the enemy's deck.

A surgeon's mate had bound his chest as he stood on the quarterdeck. He'd pulled the bandages so tight that he could only take shallow breaths and it was difficult to raise his arms far enough to steady the telescope. Nevertheless, he could see the four ships stretching away to leeward, showing the most callous disregard for the two they had left behind. Callous, certainly, but Carlisle could understand their reasoning. That commodore had a mission to perform, and it would be compromised if he tangled with even such a weak force as a fifty-gun ship and a frigate when he was only hours away from his objective. He'd have been confident, in any case, that his two ships-of-the-line could deal with a British fourth rate and a frigate, and by the time he realised his mistake his squadron was too far to leeward to intervene. By the time that Carlisle slashed the halyard on the Bourbon flag, it would have taken the remainder of the French squadron three or four hours to beat back up to them. No, that commodore had made his decision before ever a shot was fired and the steady trade wind made it impossible for him to change his mind.

'There goes *Spey's* fore topmast, sir… and his mizzen.'

The frigate's hull was hidden behind the French fourth rate, but its masts told their own story. Percival must have taken a tremendous battering from those twenty-four pounders, and it appeared that early in the engagement he'd lost the ability to manoeuvre. He could board, but the disparity in numbers made that a very risky affair. Left to themselves there was only one way that it would end.

'Stand by Mister Wishart.'

Enrico ran below to the lower gun deck. Their roles had been exchanged now that Wishart had taken on Gresham's position.

The Frenchman must have seen his consort's colours struck and he'd seen *Dartmouth* break away and come surging down towards him. He should have set all sail and left the frigate alone, but the relative positions of the two ships' masts hadn't changed.

'*Spey's* grappled the Frenchman,' shouted Whittle who had run back to the masthead as soon as *Dartmouth* set sail. 'They're trying to board.'

Ah, Percival had pinned his opponent.

'Then put me alongside, Mister Beazley, as fast as you can.'

Carlisle abandoned his plan to stand off and batter the French fourth rate into submission; there was no time for that now that *Spey* was in such deadly danger.

'One broadside, sir?'

'I think not, Mister Wishart, there'll be too many of our friends on her deck. Bring all the gun crews up and we'll board her.'

***

Dartmouth came alongside with a mighty crash that shook both the French ship and the British frigate. It was almost too easy; the Frenchman's larboard boarding nets had been robbed to bolster the starboard side and in a matter of seconds there were two hundred screaming sailors pouring onto her deck. The unfortunate defenders were caught between *Spey's* men and *Dartmouth's*, and they knew there was no point in resisting; men were dropping their weapons, and some were running below. Carlisle could see the French captain arguing with his officers beside the wheel. A pistol was raised, and a tall lieutenant knocked it from the captain's hand. Then he looked over at Carlisle and cupped his hands, shouting something that Carlisle couldn't hear. Was he trying to surrender? Carlisle grasped for the right words in French, but Enrico was quicker.

'Est-ce que vous vous rendez?'
'Oui, je me rends.'

***

CHAPTER TWENTY-EIGHT

One More Victory

Monday, Eighth of June 1761.
Dartmouth, at Anchor. Off Roseau, Dominica.

It was fortunate indeed that the rendezvous was to the west because they would have taken weeks to work those devastated ships to any destination to windward. As it was, they had spent a whole day and a night bringing some order to the chaos that the battle had left behind before they could bear away and make for St. Mary's Road, conscious all the while of the looming presence of Marie-Galante under their lee.

The anchorage was empty except for Gresham's prize, and the battered group of ships, now four strong, put theirs bows to the south to pass to windward of the Saintes. They could gain no intelligence from the shore, so they steered for Roseau, being the nearest of the likely objectives for the army.

Another weary night at sea, making no more than three knots, and that with the greatest of danger to the jury-rigged masts and spars and the knotted and spliced rigging. But at last they were in the shelter of Dominica.

'What do you think, Mister Wishart? Will we find the commodore at Roseau?'

They were walking the poop deck as seven bells sounded in the middle watch. Only a few hours to dawn and then they would see.

'I think it's likely, sir, but if not there then St. Lucia, I expect.'

It wasn't Wishart's responsibility, and he could speak of it lightly. Carlisle could have made directly for English Harbour with his prizes. If he'd hauled his wind as soon as the battle was over, he'd have weathered Guadeloupe and would now be approaching a harbour where he was certain of refuge, rather than one that may still be held by the enemy. He'd have done it as well, if it were not for his earlier stretching of his orders to wait for a convoy at the Chesapeake. He felt that he'd pushed at the commander-in-chief's orders as far as he dared, and the letter that he had picked up at English Harbour was unequivocal. He had to find the commodore at St. Mary's Road at Guadeloupe and failing that to seek him at St. Lucia and Dominica. If he'd steered for Antigua, he would have fulfilled none of those directives, even though he'd carried out the verbal part of his orders, to intercept any French squadron menacing the landings. That stock of goodwill could only stretch so far and now he was committed, and he was acutely conscious that he was moving further and further to leeward of the only naval yard in the islands.

Carlisle nodded and kept walking. Wishart could sense his unease although he felt nothing of the sort himself. He was still euphoric after the battle. He knew he had done well, and so had Gresham. He was acutely aware that many a first lieutenant had been posted after much less significant actions, and that would open the opportunity to move up to the second-in-command's billet. He barely dared to dream, and yet…

'If you're concerned about the commodore, sir… Well, just look at what you have to show for the past few days of absence.'

Both men looked astern to where the dark shapes of great ships followed them in the darkness. The French navy had forfeited two ships-of-the-line, and they could ill-afford those kinds of losses.

'You're right, of course, Mister Wishart. It was a famous victory, but I do wish I knew where the squadron and the army were, and I do hope we don't have to beat back to English Harbour until Sir James has given us the word.'

***

Dawn came stealthily, its first orange rays lighting the peaks of Dominica and slowly, so slowly, spreading its light

Carlisle's Duty

into the shadowed area in the lee of the massive island. Carlisle had kept the deck through the rest of the night and now he eagerly scanned the horizon each time his pacing brought him to the taffrail. Nothing, not the slightest hint that a mighty invasion fleet might lie ahead. He'd almost resigned himself to sailing on the St. Lucia, past the French navy at Fort Royal, with all the dangers that brought. One more turn and he'd go below…

'Sail ho! Sails on the larboard bow! It's the fleet, sir.'

Whittle again. From his lofty perch, he had been able to see through the low morning mist.

'How many, Whittle?'

'Fifty at least, sir, a hundred maybe. Ships-of-the-line, frigates, transports and store ships, all lying at anchor. And I can see sails astern of us, men-o'-war, sir. It looks like the squadron, steering for the anchorage.'

Carlisle let out a great sigh. He could breathe easily for the first time since he received the commodore's orders from his secretary in English Harbour. Now the decisions could be left to the commander-in-chief. He climbed up the maintop with his telescope slung over his shoulder and settled himself to glean what information he could before the squadron came up to him.

It hardly looked as though an invasion had taken place. There was no smoke from burning buildings, no cannon fire and no columns of red coats streaming up the hills and through the town. Roseau seemed peaceful, just as he had last seen it, with the addition of a huge fleet of transports and supply ships at anchor. In this first light of the new day he could see boats starting to move, but there didn't appear to be any urgency. Perhaps it was all over, and another French sugar island had fallen to British arms. He hoped so. One more victory was another step on the road to the end of the war, and he was so weary of it all.

***

'Just one more victory, Carlisle, one more in a war that shows no sign of ending.'

The commander-in-chief shook his head and gazed abstractedly out of the windows of his flagship at the lush green slopes of Dominica. The anchorage at Roseau was crowded with ships, and now that it was full daylight, a myriad of boats of all shapes and sizes were plying between them and the shore. Even from here he could see the union flag flying from the fort above the town.

'Lord Rollo landed on Saturday and by the evening he'd taken all the batteries and had the French commander and his second in custody. It seems that his greatest difficulty after that was finding anyone who would take the responsibility of surrendering the island. Oh, they'll ring the bells and make their proclamations in London, but it was little more than a short march on a pleasant afternoon. I understand he lost only two men killed and a few wounded, scarcely more than he'd expect on any day in an army of that size if it were kicking its heels in barracks. It appears that you lost more than that, Carlisle.'

'Yes, Sir James. I had five killed and fifteen wounded, but Captain Percival fared worse, ten or twelve killed, I believe, and he has a broken leg that may yet have to come off.'

'Well, I'm sorry for it, but you performed a great service. I shudder to think what effect it would have had on the army to see a French battle squadron on the horizon. *Mosquito* found me, you know, but we were cruising off the southern end of the island by then and by the time we reached up to the north, the French squadron – those that declined to give battle with you – thought better of the whole venture and the last that I saw of them they were stretching away to the nor'west, bound for Cape François I don't doubt. God, I'd have loved to have chased them, but the island hadn't surrendered by then, and my duty was clear.'

So that was why the commodore was looking so glum. He'd missed a fleet action by a whisker. Taking a sugar island was all very well, but it was the commander of the army's name that would be lauded back in England, and the naval commander would be largely unrecognised. Four of the line wasn't a great number – even if the two already taken were included it only made six – but with so few fleet actions in this war it would have attracted recognition out of all proportion to its significance.

'Still, as I say, it was well done. If those six of the line had appeared while we were sailing for Roseau, or worse, as the army was landing, it could have put the whole enterprise awry. Even the remaining four, if properly handled, could have delayed the whole thing by days or weeks, and then my Lord Rollo might have thought of better uses for his army, bringing in the turnip harvest in New York, in all probability.'

Carlisle was a little shocked to hear such sentiments from a commander-in-chief, but allowances had to be made for his disappointment.

'Now, what's the state of your little flotilla?'

Carlisle had to bring himself back to the present, to the discipline of composing a factual account of his four ships.

'I'm sorry to say that I rather mangled the third rate. My carpenter says that Port Royal may be able to repair her enough for use, but Portsmouth or Deptford would be better. English Harbour could patch her up enough for a passage home, so long as it's not too late in the season, but she needs a dock, and she needs temporary repairs even to make it to a dock. She won't survive a hard gale as she is.'

The land breeze had started as the sun set and *Dublin* swung at her anchor, revealing the two French prizes just a couple of cables away. It was a dramatic effect that couldn't have worked so well even if it had been planned.

'The fourth rate's in a better case; it only had to stand up to one of my broadsides and then *Spey's* twelve pounders, and we carried her by boarding. I expect English Harbour can bring her into service, if you're in need of another fifty-gun ship, sir.'

Douglas was not unaffected by the spectacle. Two French ships-of-the-line had been beaten into submission by one small British fourth rate and a frigate. It was a notable victory, more significant to the naval mind than the capture of another sugar island. There would be articles in the London broadsheets and engravings rushed out by artists who hadn't been there and had no real idea of what a battle looked like. Still, it was no good to hold the presses until any of the ships that took part returned to England, the public's interest would have moved on long before then.

'Then at least I can indulge in some promotions. How did your first lieutenant perform? Gresham, isn't it?'

Carlisle gulped. The implication was obvious, and this was an important moment for Gresham. He didn't want to lose him but, in all fairness, he couldn't stand in his way. A few months ago, before Gresham had handled affairs so well in rescuing his captain from the privateer off St. Lucia, he'd have expressed his misgivings about his fitness for command, about his ability to respond to a changing situation. But not now, and he could be entirely honest in his reply.

'Mister Gresham has always been exemplary, sir. He led the boarding party that took the sixty-four then brought her to anchor with a small prize crew with the entire complement of Frenchmen still on board. It was a notable achievement.'

Douglas nodded. He could imagine how perilous it was to take the ship in the first place and how much determination it would have needed to keep some six hundred men below deck with a makeshift prize crew.

'Is he ready for command?'

'He is sir.'

'Then I'll keep him here and make him master and commander into *Falcon,* in room of Standish who can have the fourth rate; I expect their Lordships will confirm his promotion. What was its name?'

'*Jason*, sir, fifty guns, and the sixty-four is *Fleuron.*'

'Ah yes, *Jason*, I saw it as she was anchoring. An unlucky name for the French; Lord Anson took the last one off Cape

Carlisle's Duty

Ortegal in 'forty-seven. *Fleuron's* not much better. I seem to remember a ship of that name catching fire and exploding at Brest. I do sometimes wonder what goes through the minds of the great people who choose these names. Do they have a committee, do you think, or does King Louis just decree what it'll be?'

Carlisle smiled. Sir James was well known as a student of the navy's history, and he was apt to ramble on the subject if given any encouragement.

'Our own Admiralty's not much better, Sir James. Poor old Hamilton was killed when the previous *Dartmouth* exploded off Lagos bay in the same year that *Jason* was taken. Yet she's been a lucky ship for me.'

'Lucky for us both, Carlisle,' Douglas agreed. 'I'll buy *Jason* into the service of course and unless peace is declared before *Fleuron* makes Portsmouth, she'll be taken up as well. Anson's always on the lookout for French third rates; it's just a pity you couldn't have taken one of the seventy-fours.'

Carlisle nodded; it was as he expected, with the war still raging the navy needed to bring every captured French ship into British service as rapidly as possible. It was cheaper than building a new ship, but most importantly it was quicker by far. And in terms of the balance of naval power, it had a double benefit. France had two ships less while Britain had two ships more. King George's superiority at sea grew daily, which was just as well with the prospect of Spain joining the war with its own magnificent fleet of ships-of-the-line.

He'd have to share the prizes with Percival of course, *Spey* being in sight when both of them were taken, and Douglas would take the flag officer's share; but those two ships still represented a very substantial sum of money. It was ironic. Only a few months ago he was worried about his fortune being ravaged by damages imposed by the vice admiralty court in Newport, and now he was contemplating the prospect of its increase.

'I'll send *Fleuron* home under a lieutenant, so long as the master attendant agrees with your carpenter's assessment.'

Just like that, a commander had been made post-captain, a lieutenant had been made commander, and another lieutenant had been given a prize third rate to sail back across the Atlantic. Men waited all their lives – often in vain – for such strokes of luck.

'You'll need a new third lieutenant, but I'll let you think about that.'

Now, that was generous. Not only could Wishart and Enrico move up a notch, but he could choose a master's mate or midshipman to be made acting lieutenant. Torrance perhaps, but he'd have to consider whether he was quite ready. By the time the lucky man – whoever it was – could be examined by the navy board, he'd have been long enough in post that his commission would be a foregone conclusion. So long as the war didn't end.

'Now, as for *Dartmouth*, what's the damage?'

Carlisle had been expecting this question, but until it came, he still wasn't certain how he'd answer. He paused to collect his thoughts while Douglas gazed at the two prizes, perhaps calculating their value and his share. His acting secretary offered him his notebook where he'd made some figures in the margin. Carlisle couldn't see them, but they brought a smile to the commodore's face.

What Carlisle really wanted to say was that *Dartmouth* should be sent to Portsmouth for a middling repair. He'd send for Chiara and his son and take a house near the dockyard, and he could enjoy the company of his family without feeling guilty, but he knew it wouldn't do. He'd had his stolen moments, three weeks of them, and his store of goodwill was still too low.

He sighed, which drew a questioning glance from the commodore.

'She's a tough old ship, sir, and there's nothing that the King's Yard at English Harbour can't mend.'

'Very well, then we'll see what the master attendant has to say.'

Carlisle's Duty

Douglas was keen to end the meeting, he had other affairs to deal with. He had to go ashore to meet Lord Rollo and decide the next steps in this war in the Antilles.

'You're to sail on Wednesday with *Spey* and the prizes under your command. Make directly for English Harbour. Send the French crews into the transports today and tomorrow, they can go to Portsmouth with Lord Rollo's prisoners. I'll give you some seamen from the squadron to help work the prizes. You'll have your orders within the hour.'

He looked at the secretary who bowed in agreement.

'I'll see to Mister Gresham's acting commission as soon as the master attendant has confirmed that *Jason* can be repaired.'

Douglas walked over to the chart that was hung on the cabin's bulkhead. He stepped off some distances with his fingers.

'I expect we've seen the last of that French squadron, but just in case I'll cruise off the islands for a week or so. You can expect me at English Harbour in two weeks, unless Lord Rollo decides to move on to St. Lucia. Meanwhile don't let the officers in the King's Yard fob you off with any excuses. I want a full assessment of *Dartmouth*, *Spey* and the prizes by the time I return, then I can make firm decisions. I don't want to send you back to England, not if I can avoid it. You've proved too useful, and I want you and your ship back on station as soon as possible.'

***

CHAPTER TWENTY-NINE

A Blind Eye

Friday Twelfth of June 1761.
Dartmouth, at Sea. Off Montserrat.

The four ships tossed and heaved on the great rolling swell – the legacy of a day of foul weather – as they made their way slowly and painfully towards the north. It had been a short blow, just twenty-four hours or so, but now the thick, grey murk was retreating into the west, hustled away by the trade wind that brought white clouds and sunshine to ease the minds on the quarterdecks. They had all suffered, more-or-less, in that sharp action five days before, and knots and splices were apt to fail, placing an extra burden on the meagre crews. They were short-handed even after the commodore's draft of hands, and the pumps had to be worked, and the battered ships coaxed towards a safe haven. Never before, they told themselves, had men so longed for a sight of English Harbour.

'I almost regret that it wasn't a hurricane; they're not unknown this early in the season, you know.'

Beazley looked wistfully to windward where the clear horizon and steady tops'l breeze gave him no comfort. He'd been noting the level of the mercury in his weather glass every half an hour, in case the strong winds had developed into a true tropical storm. He'd be the first seafarer to make such observations and when he said that he *almost* regretted that the hurricane hadn't materialised, it was generally understood that he wasn't telling the strict truth. Carlisle knew Beazley very well, and he'd already had to forbid him to openly wish for a hurricane to prevent him thoroughly upsetting the ship's company.

'Nevertheless, Mister Beazley, you'll have a strong case for the use of these instruments at sea. When will you send your first report? I imagine you'll address Trinity House in the first instance.'

Beazley's face spoke of the torment he'd been going through. He knew very well that he didn't have enough data to conclusively prove the value of the weather-glass, and it was better to present an unassailable case than to have his preliminary findings picked apart and ridiculed. However, he knew that it was only a matter of time before other sailing masters made the same experiments, for all he knew they could be doing so at this very moment. Being the second seafarer to present his findings was worse than useless, and he so wanted to be the first. He had continued the observations while the ship had been at anchor in Hampton Roads and he would do the same at English Harbour, but to the deeply conservative elders at Trinity House, observations at anchor were no substitute for observations taken at sea. And they were right, the instrument had to prove itself in the rough-and-tumble of seagoing service, not in the soft and easy life of a ship in a sheltered anchorage.

'Not yet, sir. I think six months is the minimum to demonstrate that it's worthy of further study. But with the storms on the passages from Newport and Hampton, and yesterday's blow, I have some good examples of the weather that follows a fall in the mercury. I'm convinced that the correlation is strong enough, at least for foretelling dirty weather. A hurricane would have just completed the picture. Still, it's only the beginning of the season.'

Carlisle smiled and turned away. He'd been sceptical at first, but with each change in the weather the evidence had mounted up. There was a long way to go before it became a reliable aid to navigation, but it was certainly not to be scorned. He'd ask Enrico to make some sketches of it. He was the best draughtsman in the ship, and he could render the glass, the mounting and the copper cage so that a reader of the data would be able to see what the instrument looked like when adapted for service at sea.

But still, all that it did was to foretell the weather and like the Pythia at Delphi, it spoke in vague and ambiguous terms that mere mortals couldn't fully understand. What it couldn't do was influence the weather, and that blow had set the little squadron far off its direct path to Antigua. The Soufrière Hills of Montserrat loomed large on the larboard beam when by rights they should be barely visible, just breaking the leeward horizon. English Harbour was dead to windward now, and with the weather moderating it was time to bring his ships hard onto the wind for what would certainly be a tedious passage and take at least a day longer than he had intended.

'Deck there! Sail ho! There's a sail on the larboard bow.'

'Aloft with you, Mister Young.'

His four ships were in no state to meet an enemy and if he had to tack back towards Dominica and the safety of the Leeward Islands Squadron and the ships sent by Colville, then he would do so without hesitation. Nevertheless, it was unlikely to be the French squadron. They would have been set to leeward as much as *Dartmouth* and her charges had been, and they were probably at Cape François by now. But still, it would be awkward to meet them with his ships undermanned and all of them more-or-less battle damaged.

Carlisle paced the poop deck, waiting for the midshipman to report. He was undisturbed up here, away from the bustle of the quarterdeck and with a panoramic view. He could see *Spey* and *Fleuron* and *Jason* in a line astern of him while over on the starboard side – to windward – the horizon was a clear-cut line dividing the blue sky from the darker blue sea, except where the high land of Antigua intruded. His squadron was perhaps two leagues off Montserrat with not the slightest danger of being set down onto its rocky eastern shore, and the world was at peace except for this unknown sail. He was irritated to see that Young was hurrying back onto deck rather than making his report from the masthead.

'I beg your pardon for coming on deck, sir, but I thought you'd like to know. The sail is hard on the wind to weather the island, sir. It's a merchantman, but the thing is that it looks very much like that Rhode Island ship, the *Hope*…'

Horace Young stood uneasily after he'd delivered his report. He wasn't at all sure that he'd done the right thing in coming back on deck, and his captain's face gave him no reassurance.

Carlisle's mind was in a turmoil; it was the very last thing that he expected to hear. And yet, it made sense. *Hope* was fast, she used to be a privateer after all, and only a fast ship would dare to sail without escort while the French privateers still scoured the oceans for British prizes. It was in the nature of John Brown to take a risk like this, and of course if *Hope* was again planning to trade with the enemy, then it could certainly not do so while under escort.

He'd delivered *Hope* to Newport at the end of March and that gave plenty of time for her to be unloaded, refitted and sent back to the islands. He wondered whether Kendrick was still the master. Probably he'd planned to weather Antigua but had been blown to leeward the same as *Dartmouth* and her squadron had. But where was he bound?

Young was still standing there uncertainly.

'Thank you, Mister Young, you acted correctly. Now go aloft and keep an eye on her. Come back to the deck and tell me if she tacks or bears away. Oh, and let me know the minute you are certain that it is *Hope*.'

***

Horace Young made only two descents during the hour that it took for the ships to close each other; the first to confirm its identity and the second to report that it appeared to be clearing away a boat, ready for swaying out. That in itself was significant. A short-handed merchantman didn't launch a boat at sea without some great necessity. It required the ship to heave-to and the mainsail to be furled and falls to be rigged. It would certainly need all hands for at least an hour, and its passage would be delayed. Carlisle could see that the boat would barely be in the water before he was past and clear.

He was tempted to ignore this intrusion, to pretend that he hadn't seen *Hope* at all. Then he wouldn't have to decide whether to tacitly condone another instance of trading with the enemy, or to bring the ship in to English Harbour again. His expression betrayed his frustration; none of the other post-captains in the navy would have paused for a moment. After the judgement of the vice-admiralty court at Newport, nobody would bring in another Brown Company ship except for the most heinous of crimes, piracy perhaps. But then those other captains weren't known throughout the service as the *colonial post-captain*, and he could imagine what would be said behind his back if he took that easy option.

He stamped his foot in exasperation. A word to the sailing master and the officer of the watch would ensure that the logs made no mention of this single passing British merchantman. He could sail on, offering a blind eye to the merchant ship and a deaf ear to the lookout, and he would never have to explain why he let a traitorous ship flying the British flag go upon its way without hindrance.

And yet… and yet…

Kendrick – he assumed that tall, confident Rhode Islander was still in command – may have a genuine emergency. He could need a surgeon, he could need a carpenter's assistance, but what he certainly didn't need was help with his navigation, not with Montserrat towering above them. No, he couldn't just pass by.

'Are we safe to heave-to here, Mister Beazley?'

The master took a bearing of the northern tip of Montserrat, just below Silver Hill, then studied the pennant far above on the main masthead.

'Wind's maybe half a point south of east, sir. If we heave-to on the starboard tack, we'll clear it by a good league, supposing we drift that far.'

'Then make a signal for all ships to heave-to, Mister Angelini.'

***

Carlisle was always surprised by the feeling of stillness

when a ship lay hove-to after days of beating into the wind. The breeze whipped across the deck less fiercely and the ship's motion settled down into a regular, predictable rising and falling to each successive peak of the swell. It gave him the peace to think about the coming meeting.

The problem – and he would admit it to nobody – was that he had a certain amount of sympathy with the New Englanders' point of view. While all the American colonies had been founded on agriculture, those northern ones had soon found that the thin, stony land provided a poor living. Now they subsisted almost entirely by trade, and they were straining at the leash to resume their old patterns of commerce. The southern colonies, Virginia in particular, may sneer at them, but in the south the land was wide and fertile, and they were not so dependent upon the sea. Of course he couldn't condone trading with the enemy, either officially or privately, and it was still possible that the Admiralty would appeal against the Newport verdict.

Well, he'd give no hint of his sympathy to Kendrick. What he'd do if he was confronted with a frank admission that *Hope* was again steering for St. Lucia, he just couldn't tell.

***

Hope hove-to ahead of *Dartmouth*, a sensible precaution as it could be assumed that the massive two-decker would make more leeway than the much smaller merchant ship, and there was no value in a collision at sea. The boat looked tiny on that huge expanse of water. It only pulled four oars and there was no obvious passenger unless the coxswain could be his visitor. Kendrick, presumably.

'My telescope, if you please.'

The boy who brought telescope wiped the lens carefully on his sleeve and handed it to his captain with an air of pride at having been entrusted with this task.

It was difficult to focus at first, the boat was moving so far up and down on the swell, and it was, in relative terms, so close. It came and then it went, but the second time the boat drifted into his view, he managed to hold it there.

Not Kendrick at all. The figure that sat in the stern grasping the tiller in a most seamanlike manner was Abraham Whipple, John Brown's star privateer captain.

'Mister Angelini, that's Captain Whipple.'

He realised as he spoke that he was again giving him the rank of captain, just as though he commanded a King's ship.

'Bring him down to the great cabin, if you please, and pass the word for Mister Simmonds.'

***

Carlisle sent Walker away. No refreshment, no welcome until he knew *Hope's* business in the Islands.

Abraham Whipple came into the cabin wearing a cautious smile, as though he wasn't at all sure what reception awaited him.

'Mister Whipple, how are you? I see you have exchanged your ship.'

Carlisle was being deliberately guarded, avoiding any hint of committing himself. He didn't know what *Hope's* purpose was in these waters, nor Whipple's reason for halting the progress of four men-o'-war.

'Good morning, Captain Carlisle, it's a pleasure to meet you again.'

Whipple looked sideways at Simmonds whose pen was in his hand, ready to record the heads of the conversation, to defend his captain's position, if it should come to that.

'I bring news of the enemy. I narrowly missed being taken by four French ships-of-the-line off St. Christopher's Island three days ago. I saw them at dawn, but by the time they sighted me I was to windward of them and I guess as soon as they saw how weatherly we were, they didn't fancy the chase. That's the joy of sailing a privateer on a trading cruise. But then you may have already met them.'

Whipple looked pointedly out of the stern window where the two French prizes rose and fell on the long Atlantic swell.

Carlisle started to relax. At least there was a good reason

Carlisle's Duty

– a good patriotic reason – for impeding his progress to Antigua. Yet he was still reluctant to give Whipple any information in return, not if he was bound for the French islands.

'How were they steering when you last saw them?'

He could hear Simmonds' pen scratching away, taking down this important information.

'South of St. Bartholomew and St. Martin. I would say they were steering to pass north of the Virgin Islands and north of Puerto Rico. They crowded on sail when they put up their helms and gave up the chase.'

'Thank you, Mister Whipple, that's useful information. I expect they're heading for Cape François.'

'Well, they won't bother you now, Captain, not with this easterly. Even if they hauled their wind as soon as they were out of sight, they'd be a day astern of me. But as you say, they'll be bound for Cape François, I expect. It would have been a sad day if I'd been taken. I would never have been able to hold up my head in Providence again.'

'And where is *Hope* bound?'

Carlisle asked that question in as neutral a tone as he could manage, just a normal conversation between two seafarers.

Whipple smiled; he wasn't fooled at all.

'Oh, I'm bound for Barbados, Captain. I'd be far to the windward of these islands if we hadn't been forced to run before a storm. I almost thought it was a hurricane, but it was only a one-day affair.'

Carlisle tried not to let his suspicions show. Martinique and St. Lucia could both be fetched on a larboard tack from Montserrat, particularly for a ship such as *Hope*. He caught a moment of disappointment on Whipple's face, it showed in the corners of his eyes that momentarily slanted downwards to meet his pursed lips. Disappointment, not anger and try as he might, Carlisle could detect no trace of subterfuge in Whipple's honest face.

Whipple recovered his poise and smiled confidentially.

'And in any case, I don't speak French. You see, this is only a temporary job for me. One trading cruise and then I'll be back to privateering.'

He could see that Carlisle was still suspicious.

'If I may be entirely frank with you, Captain Carlisle?'

Whipple cast a meaningful glance towards Simmonds who was still ready to commit to paper whatever was said.

Carlisle looked from Whipple to his secretary. It could do no harm.

'Mister Simmonds, I don't believe I'll need your services anymore but send Walker in, if you please.'

Whipple bowed slightly and waited for the clerk to leave the cabin.

'You see, Captain, although Mister Brown won his case, and he has the support of almost the entirety of the colony, he still has to deal with King George's officers, and particularly the customs houses. Now, I haven't been tainted with the suspicion of smuggling – not recently in any case – and you may not know that I'm betrothed to Governor Hopkins' niece. It's through no virtue of my own, but I do have a certain standing in the colony, which Joseph Kendrick lacks. Mister Brown felt that if I could take *Hope* on just one demonstrably legal trading voyage it would re-establish the ship's reputation. Barbados and back to Providence, a quick trip and a legitimate profit. Then I'll be back to privateering, and God send that the King of Spain feels moved to support France and join the war.'

That explained Whipple's self-confidence, his air of a man above the common level of merchant masters. Well, his explanation – his brutally and almost dangerously frank explanation – would have to do. He was in a difficult position; he could hardly accuse the man of carrying out an illegal act that a vice-admiralty court had already determined to be lawful.

'Then perhaps you'll take a drink, Captain Whipple. You've a few days passage ahead of you.'

***

Carlisle's Duty

It was like the dinner in Newport, he felt as though he'd known Whipple all his life. He liked his open, frank nature and his evident understanding of his profession. Carlisle heard the latest news from Providence and Newport, how the Browns were increasingly concerned that the court's decision would be challenged. That was partly why they'd sent *Hope* out again under a different master and on a regular trading voyage, to establish an innocent employment for the ship. Whipple told how the building boom was spreading and shipbuilding with it, and the stimulation that gave to the economy. It seemed that there was an increasing sense that it was back to business as usual in the northern colonies, back to business with a new energy to make up for the lost years.

Carlisle told him about his fight with the French squadron. Whipple, of course, had never seen an action like that, the worst violence he had seen at sea was in his privateering days when he occasionally had to fire into a French merchantman to bring them to.

'I suppose it comes naturally after so long in the King's service,' Whipple said after he'd heard the account, 'but it's not for me. I'm just waiting for the Dons to declare their hand then I'll bring the old *Gamecock* south again and increase the Browns' fortune with the minimum of risk to their property. But you, sir, if I may say, are a valuable person to Virginia. As a native, so to speak, who's fought on land and sea and can move easily from the King's service to colonial service and back again. The governor must be courting you, surely, for a position when this war is over?'

'Oh, as for that...'

Carlisle couldn't have explained why he was speaking so freely to this merchant master. There was something about Whipple, some indefinable quality that raised him above the commonplace. Perhaps he'd been so long in the exalted position of the captain of a ship-of-the-line that he craved company that he could speak to on equal terms. He couldn't do that with any of his officers, not even Enrico.

'...the governor isn't in residence of course. Mister Fauquier's the governor in all but name, and you're right, he bombards me with veiled suggestions, although I haven't committed to anything. I've only just decided to settle in Virginia.'

'Forgive me, sir, but isn't there a family plantation, down towards the river in Jamestown? I heard talk of it when I was last in Williamsburg.'

'Yes, there's a family plantation, but I've advertised it for sale. My father's not capable of managing it,' Carlisle didn't add that he was barely capable of managing himself, 'and my brother died in April while I was waiting on a convoy at Hampton. The place needs attention that I can't provide, and so it must go.'

'Ah, my condolences. It's hard to lose a brother.'

'He took his own life.'

Whipple evidently didn't know how to reply and there was silence for a few seconds.

'Then you don't see yourself as a plantation owner? That's the usual occupation for a gentleman of your standing in the southern colonies, isn't it?'

'It is, but it's not for me.'

Carlisle could only think of the way the family plantation had descended into a sort of hell in the years that he'd been at sea. It was his brother's doing, of course, and now he could see that Charles had been suffering a degenerative insanity for years. He couldn't shake off the image of those sullen workers in the tobacco fields; the contrast with the generally cheerful crew of *Dartmouth* was stark. Even more so when he remembered that a good proportion of his people had been pressed, they were themselves in a sort of slavery. Of course, he'd seen ships that resembled the plantation in the manner that the men were treated, but one way or another those captains always came to a sticky end. And now that he considered it, the captains or the first lieutenants of those ships usually had a hint of madness about them. No, he couldn't settle down to the life of a

Carlisle's Duty

plantation owner, he'd just have to find another way of occupying himself when the war was over.

'You know, life in the colonies will be different after this war, it has to be. Now I'm not suggesting for one moment that we won't be loyal subjects of King George – heaven forbid – but we surely must have a greater influence on our own fates. Mister Brown mentioned how fast the population is growing and you saw for yourself the mood of optimism. It's the same in all the colonies, from north to south, this feeling that we're not second class any longer.'

'Yes, I've seen it.'

Carlisle didn't want to dwell on the subject, it was dangerous territory for one holding the King's commission.

'And you, Captain Whipple, what will you do? Even if Spain throws its lot in with France, the war can't last very much longer, the whole of Europe will be exhausted. You may get a year or two of privateering, but what then?'

Whipple smiled broadly.

'Oh, I fancy my seagoing days will be over. I've laid enough aside to buy some land and perhaps that's my future, farming. I have a yearning to move west, into the lands across the Ohio that the French have lost. But as you say, there's more business for me at sea before I have to make any decisions.'

Carlisle didn't want the conversation to end, but both he and Whipple had only a limited time before they had to get underway again. All five ships were being set to leeward, and that preyed heavily upon their minds.

When Whipple left, with a case of Madeira lowered down into the boat, Carlisle gave the orders for his ships to beat up towards Antigua, then retreated to the poop deck where he walked and walked, trying to make some sense of the ideas that Whipple had planted in his mind.

***

CHAPTER THIRTY

A Happy Hurricane Season

Sunday, Fourteenth of June 1761.
Dartmouth, at Anchor. English Harbour.

Every seaport donned its festive face when prizes were brought in, and English Harbour was no exception. *Dartmouth* and *Spey* and their two French captures had been spotted when they arrived off the harbour just at sunset, too late for entry before dark, and they spent the night lying-to east of Standfast Point, waiting for the dawn. Before Carlisle led the procession in, the news had already spread to Falmouth and to St. John's and to all the other settlements and plantations. The King's Yard was crowded with the gentry of the island and on every overlook the common people jostled for a view of the captured French ships. The blue ensigns that flew from the sterns of *Fleuron* and *Jason* and the vast gilded lilies of Bourbon France, draped disconsolately over the taffrails, proclaimed the victory to anyone who was unsure.

'There's the master attendant, sir.'

The carpenter had been eagerly watching for the first sight of the yard's longboat that was now rowing hastily towards them. He wanted to personally conduct a tour of *Dartmouth's* battle damage, but more than that, he wanted to escort the master attendant as he made his preliminary survey of the other ships, just for the glory of the occasion.

'Then let's hope he can see to our needs here, Chips, rather than sending us back to Portsmouth, or to that wicked Port Royal.'

'Oh yes, sir, most certainly, sir.'

Chips wasn't at all in agreement that the ship should be repaired at English Harbour and his fingers were firmly crossed behind his back, where his captain couldn't see them. He had a wife and children living in Portsmouth, and a few months in the dock would suit him just fine. Carlisle was well aware of that, and he knew very well that left alone the carpenter would exaggerate every damaged knee and every splintered yard of planking. The master attendant was not a man to be easily fooled, but nevertheless…

'I think I'll walk around with you Chips, just for the first look.'

***

The master attendant toured *Dartmouth* with a growing sense of delight. It was just what he had hoped: enough damage to require a substantial repair, but nothing severe enough to need a docking; there was no dock at English Harbour. It would do nicely to keep his yard in business through the hurricane season. He countered every one of the carpenter's gross exaggerations and stated airily that there was nothing that his own shipwrights couldn't repair, she'd be good as new in a few months. Chips appeared blinking on deck after his lengthy tour and his face told his mates all they needed to know. There'd be no quiet cruise back to Portsmouth to delight the married men and no run down to Port Royal where the fleshpots of that old, sinful town could cater for the bachelors' preferred recreation. English Harbour it would be, and it was best that they got used to the idea.

A cheerful master attendant and a rather glum carpenter left for *Spey*, to assess her damage, and thence to the two French ships. Carlisle could at last retire to his cabin to consider the implications of spending the next few months at English Harbour. Three months, that was the estimate, but he knew very well that if his ship was ready for sea in September, it was unlikely that she'd sail until November. The rhythms of the year for the Leeward Islands Squadron were determined by the hurricane season which had officially already started, although the first storm rarely came until the end of June and only occasionally threatened Antigua. October was the peak of the season and every commander-in-chief planned to have his battle fleet safely at anchor from July to the start of November.

Five months then, five months of wrangling with the officers of the yard, of sitting on courts martial, at least one every week, and dealing with the inevitable indiscipline of a lengthy stay in port. He'd have to give leave, and with rum so readily available there'd be drunkenness and all the evils that followed. There'd be a few desertions as well, when merchantmen started to sail again, and he'd have to face it all without his excellent first lieutenant. He could apply for leave and take a passage to Virginia, but he was certain that Sir James wouldn't agree, and it would harm Carlisle's position if he even made such a ridiculous proposal. Every ill-considered request depleted his stock of goodwill by a measurable degree.

His desire for the war to end had never been so strong. He wanted to settle down in his new home, he wanted to carve out a new future for himself and most of all he wanted to be with his wife and his child. And to compound his misery, a knock at the door brought Simmonds and the purser for the fortnightly scrutiny of the books. He steeled himself for an hour of mental torture.

***

The morning wore on and as the sun rose the great cabin grew warmer and warmer. Walker came in and opened all the windows to let in the growing sea breeze. With *Dartmouth's* head to the sou'east, Carlisle had a vista that would have brought a gasp from anyone who had never seen it before. The Antiguan hills formed the backdrop while in the foreground the great curve of the sandy shore of Freeman's Bay extended from the far right to the centre, where the careening wharf could be seen across the spit. Fort Berkley with its row of low, pinkish stone embrasures occupied the left and, in the centre, the narrow passage led into the inner harbour with a glimpse of the King's Yard. *Spey* and the two prizes were anchored to seaward, and the harbour was otherwise deserted so there were no ships to interrupt the view.

Carlisle's Duty

The purser's voice was smooth and reassuring. He spoke in a tone that was designed to persuade his captain that everything was in order, and all he needed to do was to sign his name just here, if you please. Carlisle knew this game, he'd been playing it for years, and he was tired of it. But he also knew that with Simmonds scrutinising the books, he need do little more than decide on which items of provisions could be condemned out of hand and which would need to be investigated by a trio of his officers.

There was a bustle out on the quarterdeck. A midshipman appeared at the door.

'Lieutenant Angelini's respects, sir, and he begs to inform you that a schooner is standing into the harbour, sir. She's flying a commissioning pennant.'

A King's ship then. Probably from the commander-in-chief at Roseau. Or it could be one of those schooners that Lord Colville bought as dispatch vessels. In fact that was more likely, it was only to be expected that a dispatch vessel should arrive from the North American station. If the schooner had avoided the bad weather that *Dartmouth's* convoy had suffered it would have made a much faster passage; indeed it was a wonder that it hadn't overtaken the convoy. Letters for the commodore, no doubt. The normal communications between commanders-in-chief on distant stations who were forced to co-ordinate their activities without reference to the Admiralty or the navy board or any of the other authorities that so minutely regulated naval affairs in home waters. Still, it was a good excuse to end the purser's monotone.

'Just the one more signature, I gather. Very well.'

He took the pen that Simmonds offered and signed the final ledger.

'Now, if you would please satisfy Mister Simmonds on the final points, I'll be on deck.'

***

The view from the poop deck was even more spectacular than from the cabin. Now the vista was complete, with the Halfmoon Battery on the starboard bow and the captured third and fourth rates and the battered *Spey* anchored on the larboard bow. He could see the schooner; it had evidently crept in close to the shore around Standfast Point. Then it must have come from the north, from the American colonies, any other possibility would have brought the schooner coasting around from the west or directly from the south or east. Carlisle's heart gave a skip and his chest convulsed, bringing a stab of pain where his bandages were tight around his ribs. Perhaps it carried letters from Chiara, it was just possible, if she had written soon after he sailed from Hampton.

Now it was passing those curious natural pillars that had always reminded Holbrooke's father of the inside of Winchester Cathedral, they had that Norman-gothic look about them. Ah, that seemed a long time ago, when Carlisle was a mere master's mate under the tutelage of the senior Holbrooke.

The schooner was a thing of beauty and Carlisle watched entranced as it turned sharply around the spit of land that held the Halfmoon Battery. Even the act of wearing, when the stern passed through the wind and that huge boom swung uncontrolled across the quarterdeck, was performed with an easy grace. They were elegant craft, and fast, but they couldn't manoeuvre like a square-rigged ship, and they didn't provide a stable platform for a broadside of guns. They were useful for chasing down small privateers and French merchantmen, but not for serious battle. Half a dozen hands laid out on the yard and furled the tiny tops'l. That same operation in *Dartmouth* required thirty experienced seamen for each of the yards and couldn't be done in thrice the time in which the schooner accomplished it.

'Her anchor's ready for letting go, sir.'

Beazley was watching just as intently as his captain.

The schooner would have to pass *Dartmouth* at less than half a cable. Carlisle was aware that everyone on the upper

Carlisle's Duty

deck was watching. Normally he'd have heard the bosun's mates howling their disapproval by now, sending the men back about their business, but the ship was curiously silent, as though they were all held spellbound by the lovely little vessel.

'Ah, it looks like she's going to round-to in the bay, sir. They're standing by the staysail sheets and the main sheets and guys.'

How strange, Carlisle thought. Vessels of that size always anchored off the King's Yard unless the harbour was full, and today it was as empty as he'd ever seen it. The schooner had a boat alongside to larboard, the transom just showed beyond the schooner's stern, and it did appear as though it intended to heave-to close alongside *Dartmouth*. It was a perfectly safe manoeuvre in this gentle sea-breeze, and if it went wrong there was plenty of sea-room to recover, but even so, what news from the north could be so urgent? As the senior officer at English Harbour for the time being, any important dispatches would be brought straight to him. Was that it? Had the French been sighted descending on the islands in force? Were those six ships just a forerunner for a mighty battle squadron come to undo all of the British gains of the past few years?

Carlisle gulped; he was strangely uneasy. Well, he'd soon know.

When the schooner's bowsprit was almost abeam *Dartmouth's* foremast, he heard the helm order and saw the helmsman push the tiller to leeward. The bows swung swiftly into the wind; it was always a joy to see how fast they responded, not at all like a great fourth rate ship-of-the-line. He saw what he took to be the captain of the little vessel – a lieutenant – run forward, leaving the ship to be conned by a mate. The bows were pointing almost directly at *Dartmouth* when he reached the bowsprit.

'Captain Carlisle, sir.'

He looked uncertain for a moment as though he didn't know quite what to say.

'Lord Colville's compliments and he – he trusts that you enjoy the hurricane season.'

What the devil? Carlisle took a deep breath to blast the lieutenant for such a cryptic message. Then as the schooner's bows passed through his line of sight, the boat on its larboard side came into view. Carlisle stared, then rubbed his eyes and stared again, because there, sat in the stern sheets beside a serious-looking midshipman was Chiara, waving her hat and with her long black hair flying in the wind, little Joshua at her side.

***

HISTORICAL EPILOGUE

Europe

Broken at Lagos Bay and Quiberon Bay in 1759, and after losing a third of its ships trying to defend New France, the French navy in the middle months of 1761 was in no state to contest the mastery of the oceans and had largely abandoned any plans for an invasion of England. A diversionary raid to the north of Britain in 1760 had ended in abject failure with the loss of three frigates and two whole regiments that King Louis could ill afford. Worse still, in April 1761 the British besieged the island of Belle Île that guarded the entrance to Lorient and offered command of the Bay of Biscay south to La Rochelle.

Versailles now accepted that it was only by diverting its resources to the army in Germany that anything could be salvaged from this ruinous war. Assaulted by large and vigorous French armies, the allied forces could only hold the line in Hanover. However, for Britain, the fact that King Frederick of Prussia managed to avoid defeat on the continent could be counted as a win, while for France anything less than victory was a disaster.

North America

The long dream of New France was over and apart from some settlements in Louisiana and the far west, French power in North America was broken. For the people of the British colonies and Canada, it was a time to make plans for the future, and to decide what should be made of these vast new territories that had been opened up.

The Long War

With the sole exception of Minorca, France had nothing to bring to the table in peace negotiations and fought on in the hope of luring Spain into the conflict to turn the tide. Without Spain, and its undamaged fleet, France could not see a way to end the war before it lost the rest of its colonies, yet Spain couldn't afford to enter the war and was fearful of the consequences if it did.

FACT MEETS FICTION

The Molasses Act

According to Historian John C. Miller, '*the Molasses Act of 1733 threatened New England with ruin, struck a blow at the economic foundations of the middle colonies, and at the same time opened the way for the British West Indians—whom the continental colonists regarded as their worst enemies—to wax rich at the expense of their fellow subjects on the mainland.*'

Molasses was used in the eighteenth century to make rum, and for the New England colonies, and Rhode Island in particular, its manufacture had become an important part of their economy. In France, the great brandy houses successfully lobbied to prevent molasses being imported, fearing that if rum became a popular drink, it would harm their near-monopoly on spiritous liquors. Consequently, molasses, which is a by-product of sugar production, could be had cheaply in the French sugar islands. It didn't take long for the New Englanders to notice this opportunity to reduce the cost of the raw materials for rum production.

This didn't please the British West Indies sugar planters who commanded a large and vigorous lobby in Parliament, which in 1733 dutifully passed the Molasses Act. This act imposed a tax of six pence per gallon when the product originated from anywhere but the British possessions, making the French molasses uncompetitive against that produced in Jamaica, Barbados, Antigua and the other islands.

The New England colonies recognised that the tax struck a blow at their economic foundations. In the event, a flourishing trade in smuggled molasses, and the reluctance of the British government to pick a fight with its American colonies, meant that the tax was rarely paid. Smuggling, bribery and intimidation of customs officials effectively nullified the law, leading to the quasi-official policy of *wise and salutary neglect*, which lasted from the 1730s until the seven years war.

It was against this background, and his own feelings of professional insecurity, that the fictional Captain Carlisle brought the fictional Providence privateer *Hope* into English Harbour on the charges of trading with the enemy and smuggling.

John Brown

John Brown was an American merchant and statesman from Providence, Rhode Island and a noted slave trader. He was instrumental in founding Brown University, serving as its treasurer for 21 years, and was involved in many other public functions. He was active in the American Revolution, notably as an instigator of the 1772 Gaspee Affair. Brown is portrayed in this book in just the way that the contemporary accounts describe him – loud, forthright and domineering, with a keen nose for a business opportunity – not a man to be crossed.

Abraham Whipple

Abraham Whipple was born near Providence, in Rhode Island and early in his life chose to be a seafarer. He embarked on a career in the lucrative West Indies trade, working for Moses and John Brown. During the seven years war, he became a privateersman and commanded *Gamecock*, and in one six-month cruise, he was said to have captured twenty-three French ships. In 1772, Whipple attacked and burned the British cutter *Gaspee* in Narragansett Bay, the first British naval casualty of the American Revolution. He went on to become a commodore in the Continental Navy and to make a significant contribution to the colonies' struggle for independence. We will likely meet Abraham Whipple in future instalments of the Carlisle & Holbrooke Naval Adventures.

The Post-War Building Boom

You have only to walk through the old parts of Newport and read the dates on the buildings to see the extent of the building boom that started in late 1759. It truly was a period of optimism and that was largely due to the frustration of France's aspirations in North America.

The Careenage, St. Lucia

The small port of Carénage in the northwest of St. Lucia was renamed Castries in 1785, after Charles Eugène Gabriel de La Croix de Castries, the French Minister of the Navy. It is now the bustling capital of the island nation, visited by thousands of cruise ship passengers every year.

Dominica

The French island of Dominica was captured in 1761 by Lord Rollo's army in much the way that I have described.

***

Chris Durbin

THE CARLISLE AND HOLBROOKE SERIES

Book 1: The Colonial Post-Captain

Captain Carlisle of His Britannic Majesty's frigate *Fury* hails from Virginia, a loyal colony of the British Crown. In 1756, as the clouds of war gather in Europe, *Fury* is ordered to Toulon to investigate a French naval and military build-up.

While battling the winter weather, Carlisle must also juggle with delicate diplomatic issues in this period of phoney war and contend with an increasingly belligerent French frigate.

And then there is the beautiful Chiara Angelini, pursued across the Mediterranean by a Tunisian corsair who appears determined to abduct her, yet strangely reluctant to shed blood.

Carlisle and his young master's mate, George Holbrooke, are witnesses to the inconclusive sea-battle that leads to the loss of Minorca. They engage in a thrilling and bloody encounter with the French frigate and a final confrontation with the enigmatic corsair.

Book 2: The Leeward Islands Squadron

In late 1756, as the British government collapses in the aftermath of the loss of Minorca and the country and navy are thrown into political chaos, a small force of ships is sent to the West Indies to reinforce the Leeward Islands Squadron.

Captain Edward Carlisle, a native of Virginia, and his first lieutenant George Holbrooke are fresh from the Mediterranean and their capture of a powerful French man-of-war. Their new frigate *Medina* has orders to join a squadron commanded by a terminally ill commodore. Their mission: a near-suicidal assault on a strong Caribbean island fortress. Carlisle must confront the challenges of higher command as he leads the squadron back into battle to accomplish the Admiralty's orders.

Join Carlisle and Holbrooke as they attack shore fortifications, engage in ship-on-ship duels and deal with mutiny in the West Indies.

Book 3: The Jamaica Station

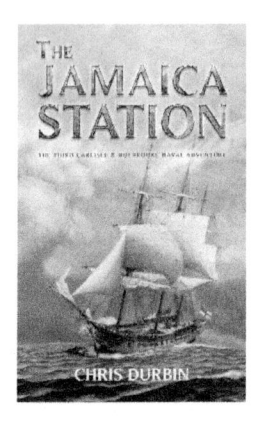

It is 1757, and the British navy is regrouping from a slow start to the seven years war.

A Spanish colonial governor and his family are pursued through the Caribbean by a pair of mysterious ships from the Dutch island of St. Eustatius. The British frigate *Medina* rescues the governor from his hurricane-wrecked ship, leading Captain Edward Carlisle and his first lieutenant George Holbrooke into a web of intrigue and half-truths. Are the Dutchmen operating under a letter of marque or are they pirates, and why are they hunting the Spaniard? Only the diplomatic skills of Carlisle's aristocratic wife, Lady Chiara, can solve the puzzle.

When Carlisle is injured, the young Holbrooke must grow up quickly. Under his leadership, *Medina* takes part in a one-sided battle with the French that will influence a young Horatio Nelson to choose the navy as a career.

Book 4: Holbrooke's Tide

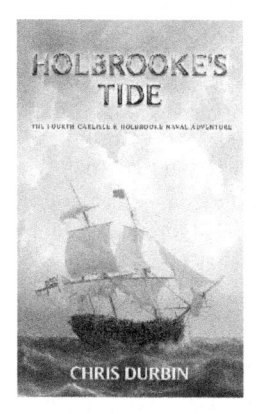

It is 1758, and the Seven Years War is at its height. The Duke of Cumberland's Hanoverian army has been pushed back to the River Elbe while the French are using the medieval fortified city of Emden to resupply their army and to anchor its left flank.

George Holbrooke has recently returned from the Jamaica Station in command of a sloop-of-war. He is under orders to survey and blockade the approaches to Emden in advance of the arrival of a British squadron. The French garrison and their Austrian allies are nervous. With their supply lines cut, they are in danger of being isolated when the French army is forced to retreat in the face of the new Prussian-led army that is gathering on the Elbe. Can the French be bluffed out of Emden? Is this Holbrooke's flood tide that will lead to his next promotion?

Holbrooke's Tide is the fourth of the Carlisle & Holbrooke naval adventures. The series follows the exploits of the two men through the Seven Years War and into the period of turbulent relations between Britain and her American colonies in the 1760s.

Chris Durbin

Book 5: The Cursed Fortress

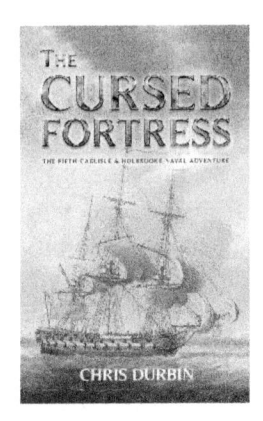

The French called it *La Forteresse Maudite*, the Cursed Fortress.

Louisbourg stood at the mouth of the Gulf of Saint Lawrence, massive and impregnable, a permanent provocation to the British colonies. It was Canada's first line of defence, guarding the approaches to Quebec, from where all New France lay open to invasion. It had to fall before a British fleet could be sent up the Saint Lawrence. Otherwise, there would be no resupply and no line of retreat; Canada would become the graveyard of George II's navy.

A failed attempt on Louisbourg in 1757 had only stiffened the government's resolve; the Cursed Fortress must fall in 1758.

Captain Carlisle's frigate joins the blockade of Louisbourg before winter's icy grip has eased. Battling fog, hail, rain, frost and snow, suffering scurvy and fevers, and with a constant worry about the wife he left behind in Virginia, Carlisle will face his greatest test of leadership and character yet.

The Cursed Fortress is the fifth of the Carlisle & Holbrooke naval adventures. The series follows the two men through the Seven Years War and into the period of turbulent relations between Britain and her American colonies in the 1760s.

Book 6: Perilous Shore

Amphibious warfare was in its infancy in the mid-eighteenth century, it was the poor relation of the great fleet actions that the navy so loved.

That all changed in 1758 when the British government demanded a campaign of raids on the French Channel ports. Command arrangements were hastily devised, and a whole new class of vessels was produced at breakneck speed: flatboats, the ancestors of the landing craft that put the allied forces ashore on D-Day.

Commander George Holbrooke's sloop *Kestrel* is in the thick of the action: scouting landing beaches, duelling with shore batteries and battling the French Navy.

In a twist of fate, Holbrooke finds himself unexpectedly committed to this new style of amphibious warfare as he is ordered to lead a division of flatboats onto the beaches of Normandy and Brittany. He meets his greatest test yet when a weary and beaten British army retreats from a second failed attempt at Saint Malo with the French close on their heels.

Perilous Shore is the sixth of the Carlisle & Holbrooke naval adventures. The series follows Holbrooke and his mentor, Captain Carlisle, through the Seven Years War and into the period of turbulent relations between Britain and her American colonies in the 1760s.

Book 7: Rocks and Shoals

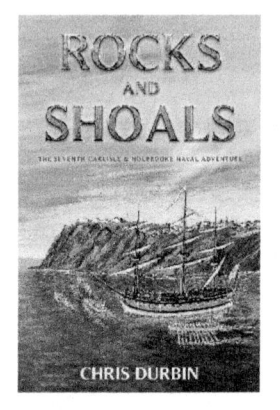

With the fall of Louisbourg in 1758 the French in North America were firmly on the back foot. Pitt's grand strategy for 1759 was to launch a three-pronged attack on Canada. One army would move north from Lake Champlain while another smaller force would strike across the wilderness to Lake Ontario and French-held Fort Niagara. A third, under Admiral Saunders and General Wolfe, would sail up the Saint Lawrence, where no battle fleet had ever been, and capture Quebec.

Captain Edward Carlisle sails ahead of the battle fleet to find a way through the legendary dangers of the Saint Lawrence River. An unknown sailing master assists him; James Cook has a talent for surveying and cartography and will achieve immortality in later years.

There are rocks and shoals aplenty before Carlisle and his frigate *Medina* are caught up in the near-fatal indecision of the summer when General Wolfe tastes the bitterness of early setbacks.

Rocks and Shoals is the seventh of the Carlisle & Holbrooke naval adventures. The series follows Carlisle and his protégé George Holbrooke, through the Seven Years War and into the period of turbulent relations between Britain and her American colonies in the 1760s.

Book 8: Niagara Squadron

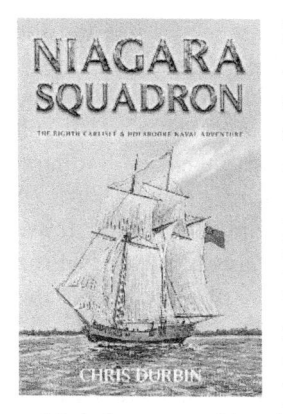

Fort Niagara is the key to the American continent. Whoever owns that lonely outpost at the edge of civilisation controls the entire Great Lakes region.

Pitt's grand strategy for 1759 is to launch a three-pronged attack on Canada. One army would move north from Lake Champlain, a second would sail up the Saint Lawrence to capture Quebec, and a third force would strike across the wilderness to Lake Ontario and French-held Fort Niagara.

Commander George Holbrooke is seconded to command the six hundred boats to carry the army through the rivers and across Lake Ontario. That's the easy part; he also must deal with two powerful brigs that guarantee French naval superiority on the lake.

Holbrooke knows time is running out to be posted as captain before the war ends and promotions dry up; his rank is the stumbling block to his marriage to Ann, waiting for him in his hometown of Wickham Hampshire.

Niagara Squadron is the eighth Carlisle and Holbrooke novel. The series follows Carlisle and his protégé Holbrooke through the Seven Years War and into the period of turbulent relations between Britain and her American colonies in the 1760s.

Book 9: Ligurian Mission

It is the summer of 1760 and the British navy reigns supreme on the oceans of the world; only in the Mediterranean is its mastery still seriously challenged. Admiral Saunders is sent with a squadron of ships-of-the-line to remind those nations that are still neutral of the consequences of siding with the French.

Edward Carlisle's ship *Dartmouth* is sent to the Ligurian Sea. His mission: to carry the British envoy to the Kingdom of Sardinia back to its capital, Turin, then to investigate the ships being built in Genoa for the French.

He soon finds that the game of diplomacy is played for high stakes, and the countries bordering the Ligurian Sea are hotbeds of intrigue and treachery, where family loyalties count for little.

Carlisle must contend with the arrogance of the envoy, the Angelini family's duplicity and a vastly superior French seventy-four-gun ship whose captain is determined to bring the Genoa ships safely to Toulon.

Ligurian Mission is the ninth Carlisle and Holbrooke novel. The series follows Carlisle and his protégé Holbrooke through the Seven Years War and into the period of turbulent relations between Britain and her American colonies prior to their bid for independence.

Book 10: Nor'west by North

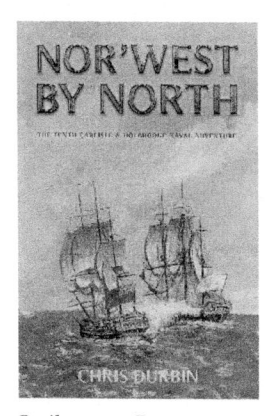

By late 1759 it is clear that France is losing the Seven Years War. In a desperate gamble, the French Atlantic and Mediterranean fleets combine to dominate the Channel and cover a landing in the south of England, but they are annihilated by Admiral Hawke at Quiberon Bay. Meanwhile, a diversionary landing is planned in the north of Britain, and it sails from Dunkirk before news of the disaster at Quiberon Bay can reach its commander. The ill-fated expedition sets out to circumnavigate Britain in an attempt to salvage something from the failed strategy.

George Holbrooke, newly promoted to post-captain and commanding the frigate Argonaut, joins a squadron sent to intercept the French expedition. The quest takes him to Sweden, the Faroes, the Western Isles of Scotland and then to Ireland and the Isle of Man. The final act is played out at a secluded anchorage in the Bristol Channel.

Nor'west by North is the tenth Carlisle and Holbrooke novel. The series follows Carlisle and his protégé Holbrooke through the Seven Years War and into the period of turbulent relations between Britain and her American colonies prior to their bid for independence.

BIBLIOGRAPHY

The following is a selection of the many books that I consulted in researching the Carlisle & Holbrooke series:

Definitive Text

Sir Julian Corbett wrote the original, definitive text on the Seven Years War. Most later writers use his work as a steppingstone to launch their own.

Corbett, LLM., Sir Julian Stafford. *England in the Seven Years War – Vol. I: A Study in Combined Strategy*. Normandy Press. Kindle Edition.

Strategy and Naval Operations

Three very accessible modern books cover the strategic context and naval operations of the Seven Years War. Daniel Baugh addresses the whole war on land and sea, while Martin Robson concentrates on maritime activities. Jonathan Dull has produced a very readable account from the French perspective.

Baugh, Daniel. *The Global Seven Years War 1754-1763*. Pearson Education, 2011. Print.
Robson, Martin. *A History of the Royal Navy, The Seven Years War*. I.B. Taurus, 2016. Print.
Dull, Jonathan, R. *The French Navy and the Seven Years' War*. University of Nebraska Press, 2005. Print.

Sea Officers

For an interesting perspective on the life of sea officers of the mid-eighteenth century, I'd read Augustus Hervey's Journal, with the cautionary note that while Hervey was by no means typical of the breed, he's very entertaining and devastatingly honest. For a more balanced view, I'd read British Naval Captains of the Seven Years War.

Erskine, David (editor). *Augustus Hervey's Journal, The Adventures Afloat and Ashore of a Naval Casanova*. Chatham Publishing, 2002. Print.

McLeod, A.B. *British Naval Captains of the Seven Years War, The View from the Quarterdeck*. The Boydell Press, 2012. Print.

Life at Sea

There are two excellent overviews of shipboard life and administration during the Seven Years War.

Rodger, N.A.M. *The Wooden World, An Anatomy of the Georgian Navy*. Fontana Press, 1986. Print.

Lavery, Brian. *Anson's Navy, Building a Fleet for Empire, 1744 to 1793*. Seaforth Publishing, 2021. Print.

John Brown

John Brown was a larger-than-life and highly controversial figure in Rhode Island in the latter part of the eighteenth century. His legacy is tarnished by his involvement in the slave trade and his biographer makes no attempt to hide this facet of his life.

Rappleye, Charles. *Sons of Providence, the Brown Brothers, the Slave Trade, and the American Revolution*. Simon & Shuster, 2006, Print.

Abraham Whipple

Abraham Whipple was one of the most important figures in the birth of the United States Navy and is well-known for his involvement in the burning of the British sloop Gaspee. He was in many ways typical of his age and background yet remarkable for his willingness to take the law into their own hands.

Cohen, Sheldon S. *Commodore Abraham Whipple of the*

Chris Durbin

Continental Navy, Privateer, Patriot, Pioneer. University Press of Florida, 2010, Print.

THE AUTHOR

Chris Durbin grew up in the seaside town of Porthcawl in South Wales. His first experience of sailing was as a sea cadet in the treacherous tideway of the Bristol Channel, and at the age of sixteen, he spent a week in a tops'l schooner in the Southwest Approaches. He was a crew member on the Porthcawl lifeboat before joining the navy.

Chris spent twenty-four years as a warfare officer in the Royal Navy, serving in all classes of ships from aircraft carriers through destroyers and frigates to the smallest minesweepers. He took part in operational campaigns in the Falkland Islands, the Middle East and the Adriatic and he spent two years teaching tactics at a US Navy training centre in San Diego.

On his retirement from the Royal Navy, Chris joined a large American company and spent eighteen years in the aerospace, defence and security industry, including two years on the design team for the Queen Elizabeth class aircraft carriers.

Chris is a graduate of the Britannia Royal Naval College at *Dartmouth*, the British Army Command and Staff College, the United States Navy War College (where he gained a postgraduate diploma in national security decision-making) and Cambridge University (where he was awarded an MPhil in International Relations).

With a lifelong interest in naval history and a long-standing ambition to write historical fiction, Chris has completed the first ten novels in the Carlisle & Holbrooke series, which follow the fortunes of a colonial Virginian and a Hampshire man who both command ships of King George's navy during the middle years of the eighteenth century.

The series will follow its principal characters through the Seven Years War and into the period of turbulent relations between Britain and her American colonies in the 1760s. They'll negotiate some thought-provoking loyalty issues when British policy and colonial restlessness lead inexorably to the American Revolution.

Chris lives on the south coast of England, surrounded by hundreds of years of naval history. His three children are all busy growing their own families and careers while Chris and his wife (US Navy, retired) of thirty-nine years enjoy sailing their Cornish Shrimper 21 on the south coast.

Fun Fact:

Chris shares his garden with a tortoise named Aubrey. If you've read Patrick O'Brian's *HMS Surprise* or have seen the 2003 film *Master and Commander: The Far Side of the World*, you'll recognise the modest act of homage that Chris has paid to that great writer. Rest assured that Aubrey has not yet grown to the gigantic proportions of *Testudo Aubreii*.

FEEDBACK

If you've enjoyed *Carlisle's Duty*, please consider leaving a review on Amazon.

This is the eleventh of a series of books that will follow Carlisle and Holbrooke through the Seven Years War and into the 1760s when relations between Britain and her restless American colonies are tested to breaking point. Look out for the twelfth in the Carlisle & Holbrooke series, coming soon.

You can follow my blog at:

www.chris-durbin.com.

Printed in Great Britain
by Amazon